M000274282

Inferno
The Wolf Pack Series

MAUREEN SMITH

Wordsmith Enterprises

INFERNO (The Wolf Pack Series)

Copyright © 2012 by Maureen Smith

All rights reserved. Except for use in any review, the reproduction or utilization of this work in whole or in part in any form by any electronic, mechanical or other means, now known or hereafter invented, including xerography, photocopying and recording, or in any information storage or retrieval system, is forbidden without the written permission of the author.

This is a work of fiction. Names, characters, places and incidents are either the product of the author's imagination or are used fictitiously, and any resemblance to actual persons, living or dead, business establishments, events or locales is entirely coincidental.

For questions and comments about this book, please contact Maureen Smith at author@maureen-smith.com. Visit the author's official Web site at: www.maureen-smith.com

ISBN-13: 978-0615599588
ISBN-10: 0615599583

Inferno
The Wolf Pack Series

*To firefighters everywhere who don the bunker gear
and put your lives on the line every day to rescue others
Thank you for your courage, bravery and sacrifice*

The Firefighter's Prayer

When I'm called to duty, God
wherever flames may rage
give me strength to save a life
whatever be its age

Help me to embrace a little child
before it is too late
or save an older person from
the horror of that fate

Enable me to be alert
to hear the weakest shout
and quickly and efficiently
to put the fire out

I want to fill my calling
and to give the best in me
to guard my neighbor and
protect his property

And if according to your will
I have to lose my life
bless with your protecting hand
my children and my wife.

—Author Unknown

Chapter 1

Coronado, Colorado
A suburb of Denver
November 1980

Prissy Wolf's body glistened with sweat as she thrust her hips upward, feeling her stomach muscles quiver as she held the position. She counted silently to twenty, then lowered her butt to the exercise mat with a grateful sigh.

"And up we go again!"

Prissy shot an aggrieved look at the smiling fitness instructor displayed on her television screen. The perky blonde hadn't broken so much as a sweat, while Prissy was drenched from head to toe. And she'd barely made it halfway through the thirty-minute aerobics video.

"Well, what're you waiting for? You heard the woman. Get those hips back up."

Prissy whipped her head toward the amused voice.

Her husband stood in the doorway of her study, which doubled as her exercise room. He looked rumpled and sexy in black sweat shorts and a gray Coronado Fire Department T-shirt. The soft fabric clung to his broad chest and showed off thick, muscular biceps that Prissy never grew tired of admiring. Of course, when it came to Stanton Wolf's looks, there was *plenty* to admire. For starters, he was six foot five with rich mahogany skin and full, sensual lips framed by a neat goatee. His eyes were dark and heavy lidded, and so damn piercing that Prissy *still* shivered sometimes when he gazed at her.

The man had the kind of looks that were made for gracing the glossy pages of a firefighter's calendar—all twelve months. Which was why Prissy adamantly refused to let him pose for one. God knows he didn't need any more women fawning over him than he already had.

"How long have you been standing there?" she asked him.

Stan's eyes glinted wickedly as he looked her over. "Long enough for me to gain a whole new appreciation for the female body—specifically, *yours*."

Prissy guffawed, hyperconscious of her soft belly and thick thighs sheathed in black spandex that was supposed to be slimming—the color, not the material. For the past year, she'd been trying to lose weight by exercising regularly and cutting back on the unhealthy sugar and carbs that had helped her put on unwanted pounds over the years. She was making progress, slowly but surely getting herself down to a size twelve.

Four times a week, she dragged herself out of bed before the crack of dawn and crept to her study, where she changed into her exercise clothes and popped in one of the aerobics tapes from her growing collection. She was usually finished by the time her husband came home from his shift and her sons began getting ready for school.

"Why are you frowning at me like that?" Stan asked, his deep voice breaking into Prissy's thoughts.

Her eyes narrowed suspiciously. "Because I could have sworn I locked that door, like I do every morning."

Stan grinned, his teeth flashing white against his dark skin. "Guess you forgot."

Prissy's frown deepened. "Well, I'm not finished yet, so..." She trailed off pointedly.

Instead of taking the hint and leaving, Stan stepped into the room and closed the door behind him. Suppressing an exasperated sigh, Prissy sat up on the mat and grabbed the remote control to pause the aerobics video as Stan sauntered over and crouched down beside her.

"Good morning," he murmured, leaning down to brush a kiss across her mouth. His lips were soft, and he tasted like fresh, minty toothpaste.

"If you wanted a workout," he murmured, nibbling her lower lip, "all you had to do was ask."

"Maybe I would have," Prissy retorted, "if you'd actually been there when I rolled over in bed this morning."

Stan tensed, then drew back to meet her accusing gaze. "You're mad because I slept on the sofa last night," he said evenly.

"What do *you* think?"

He frowned. "Pris—"

"I mean, come on, Stan. You work over seventy hours a week. You're only here half the time, so is it asking too much for you to sleep with me when you *are* home?"

Stan heaved a ragged sigh. "Come on, baby. Don't be mad about this. I couldn't sleep last night, so rather than keep you awake with my tossing and turning, I got up and went to the living room."

"Where you apparently had no trouble sleeping like a baby," Prissy said bitterly.

Stan hesitated. "Not right away. It took me a while to doze off."

"I wonder why."

Stan frowned, staring at her. "What's that supposed to mean?"

Prissy met his gaze directly. "It's not as though this is the first time you've snuck out to the living room during the night. Over the past few months, you've slept on the sofa almost as often as you've slept in our bed. So I can't help but wonder if there's more to your story than insomnia."

"My *story*?" Stan's eyes narrowed on hers. "Are you accusing me of something, Pris?"

She just looked at him, wishing she had the courage to come right out and ask him the question that had been tormenting her for the past several months, keeping her awake many nights and wreaking havoc on her soul.

A question that no loving, devoted wife should ever have to ask her man.

Are you having an affair?

The words hovered on the tip of her tongue—a powder keg set to detonate, an accelerant waiting to ignite the inferno that would blaze through their lives and destroy them.

"Look, baby, you have no reason to be upset," Stan said calmly. "Whenever I'm having insomnia, it's better for me to sleep on the sofa so I won't disturb you. I know you have to get up early for work every morning, so you need your eight hours of rest. Hell, woman, I don't understand why you're not thanking me for being so considerate."

Because I think you're lying to me, Prissy silently accused. *I think you've met someone else, but I'm too much of a coward—*

and too damn afraid of losing you—to confront you with my suspicions.

"Anyway," Stan continued, gently caressing Prissy's cheek, "I didn't come in here to argue with you. I was hoping we could spend some time together before the boys wake up."

Prissy knew what "spending time together" meant, and she wasn't interested. Or so she told herself.

"In case you haven't noticed," she said archly, "I was in the middle of exercising."

"I noticed." Stan's eyes glinted wickedly as he gripped the waistband of her leggings. "I came to offer my services."

"Your *services*?"

"That's right." He began peeling the spandex over her hips. "You're not getting a full-body workout. I can give you one."

Prissy's belly quivered even as she feebly protested, "Come on, Stan. I'm all sweaty."

"And I intend to make you even sweatier," he promised, pulling her leggings all the way off.

"Stan—"

"I don't know why you're trying to lose weight." Lowering his head, he kissed the inside of her damp thigh, sending delicious shivers to her groin. "Don't you know how beautiful you are? Don't you know how turned on I get every time you strut naked across our bedroom, shaking this bodacious ass of yours? Don't you realize how much I enjoy having these juicy thighs wrapped around me when I'm buried deep inside you?"

Prissy trembled hard as he kissed her other leg. "Stan—"

"Mmmm," he purred, running his tongue up her thigh. "Even the taste of your sweat turns me on."

Oh, God, Prissy thought, closing her eyes as a rush of heat filled her belly. No matter how angry she was at Stan, she'd never been able to resist him. But it certainly wasn't for lack of trying.

"Baby, this really isn't a good— *Oh!*" she cried out when he stroked his tongue over the silk crotch of her panties. As jolts of pleasure tore through her body, her back arched off the floor.

Stan chuckled softly. "What were you saying?"

Prissy scarcely heard the question. She wanted him inside her. His tongue, his fingers, his heavy shaft—any and every part of him. So she didn't protest when he peeled off her panties and tossed them aside. As he lowered his mouth to her sex, she fell back against her exercise mat, eager for the sensual workout his tongue was about to give her.

There was a sudden knock at the door. "Ma!"

Prissy nearly jumped out of her skin.

Swearing under his breath, Stan lifted his head and met her panicked gaze.

Did you lock the door? Prissy mouthed.

Before Stan could respond, their youngest son knocked again. "Ma? Are you in there?"

"Um, just a sec—"

But Mason was already opening the door.

With lightning-quick reflexes, Stan grabbed Prissy's exercise towel from the floor and covered her nudity just as Mason burst into the room, a flash of blue and white in Star Wars pajamas.

"Ma, I can't find my—"

"Boy," Stan interrupted sternly, "how many times have we told you to knock before you enter a room?"

Mason pulled up short, frowning at his father as Prissy discreetly used her foot to drag her underwear out of the boy's view. "But I *did* knock."

"And what are you supposed to do after that?" Stan demanded.

Dropping his gaze to the hardwood floor, Mason mumbled, "Wait for permission to enter."

"That's right," Stan confirmed. "So why didn't you do that?"

Taking pity on their son, Prissy gently intervened, "It's okay, Mason. I know you'll remember next time. Now what were you saying that you can't find?"

Darting a wary glance at his father, Mason replied, "I can't find my firefighter T-shirt. I wanna wear it today 'cause Dad's coming to my school. Remember, Daddy?"

Stan smiled indulgently. "Of course I remember. But the presentation's tomorrow, champ. Not today."

"Nuh uh," Mason argued, wagging his head. "It's today."

Stan frowned. "I think you're mistaken, son."

"Actually, he's not," Prissy interjected. "Your visit to Mason's class *is* today."

"*It is?*"

"Yes," Prissy and Mason chorused.

"Aw, hell," Stan muttered, scrubbing a hand over his face. "I must have gotten the dates mixed up."

"I don't see how," Prissy said reproachfully. "It's all our son has been talking about for weeks, and his teacher sent home a reminder a few days ago."

Mason eyed his father worriedly. "Are you still coming, Daddy?"

"Of course, son. I'm looking forward to it." Stan smiled, but it didn't quite reach his eyes. He glanced at Prissy. "I'll help Mason find his shirt so you can finish your workout."

Prissy nodded, watching as he got to his feet. "He needs to wear the T-shirt over the turtleneck I laid out for him. It's cold outside."

Stan gave a mock salute. "Yes, ma'am. Let's go, champ."

As father and son started from the room, Mason glanced back curiously at Prissy, then looked up at Stan. "Daddy?"

"Hmm?"

"How come Ma's underwear was on the floor?"

As Prissy's face flamed with embarrassment, Stan threw back his head and roared with laughter.

Chapter 2

When Prissy reached the kitchen doorway an hour later, the scene she encountered could only be described as one of chaotic harmony.

Stan stood at the stove stirring a pot of grits and frying bacon in a pan while quizzing their son, Montana, for a history test.

Magnum was smearing grape jelly on several slices of toast while rapping to his favorite song by the Sugarhill Gang.

Maddox had his nose buried in a Hardy Boys novel, blissfully ignoring Mason's animated monologue about his football team's upcoming game.

As Prissy stood there observing her family, a soft, poignant smile curved her lips. These were her men, her heart and soul. She couldn't imagine what her life would be like without them. She prayed to God that she'd never have to find out.

Mason was the first to notice her standing in the doorway. "Hey, Ma," he called out cheerfully. "Daddy's making breakfast."

Prissy's smile deepened. "I see that."

As the others turned to look at her, she couldn't help marveling at the striking resemblance between her husband and sons. All of the boys had inherited Stan's beautiful dark skin, deep-set eyes and strong, handsome features. Wherever they went, strangers always remarked on the familial resemblance, which was strong enough to turn any skeptic into a staunch believer of human cloning.

As Prissy padded into the large kitchen, Stan's appreciative gaze roamed over her tailored gray skirt suit, which she wore with a red camisole and a wide belt.

"You look good, baby," he told her.

"Thank you," Prissy said, warming with pleasure. No matter what was going on with her husband, it felt good to know that he still found her attractive. "I have a lot of meetings today, so you know I have to look my best."

"Which you always do," Stan said with a wink.

Prissy smiled gratefully at him. Reaching the large oak breakfast table where Maddox and Mason were seated, she kissed the top of her sons' heads before exclaiming to Maddox, "I can't believe you started that book last night and you've almost finished it!"

"It's *good*, Ma," Maddox declared.

"Apparently so. We'll have to make another trip to the library soon." Prissy glanced across the room at Magnum. "Boy, how much jelly are you going to put on that toast?"

"What?" He glanced down at the slice of toast in question. "This ain't too much."

"Isn't," Prissy corrected, crossing the room to retrieve a mug from the cabinet. "And, yes, it *is* too much."

Magnum merely grinned.

"I was just about to make the eggs," Stan told Prissy as she helped herself to some of his strong black coffee—typical firefighter's brew. "Everything else is ready."

"Thank you, baby." Prissy kissed his stubble-roughened jaw and rubbed his broad back. After adding cream and sugar to her coffee, she took a careful sip, eyeing Montana over the rim of her mug. "Ready for the test?"

"I think so."

Stan cocked a brow at Montana. "You *think* so?"

The boy grinned weakly, flashing dimples. "Yeah, I'm ready."

Stan nodded approvingly. "That's more like it."

Prissy looked around the kitchen, belatedly noticing the absence of her eldest son. "Where's Manny?"

His brothers exchanged glances and shrugged. "Probably still asleep," Magnum suggested.

"He'd better not be," Prissy muttered, setting her mug down on the counter and striding purposefully from the kitchen.

She made her way past the tastefully furnished living room and up the staircase to the second floor. When she reached Manning's bedroom at the end of the hallway, she knocked on the door.

"Manny?" she called.

There was no answer.

She knocked again. "Manny? Are you awake?"

Silence.

Frowning, Prissy opened the door and poked her head into the shadowy room.

Manning was sprawled across his bed, eyes closed, one long leg dangling crookedly over the side.

Shaking her head in exasperation, Prissy marched over to the bed and shook his shoulder. "Manny, wake—"

He jumped, his dark eyes snapping open. "Ma?"

It was only then that Prissy saw that he was wearing headphones that connected to his Walkman, which was why he hadn't heard her calling him. "Why haven't you finished getting dressed?" she fussed, gesturing at his bare chest. "Don't you know what time it is? You're gonna miss your bus!"

Manning sat up slowly, plucking the headphones off. "Do I have to go to school today?"

"Of course you do! Why would you ask that?"

When Manning said nothing, Prissy felt his forehead. "You don't have a fever."

"I know. I just..." He trailed off with a listless shrug. "I just don't feel like going today."

Prissy frowned. "Now you know that's not a good reason for missing school."

Again Manning shrugged.

With another shake of her head, Prissy strode to the windows and yanked the curtains open. Manning winced as pale sunlight flooded the room, which looked like a tornado had swept through it, leaving clothes, sneakers and books strewn haphazardly across the floor.

Prissy clucked her tongue. "This room is a pigsty! I want it cleaned up when you get home from school today, you hear?"

"Yes, ma'am," Manning mumbled, dragging on a blue sweater over his jeans.

As Prissy headed from the room, she added over her shoulder, "And hurry up so you can eat breakfast."

"I'm not hungry."

Prissy froze, then turned and stared at her firstborn. She couldn't have heard right. Manning Wolf never missed a meal. *Ever.*

She eyed him worriedly. "What's wrong, baby?" she asked, even as she acknowledged that her son wasn't such a "baby" anymore. At fourteen, he was already six foot one, with broad shoulders and a sprinkling of facial hair. Even his voice was changing, deepening into what would soon become a rich baritone like his father's. He was morphing into a man right before Prissy's very eyes.

"Is everything okay at school?" she prodded gently. "I know being a freshman can take some getting used to. And it probably doesn't help that your mother is the school superintendent."

Manning grunted noncommittally, bending to tie his huge sneakers.

Watching him, Prissy felt a familiar pang of guilt. Although it had been two years since they moved from Atlanta, she knew that Manning and his brothers were still adjusting to life in Coronado. They missed their old neighborhood, their schools, their friends, and—most of all—their cousins Michael and Marcus. Living in a five-bedroom house with a pool had done little to cure their homesickness. They wanted to go back to Atlanta so badly that Prissy couldn't help second-guessing her decision to uproot them.

As Manning rose and walked to the dresser, she remarked conversationally, "I heard that Coach Delaney really wants you to play for the basketball team. He even called your daddy at work, hoping he could persuade you to try out for the team."

"I don't wanna play basketball," Manning mumbled, picking out his short afro with a long-toothed comb.

Prissy frowned. "Why not? You played back in Atlanta."

"It's not the same here."

"Really?" Prissy countered wryly. "Do they play basketball by different rules in Coronado?"

"That's not what I meant."

"No? Then what *did* you mean?"

Manning sighed heavily, meeting her gaze in the dresser mirror. "Look, Ma, I know why you want me to try out for the team. It's the same reason you have Mason and Magnum playing football, Madd in Boy Scouts, and Monty in the school band. You're trying to keep us all busy because you think the more activities we're involved in, the less we'll miss home."

Busted, Prissy thought.

"Is it a crime to want the best for my family?" she countered defensively. "The reason I took the superintendent job was to give you and your brothers a better quality of life than we had in

Atlanta. Someday when *you're* a parent faced with making difficult decisions for your family, you'll understand why I made the choice that I did."

She watched as Manning stalked over to his bed, snatched his backpack off the floor and began shoving books inside.

She heaved a weary sigh. "We've been living here for over two years, Manny. Like it or not, this is your home now."

"No, Ma," he said quietly, shaking his head at her. "This might be where we live, but it will *never* be home."

Prissy held his gaze for a long moment, then turned and left without another word.

After walking his youngest sons to the bus stop and seeing them off, Stan returned to the house and cleaned up the kitchen. On his days off from work, he always tried to help out around the house so Prissy wouldn't feel taken for granted. The woman did everything, balancing the demands of her job with cooking, cleaning, washing laundry, checking homework, carpooling, planning birthday parties and faithfully attending parent– teacher conferences. Stan and the boys would be lost without her.

Which was why he felt so damn guilty for deceiving her.

He knew he should come clean and tell her the truth about everything.

But he couldn't.

And that made him a bigger coward than he cared to admit.

As soon as Prissy and Manning left the house, Stan grabbed the phone and placed a call. When a woman's smooth voice came on the line, he said quietly, "Hi, this is Stan."

"Hello, Stan. How are you?"

"I'm good." He wiped crumbs off the counter. "Listen, I can't see you today."

"Oh? Is everything okay?"

"Yeah. Remember when I told you that I'd be giving a fire prevention talk to my son's first grade class?"

"Of course. Tomorrow afternoon, right?"

"Actually, it's today. I must have gotten the dates mixed up."

"Oh, that's too bad. I was really looking forward to seeing you today, Stan."

He was silent, guilt gnawing at his insides as he wrung out the dishrag in the sink.

"I have some time tomorrow afternoon," the woman offered.

Catching a flash of color out of the corner of his eye, Stan whipped his head around to find Manning standing in the doorway with his bookbag slung over his back. He was watching Stan, his eyes narrowed speculatively.

Swallowing hard, Stan turned away to murmur into the phone, "I need to go. I'll call you back later."

Hanging up the wall phone, he turned to face his son. "What're you doing back home?"

"I missed my bus," Manning mumbled.

"Again? This is the second time in two weeks."

Manning just looked at him.

Stan heaved an exasperated breath. "Let me get my keys, and I'll drive you to school."

Manning nodded, stepping aside as Stan stalked past him and headed down the hall toward the master bedroom.

"Who was on the phone, Dad?"

Stan halted midstep, then glanced over his shoulder to meet his son's suspicious gaze. "No one," he replied.

Manning frowned. "But I heard you talking to somebody."

"It was just a telemarketer selling life insurance. I told her I wasn't interested."

Manning looked skeptical. "Is that why you're calling her back?"

Stan faltered, unnerved that he'd been caught in a bald-faced lie.

"Don't worry about who I was talking to," he snapped. "Last I checked, boy, I don't answer to you."

Manning clenched his jaw as his expression darkened. Averting his gaze, he muttered something under his breath.

"*What?*" Stan demanded, his brows raised as he took a threatening step toward the boy. "You got something to say to me?"

Before Manning could respond, the doorbell rang.

Shooting a dark glance at his son, Stan went to answer the front door.

Standing on the porch was a beautiful biracial girl wearing a tight V-neck sweater over a denim miniskirt with pink leg warmers. Stan recognized her as one of the neighbor's teenage daughters, though her name escaped him at the moment.

"Good morning, Mr. Wolf," she gushed, batting her heavily mascaraed lashes at him.

Stan smiled indulgently. "Hello, uh—"

"Caitlyn," the girl supplied. "I live down the street."

"Right, right. What can I do for you, Caitlyn?"

"Well, I was just getting dressed for school when I looked out my bedroom window and saw Manning walking back from the bus stop. I figured he must have missed the bus, so I just thought I'd swing by to see if he needs a ride to school."

Stan chuckled. "That's very kind of you, Caitlyn, but I was going to take—"

"That's okay, Dad," Manning interrupted, appearing beside Stan in the doorway. He gave Caitlyn a slow once-over, lingering on the swell of her cleavage. "She can give me a ride."

The girl smiled with pleasure. "Hey, Manning," she purred, a predatory gleam in her hazel eyes. "Are you ready?"

He nodded quickly. "Let's go."

"Not so fast," Stan interjected, holding up a hand to detain his son as he gave Caitlyn a shrewdly appraising look. "How old are you?"

"Dad—" Manning groaned.

The girl laughed. "I just turned sixteen, Mr. Wolf. I'm a junior at the high school."

"So that means you haven't had your driver's license very long."

As Manning slapped a hand to his forehead, Caitlyn grinned unabashedly. "That's true, but I've been driving for over a year with my learner's permit. And I have a spotless record so far—no tickets or accidents whatsoever." Her eyes danced with mirth. "Don't worry, Mr. Wolf. You have my word that I'll get your son to school safe and sound."

"Hmm." Stan's gaze strayed past her to the shiny red Camaro parked at the end of his driveway. "Is that your car?"

"Yup." Caitlyn beamed proudly. "My parents gave it to me for my birthday. Totally awesome, right?"

Stan smothered a laugh. "Totally."

Manning shot him an aggrieved look. "Can we go now?"

Stan hesitated another moment, then relented with a nod. "You kids have a good day. And thanks for giving my son a ride to school, Caitlyn."

"Oh, you don't have to thank me," she purred, smiling coyly at Manning. "It's my pleasure."

I'll bet, Stan mused, watching as the teenagers walked to the Camaro and climbed inside. As Manning buckled his seatbelt, Caitlyn cupped his cheek in her hand and made a comment that brought a slow, lazy smile to his face.

Stan chuckled softly, shaking his head. His son was definitely a chip off the old block.

Which wasn't necessarily a good thing.

As Stan moved to close the door, Manning glanced out the passenger window and met his gaze. The boy's smile faded, letting Stan know that he hadn't forgotten about their near-confrontation.

Stan hesitated, then lifted his hand in a small wave.

Manning nodded shortly.

Long after the Camaro pulled off, Stan stood there wondering how much longer he could keep his secret from destroying his family.

Chapter 3

"Good morning, Dr. Wolf," Gayle Abrams greeted Prissy when she arrived at work that morning.

Prissy smiled at her secretary, a pretty Jamaican sister with beautifully braided hair and a liltingly accented voice that always transported Prissy back to her romantic honeymoon in Ocho Rios.

"Good morning, Gayle," Prissy greeted her warmly. "Got any messages for me?"

"Yes, ma'am." Her efficient secretary passed her a small stack of phone messages. "Mrs. Cohen called to confirm that you're still coming to speak to their group today about the upcoming bond election."

Prissy nodded. "Absolutely."

With $17.4 million of taxpayer dollars at stake, Prissy had made it a priority to meet with as many civic organizations as possible to address their questions and concerns about the school district's proposed capital improvement plan. Since Rose Cohen's auxiliary league had many members who were active in the community, Prissy knew that having the group's support could be crucial to the passage of the bond proposal.

"Would you like some coffee?" Gayle offered.

"No, thanks," Prissy declined, sifting through her phone messages. "I'm still wired from the brew Stan made this morning."

Gayle grinned suggestively. "Why doesn't it surprise me that that husband of yours makes potent coffee?"

Prissy laughed as she left the reception area to head toward her office. It was early, so the other members of her staff hadn't arrived yet.

At the end of the corridor, her office was identified by a brass nameplate on the door that read DR. PRISCILLA WOLF, SUPERINTENDENT.

For the past two years, Prissy had served as chief officer of a small school district right outside of Denver. Although she had a Ph.D. in education administration and several years of experience as a high school principal, her status as an outsider was what had given her an edge over the other candidates vying for the job. In an unprecedented move, Coronado's school board had hired Prissy to improve relations between the district's administrators and the board of education, whose bitter stalemates had become notorious. Since Prissy had no baggage, no alliances and no axes to grind, she—unlike her predecessor— had been able to propose a $17.4 million bond to address the district's educational and infrastructure needs.

Entering her office, Prissy strode across the large room to her desk and set down the monogrammed leather briefcase that Stan and the boys had given to her for Mother's Day last year. She'd just sat in her chair when the intercom on her desk buzzed.

"Dr. Wolf, you have a call."

"Who is it, Gayle?"

Her secretary paused for a long moment. "Celeste Wolf."

Prissy tensed, her chest tightening with anger. She considered instructing her secretary to take a message, but she'd been doing that for the past two months. Sooner or later, she'd have to break her silence and talk to her ex sister-in-law.

"Dr. Wolf?" Gayle prompted tentatively. "Should I tell her you're not available?"

"No," Prissy murmured. "I'll speak to her. Thanks, Gayle."

When the call was transferred, Prissy drew a deep, calming breath before lifting the receiver. "Hello," she said coolly.

"Hey, Pris." Celeste sounded nervous. "Thank you for taking my call this time. I was afraid you wouldn't."

Prissy stared up at the ceiling. "I've got a full afternoon of meetings that I need to prepare for, so I don't have a lot of time to talk."

"I understand," Celeste said meekly. "The reason I'm calling is to find out whether you're still attending the educators' leadership conference this weekend."

"Of course I am. I told you before that I'm one of the workshop presenters."

"I know." Celeste paused for a moment. "Since the conference is in Minnesota this year, I was hoping I'd get an opportunity to see you."

Prissy frowned. "What do you mean? Are you going to be in Rochester?"

"Um, actually, I'm already here. Have been for over a week."

"Why?"

Another pause, this one longer. "I'm here with Grant. He's working at the Mayo Clinic."

"What? I thought he changed his mind about accepting the surgeon position because he wanted to stay in Atlanta with you."

"He did. But then the clinic's head of neurosurgery came back to him about working on a major research project. Grant's participation in the groundbreaking study would bring so much publicity to Atlanta General that they agreed to loan him to the Mayo Clinic for four months. Grant asked me to join him here, and I agreed."

Prissy was stunned. "What about your job at the hospital?"

"I resigned."

"*What?*"

"I would have done that eventually anyway," Celeste hastened to explain. "Since I'm starting my master's in nursing program next fall, Grant wants me to be able to concentrate on my studies and not have to worry about working. Far be it from me to argue with the man who will be paying my tuition."

Which Sterling was unable to, Prissy thought. "Congratulations," she drawled sarcastically. "Looks like you found your Sugar Daddy."

Celeste sighed. "Don't be like that, Pris. You know how much—"

Prissy cut her off. "Does Sterling know you're in Minnesota?"

Celeste's prolonged silence gave Prissy her answer.

"I don't believe this," she hissed. "The ink on your divorce papers is barely dry—you haven't even changed your last name yet—and you've already relocated to another state with Grant?"

"I haven't relocated—"

"What about Michael and Marcus?" Prissy demanded. "How the hell are you supposed to spend any time with them if you're living in Minnesota for the next four months?"

"I'll work out an arrangement with Sterling," Celeste said defensively.

"The same man who doesn't even know where you are?"

Celeste heaved a frustrated breath. "Look, I didn't call to argue with you, Pris. I called to invite you to have dinner with me while you're in town."

"I don't think so," Prissy said flatly.

"Please, Pris," Celeste entreated. "I really need to see you and explain some things to you—"

"It's too late for explanations."

"What do you mean?"

"You could have confided in me a long time ago that you and Sterling were having problems, but you didn't. You could have told me this past summer, when *I* was pouring out my heart to *you* about my issues with Stan. But you didn't say a damn word."

"Because I was ashamed!" Celeste burst out desperately. "I was ashamed of my behavior, I was scared of losing my family and I was afraid that you wouldn't understand what I was going through! And considering the way you've completely shunned me since the divorce, can you really blame me for not confiding in you?"

"Don't you *dare* put this back on me!" Prissy spat furiously. "*You're* the one who's been keeping secrets for God only knows how long. *You're* the one who cheated on your husband and got caught. *You're* the one who walked out on your children—your *children*, for God's sake!—to be with a man you barely know. So don't you *dare* point any fingers at me, because the only one who's to blame for our broken friendship is *you!*"

Celeste was silent for so long that Prissy wondered whether she'd hung up on her.

She waited tensely, the receiver gripped tightly in her hand.

After what seemed an eternity, Celeste spoke. "I really don't want to have this conversation over the phone, Pris. Let me take you to dinner while you're in town. *Please.*"

Prissy swiveled toward the office window, too angry to enjoy the scenic view of the Rocky Mountains in the distance.

"I miss you, Prissy," Celeste said plaintively. "I miss being able to pick up the phone and talk to you anytime. I miss gossiping about our coworkers and our favorite celebrities. I miss swapping recipes and discussing our boys' latest antics. I miss your friendship. And even though you're upset with me right now, I know you feel the same way."

Prissy swallowed tightly, wishing she could deny it. But she couldn't, because the truth was that she *did* miss Celeste. Over the past sixteen years, Celeste had become the sister Prissy never had. She'd been her matron of honor, and had been present for the birth of all five of Prissy's children. They'd shared everything with each other—or so Prissy had always believed.

But she'd been wrong. Celeste wasn't half the woman she'd thought she was, and the way she'd betrayed her husband and children was unforgivable.

So Prissy had nothing to say to her other than, "I'm sorry, Celeste, but I won't be able to meet you for dinner."

"What about drinks? Surely you can make time for drinks?"

"I don't think so."

"So that's it? Just because I made a decision you don't agree with, we can't be friends anymore?"

"I have to go, Celeste," Prissy said with quiet finality. "Take care of yourself."

Before Celeste could utter another word, Prissy hung up the phone.

Blinking back tears of anger and regret, she swiveled away from the window and exhaled a deep, shaky breath. She told herself that she'd done the right thing by severing ties with Celeste.

So why didn't she feel better?

Shaking her head, she swiped at the corners of her eyes. At that moment her gaze landed on a framed portrait on her desk. In the old photograph, Prissy sat with three-year-old Mason on her lap. Stan stood behind them with one hand resting lovingly on Prissy's shoulder. Manning, Montana, Magnum and Maddox flanked her, two on each side. All of them wore big smiles as they beamed into the camera, their eyes shining with happiness and laughter.

Prissy slowly reached across her desk and picked up the photo. A soft smile curved her lips as she tenderly traced her fingertips over the beloved faces of her husband and sons. She remembered how overjoyed she and Stan had been when they'd learned that she was pregnant—the first time, and every time after that. She remembered Stan kneeling before her with his arms wrapped around her expanding waist and his face pressed to her swollen belly as he marveled at the life growing inside her.

She remembered his delighted shouts of laughter whenever the baby kicked him, and she remembered the lazy nights they'd lain in bed together reading from a pregnancy book while Stan gently rubbed her stomach and talked to their unborn son.

Prissy wasn't like Celeste. No matter how bad things might become between her and Stan, she could never walk out on her family.

But what if Stan's having an affair? challenged an inner voice. *Would you stay with a man who's unfaithful to you? What if the decision is taken out of your hands, and Stan leaves you and the kids for another woman?*

Prissy's smile faded.

Holding the family portrait close to her heart, she silently prayed, *Please don't let my worst fears come true, God. Please keep my precious family together.*

Two hours later, Prissy was adding the finishing touches to a budget report she planned to present at tonight's school board meeting. When a knock sounded at her door, she glanced up. She was surprised to find her husband standing in the doorway behind her secretary.

"Sorry to disturb you," Gayle announced in a singsong voice that was far from apologetic, "but you have a visitor, and the gentleman insisted on seeing you right away."

"Did he, now?" Amused, Prissy arched a brow at Stan. "Has the gentleman ever heard of calling first or making an appointment?"

Holding her gaze, Stan said dryly, "The gentleman is offended at the notion that he'd have to call or make an appointment to see his own damn wife."

"Touché." Lips quirking, Prissy glanced at Gayle. "Would you please hold my calls for ten minutes?"

"Make that twenty," Stan corrected, sidestepping Gayle to enter the office.

"As you wish, Mr. Wolf." Grinning wickedly at husband and wife, Gayle closed the door behind her.

Shaking her head in exasperation, Prissy watched as Stan sauntered toward her. He wore black boots and his department-issue uniform—the navy blue one with a gold badge and a patch bearing the CFD emblem sewn onto each sleeve. Prissy had never been the type to lose her mind over a man in uniform...until the first time she'd seen her husband in one. He'd looked so damn fine that her mouth had watered, and all she'd wanted to do was jump his bones.

Fourteen years later, nothing had changed.

He *still* looked mouthwateringly good, and she *still* wanted to devour him.

But this was not the time or the place.

She eyed him warily as he reached her desk. "What're you doing here, Stan?"

"Since we got interrupted this morning," he drawled, "I came to finish what we started."

"*What?*" She shook her head quickly. "I don't think so."

"Then don't think," he suggested, rounding the desk. "Just go with the flow."

"Are you crazy?" Prissy demanded, watching as he knelt beside her and swiveled her chair around to face him. "I'm at *work*, Stan. I can't be fooling around—"

"Says who?" he challenged, kissing her bare knees. "Aren't you the boss?"

"That's not the point!" As he began reaching under her skirt, she shot a panicked glance toward the closed door. "I'm *serious*, baby. This isn't a good time. Someone could walk in at any moment—"

"Gayle won't let 'em."

"—and I've got a million things to do—"

"Starting with me."

Prissy groaned, even as her pulse went haywire. "Stan—"

He leaned forward and kissed her, silencing her protests. Though Prissy knew she should resist, she couldn't find the willpower to do so. Because the truth was that she wanted him. Craved him. Needed him like her body needed water and oxygen. And it would always be this way.

Tasting her surrender, Stan dragged her silk panties off her legs and over her red stilettos, then set them on the desk. Without breaking their kiss, he lifted her effortlessly from the chair and sat down, leaving her no choice but to straddle his hard thighs. Their mouths opened and closed over each other's, tongues dancing to the same slow, sensual rhythm.

Prissy shivered at the feel of Stan's callused hands sliding underneath her skirt to cup her bare bottom. As he kneaded the plump flesh, she ground her hips against his thick, straining erection.

He reacted with a husky groan. "Baby..."

Sucking his bottom lip, Prissy admonished, "See what you started."

"Umm-hmm," he murmured, unzipping his pants. "And I intend to *finish* it."

Pulse hammering, Prissy hitched her skirt up her thighs and lowered herself onto his long, hard shaft. They both groaned softly with pleasure.

As Stan began thrusting into her, she wrapped her arms around his neck and whispered breathlessly, "This is crazy. I'm supposed to be working."

Stan's eyes glittered wickedly. "You know what they say about all work and no play."

"Mmmm." Prissy's head fell back, eyes closing as she surrendered to the delicious sensations pounding through her body. She rocked her hips up and down as Stan drove into her, plunging deeper and harder with every stroke.

Their coupling felt so incredible that Prissy never wanted it to end. But all too soon she was coming apart, her back arching with the force of her sudden orgasm. Stan crushed his mouth to hers, smothering her helpless cry just in time.

Moments later he exploded, his hands tightly gripping her butt as he spent himself inside her.

Weak and trembling, Prissy dropped her head onto his shoulder and nibbled his jaw, savoring the subtle spice of his aftershave. As he kissed her forehead and gathered her closer, she sighed contentedly, wishing she could remain in his arms for the rest of the day.

"You know you are *so* wrong for this."

Stan grinned, lazily stroking her back. "If loving you is wrong, I don't wanna be right."

Prissy laughed, lifting her head to give him an accusing look. "If I'm unprepared for my meetings this afternoon, I'm blaming *you*."

His eyes glinted wickedly. "In that case," he drawled, "we might as well go for round two—"

"Don't even *think* about it," Prissy warned, hurriedly scrambling off his lap before she could succumb to temptation. God knows she wanted nothing more than to blow off her meetings and spend the rest of the day making love to Stan. But duty called, and she'd never been one to shirk her responsibilities.

Watching as she plucked her panties off the desk and slipped them on, Stan said huskily, "We'll finish this later."

It wasn't a request, and Prissy knew it. As her body heated with anticipation, she smiled demurely. "I'll see what I can do."

Stan laughed. As he tucked himself back into his pants and zipped up, his pager went off. He hesitated for a moment, then reached down and removed the device clipped to his waistband. As he checked the display screen, Prissy felt rather than saw him tense.

Smoothing the wrinkles from her skirt, she teased, "Don't tell me they're calling you from the station. Don't those people know you're off for the rest of the week?"

Stan smiled absently, returning the pager to his waistband.

"Do you want to use my phone to call them back?" Prissy offered.

"No," he said quickly. Too quickly.

Prissy frowned as a whisper of unease ran through her.

She watched as Stan rose from the chair and began straightening his uniform. A change had come over him, so subtle she might have missed it if she didn't know him as well as she did.

Struck by a sudden realization, she glanced at her wristwatch. "You don't have to be at Mason's school until one-thirty. Are you going somewhere before then?"

"No." He paused, seeming to reconsider his answer before he amended, "I'm just dropping by the station to pick up some prep materials for the exam. The test date will be here before I know it."

After fourteen years of distinguished service as a firefighter—climbing his way up the ranks to lieutenant—Stan was now up for a promotion to captain pending the results of written and oral exams he was scheduled to take in January.

"You know," Prissy remarked, folding her arms across her busty chest, "you're supposed to stay *away* from the station on your days off. If the alarm sounds while you're there—"

"I'll let the fellas who are on duty handle the emergency. That's what shifts are for."

Before Prissy could argue, Stan pressed a quick, hard kiss to her mouth. "I'll see you this evening."

She nodded, walking him to the door. "Are you still taking the boys to the movies after school?"

"Yeah. It's supposed to be a surprise. You didn't tell them, did you?"

"Of course not. Besides," Prissy added wryly, "I didn't have the heart to tell Manny that he's going to miss out on seeing a movie just because he gets out of school much later than his brothers."

Stan grinned ruefully. "I'll make it up to him."

"You'd better."

Stan kissed her again, then winked. "I'll pick up dinner on the way home."

"Okay." She smiled softly. "Good luck on the presentation."

"Thanks, honey. Hope your meetings go well."

"Me, too."

After Stan left, Prissy closed the door and headed to her private bathroom to freshen up and change her underwear. She kept an extra pair at the office in case of emergencies, which now, apparently, included midday quickies.

Blushing at the thought, Prissy surveyed her reflection in the mirror. She'd been called pretty, even beautiful on a good day. Her skin was the color of mocha and she had dark, almond-shaped eyes. Her forehead was round, her lips were full and her dimpled chin made her look younger than thirty-three. Before interviewing for the superintendent job two years ago, she'd exchanged her big afro for feathered tresses that framed her face. As much as she may have wanted to believe that her qualifications would matter more than her appearance, she'd known better than to take any chances.

After washing her hands at the sink, Prissy emerged from the bathroom and returned to her desk.

Five minutes later, she found herself unable to concentrate on the report she'd been working on before Stan arrived.

Because try as she might, she couldn't shake the feeling that he'd been hiding something from her. Something to do with the page he'd supposedly received from someone at work.

Supposedly?

Prissy frowned, her mind churning with speculation. After another moment, she picked up the phone and called the fire station.

After exchanging pleasantries with Dora—Engine Company 8's only female firefighter who was on watch desk duty—Prissy said very casually, "Someone just paged Stan, but he couldn't get to the phone right away to return the call. Do you know if anyone there might have been looking for him?"

"Not that I know of. But I can check with the other guys on duty, if you don't mind holding?"

"I don't mind. Thanks, Dora." Prissy waited tensely, drumming her manicured fingernails on the desk.

After a few minutes, Dora came back on the line. "I was right. No one here paged Stan—"

Prissy's heart sank.

"—but the fellas said he's more than welcome to come to work if he's bored."

Prissy forced out a laugh. "Thanks for checking for me, Dora."

"Anytime, hon."

Prissy's hand trembled as she hung up the phone.

Stan's pager had been issued to him and other senior firefighters who had paramedic training so that they could be reached in case of an emergency that required additional personnel. Stan had never used his pager for personal reasons; his colleagues were the only ones who even had the number.

Prissy frowned, leaning back in her chair.

If someone from work didn't page my husband, she wondered suspiciously, *who the hell did?*

Chapter 4

Erin Gilliard slid a tube of red lipstick across her mouth, then inspected her reflection in the compact mirror she'd retrieved from her purse. With her honey complexion, flawless features and lustrous mane of dark hair, she bore such a striking resemblance to Jayne Kennedy that she was often mistaken for the popular model.

Smiling at the thought, Erin fluffed her hair in the mirror, wanting to look her best for her man in case he showed up today.

She couldn't pinpoint the exact moment she'd begun to think of Stanton Wolf as her man. All she knew was that she'd wanted him from the moment she met him.

And who could really blame her?

With skin slathered in dark chocolate, piercing bedroom eyes, juicy lips and mountain-wide shoulders that would make any woman fantasize about being swept up in a fireman's carry, Stan was a god. He'd sauntered into her life wearing his firefighter's uniform, exuding so much testosterone and raw sex appeal that she'd had to cross her legs tightly under her desk. He'd paused at the door to offer a sheepish apology as he stamped the dust off his work boots before entering the room. When she'd heard that voice—that deep, dark, wicked voice— her panties had gotten embarrassingly wet.

From that moment on, she'd known she had to have him.

It didn't matter that he had a wife and five children—five strapping *sons*, as if she needed any further proof of his overwhelming virility.

And it didn't matter that, as a rule, she never mixed business with pleasure.

Nothing else mattered but her need to stake her claim to Stan.

And now, after three months of spending time with him and getting to know him better, she was *so* close to making him hers.

Erin admired her reflection another moment, then returned the compact mirror to her purse and leaned back in her chair with a satisfied smile on her face.

She couldn't *wait* to see Stan again.

The sooner, the better.

Chapter 5

Manning gazed out the classroom window as his precalculus teacher's voice droned on and on, explaining complex mathematical theorems that failed to hold Manning's attention. Since leaving the house that morning, he'd been unable to concentrate on anything other than the conversation—argument?—he'd had with his father.

Something was going on between his parents.

Something bad.

Last night when Manning crept downstairs to get a drink of water, he'd found his father sleeping on the living room sofa. And it wasn't the first time, either. When it happened last month, his dad told him that he'd fallen asleep watching a late football game. But over breakfast that morning, Manning had sensed some tension between his parents. They'd hardly spoken to each other, and whenever their eyes met across the table, they couldn't seem to look away fast enough.

So when Manning saw his father on the sofa last night, he knew something was wrong. His suspicions were confirmed when he caught his dad outright lying about his phone conversation.

Why did he lie about who he was talking to? Manning wondered apprehensively. *What is he hiding?*

Manning was afraid to find out, because he didn't want to end up like his cousins Michael and Marcus, whose parents had recently gotten divorced. Poor Marcus hadn't been the same ever since he'd caught his mother making out with another man. The last time Manning spoke to Mike on the phone, Mike told him that Marcus still had nightmares and often cried himself to sleep at night. Even though Mike tried to act all tough and brave, Manning knew that he was hurting just as much as Marcus. They missed their mom, and they didn't understand how she could abandon them the way she'd done. Manning didn't understand, either.

He loved his parents more than anything. He didn't want to be forced to choose between them if they got divorced. If his dad returned to Atlanta, he wouldn't want to be left behind, nor would his brothers. On the other hand, Manning couldn't bear the thought of his mother living alone in that big ol' house. She'd be sad and lonely, and Manning would miss the hell out of her.

"Am I boring you, Mr. Wolf?"

Snapped out of his reverie, Manning turned from the window to meet the reproachful glare of his teacher, a middle-aged white dude with shaggy brown hair that matched his corduroy slacks and Hush Puppies.

Manning eyed him blankly. "Huh?"

As his classmates snickered, Mr. Langenkamp frowned with displeasure. "I asked whether I was boring you, since you'd obviously rather daydream than pay attention to the lesson."

"I wasn't daydreaming," Manning objected.

"No?" Mr. Langenkamp challenged, raising a bushy brow. "Then you heard my explanation for how to solve the equation on the board?"

Manning hesitated for a moment, darting a glance around the room. While most of his classmates gave him *better-you-than-me* looks, one bespectacled girl smiled encouragingly at him. Something about her smile tugged at Manning, and he stared at her until she blushed and dropped her eyes.

"Mr. Wolf?"

Glancing away from the girl, Manning met his teacher's stern gaze. "Yeah, I heard your explanation."

"Oh, really?" Mr. Langenkamp countered skeptically. "In that case, why don't you tell us the answer."

"Sir?"

Mr. Langenkamp gestured to the chalkboard. "Prove that you were paying attention. Solve the problem."

A hushed silence swept over the room. Manning could sense the other kids holding their collective breath, waiting to witness the outcome of this showdown between him and the teacher who struck fear in the hearts of every student unlucky enough to be assigned to his class.

Mr. Langenkamp smirked at Manning. "Any day now, Mr. Wolf."

Taking a deep breath, Manning rose from his chair and walked to the front of the classroom. Lips pursed, eyes narrowed in concentration, he studied the quadratic equation scrawled across the chalkboard.

$$3x^3 = -13x^2 + 10x$$

After several moments, he picked up a piece of chalk and went about solving the problem.

When he'd finished, he set the chalk down and turned to face Mr. Langenkamp.

Dude looked stunned.

"Sir?" Manning prompted. "Is this correct?"

Mr. Langenkamp blinked rapidly and glanced around at the shocked faces of his other students, then nodded grudgingly.

"Explain how you reached the solution," he instructed tersely.

"Okay, check this out." Pointing to the chalkboard, Manning rattled off the steps he'd taken. "Using the factoring method, I moved the non-zero terms to the left side of the equation, setting the polynomial equal to zero. Next I factored the quadratic and set each factor equal to zero to solve the smaller equations. After that I plugged each answer into the original equation to make sure the quadratic equation was true and—*Shazam!*—problem solved."

As laughter erupted around the room, Mr. Langenkamp scowled.

Smothering a triumphant grin, Manning asked innocently, "Would you like me to demonstrate how to solve the equation using the quadratic formula? Or by completing the square?"

"Ah, no, that won't be necessary. Please have a seat, Manning." Mr. Langenkamp paused, then added gruffly, "And stop daydreaming in my class. I won't go so easy on you next time."

"Yes, sir," Manning said with mock solemnity.

As he sauntered back to his desk, his classmates stared at him with varying degrees of admiration, amusement and envy. A pretty blonde seated near the front winked flirtatiously at him. Even as Manning smiled back, his gaze was already skipping past her to rest on the girl with the thick eyeglasses. But her head was bent as she scribbled furiously in her notebook.

When the dismissal bell rang, the teacher asked Manning to stay behind.

As the other students filed noisily out of the classroom, Mr. Langenkamp leaned a hip against the corner of his desk and folded his arms across his chest. "You set me up, Mr. Wolf."

Manning eyed him blankly. "What do you mean?"

"You were never worried about not being able to solve the equation. But you pretended you were so the joke would be on me."

Manning gave him a look of exaggerated innocence. "I don't know what you're talking about, Mr. Langenkamp."

"Sure. Whatever you say." The man smiled wryly at Manning. "Do you know how rare it is for ninth graders to take precalculus? You and Miss Chastain are the only freshmen enrolled in precalculus in the entire school. We've barely started the unit on quadratic equations, and you already know all the methods for solving them. How do you explain that?"

Manning shrugged. "Every summer my mom makes me and my brothers read a certain number of books, and she gives us math and science lessons to get us prepared for each new school year."

"Why doesn't that surprise me?" Mr. Langenkamp mused, shaking his head. "Your mother's the youngest superintendent we've ever had. Of course her children are wunderkinds."

Recognizing the term, Manning chuckled. "I wouldn't say all *that*."

"You don't have to. Everyone else will." Mr. Langenkamp smiled. "On that note, have you ever considered becoming a math tutor? For a few hours a week after school, you could earn some extra cash and help your less fortunate peers who weren't gifted with your mathematical brilliance."

Manning thought about the conversation he'd just had with his mother about him and his brothers getting involved in various activities. He knew she'd be pleased with him becoming a math tutor, even if *he* wasn't exactly sold on the idea.

"What do you say?" his teacher prodded.

"I'll think about it," Manning said, making no promises.

"Please do."

After leaving Mr. Langenkamp's classroom, Manning headed down the noisy hallway toward his locker, sidestepping a group of rowdy freshmen who were tossing wads of paper at one another. Not for the first time, Manning wished he were back in Atlanta attending high school with Mike, Quentin Reddick and the rest of the crew from their neighborhood. Although Manning had made a few good friends here, none of them could replace the homeboys he'd left behind.

"Nice work in class."

Glancing over his shoulder, Manning saw the nerdy-looking girl from precalculus. The girl with the beautiful smile.

"Thanks," he told her.

"I knew you could do it," she stated, falling in step beside him.

Manning cocked a brow at her. "How'd you know that?"

"You're smart. Gifted."

Manning shook his head with a grimace. "That word gets thrown around too much."

She eyed him knowingly. "If you weren't gifted, how else could you have spaced out for most of class and still come up with the right answer to the equation?"

Manning smiled at her. "I got lucky." When he noticed that she was struggling to keep pace with his long-legged stride, he automatically slowed down. "What's your name, shorty?"

She smiled shyly. "Taylor Chastain."

He shook her small, proffered hand. "Manning—"

"Wolf. I know." She laughed. "Mr. Langenkamp must have called your name a hundred times today. He probably regrets that now."

Manning chuckled, discreetly checking out Taylor's appearance. She wore a baggy beige sweater over a plaid wool skirt that fell past her knees. The frumpy outfit was topped off by ugly wooden clogs that made an annoying *clip-clop* sound as she walked. Her dark hair was pulled back into a messy ponytail, and black horn-rimmed glasses rested on the bridge of her nose. On the plus side, her skin was smooth, without a trace of the acne that plagued many of their peers. The color reminded Manning of his great-grandmother's brown sugar pecan pie.

Between the bulky sweater Taylor wore and the books clutched to her chest, he couldn't tell how big her breasts were. But he knew they couldn't compare to Caitlyn's bodacious boobs, which he'd ogled the entire ride to school that morning.

"So," Taylor interrupted before his mind began to wander, "did Mr. Langenkamp ask you to be a math tutor?"

"Yeah." Manning shot her a surprised look. "How'd you know?"

Taylor grinned mysteriously. "I know everything."

Manning laughed. "I'm starting to believe that."

Taylor's grin widened. Looking at her, Manning had a sudden urge to pluck her glasses off her face so he could see her eyes better.

"I was just kidding," she continued. "I knew because Mr. Langenkamp asked me the same thing before class started."

"What'd you tell him?"

"That I'd get back to him tomorrow."

"You wanna be a tutor?"

"Maybe." She shrugged. "Beats babysitting my little brother after school every day."

Manning pulled a wry face. "I know what you mean."

"Really? Do you have any sib—" She broke off at the sight of three pretty cheerleaders coming toward them. As the girls drew near, Taylor smiled brightly. "Hey, Janelle. How's it—"

Rudely ignoring Taylor's greeting, Janelle beamed at Manning and cooed, "Hiii, Manning."

He nodded briefly at her. "Wassup."

Taylor looked crestfallen as Janelle and her giggling companions continued down the hallway without acknowledging her presence.

Manning eyed Taylor sympathetically. "Friend of yours?"

"Used to be," she mumbled.

"What happened?"

A small, humorless smile twisted Taylor's mouth. "She sprouted breasts and made the junior varsity cheerleading squad."

"Ah." Manning nodded understandingly. Deciding it was best to change the subject, he said curiously, "By the way, what were you writing in your notebook at the end of class?"

Taylor looked surprised. "You saw me?"

"Yeah."

"Oh." She hesitated, pushing her glasses up on her nose. "Well, I was, um, copying your answer off the board."

Now it was Manning's turn to be surprised. "Why'd you do that?"

Taylor grinned sheepishly. "Turns out I *don't* know everything."

They both laughed.

As they reached Manning's locker, he noticed a group of upperclassmen approaching from the other direction. As the boys sauntered past, one of them knocked Taylor's books out of her arms.

"Hey!" she protested as the posse burst out laughing.

"Oops!" taunted the ringleader—a beefy, dark-haired white boy. "Guess you'd better be more careful next time, dweeb."

As another wave of raucous laughter erupted, Manning's temper flared. "Hey, asshole."

The retreating boys froze in their tracks.

After exchanging startled glances, they turned slowly to stare at Manning. The ringleader looked stunned, as if he couldn't believe that a lowly freshman had addressed him so disrespectfully.

He pointed to his chest. "Are you talking to *me*?"

"Hell, yeah, I'm talking to you," Manning growled. "What the hell do you think you're doing?"

The boy's eyes widened incredulously. "*Excuse me*?"

"Yo, you got a hearing problem or something?" Manning pointed at Taylor's fallen books. "You need to pick those up and apologize to the young lady."

Huddled beside him, Taylor muttered nervously, "It's okay, Manning."

"Yeah, *Manning*," the bully jeered mockingly. "You'd better listen to the little dweebette before someone gets hurt."

Manning didn't blink. "The only one who's about to get hurt up in here is you, motherfucker."

The boy's face reddened as his friends exclaimed in angry protest. An excited buzz was sweeping through the hallway as other students crowded closer to watch the unfolding showdown.

The ringleader looked Manning over, sizing him up before he smirked at his friends. "Can you believe this little dipshit?"

Their answering grins were full of tense bravado as they watched Manning saunter toward them. One of the boys—the token Negro in the group—couldn't even look Manning in the eye.

Stopping in front of his adversary, Manning warned through clenched teeth, "I'ma tell you one more time, asshole. Pick up those books and apologize to my friend."

"Or what?" the bully challenged, sneering as he pushed his face into Manning's. "Who's gonna make me?"

Deciding they'd done enough talking, Manning threw a punch that connected with the boy's jaw and rocked his head backward. Before the chump could recover, Manning was all over him.

The blows he landed felt *damn* good, but he knew there'd be hell to pay later.

Chapter 6

Prissy was livid.

Half an hour ago, she'd been on her way out the door to meet with Rose Cohen's auxiliary league when Manning's high school principal called to inform her that Manning had gotten into a fight with another student.

She'd rushed right over to Coronado High. Upon her arrival, she'd found her son sprawled in a chair across from Principal Henderson's desk, an ice pack pressed to his left eye. When he saw Prissy, a look of dread had crossed his face before his expression turned sullen.

Seething with fury, Prissy listened with forced composure as the principal explained to her what had happened that morning. "According to other students who witnessed the fight," Henderson said at the end of his account, "Manning threw the first punch."

Prissy glanced sharply at her son. "Is that true?"

Lowering the ice pack from his face, Manning mumbled, "Yeah."

"*What?* Why did you do that?"

Manning fell mutinously silent, glaring down at his sneakers.

"I asked you a question," Prissy snapped. "Why did you start the fight?"

Her son scowled. "I didn't start it. I finished it."

Taken aback by his brash response, Prissy shot a glance at Principal Henderson. The man was frowning, his eyes narrowed with disapproval.

Striving for patience—and resisting the maternal instinct to fuss over her son's swelling eye—Prissy prodded, "So you threw the first punch, but you didn't start the fight?"

"No, ma'am."

When Manning stubbornly offered no more, it took everything Prissy had not to reach over and smack him upside his head.

"I certainly share your frustration, Dr. Wolf," Principal Henderson interjected. "None of the eyewitnesses saw what actually led to the altercation, or so they claim. The other boy and his friends aren't cooperating, and neither is Manning."

"Where *is* the other student?" Prissy asked. "I'd like to meet with him and his parents to get to the bottom of this incident."

Principal Henderson grimaced. "I'm afraid that won't be possible today. Rory had to be taken to the hospital. His, ah, nose may be broken."

Prissy gasped, whipping her head around to stare incredulously at Manning. She couldn't believe that her own child had sent another student to the hospital. *The hospital!*

"What on earth has gotten into you?" she demanded furiously.

Manning slumped lower in his chair, radiating teenage rebellion and resentment.

Principal Henderson cleared his throat, drawing Prissy's angry gaze back to him. "Because Manning violated our no-fighting policy, I'm afraid I have no choice but to suspend him for three days." The man wore a pained expression. "I'm sorry, Dr. Wolf. I wish I could offer an alternative—"

"Oh, no," Prissy interrupted, holding up a hand. "You have *nothing* to apologize for, Mr. Henderson. My son broke the rules, so he has to suffer the consequences of his actions. Believe me, he knows better than to expect preferential treatment just because I'm the superintendent."

Principal Henderson looked immensely relieved, and Prissy knew why. Her predecessor had been known to hold grudges, retaliating against anyone she even *suspected* of opposing her. Principal Henderson undoubtedly feared that Prissy would find a way to punish him for suspending her son. But right now, the only one who needed to fear her wrath was Manning.

"Since this was his second offense," Principal Henderson volunteered, "Rory Kerrigan will be suspended for six days."

Prissy arched a brow. "A repeat offender?"

"You could say that." Principal Henderson glanced at Manning, wry humor tugging at his lips. "But after today, I think it's safe to assume that Rory will choose his battles more wisely."

Prissy didn't share the principal's amusement. Turning to her son, she said sternly, "Do you have something to say to Principal Henderson?"

With obvious reluctance, Manning looked at the principal and mumbled dutifully, "I'm sorry for—"

"Sit up," Prissy snapped.

He straightened in the chair. "I'm sorry for getting into a fight with Rory."

"And?" Prissy prompted.

Manning clenched his jaw. "It won't happen again, sir."

Principal Henderson nodded graciously. "Apology accepted. You're a good student, Manning. I've heard nothing but great things about you from your teachers, all of whom have high expectations of you. So I don't want to see you back in my office again. Understood?"

Manning nodded. "Yes, sir. I understand."

"Good."

After answering some of Principal Henderson's questions about the upcoming bond election, Prissy thanked him for his time and ushered her son out of the office.

In the outer reception area, a mousy-looking girl with horn-rimmed glasses was speaking urgently to the secretary. "It's very important that I see Principal Henderson and tell him—" She broke off at the sight of Prissy and Manning.

As Prissy watched in openmouthed astonishment, the girl suddenly rushed over and threw her arms around Manning's waist. He looked startled, then adorably abashed.

Drawing away, the girl gazed up at him and whispered earnestly, "Thank you."

He winked at her with his good eye. "Keep your head up."

The girl nodded with the solemnity of an embattled soldier pledging to carry on the fight in honor of a fallen comrade.

As Prissy and Manning left the main office, the girl's wistful gaze followed them out.

Prissy waited until she and Manning were in the car before she asked, "Who was that young lady?"

"Her name's Taylor," Manning mumbled, staring out the passenger window. "She's in my math class."

"Is that why you got into a fight with that boy? Because he was bullying Taylor?"

Manning merely shrugged.

Prissy frowned. "That's not an answer."

"Does it really matter?"

"*Excuse you?* Of course it matters!"

"Why, Ma?" Manning challenged, meeting her angry gaze. "What difference does it make why I was fighting? Even if I tell you that I punched Rory 'cause he was picking on Taylor, I'd *still* be in trouble. So what's the point?"

"The point is that I asked you a question, and I expect an answer!"

Manning turned back to the window, ignoring her.

As her temper snapped, Prissy reached over and grabbed his chin in her hand, forcing his gaze back to hers as she scolded sharply, "*Manning Josiah Wolf!* Don't you dare look away from me when I'm talking to you!"

He glowered at her, nostrils flaring, dark eyes flashing with tumultuous emotions.

Prissy stared at him, wishing she could see into his troubled soul. "What's this really about, Manny?" she probed, striving for composure. "Are you trying to get back at me for making you go to school today? Or are you trying to punish me for uprooting you from Atlanta? Which is it?"

A muscle clenched in his jaw. "You don't understand."

"*Then help me understand!*" Prissy burst out shrilly. "Help me understand how a boy who has everything going for him could still manage to be so damn miserable! Help me understand how you could become so enraged that you'd break someone's nose! Help me understand just what the *hell* is going on with you!"

He was silent, his surly gaze shifting past her to stare out the window.

Glancing over her shoulder, Prissy saw a woman fumbling to unlock the door of a yellow Volvo nearby; she was so busy watching Prissy and Manning that she kept missing the keyhole.

Frowning at the realization that her shouting had attracted an audience, Prissy abruptly released her son's chin and started the engine. She waited until they'd left school grounds before she resumed her tirade.

"We don't live in Atlanta anymore, Manny. We left behind the old neighborhood where you and your brothers had to worry about fending off bullies on your way to the bus stop every morning. You don't have to fight for your survival anymore."

"I know that," Manning mumbled.

"Then you need to act like it!" Exasperated, Prissy shook her head at him. "Do you have *any* idea what people are going to think when they hear about this incident? You're the superintendent's son, and like it or not, folks expect more from you. So you can't go around getting into brawls and breaking people's noses like you're some hoodlum off the street!"

Once again, Manning was broodingly silent.

"Do you realize how much you've disrupted my day?" Prissy continued. "I was on my way to an important meeting with a large community organization when Principal Henderson called me. Thanks to you, the meeting will have to be postponed, which is a damn shame considering how hard it was for me to even *get* on this group's calendar. And God only knows what's going to happen with Rory and his parents. If you really broke his nose, they might decide to sue us. So while I'm over here trying to improve our school district and convince voters to approve a $17.4 million bond proposal, my family could be battling a *lawsuit!*"

Staring down at the melting ice pack in his lap, Manning grumbled, "I'm sorry."

"Oh, you're *gonna* be sorry," Prissy promised. "If you think that getting three days off from school translates into a vacation, you're in for a rude awakening. By the time you finish washing and folding your brothers' laundry, cleaning their rooms, mopping the kitchen floor, vacuuming the house, mowing the yard, reorganizing the garage and doing whatever else needs to be done, you're gonna *beg* to return to school."

At that, Manning leaned back against the headrest, closed his eyes and groaned.

And for the first time that afternoon, Prissy found something to smile about.

Everything had been going so well.

The roomful of first graders listened raptly as Stan described his job as a firefighter and demonstrated fire prevention safety measures. Assisted by Sparky the Fire Dog—which was really his colleague, Jake Easton, in a Dalmatian costume—Stan taught Mason and his classmates how to Stop, Drop and Roll to smother burning clothes, and to crawl under smoke and stay low to the floor during a fire. He led them in a spirited rendition of the fire safety song—which was sung to the tune of "Frère Jacques"—and answered some of their amusing questions, like whether he'd ever hurt himself sliding down the pole at the fire station. (Which, for the record, he never had.)

He was almost home free.

Until Miss Dominguez cheerfully informed her students that they had time for just one more question before Stan's visit ended.

A small hand shot into the air, rising above the others.

Stan smiled, pointing to the child attached to the urgently waving hand. "What's your name, buddy?"

"Colton, sir. Colton Cobb." He was a cute kid with bright green eyes, freckled cheeks and a voice that squeaked.

Again Stan smiled. "What's your question for me, Colton?"

The boy rose from his little desk, looked Stan in the eye and asked bluntly, "When you run into a burning house, do you ever get scared of dying?"

Stan's throat locked.

Shit.

As a hushed silence swept over the classroom, Stan shot a glance at Miss Dominguez. But she seemed as stunned as he was.

He swallowed hard as Colton waited, oblivious to the havoc his perfectly innocent question had wrought on Stan's nervous system.

As he floundered for a response, Mason piped up confidently, "My daddy's the best fireman in the world. So he's *never* gonna die!"

Jesus.

Stan saw Jake staring at him with his huge, spotted head cocked to one side, mimicking the perplexed gesture of a real dog. And like a faithful furry friend, he came to Stan's rescue.

Turning to the whispering schoolchildren, he asked animatedly, "Who wants a fire hat?"

"*I do! I do!*" came the delighted squeals.

Relieved that the diversion tactic had worked, Stan watched as Jake reached inside his large "doggy bag" and began distributing red plastic fire hats with all the joviality of Santa Claus handing out presents at Christmastime.

"Okay, children," Miss Dominguez called out brightly. "Let's show our appreciation to Lieutenant Wolf and Sparky the Fire Dog for visiting our class today!"

Stan smiled weakly as the first graders showered him and Jake with a boisterous round of applause.

Afterward, as most of the kids flocked to Sparky to cop a feel of his costume, Miss Dominguez approached Stan. She was a pretty young thing who looked barely old enough to drive, let alone be a schoolteacher.

"Thanks again for coming today, Mr. Wolf," she gushed. "You were *wonderful* with the children. You had them hanging on to your every word."

Until the end when I froze like a deer in headlights, Stan thought grimly. "Thanks for inviting me," he told Miss Dominguez. "I'm glad the kids enjoyed the presentation."

"*Enjoyed it?* Are you kidding? This is all they're going to talk about for the rest of the school year!"

Stan smiled absently, watching as Jake crouched down so that the children could play with his—Sparky's—floppy ears.

"Maybe you could come back for Career Week," Miss Dominguez suggested hopefully as she tucked her long, dark hair behind one ear. "I know my class would *love* to have you again."

Stan chuckled. "Thanks for the invitation, but I'd better pass. I don't want the other parents to accuse me of hogging up the limelight."

Miss Dominguez laughed, wagging her head at him. "Now I see where Mason gets his sense of humor."

"Uh-oh. Don't tell me that boy's been cutting up in class."

"Oh, no. Not at all. Mason is *such* a delight, Mr. Wolf. He's one of my smartest students, and he has a way of getting the other children to listen to him." Miss Dominguez smiled warmly. "But I guess I should wait until next week's parent–teacher conference to tell you how he's doing."

"That's okay. I'm back on day shift all next week, so I won't be able to make the meeting anyway. But my wife will fill me in."

"Oh." Miss Dominguez's smile slipped a notch. "Right. Of course."

Just then Mason ran over and threw his small arms around Stan's waist. "You were *awesome*, Daddy!"

Stan smiled indulgently. "Think so?"

"Yeah!" Mason beamed up at him. "Magnum and Maddox are gonna be jealous!"

Stan laughed, affectionately rubbing the back of his son's head. "Speaking of your brothers, we need to pick them up from their classes, then swing by the middle school to get Monty. So you need to gather your things so we can leave."

Miss Dominguez glanced at the clock on the wall. "Goodness! It *is* almost time for the bell to ring." With a brisk clap of her hands, she called out to the children, "Okay, class! Take out your planners and write down your homework assignments, then pack up and get ready for dismissal."

As the kids raced back to their desks, Stan and Jake stepped into the hallway and closed the classroom door behind them. Jake wasted no time removing the humongous dog head.

"I couldn't *wait* to do that," he muttered, using one pawed hand to smooth his wavy blond hair. "This thing is scratchy and hot as hell."

Stan chuckled sympathetically.

Jake was a rookie firefighter who'd had the misfortune of being around that morning when the guy who normally did the Sparky public appearances called in sick.

"Norris owes me *big time*," Jake grumbled.

"Oh, I don't know about that," Stan teased, studying the row of childish drawings displayed along the wall. "You looked like you were enjoying yourself in there. You were a natural. Norris should be worried."

Jake snorted out a laugh. "Believe me, I have no interest in replacing him as Sparky the Fire Dog. What *does* interest me is Miss Dominguez. Why didn't you tell me that your kid's teacher is a total babe?"

Stan chuckled. "Maybe because she looks like she just graduated from high school."

Jake grinned. "Well, *I'm* not exactly Methuselah."

Stan laughed. "That you aren't, rookie."

Sobering after another moment, Jake eyed Stan curiously. "So what happened to you in there?"

Stan automatically tensed. "What're you talking about?"

"What happened when that kid asked you that question? You looked...well, you looked terrified." Concerned blue eyes searched Stan's face. "What spooked you?"

Instead of responding, Stan turned back to the wall to survey Mason's colorful drawing of their family. He'd posed them against the backdrop of their large white house with the black shutters and pretty rose beds that Mama Wolf had planted for them during her first visit to Coronado. In the sketch, Stan was practically a giant who towered above everyone else. Larger than life.

My daddy's the best fireman in the world. So he's never gonna die!

Undaunted by Stan's stony silence, Jake continued, "You've been doing school visits for fourteen years now, so I'm sure you've heard that question before. What made today different?"

Stan swallowed hard.

Thankfully he was spared from answering when the dismissal bell rang, releasing hordes of noisy children from their classrooms.

As soon as Mason appeared, Stan scooped him up and swung him onto his shoulders, making the boy squeal with delight as his peers looked on enviously.

"Come on," Stan told Mason, "let's go get your brothers."

"Okay!" He waved at Jake. "Bye, Sparky!"

Jake winked at him. "Bye, Mason. Be good."

"That's what *I* should be telling *you*," Stan said, watching as Jake edged toward the open doorway of Mason's classroom. "What're you up to?"

Jake grinned mischievously. "I'm just gonna see if Miss Dominguez needs any help, you know, erasing the chalkboard."

Stan chuckled. "*Riiight.*"

As he moved off with Mason perched astride his shoulders, Jake called after him, "Enjoy your time off, lieutenant."

"Thanks, rookie," Stan called back. "Stay out of trouble."

"You, too."

I'm trying, Stan thought as he strode down the bustling hallway, oblivious to the awestruck stares of children he passed. *God knows I'm trying.*

Chapter 7

Stan knew something was wrong the moment he stepped through the front door that evening and took one look at Prissy's face.

"Hey, baby," he greeted her, balancing three extra-large pizza boxes as he leaned down to kiss her cheek. "What's the matter?"

Before she could respond, Montana, Magnum, Maddox and Mason stampeded past him into the house, still buzzing with excitement over the sci-fi adventure film they'd just watched.

"Hey, Ma!" they chorused, peeling off their coats. "Dad took us to the movies!"

Prissy smiled wanly. "I know. Did you enjoy it?"

"Yeah!" They began recapping their favorite scenes, their animated voices tumbling over one another's until Stan interrupted with a sharp whistle that cut through the cacophony.

He glanced at each of them in turn. "I thought you boys said you were hungry?"

"We are!" Montana confirmed.

"Starving!" Magnum added.

"Then take these"— Stan handed the pizza boxes to Montana —"and go eat."

They didn't have to be told twice. As they took off for the kitchen, Prissy—who'd somehow wound up with an armful of coats—began hanging them neatly in the mud room, where they also stored boots and mittens, backpacks, sports gear and umbrellas.

Stan followed Prissy inside the cheery room and touched her shoulder, feeling the tension beneath her suit jacket. "What's going on, baby? Is everything okay?"

"No." Finished with her task, Prissy turned to look at him. Instinctively fearing the worst—that she'd somehow uncovered his secret—Stan braced himself for the confrontation he'd been dreading for months.

But then she said, "Your son was suspended from school today."

It was the last thing Stan had expected to hear. "*What?*" he exclaimed, staring at her. "Suspended for what?"

"Fighting."

"*Fighting?*"

Prissy nodded, looking grim. "According to the principal, Manny started the fight by throwing the first punch."

Stan frowned. "He must have been provoked."

"That's no justification for what he did," Prissy countered sharply. "Anyway, I don't know whether he was provoked or not because he wouldn't tell me or Principal Henderson what really happened."

"What do you mean he wouldn't tell you?" Stan demanded.

Prissy sighed, wearily pinching the bridge of her nose between her thumb and forefinger. "He's being difficult. Uncooperative."

Stan scowled. "We'll see about that. Where is he?"

"Upstairs cleaning his room, which he was *supposed* to do earlier when I dropped him off at home. But when I got back from the board meeting ten minutes ago, I found him lying across his bed fast asleep. He hadn't picked up a damn thing."

Clenching his jaw, Stan left the mud room and strode to the bottom of the staircase. "Manny!" he called up. "Get your behind down here!"

Moments later he heard the heavy thud of footsteps moving across the second floor, and then Manning appeared at the top of the stairs. When Stan saw the shiner his son was sporting, he swore under his breath.

"Boy," he warned, "don't let me find out that you got your butt kicked."

Prissy gasped. "*Stanton!*"

"I'm just sayin', baby. If he started the fight, he'd damn well better had finished it."

Prissy sucked her teeth. "He said pretty much the same thing in the principal's office. I should have known he got that nonsense from *you!*"

Stan made no reply, watching as Manning descended the staircase and came toward him with the reluctant dread of a condemned prisoner being marched out to face a firing squad. When the boy reached him, Stan cupped his chin in his hand

and angled his face toward the chandelier light, frowning as he examined the bruised flesh surrounding Manning's left eye.

After a few moments, he grunted, "You'll live."

"Of course he will," Prissy said tightly. "*He's* not the one who wound up in the emergency room with a broken nose."

"*What!*" Stan stared incredulously at his son. "You broke the kid's *nose?*"

Manning dropped his gaze. "I didn't mean to."

"Try telling that to Rory's parents," Prissy snapped. "That is, if they ever decide to return my phone call."

"Hold up. Wait a minute." Stan divided a wary glance between his wife and son. "Rory who? Rory *Kerrigan?*"

Manning shrugged a shoulder. "I don't know his last name."

"Yes," Prissy confirmed, staring at Stan. "It's Kerrigan. Why?"

"Aw, hell," Stan groaned, covering his face with his hands. "*Shit.*"

"What is it?" Prissy asked, too alarmed to chastise him for using profanity in front of Manning.

"I work at the same firehouse as Rory Kerrigan, Senior," Stan explained. "He's on a different shift, but I know who he is."

Prissy shot him a stricken look. "Please tell me you're joking."

"I wish I was," Stan muttered.

Prissy threw her hands up in the air. "I can't deal with this anymore," she fumed, her bare feet slapping against the hardwood floor as she started from the foyer. "I'm going to have a hot bath and take some aspirin and lay down before I end up killing someone."

Stan and Manning watched her stalk off, then looked at each other.

Stan smiled narrowly. "Looks like it's just you and me, son."

Manning gulped hard.

Over his shoulder, Stan saw Montana, Magnum, Maddox and Mason huddled around the kitchen doorway with their mouths hanging open, eyes wide with unabashed curiosity as they watched the unfolding drama. Catching their father's ominous glare, they wasted no time scurrying back into the kitchen.

"Let's take this conversation downstairs," Stan told Manning.

The boy gave a jerky nod.

They left the foyer and descended a narrow flight of stairs to reach the finished basement. The sprawling area—which Stan and the boys had affectionately dubbed the "Wolf Den"—was furnished with a black leather sofa and matching armchairs, a big-screen television, a pool table, a poker table, a pinball machine and an indoor basketball hoop with an electronic scoreboard. The wood-paneled walls were adorned with framed posters of famous black athletes from the past and present: Joe Louis, Muhammad Ali, Walter Payton and Dominique Wilkins, to name just a few.

The basement was a breeding ground for testosterone, hence it was the only part of the house that Prissy rarely ventured into.

As soon as Manning sat down on the sofa, Stan barked, "Start talking."

When Manning hesitated a second too long, Stan reached for his belt buckle.

That loosened the boy's tongue *real* quick. "The reason I punched Rory is 'cause he was picking on this girl from my math class. We were walking to our lockers after precalculus, and Rory just came along and knocked Taylor's books out of her arms. I got mad—"

"So you decided to take a swing at him."

Manning hesitated, then nodded tightly. "I told him to apologize to her, but he wouldn't. He started calling us names and talking trash, so..." Manning gave a helpless shrug, shaking his head at Stan. "I'm sorry, Dad, but he had it coming."

"That may be so," Stan growled, "but you shouldn't have lost your cool like that. How many times have we told you and your brothers that violence never solves anything? And now look where we are. Because you couldn't control your temper, you sent a boy to the hospital and got suspended from school, and you've put your mother's reputation in jeopardy."

Manning hung his head. "I'm sorry," he mumbled.

"You should be. You're the superintendent's son, so you know damn well that everything you do—good or bad—is a reflection of your mother. So that means you need to be mindful of your behavior and make better decisions."

Glaring down at the floor, Manning muttered resentfully, "I didn't ask to be the superintendent's son."

"*But you are!*" Stan roared, losing his patience. "You *are* the superintendent's son, boy, and there ain't a damn thing you can do about it!"

Manning was silent, a muscle throbbing in his clenched jaw.

Stan jabbed a finger at him. "See, what you fail to realize is that I know you, Manny. I know you even better than you know yourself. So I understand that there was more to that fight than you defending some girl from a bully. You left the house this morning just spoiling for a fight, and Rory Kerrigan gave you the perfect excuse to take out your frustrations on him."

"That's not true!" Manning protested vehemently. "He was being an asshole!"

"*Excuse you?*" Stan thundered, leaning down to get in Manning's face. "Who do you think you're talking to?"

Manning's eyes widened with alarm as he swallowed nervously, Adam's apple bobbing in his throat.

Stan searched the boy's face, which was so strikingly similar to his own that it was like looking into a time-warped mirror.

"What's going on with you?" he asked, striving for calm. "Talk to me, son. Unburden yourself."

Manning just looked up at him, nostrils flaring with suppressed emotion.

"I'm waiting."

"I hate it here!" Manning burst out furiously.

Stan nodded slowly. "Tell me something I *don't* know."

"I wanna go back to Atlanta!"

"You will." At the hopeful gleam that lit Manning's eyes, Stan calmly elaborated, "When you turn eighteen in four years, you'll go back to Atlanta to attend Morehouse with Michael. That's always been the plan. Of course, if you keep getting suspended from school, Morehouse won't take you, nor will any other college or university."

Manning frowned, as if such an outcome had never occurred to him.

Typical teenager. Act first, think later.

"You're treading on thin ice here," Stan continued, driving home the point. "The next time you get suspended, the punishment will be for six days. Get in trouble a third time, and you're gonna be expelled from school. Is that what you want?"

"No," Manning mumbled.

"Then I suggest you get your act together. Fighting at school won't be tolerated. The next time it happens, getting suspended will be the *least* of your worries. Are we clear?"

Manning nodded obediently. "Yes, sir."

"Good." Stan exhaled a deep breath, then sat down beside his son.

"You hate Coronado as much as I do," Manning grumbled.

Stan shot him a surprised glance. "No, I don't."

"Yes, you do. I've heard you talking to Uncle Sterling—"

"First of all," Stan cut him off, "you need to stop eavesdropping on my phone conversations. I've never told your uncle that I hate Coronado because I don't. Yes, living here has taken some getting used to, and there are many things about Atlanta that I'll always miss. Like hanging out with your uncle, and being able to watch Michael and Marcus grow up. I miss our Wolf Pack cookouts and birthday parties and pick-up games. I miss being able to drive down to Savannah to visit Mama Wolf on the spur of the moment. I miss our barber shop and the fellas from the old fire station, especially the ones I started my career with. I miss—" He broke off at the knowing look on Manning's face, a look that told him he'd probably revealed too much.

He briskly cleared his throat. "What I'm trying to say is that you're not alone in missing Atlanta. But you shouldn't allow your homesickness to keep you from appreciating everything Coronado has to offer."

"Like what?"

"Well, I don't know about you, but I love looking out the window every morning and seeing those beautiful mountains. Makes me feel like I'm in God's country. And the parks and lakes are amazing—"

"You sound like a tour guide," Manning mocked.

Stan laughed. "The point is, Coronado's not as bad as you think. Even your brothers are starting to enjoy living here, and *they* hated leaving Atlanta as much as you did. Not only that, but your mother loves her job, and she's doing good things for your school district and the community. So as much as you want us to go back to Atlanta, it's not gonna happen. The sooner you accept that and move on, the better off you'll be."

Manning was silent, staring broodingly at the floor.

After several moments, Stan decided to change the subject before Manning turned the tables on him and asked about the phone conversation he'd overheard that morning.

"So," Stan ventured, "is she pretty?"

His son gave him a blank look. "Who?"

Stan smirked. "The girl you chivalrously defended and got suspended for. Is she pretty?"

Manning shrugged. "I dunno."

"What do you mean?"

"I can't really tell if she's pretty. I guess she could be, but she wears these big ugly glasses that practically cover her whole face. And the way she dresses..." Manning shook his head with a pained grimace.

Stan chuckled wryly. "So I take it she's no Caitlyn."

"No way," Manning agreed with a rueful laugh. "Not even close."

"But you came to her rescue anyway."

"Of course. Taylor's a nice girl, really smart and funny. She doesn't deserve to get picked on by assho— jerks like Rory."

"So if it happens again—if you see Rory or another bully picking on Taylor—what're you gonna do?"

Manning eyed him darkly. "Please don't ask me that question, Dad."

Stan chuckled, reluctantly impressed by Manning's overprotectiveness toward Taylor. Could he really fault the boy? Wasn't he raising his sons to be gentlemen who cherished and protected women and looked out for underdogs? Under the circumstances, could he punish Manning for defending Taylor when *he* would have done the exact same thing?

Stan scratched his ear, unnerved by the realization that he bore partial responsibility for his son's behavior. Damn, he hated it when that happened.

"Speaking of Caitlyn," he said gruffly, "you need to watch out for that one."

Manning shot him a puzzled look. "Why?"

"The girl may be beautiful, but she's trouble with a capital *T*."

"How do you know?"

Stan smiled wryly. "I've been around long enough to know a troublemaker when I see one, son. Take my word for it."

Manning sniffed. "I'm not worried about Caitlyn," he declared with a dismissive flap of his hand. "I can handle her."

"Oh, really?" Stan challenged. "Because you've got all this experience with women, right?"

Manning grinned weakly. "Of course."

Stan let out a bark of laughter. "Boy, who you trying to fool? You're still wet behind the ears!"

"No, I'm not," Manning protested.

"Yes, you are. I know good and damn well you're still a virgin. And when that's no longer the case, I'll know just like your uncle knew when Michael lost his virginity last summer. Sooner or later, you boys will learn that you can't get anything past us."

Manning shook his head, a surly grin tugging at the corners of his mouth.

"Seriously though, Manny," Stan continued. "As much as you may want to outdo Mike by losing your virginity at a younger age than he did, believe me when I tell you that you're not ready to start having sex. You're only fourteen years old. So you've got plenty of time to, ah, experience the pleasures of lovemaking. With the right girl," he added pointedly.

"Girls," Manning corrected.

"What?"

"You said 'girl.' Like there'd only be one."

"And what would be so terrible about that?" Stan demanded. "Your mother was a virgin when we started dating in high school. I'm the only lover she's ever had."

"But was she the only lover *you've* ever had?" Manning challenged.

That shut Stan up.

"I didn't think so," Manning said with a laugh.

Stan scowled.

"Anyway," he blurted, abruptly rising from the sofa, "we'd better head back upstairs and see if your greedy brothers left us any pizza."

"They'd better have," Manning muttered, pushing to his feet.

Stan snorted. "After all the trouble you've caused today, you're lucky I'm not feeding you a peanut butter and jelly sandwich for dinner. Tomorrow morning, after your mother has had a chance to cool down, I expect you to apologize to her for your behavior."

"Yes, sir."

As they approached the stairwell, Stan unbuckled and removed his leather belt. "You're the oldest, Manny. So like it or not, your mother and I expect you to set a better example for your brothers. When you fail to do that, you have to suffer the consequences."

A look of dread crossed Manning's face. "But, Dad—"

"But nothing, boy!" Lips quirking with amusement, Stan pulled Manning close and murmured in his ear, "Your nosy brothers are probably eavesdropping at the door. When I hit the banister with my belt, I want you to holler so they'll think I'm whipping you. Okay?"

Manning nodded quickly, flashing a wobbly grin of relief.

Sure enough, when they emerged from the basement a few minutes later, Montana, Magnum and Maddox scattered like rats scurrying from light. Only Mason lingered behind to point a finger at Manning and taunt gleefully, "Oooh, you got a butt whupping!"

"Shut up," Manning grumbled, swiping at an imaginary tear for good measure.

As Mason scampered off giggling impishly, Stan and Manning traded conspiratorial grins.

Chapter 8

Two hours later, Prissy glanced up from a report she'd been perusing to watch as Stan entered their bedroom suite and closed the double doors behind him.

"Boys in bed?" she asked.

"Yes, ma'am. Homework completed, baths taken, teeth brushed, clothes laid out for tomorrow. Check, check, check and check."

"Thanks, honey." Prissy smiled ruefully. "I didn't mean to desert you like that, but I needed to put as much distance as possible between myself and our firstborn."

Stan chuckled. "He's lucky you did. I honestly thought you were gonna strangle him with your bare hands."

"I certainly wanted to," Prissy muttered darkly. "If I didn't think it would traumatize our other children, I just might have."

Stan laughed, tugging off his undershirt as he sauntered to the walk-in closet. The sight of his thick, rippling muscles defused some of Prissy's anger. Some, not all.

Setting her paperwork on the cherry nightstand, she asked, "Did you get the full story out of him?"

"Of course. You know I don't play that."

Prissy waited not so patiently as Stan disappeared into the closet to change his clothes. Two minutes later he reemerged wearing gray pajama bottoms and no shirt. Prissy bit her bottom lip as her gaze latched onto his broad, muscular chest. It was downright criminal how utterly virile and sexy the man was.

Heading to the master bathroom to brush his teeth, he explained, "Manny told me he was defending a girl that Rory Kerrigan was picking on."

"Taylor," Prissy supplied.

"Right."

"I saw her at the school. When we were leaving the principal's office, she came up and hugged Manny and thanked him. So I figured he must have gotten into the fight because he was standing up for her." Prissy frowned, folding her arms across her chest. "Why couldn't he have just told me that?"

"Guess he figured it wouldn't matter," Stan said pragmatically. "Regardless of the reason he was fighting, he knew he was in deep trouble."

"That's *exactly* what he said." Prissy scowled. "He really *is* your son."

Stan chuckled around a mouthful of toothpaste.

"He's always been stubborn," Prissy continued, adjusting the heavy bed covers at her waist. "But it seems that the older he gets, the more hotheaded he becomes."

Stan finished brushing his teeth, then switched off the light and left the bathroom. "Don't be too hard on him, babe. You know boys will be boys."

"*Excuse me?*" Prissy sputtered indignantly. "What's that supposed to mean?"

"Boys fight," Stan stated matter-of-factly. "Back in Atlanta, Michael and Manning brawled with other boys all the time. It was practically a rite of passage."

"Only because the neighborhood was overrun by hoodlums who terrorized anyone who was afraid to fight back. The boys had no choice but to defend themselves and protect their younger brothers." Prissy gestured around the large, elegantly furnished bedroom. "In case you haven't noticed, we're not in the old neighborhood anymore."

Stan looked amused as he climbed into the king-size bed. "So I guess there are no hoodlums in Coronado, huh?"

"That's not what I'm saying," Prissy protested. "And I can't believe you're defending Manny's behavior when you know what the repercussions might be."

"I'm not defending his behavior," Stan countered mildly. "I'm just asking you to cut him some slack. What he did today was honorable, standing up for a young lady who couldn't stand up for herself. You know as well as I do that if he'd let Rory get away with bullying Taylor, we *both* would have been disappointed in him."

Prissy couldn't deny it. Even as angry as she was that afternoon, she'd been undeniably moved by the touching encounter between Manning and Taylor. What mother *wouldn't* have appreciated witnessing her teenage son's kinder, gentler side?

Watching her expression soften, Stan smiled. "I seem to recall a few fights *I* got into while defending your honor when we were in high school. Do you remember?"

A tender, reminiscent smile curved Prissy's lips. "Yes, I remember," she admitted, awash with memories of being a shy, brainy student who'd miraculously captured the heart of one of the most popular boys at school. While Prissy had never been as woefully frumpy as poor Taylor, she'd been enough of a Plain Jane to go largely unnoticed by most guys...until Stan came along and turned her world upside down.

For as long as she lived, she would never forget the day their paths had collided—literally. She'd been rushing to class when suddenly she'd run right into the solid wall of Stan's chest. The impact had sent her books scattering across the floor, but that was nothing compared to the way her heart had somersaulted when Stan grabbed her arms to keep her from falling backward.

She'd fallen anyway...fallen hopelessly in love.

Sighing deeply at the memory, Prissy shifted onto her side to face Stan, imitating his pose with her head propped in her hand. She wore one of his oversize CFD T-shirts and had her hair wrapped in a satin scarf.

"Okay," she relented, "so maybe I can cross one or two things off my chore list for Manny. But only *after* we know what the fallout will be from Rory's injury."

Stan chuckled, affectionately tweaking her nose. "Rory's parents aren't gonna sue us, if that's what you're worried about."

Prissy raised a brow at him. "How do *you* know that?"

"For starters, hiring a lawyer is expensive, and I know the Kerrigans don't have money like that. Second, I've worked with Rory's father, so I know the type of man he is. I'm sure he realizes that filing a lawsuit against us would only draw attention to the fact that his son got his punk ass whupped by *our* son, who happens to be a freshman. Believe me, no self-respecting man would subject his own kid to that kind of public humiliation. Right now he's probably just hoping that this whole thing will die down as quickly and quietly as possible."

Prissy sighed. "I sure hope you're right. Because the timing of this incident couldn't be worse."

"I know," Stan agreed, gently stroking her cheek. "Tell you what. If you don't hear back from Mrs. Kerrigan tomorrow, after

I drop you off at the airport on Thursday, I'll swing by the firehouse to have a man-to-man talk with Rory's father. How does that sound?"

"It sounds good." At the mention of her upcoming business trip, Prissy was suddenly reminded of the phone call she'd received from Celeste that morning.

After a brief hesitation, she murmured, "I spoke to Celeste today."

Stan's expression instantly darkened. "What did *she* want?"

Again Prissy hesitated, knowing all too well how Stan felt about his former sister-in-law. "She wants to see me while I'm in Rochester for the conference. She's spending the next four months there with Grant, who's working on a research project for the Mayo Clinic."

Stan stared at Prissy. "You're joking, right?"

"You know I wouldn't joke about something like this."

"So let me get this straight," Stan growled, angrily pushing himself up to a sitting position. "While my brother is working his ass off to make ends meet, keep food on the table and raise two sons who're still reeling from the divorce, Celeste is off playing house with her fucking *boyfriend*?"

Prissy grimaced. "In a nutshell, yes."

"That selfish bitch!" Stan exploded, his dark eyes flashing with fury. "Just when I thought she couldn't get any more shameless, she proves me wrong!"

"I know," Prissy murmured. "I couldn't believe she had the audacity to call and invite me to dinner."

"And what'd you tell her?"

"I told her no, of course. I have no interest in hearing anything she has to say at this point."

Stan scowled. "How the hell does she plan to keep her court-appointed visits while she's in Minnesota? Does she plan to fly back to Atlanta every weekend?"

"I don't know. She claims she's going to work out an arrangement with Sterling. That is, whenever she gets around to telling him that she's in Minnesota."

"*What?* She hasn't told him yet?"

"Apparently not."

"Son of a bitch," Stan growled, shaking his head in angry disbelief. "No wonder Sterl didn't say anything to me when we talked yesterday. He doesn't even know that Celeste has flown the damn coop."

"And I don't think we should be the ones to tell him." At the dark look Stan shot her, Prissy elaborated, "As furious as we both are, and as much as we want to intervene on Sterling's behalf, we have to let him and Celeste work through these issues on their own. They were married to each other for sixteen years. Ultimately, *they're* the only ones who know what truly went wrong in their marriage. But they both love Michael and Marcus, so I believe they'll do what's best for their sons."

Stan scowled, muttering an expletive under his breath.

"Do I have your word that you won't interfere?" Prissy pressed gently.

Stan didn't answer.

"Stanton?"

He blew out a harsh breath. "Yeah," he grumbled darkly. "I won't interfere. Damn it."

"Good." Suppressing a small smile, Prissy curved an arm around his waist and laid her head against his muscled bare chest. She felt the tension ebb from his body moments before he kissed the top of her head and wrapped an arm around her, drawing her protectively closer. She sighed and closed her eyes, enjoying the sinewy warmth of his skin and the strength of his heartbeat beneath her cheek.

They were silent for a few minutes, content to just hold each other. Since Stan spent half the week at the fire station, Prissy cherished these moments of togetherness when she could enjoy having him all to herself. As the wife of a firefighter, she understood the dangers that Stan faced every time he went out on an emergency call. She knew that he could be taken from her at any time. So she never, *ever* took his presence for granted.

"You'd better not be falling asleep," Stan murmured, his deep baritone rumbling through her.

"Why not?" she teased without opening her eyes. "It's been a long, stressful day. I'm tired."

"You can sleep after I collect on my rain check."

"What rain check? I don't remember promising any—"

She was silenced by the warm pressure of Stan's mouth covering hers. As a soft sigh of pleasure escaped her, Stan shifted on the bed until they were lying on their sides facing each other.

Prissy opened her mouth as his tongue slid inside, sensually stroking hers. As her nipples tightened, she lifted her leg and draped her thigh across his waist. Groaning softly, Stan pressed the hard, heavy ridge of his shaft against her belly and reached around to cup her butt cheek.

Prissy moaned as moisture seeped onto her panties, making the cotton crotch stick to the pulsing folds of her sex. As Stan deepened the kiss, she sucked on his tongue and rocked her hips against his.

Through the hazy fog of desire clouding her mind, her conscience nagged at her, demanding an answer to the question that had taunted her all day.

With a supreme effort, she broke the kiss and pulled back, ignoring Stan's protesting groan. As his lashes slowly lifted, she searched his face. "Baby?"

"Yeah?"

She looked him in the eye. "Who paged you today?"

He blinked at her, nonplussed. "When?"

"This morning after we made love in my office. Someone paged you."

"Oh." His heavy brows furrowed in confusion. "I thought I told you it was someone from work."

"No," Prissy countered evenly, "*I* assumed it was someone from work, and you never actually corrected my assumption."

"Because you were right. It *was* one of my coworkers."

Prissy shook her head slowly at him. "No, it wasn't."

He frowned. "What're you talking about?"

"I called the station after you left my office. I asked Dora to check if anyone there had paged you. No one had. So again I ask, Stanton. Who paged you?"

He eyed her incredulously. "I can't believe you called my workplace to check up on me, Pris."

"Just answer the question."

"I've given you no reason to—"

She bolted upright. "*Just answer the damn question!*"

"I did, woman, but you ain't trying to hear it!"

"Because I know you're lying to me!"

Stan stared at her, his face as hard and impenetrable as granite.

Prissy stared back at him, her heart pounding violently against her ribs. She could feel the white-hot flames of that inferno sweeping dangerously closer, licking at her, threatening to consume her.

As tears scalded her eyes, she abruptly rolled away, turning her back on Stan.

Without warning he hauled her against him, his muscular arms banding tightly around her resistant body.

"*Let me go, Stan.*"

"No, goddamn it! You're not going anywhere, and neither am I!"

Prissy squeezed her eyes shut, letting the tears escape as she cried out, "I don't know what's going on with you. I feel like I'm losing you, and I don't know why!"

"I'm sorry, sweetheart," Stan groaned against the nape of her neck. "I'm so sorry."

What are you apologizing for? Prissy wanted to scream. *What have you done?*

But suddenly she thought of the weekend they'd flown back to Atlanta to visit Sterling, Michael and Marcus after Celeste moved out. She thought of how devastated they'd all been, how utterly lost and bereft Sterling had looked.

And she'd realized, then, that sometimes ignorance could be bliss. Because if Celeste's infidelity had never been discovered, her family would still be intact.

"I love you," Stan whispered fiercely, rubbing his face back and forth against Prissy's hair. "I love you so damn much, baby."

"Then just hold me," Prissy pleaded tearfully. "Hold me, and don't ever let go."

"I won't." His arms tightened around her, as if he were trying to absorb her into his body. "I *swear* I won't."

And for now, that was enough.

Sometime around midnight, Manning was awakened by a light tapping noise.

Groggily opening his eyes, he peered around his darkened bedroom. When he realized that the sound was coming from the window, he threw back the covers, climbed out of bed and padded across the room.

Reaching the window, he shoved the curtains open and was shocked to see Caitlyn's face pressed to the glass.

She smiled and waved at him, as if it were perfectly normal for her to be crouched outside his bedroom window in the middle of the freakin' night.

When he stood there gaping at her, she grinned mischievously and mouthed, *Aren't you gonna let me in?*

Manning hesitated, casting a furtive glance at his closed bedroom door. He was in enough trouble as it was. If his parents caught him with a girl in his room, he'd be grounded till he graduated from high school—assuming he lived that long.

Another tap on the glass drew his gaze back to the window.

Please? Caitlyn silently cajoled, batting her lashes at him.

Needing no further encouragement, Manning quickly raised the windowpane and reached down to lift her through the opening.

"Mmmm," she purred appreciatively, gripping his biceps as he set her down on the floor. "So *strong.*"

"Shh!" Clapping his hand over her mouth, Manning whispered sharply, "What the hell are you doing here?"

Her hazel eyes glittered in the moonlight as she responded to his question. When her words came out muffled, Manning frowned. "Huh?"

She lowered her eyes, pointedly staring at his hand over her mouth.

"You have to keep your voice down so no one will hear you," Manning warned. "I'm serious. All right?"

At her obedient nod, he removed his hand.

She smiled coyly, sliding her arms around his neck and pressing her soft body against his. Her dark hair was swept into a bun, and she had on a pink trench coat that made him wonder what she wore beneath.

"I came to congratulate you, slugger," she whispered, her candy-scented breath fanning his face. "Everyone at school is talking about how you totally kicked Rory Kerrigan's ass, had him bleeding everywhere and whimpering for his mommy." She snickered. "No one's ever stood up to that douchebag before. You're a hero, Manning."

"Yeah?" he murmured with a wry half smile. "Tell that to my parents."

"I will if you want me to. Seriously."

"Uh, thanks, but I don't think it'd do any good. How'd you get up here?"

"I climbed up the trellis."

"The what?"

"The trellis."

An image of the rose-draped ladder attached to the side of the house filled Manning's mind, and he chuckled. "I didn't know that's what it was called."

A delighted grin curved Caitlyn's lips. "God, you're cute."

Manning suddenly remembered that on the ride to school that morning, she'd casually asked him whether he had his own bedroom and where it was located. Now he knew why she'd been so interested.

As a cold gust of wind swept into the room, he pulled away from Caitlyn to close the window. As he turned around, she caught his face between her hands and kissed him. He kissed her back, sucking on the cherry-flavored tongue she plunged into his mouth.

Moaning softly with pleasure, she backed him toward the bed and pushed him down. Heart pounding with excitement, Manning watched as she unbuttoned her trench coat and slipped it from her shoulders.

His eyes flew wide. *"Shit!"*

Her naked body glowed softly in the moonlight as she climbed onto the bed. She helped Manning pull off his shorts, then reached up and removed a foil packet tucked inside her bun.

It was all Manning could do to hold still as she covered him with the condom and straddled his waist.

"Are you a virgin?" she whispered.

He swallowed hard. "Hell, no."

Her eyes twinkled. "That's too bad," she lamented.

"Why?"

"I wanted to have the bragging rights of popping your cherry."

That sounded fair enough.

"Okay," Manning quickly amended. "I'm a virgin."

Caitlyn laughed, low and wicked. "They say you never forget your first. Do you think you could ever forget me, Manning?"

Not in this lifetime.

"Depends."

"On what?"

"What you're working with."

This startled another laugh out of her. "What I'm *working* with?"

"Yeah." Manning grinned cockily. "You might be my first, but you damn sure won't be my last. So I can't answer your question till I see how many moves you got."

Caitlyn smiled seductively. "Oh, I've got *plenty*."

"Show me."

So she did.

Chapter 9

Something was different about Manning.

Stan knew it the moment his son strolled into the kitchen the next morning, freshly showered and dressed in his favorite Atlanta Falcons T-shirt, black sweatpants and high-top sneakers.

"Morning, pops," he greeted Stan, who was seated at the breakfast table sipping his second cup of coffee while reading *The Denver Post*.

"Good morning." Peering over the top of the newspaper, Stan watched as Manning sauntered over to the microwave to heat up the plate of pancakes and bacon his mother had left for him. Even when Prissy was mad at the boy, she couldn't suppress her maternal instinct to coddle and pamper him.

Stan took another sip of coffee. "Did you talk to your mother before she left for work?"

"Yeah," Manning answered, pouring himself a glass of orange juice. "We're cool."

Which meant he'd laid on the charm—draping an arm around Prissy's shoulders, resting his head on top of hers and calling her "Mommy" until she melted, as she always did.

Stan chuckled inwardly. "Did she give you the list of chores you're supposed to be doing?"

"Yup." Manning patted his shorts pocket. "Got it right here."

Stan nodded, setting down his mug. "As soon as you finish your breakfast, I expect you to get to work."

"Yes, sir."

Stan's eyes narrowed. Manning looked and sounded *way* too chipper for a kid who was facing three days' worth of grueling manual labor.

"How's that eye?" At the blank look Manning gave him, Stan pointed to the shiner on his face.

"Oh." The boy reached up and touched the discolored skin, then shrugged a shoulder. "Forgot all about it."

Stan's brows went up.

When the microwave beeped, Manning removed his plate and poured syrup over the stack of pancakes, then grabbed a fork from the cutlery drawer and scooped up his drink. Walking over to the table, he plopped down across from Stan and said a quick grace before attacking his food with even more gusto than usual.

Amused, Stan watched him for a few moments. "Looks like *someone* woke up with a huge appetite."

Manning grunted, shoveling a syrupy forkful of pancake into his mouth.

"Just out of curiosity, why'd you take a shower?"

"Huh?"

"Why'd you bother to take a shower," Stan elaborated, "when you're gonna be doing chores all day and getting sweaty?"

Manning shrugged, not glancing up from his plate. "I forgot I wasn't going to school."

"Really?"

"Yeah."

Laying aside his newspaper, Stan stood and leaned across the table to sniff at Manning.

The boy eyed him quizzically. "What're you doing, Dad?"

"You smell different."

Manning looked wary. "Different how?"

"I don't know." Stan took another whiff. "But you do."

Manning huffed a shaky laugh. "You be buggin', pops. All you smell on me is soap and water."

"Hmm." As a firefighter, Stan had developed a keen sense of smell that enabled him to detect gas leaks and smoke with the precision of a bloodhound. So when he told Manning that he smelled different, he knew he wasn't imagining things.

Slowly he returned to his chair, eyes narrowed speculatively as he searched his son's face.

Manning resumed eating, but there was a new guardedness to him.

Picking up his coffee mug, Stan casually remarked, "I saw Caitlyn on my way back from walking your brothers to the bus stop."

Manning bit into a slice of bacon. "Yeah?"

"Yeah. She was heating up her car in the driveway." Stan sipped his coffee, watching his son over the rim of the mug. "She wanted me to tell you that she's ready to give you another ride whenever you want."

Manning choked on the bacon. Coughing and gasping, he grabbed his glass of orange juice and downed half the contents.

"You all right?" Stan drawled.

Manning quickly bobbed his head. "It just, uh, went down the, uh, wrong way," he rasped, plunking down the glass.

"You should be more careful," Stan warned mildly. "Eating, like anything else in life, should never be done in a hurry."

Manning nodded and dropped his gaze to his plate, his lips twitching with amusement.

"I assume, of course, that Caitlyn was referring to giving you another ride to *school*."

"Of course." But Manning could barely keep the smirk off his face.

Stan grew still. "Look at me."

Manning hesitated for a moment, then slowly lifted his head to meet Stan's suspicious gaze.

"Something you wanna tell me?"

Long pause. "Like what?"

Stan frowned. "Boy—"

Suddenly the phone rang.

Father and son stared at the ringing instrument, then at each other.

A second later, Manning jumped up from the table as if his chair had suddenly caught on fire. "I'd better get to work. Lots to do, you know?"

After dumping his empty plate in the sink, he beat a hasty retreat as Stan stood and crossed to the wall phone. He picked up on the last ring. "Hello?"

"Hello, Stan," a warm female voice greeted him. "Did I catch you at a bad time?"

Hell, yeah!

"Um, sort of. Hold on."

Quickly setting down the receiver, Stan crept to the kitchen doorway. After several moments, Manning jogged down the staircase and headed into the garage, bopping his head to the beat of whatever song was playing on his Walkman.

Heart thudding, Stan strode back to the phone. "Sorry about that."

"No, I'm the one who should apologize. It's after eight, so I just assumed you had the house all to yourself by now."

"I would have," Stan said with wry humor, "but my eldest had other plans."

"Manning?"

"Yeah."

"Is he sick?"

"Not quite." Stan kept one eye on the doorway, lest the child in question sneak up on him again. "I'll fill you in when I see you."

"So we're still on for Friday afternoon?"

Stan hesitated as his mind flashed on an image of Prissy, her face contorted with pain and fury as she hurled accusations at him. Her words, and the raw anguish behind them, had haunted him for the rest of the night. Long after she fell asleep, he'd stayed awake holding her, whispering promises he wished he could keep.

His stomach churned now, coating his throat with bile and guilt.

"Stan?" the woman prompted gently. "I'd really like to see you on Friday."

"I know." He closed his eyes, swallowing the bitter taste of his deception. "I'll be there."

After dinner that evening, Manning helped Prissy clear the table while Stan and the boys headed downstairs to the basement to set up a new video game system.

Prissy was in a better mood tonight, thanks in large part to a phone call she'd received at work. Rory Kerrigan's mother had called to inform her that Rory's nose wasn't broken after all, but even if it had been, it would have served him right. She'd gone on to explain her shocked disappointment at learning from the principal that her son was a bully who regularly tormented other kids at school. She'd claimed complete ignorance, even though Rory had been suspended once before for bullying.

At the end of their conversation, Mrs. Kerrigan had assured Prissy that her son had learned his lesson, and there were no hard feelings between them.

When the rest of the day passed with no concerned phone calls from any of the school board members, Prissy had breathed a huge sigh of relief before grabbing her briefcase and heading home.

She'd just playfully flicked some sudsy water at Manning's face when the doorbell rang. Leaving her laughing son to the dishes, she went to answer the door.

She was surprised to find Manning's classmate, Taylor, standing on the porch. The girl wore a camouflage army jacket that was several sizes too big, bright orange bellbottoms and a pair of black-and-white Converse All-Stars that had seen better days.

She smiled nervously at Prissy. "Um, hi, Dr. Wolf. My name's—"

"I know who you are, Taylor." Prissy smiled warmly. "What brings you here this evening?"

The girl pushed her horn-rimmed glasses up on her nose. "Is, um, Manning here?"

"Yes, he is. Come in and I'll get him for you."

"Oh, I can just wait outside. I don't want to impose—"

"You're not imposing," Prissy assured her, opening the door wider. "Please come inside, Taylor. I insist."

The girl hesitated another moment, then tentatively stepped into the house and swept an admiring glance around. "You have a beautiful home," she said.

"Why, thank you, baby." As Prissy moved to close the door, she saw a boy's old ten-speed bicycle lying at the end of the driveway behind the family minivan. "Is that your bike, Taylor?"

"Yes, ma'am. Well, technically, it's my brother's, but I'm using it while he's away. Not that he'd be riding it if he were here anyway. Do you want me to move it from the driveway? The kickstand's broken, otherwise I wouldn't have laid—"

"The bike's just fine where it is," Prissy gently interrupted the girl's breathless chatter.

Closing the door, she smiled at Taylor and had a sudden flashback to how nervous she'd been the very first time she visited Stan's home and met his grandmother, who'd lovingly welcomed her into the fold.

On impulse, Prissy reached out and smoothed back Taylor's windblown ponytail. When the girl gave her a winsome smile, Prissy felt a sharp pang of longing for the daughter she'd never had.

"Did you say your brother's away?" she inquired curiously.

"Yes, ma'am," Taylor answered. "He's in the army, stationed in Iran."

"Really?" Prissy couldn't help thinking of the disastrous Iran hostage crisis that had sent shockwaves through the world earlier that year when the U.S. military's failed rescue operation had resulted in the deaths of eight American soldiers and an Iranian civilian.

"This is my brother's army jacket," Taylor shyly explained, pointing to the T. CHASTAIN nameplate stamped across the front lapel. "He always called me his good luck charm, so I wear it every day to, um, bring him luck."

Prissy's heart melted. She smiled, gently clasping Taylor's hands between hers. "We'll pray for his safe return home."

Taylor's expression softened with gratitude. "Thank you."

Prissy hugged her, then drew back to call over her shoulder, "Manny! There's someone here to see you!"

Moments later Manning emerged from the kitchen wiping his hands on a dishtowel. His eyes widened with surprise when he saw who stood in the foyer. "Taylor?"

She smiled shyly. "Hi."

"Hi, yourself." Manning grinned, tossing the dishtowel over his shoulder as he came forward. "What're you doing here?"

Removing a bookbag strapped to her back, Taylor explained, "I asked my friend who works as an aide in the main office to give me a copy of your class schedule, then I went to all your teachers and got your classwork and homework assignments so you won't fall behind while you're on, um, suspension."

"Really?" Manning was clearly touched as he accepted the handouts from her. "Thank you, Taylor. I really appreciate this."

"Yes," Prissy added warmly, "it was *very* kind and thoughtful of you, Taylor."

The girl waved off their gratitude, looking thoroughly embarrassed. "It was the least I could do, considering it was my fault that you got in trouble, Manning."

"It wasn't your fault," he and Prissy assured her.

As Taylor opened her mouth to argue, Stan emerged from the basement trailed by the boys.

"I thought I heard voices up here," Stan said, smiling easily at their guest. "Hello. You must be Taylor."

The girl's eyes widened behind the thick lenses on her glasses. She looked from Stan to Manning to the rest of the boys, then blinked rapidly as if to clear her vision.

Prissy inwardly smiled. Taylor's stunned reaction was the same one that most people had upon encountering the fellas, who were like those wooden Russian dolls of decreasing size that were stacked one inside the other.

Amused by his classmate's dumbfounded silence, Manning smoothly interjected, "Taylor, I'd like you to meet my dad and my brothers Montana, Magnum, Maddox and Mason."

Recovering her composure, Taylor smiled brightly and thrust her hand forward. "Nice to meet all of you," she enthused, shaking their hands in turn. "I didn't realize Manning had such a big family, not to mention *five* identical twins."

Everyone laughed.

Everyone but Mason, who stared at Taylor as if she were an oddity his young mind couldn't comprehend. Pointing at her, he leaned close to Montana and whispered loudly, "Look at her clothes. She looks like—"

Monty clapped a hand over his baby brother's mouth.

Taylor blushed, uncomfortably shifting from one foot to another.

Prissy cleared her throat. "Manny, why don't you take Taylor to the kitchen and offer her some of Mama Wolf's pound cake?"

"Sure—"

"Oh, that's okay," Taylor quickly interjected. "I don't want to impose—"

"You're not imposing," Prissy told her.

"Are you sure? I should probably go before it gets dark anyway."

"Where do you live?" Prissy asked curiously.

Taylor hesitated, biting her full lower lip. "Cedar Creek."

At the mention of the old subdivision populated by modest brick ramblers, Prissy exclaimed, "You mean you rode your bike from all the way over there?"

Taylor nodded. "It's not that far."

Prissy frowned. "It's certainly too far for a young lady to be riding back and forth from there at this time of night."

Stan gave her a warning look, recognizing that she was about to launch into overprotective-mother-lioness mode. "Pris—"

"Where are your parents?" she fussed.

Taylor looked discomfited. "My parents are divorced," she explained. "I live with my dad, but he had to go out of town this week. My aunt's staying with me and my younger brother until Dad gets back."

"I see," Prissy murmured, trying not to pass judgment on the woman who'd left her children to be raised by their father. *Like Celeste.*

"Well," Prissy said decisively, draping an arm around Taylor's shoulders, "if you call and ask your aunt, I'm sure she won't mind if you stay a while longer and have some pound cake. Manning's great-grandmother mails us care packages every month, and her cakes are to *die* for. She always sends two, so there's plenty to share. After you eat, Manning and I will take you back home."

Lips twitching with humor, Stan graciously volunteered, "I can drive her."

"Thank you, honey," Prissy said warmly. She smiled at Taylor. "So what do you say, little missy?"

"Well, um, I'm not, um—" Faltering, Taylor looked askance at Manning, who grinned ruefully and shook his head at her.

"She's not gonna leave you alone," he warned, the amused voice of experience. "So you might as well say yes."

Taylor smiled sheepishly. "Well...I *could* use some help with our precalculus homework."

Manning's grin broadened. "Say no more. I'm your man."

Taylor beamed at him.

Bored with the entire transaction between their eldest brother and Taylor, the boys raced back downstairs to the basement to resume playing their new video games.

As Prissy watched Manning and Taylor head off to the kitchen, Stan curved an arm around her waist, affectionately nuzzling her earlobe. "What're you up to, woman?"

"What?" Prissy asked innocently.

Stan chuckled. "You know what I'm talking about. You practically kidnapped that girl."

Prissy smiled, shivering at the soft rasp of his goatee against her cheek. "I really like her."

"Gee, I couldn't tell."

Prissy laughed. "Don't make fun of me. Taylor's a sweetheart. Not only did she defend Manny to Principal Henderson, but then she came all the way out here tonight just to bring Manny his schoolwork so he wouldn't fall behind while he's suspended."

"Well, considering that he got suspended over *her*—" Stan broke off with a laugh as Prissy poked him in the ribs. "I'm just kidding, babe. You're right. It was very considerate of Taylor to bring our son his schoolwork. I can see why you've taken such a shine to her."

"I really have." Prissy sighed, savoring the warmth and solidity of Stan's body as she rested her head against his shoulder. "It's nice to have another woman in the house."

Stan raised a brow at her. "You say that as if you intend to make Taylor a regular fixture around here."

Prissy smiled. "That's not such a bad idea."

Just then a girlish peal of laughter wafted from the kitchen, followed by Manning's rumbling chuckle.

Stan and Prissy exchanged amused looks.

"Do they remind you of anyone?" she asked knowingly.

He smiled into her eyes. "Now that you mention it, they *do* remind me of a certain young couple from another time. But that doesn't mean we should start planning their wedding."

"Of course not. They're only fourteen. We were eighteen when we got married."

"*And* we were in love," Stan pointed out humorously. "Manny and Taylor barely know each other, so let's not get ahead of ourselves."

"I'm not," Prissy insisted.

"Umm-hmm." Stan gave her a look that told her he knew better.

She grinned sheepishly. "Just because I— *Hey!*" she exclaimed as Stan suddenly bent and swept her easily into his arms. As he strode purposefully from the foyer, she eyed him in disbelief. "What're you doing?"

Kissing her softly, he murmured, "I'm taking you to bed, woman."

"*Now?*" Prissy protested, even as her body heated at the prospect of reconnecting intimately with him after the emotionally trying night they'd had. "But you're supposed to be driving Taylor home when she and Manny finish their math homework."

"It'll take them at least an hour," Stan reasoned, carrying her into their darkened bedroom. "So that means we can start with an appetizer, and finish with the main course later."

"In that case," Prissy purred as he kicked the door shut behind them, *"bon appétit...."*

Chapter 10

"Okay. Let me try this again." With her thick brows furrowed in concentration, Taylor methodically went through the steps for solving a quadratic equation by factoring. When she'd finished the problem, she slid her paper over to Manning and asked hopefully, "Is that right?"

He scanned her work, then nodded approvingly and raised his hand to her. "High five."

Whooping with delight, Taylor slapped her palm against his. "Finally!"

Manning grinned. "I knew you could do it."

She beamed with gratitude. "Thank you *sooo* much, Manning. I was beginning to think I'd *never* be able to solve the problem, even after two days of listening to Mr. Langenkamp's explanations." She gave Manning an awed look. "You're a good teacher."

"Not really," he said, shrugging off the praise. "You were on the right track. You were just making it harder than necessary."

"Precalculus *is* hard."

Manning grinned, rising from the table with their dessert plates. "Piece of cake?"

Taylor snorted. "Maybe to *you*, but not—"

"No," Manning said with a chuckle, "I was offering you another piece of cake."

"Oh." Taylor laughed, then shook her head at him. "I'd better not. I've already had two slices."

"So what? Who's counting?"

"*I* am, obviously."

"Well, you shouldn't," Manning told her, crossing to the counter where his great-grandmother's famous pound cake was on display on a glass dessert stand. Removing the lid, he cut into the dense, moist cake and added a thick wedge to each plate.

As he returned to the table and handed Taylor her plate, she laughingly groaned. "If I eat this, you're gonna think I'm such a pig."

"No, I'm not. I'm gonna think you're someone who appreciates a good pound cake."

Taylor grinned. "It *is* good." Biting into her piece, she closed her eyes with a dreamy moan. "It's *better* than good. It's the best thing I've ever tasted."

Manning chuckled. "Mama Wolf would love to hear that."

Taylor laughed, her eyes twinkling behind her glasses. "Believe me, if I ever have the pleasure of meeting her, I'll be sure to tell her what I just said."

Manning smiled, polishing off his cake as he covertly studied his new friend. When she'd removed her camouflage jacket earlier, he'd tried not to cringe at the sight of the bulky, multicolored sweater she wore. Even more hideous were her bright orange pants, which hurt his eyes so bad that he'd been more than relieved when she sat down and pushed her chair under the table, sparing his retinas from further damage.

"I didn't abandon you yesterday," Taylor suddenly blurted.

Manning blinked, staring at her. "What're you talking about?"

She hesitated, biting her lip. "Yesterday when Principal Henderson and Coach Delaney came to break up the fight, people were pushing and shoving really bad. I get extremely nervous in crowds, so I reached down to rub my charm because that usually calms me down. But my necklace was gone. So I panicked. While you and Rory were hauled off to the principal's office, I ran back to all of the classes I'd had so far to see if I could find my necklace. After searching for a while, I gave up and went to the bathroom, where I locked myself in the stall and bawled my eyes out."

Manning regarded her sympathetically. "The necklace must mean a lot to you."

"It does." Taylor smiled softly. "My mother gave it to me after I performed in my first violin recital."

"You play the violin?" Manning asked.

"Yeah." Her expression clouded. "Well, I used to. I haven't played since we moved to Coronado last year."

"Why not?"

She shrugged, averting her gaze to her plate. "I haven't felt like it."

Manning thought of what he'd told his mother when she'd asked him about playing basketball. *It's not the same here.*

Maybe Taylor felt the same way.

"My brother plays the saxophone," he told her.

"Really? Which brother?"

"Monty. He's in the seventh grade jazz band. Sometimes when I'm feeling down, he comes into my room and plays songs for me. He's really good. You should hear him sometime."

Taylor smiled warmly. "I'd like that."

"Yeah, I think you would." Manning hesitated, then added gently, "You should keep playing the violin, Taylor. If you're good at it, and it's something you enjoy doing, you shouldn't give it up."

She held his gaze for a long moment, then glanced down at the table and swallowed tightly. "Maybe you're right," she whispered.

"It happens every once in a while," he joked.

She looked up at him, and they shared a quiet smile.

When the moment passed, Taylor ate the rest of her cake, then brushed the crumbs from her fingers. "Let me finish my story."

"Go ahead."

"Well, as I was saying, I was in the bathroom stall feeling sorry for myself when I suddenly remembered that you were, at that very moment, getting in trouble for defending me. So I wiped my tears and ran down to the principal's office to tell him what had really happened, because I know about the stupid 'code of silence' that kids have been brainwashed to follow to protect bullies like Rory Kerrigan." She rolled her eyes in disgust. "Anyway, by the time the office secretary finished taking phone calls, setting up appointments, signing hall passes—giving her attention to everyone but me—you and your mom were already coming out of Principal Henderson's office." She eyed Manning apologetically. "I'm so sorry I didn't get there sooner."

"It's okay. You couldn't have stopped Henderson from suspending me."

"Maybe not, but I should have been there to plead your case."

"You did. Principal Henderson called my mom at work today to tell her everything you said on my behalf. Not only that, but you convinced some other kids to come forward to complain about Rory's bullying." Manning grinned, shaking his head. "That dude's in so much trouble that if he even *looks* at anyone the wrong way, he's getting expelled."

"Good," Taylor said with such vehement satisfaction that Manning laughed.

She smiled shyly at him. "I just want to thank you again for what you did. No one's ever stood up for me like that before. Well, except for my brother, and he's family so he doesn't count."

Manning chuckled. "You don't have to keep thanking me, Taylor. If the situation were reversed, I know you would have done the same thing for me."

"Maybe." She grinned ruefully. "The only difference is that *I* don't have a killer left hook, so I would have gotten my butt kicked."

They both laughed.

Sobering after several moments, Manning told her, "I'm sorry you lost your necklace."

"Oh, but I didn't!" Taylor exclaimed, grabbing his arm in her sudden excitement. "When I got home from school yesterday, I found my necklace *right* where I'd left it on top of the dresser. I must have forgotten to put it on that morning, which is something I almost *never* do. I'm absentminded about a lot of things, but not when it comes to wearing my necklace. But this is one time that being forgetful worked out for me."

"That's great, Tay," Manning said warmly. "I'm glad you didn't lose the necklace after all. I know you would have been—" He broke off, puzzled by the odd look she was giving him. "What's wrong?"

"You called me Tay."

"I know. It's short for Taylor." He paused. "You don't mind if I call you that, do you?"

"No." She smiled shyly. "You can call me whatever you want, Manning."

He smiled, feeling something swell in his chest. "So are you wearing it now?"

She blinked at him. "What?"

"The necklace."

"The...? Oh! Right. My necklace. Yes, it's right here." She reached inside her thick sweater and pulled out a delicate gold chain with a charm. "See? It's a violin."

Manning leaned over to get a better look. "Oh, yeah, it *is* a violin." He touched the small gold pendant, which was warm from Taylor's skin. "It's pretty."

"Thank you, Manning."

Hearing the breathless catch in her voice, Manning lifted his eyes to hers.

She was staring at him.

He stared back, suddenly feeling like a colony of butterflies was flapping around in his stomach.

"Manning...I..." Taylor trailed off as a pretty flush spread over her cheeks.

Unable to resist, Manning leaned closer to her.

She met him halfway.

As their lips touched, he closed his eyes and felt a delicious shock. As if a thousand volts of electricity were charging through his body, but in a good way.

"*OOOH!*"

Manning and Taylor sprang apart, whipping their heads around to find Mason gawking at them from the doorway.

Manning inwardly groaned.

"Oooh," Mason breathed, scandalized. "You were kissing a *girl!*"

"Mas—"

"I'm tellin'!"

As Mason spun on his heel, Manning shot from his chair and chased him down—no easy feat considering that Mason was the fastest runner in his citywide football division's age group. But Manning was bigger, stronger and much more determined.

Catching Mason around the waist, Manning hefted him under his arm like a sack of potatoes and carried him back into the kitchen.

"*Put me down!*" Mason howled, kicking and squirming against Manning. "I'm gonna tell on you. Da—"

Manning clapped a hand over his baby brother's mouth, then set him on the floor and crouched down to bring himself to eye level with the little runt.

"Be quiet," he warned, "or I'm gonna tell Santa Claus that you're the one who killed your class's pet hamster by overfeeding him."

As Mason's eyes widened with dismay, Taylor let out a shocked gasp. "*Manning!*"

He grinned diabolically at Mason. "So what's it gonna be, pipsqueak? Are you gonna keep your mouth shut about what you just saw here? Or am I ratting you out to Santa?"

Mason eyed him anxiously.

Removing his hand from his brother's mouth, Manning arched an expectant brow at him. "Well?"

Mason hung his head and mumbled, "I won't tell on you."

"Atta boy." Manning kissed his brother's forehead and swatted his backside. "Now go on. Get outta here."

As the boy turned and trudged from the kitchen with slumped shoulders, Manning took pity on him.

"Mason."

He glanced back.

"I've got a few candy bars under my bed. You can have them." As Mason's face lit up, Manning put his finger to his lips and winked. "But don't tell the others, or they'll know you're my favorite."

Mason beamed with sheer delight. "I won't tell 'em!" he promised before dashing off to raid the secret stash.

Manning grinned ruefully at Taylor. "Sorry about that."

"It's okay." She was blushing hard, not meeting his gaze. "I-I should be going anyway."

"But we haven't finished our math homework yet."

"I know, but I need to get home before my brother goes to bed."

"Why?"

"Well, I always read him a bedtime story. It's our nightly ritual."

Manning was impressed. "You two must be pretty close."

"We are." She gave him a stern look. "So I'm not a fan of tormenting little brothers."

When Manning ducked his head in shame, she grinned. "But you redeemed yourself with the candy."

"Thank you," he said humbly.

Taylor laughed.

Manning smiled at her. He wanted to kiss her again to see if he'd only imagined those electric shocks, but he was afraid she'd bolt if he went near her, and the last thing he wanted to do was scare her off.

"I'll go get my dad so we can take you home."

Taylor hesitated for a moment, then nodded. "Okay. Thank you."

Manning left the kitchen and made his way down the hall and around the corner to his parents' bedroom. The double doors were closed, so he just figured that his parents wanted privacy to talk and catch up on each other's day.

But as he raised his hand to knock, he heard faint noises coming from within the room. Low moans punctuated by squeaking bed springs.

Manning jumped back from the door.

As a slow flush crawled up his neck, he made a disgusted face, then turned and beat a hasty retreat.

When he returned to the kitchen, Taylor was packing up her books. As Manning dropped back into his chair, she glanced up and asked curiously, "Where's your dad? Is he coming?"

Manning shuddered with revulsion. "I don't wanna know."

Taylor gave him a puzzled look. "What do you mean?"

"Nothing. Why don't we, um, finish our homework? I wanna make sure you can solve the rest of the problems."

"Okay," Taylor agreed slowly. "But your dad's coming, right?"

Manning grimaced. "If he isn't now, he will be soon enough."

Chapter 11

When Stan and Manning returned from dropping Taylor off at home, Prissy had already tucked the boys into bed. After saying good night to Manning—who was visibly exhausted from a long day of doing chores—Stan headed to his bedroom hoping to pick up where he and Prissy had left off earlier.

When he reached the darkened room, he found his bathrobe lying on his side of the empty bed. On the nightstand, a candle glowed softly beside a folded note.

With mounting curiosity and excitement, he crossed to the nightstand and picked up the piece of paper.

Strip down to the bare essentials, Prissy had written, *and meet me outside for the main course.*

Stan grinned, anticipation and desire heating his blood.

He quickly undressed and donned his bathrobe, then opened the French doors that led outside to the private deck.

He found his wife in the Jacuzzi surrounded by flickering votive candles. Her black hair clung wetly to her face and bare shoulders.

Languidly sipping from a glass of wine, she watched as Stan approached. "Took you long enough," she purred.

"Believe me," Stan drawled, "I hurried back as fast as I could."

"Mmm," Prissy murmured, admiring his naked body as he removed his robe and laid it over hers on the edge of the Jacuzzi.

As the chilly night air hit his bare skin, Stan shivered and exclaimed, "Woman, you must be trying to freeze my balls off."

Prissy laughed. "Now why would I wanna do that? I happen to be very fond of your, ahem, balls."

Stan grinned, climbing inside the Jacuzzi. As the heated water enveloped his body, he groaned with appreciation. When he sat down beside Prissy and lay back, she handed him a glass of wine.

"I thought we could have a late-night rendezvous before I leave for my trip tomorrow," she explained.

"Sounds good to me." Stan sipped his wine as he looked down at her round, voluptuous breasts, enjoying the way her dark nipples played peek-a-boo with the steamy water. The longer he stared, the more aroused he became.

Observing his riveted gaze, Prissy chuckled softly. "Like what you see?"

He lifted his eyes to her face, which was certainly no hardship. Even without a stitch of makeup on, his wife was beautiful. And now, with her eyes sparkling and soft candlelight dancing across her features, she was downright radiant.

Unable to resist, Stan reached over and tenderly cupped her smooth cheek in his hand. As they gazed into each other's eyes, he felt his chest swell with all the love he had for her. It killed him to think of how much pain he'd been causing her lately.

Then tell her the truth, his conscience urged.

I can't, he silently insisted. *Not yet.*

Watching the play of emotions across his face, Prissy whispered, "Penny for your thoughts?"

Stan hesitated, then mustered a small smile. "I was just remembering the very first time we were in a Jacuzzi together. Do you remember?"

"Of course." Prissy's eyes glimmered. "It was on our honeymoon in Ocho Rios. We had a Jacuzzi in our hotel room."

Stan grinned wickedly. "Which we took full advantage of."

She laughed demurely. "We sure did."

Even though they'd barely had two pennies to rub together, they'd enjoyed a simple yet beautiful church wedding followed by an all-expenses-paid trip to Jamaica, courtesy of Mama Wolf.

"That was the most unbelievably romantic week of my life," Prissy reminisced with a dreamy sigh. "It's a miracle that Manny wasn't conceived the first night we were there."

Stan chuckled. "That's true, considering how many times we made love that night alone."

Sharing an intimate smile, husband and wife intertwined their arms and leisurely sipped from each other's glasses. When they'd enjoyed their fill, Prissy took their drinks and set them down. As she snuggled against Stan, he affectionately kissed her forehead and draped an arm around her shoulders.

They were silent for a few minutes, basking in the romantic ambiance provided by the soft candlelight, the soothing water and the glittering shower of stars across the night sky.

"This is nice," Stan murmured contentedly.

"Umm-hmm," Prissy agreed, her head resting on his shoulder. "We need to unwind in the Jacuzzi more often."

"Definitely." Stan rubbed his cheek against her damp, silky hair. "I wish you didn't have to leave tomorrow."

"I know," she lamented with a sigh. "But I've already committed to teaching the workshop on educating tomorrow's leaders. And it's important for me to network with my peers around the country."

"I know," Stan conceded with a low chuckle. "I'm just being greedy, wanting to keep you all to myself for as long as possible."

"Mmm, I love it when you're greedy. In fact," Prissy purred as she reached underwater to wrap her fingers around his shaft, "I'm feeling a little greedy myself."

Stan groaned with pleasure as she stroked him slowly and provocatively, gliding her hand up and down his rigid length. Pulse pounding violently, he lowered his head and slanted his mouth over hers. She moaned softly as he suckled her plush lower lip before sliding his tongue into her mouth, savoring the cool sweetness of the wine mingled with her own intoxicating nectar.

Prissy sensually twirled her tongue around his as her hand continued caressing his shaft, pumping him from base to tip while massaging his painfully tight balls. When he couldn't take any more, he pulled away and whispered roughly, "Stand up so I can taste you."

She smiled, her eyes as darkly shimmering as the water. Slowly she rose, looking like some voluptuous water nymph surfacing from an enchanted lake, beautiful brown skin glowing in the candlelight. Spellbound, Stan watched as she stood over him with rivulets of water streaming down her generous breasts and soft belly before disappearing into the neat triangle of curls between her thick thighs.

Stan swallowed hard, lust pounding through his blood as he devoured her luscious, womanly curves. Her body was built for sex, for giving a man the kind of scorchingly erotic pleasure that enslaved him for life.

As Prissy straddled his legs, Stan cupped her round butt cheeks and leaned forward to place a gentle, reverent kiss upon her belly. She quivered, her hands latching onto his shoulders for support.

"Sweet, beautiful wife," he husked, trailing kisses down to the silken vee between her thighs. When he flicked his tongue over her taut clit, her hips bucked and her legs wobbled. He tightened his grip on her, holding her upright as he licked her swollen lips.

Prissy mewled and arched backward, her hands clutching the back of his head.

Groin throbbing with need, Stan buried his mouth in her warm, fleshy mound and went to work nibbling her clit and sucking her labia.

"Baby," Prissy whimpered, helplessly grinding her hips against his face. "Oh, baby, that feels so damn *good...*"

Keeping one hand firmly around her waist, Stan used his thumb and forefinger to gently pull back the hood of her clit, exposing the sensitized nerve endings. When he drew the slick nub deep into his mouth, Prissy came with a wild cry, her body shaking uncontrollably as her orgasm flooded her.

As her knees gave out, Stan caught her and eased her down onto his lap.

She smiled weakly, looping her arms around his neck as she straddled his waist. "You know you get me every time you do that," she whispered.

"Good," Stan murmured as they shared an openmouthed kiss, tongues tangling erotically. His shaft, wedged between their wet bodies, was painfully erect and throbbing. As Prissy deepened the carnal kiss, he closed his eyes, unbearably aroused by the stiffness of her nipples poking his chest and the pulsing heat of her sex pressed against his thigh.

Dragging her lips to his ear, Prissy whispered seductively, "Your turn."

His breath snagged inside his throat. When she climbed off his lap, he rose from the water and stared down at her as she knelt before him.

"Mmmm," she purred, admiring his engorged penis jutting toward her face. "Looks like *somebody* wants some special attention."

Stan shivered at the feel of her wet, warm fingers curling around the thick base of his shaft. She stroked him slowly and sensually until pearly drops of precome began dripping out of him, lubricating her hand.

"Ummm," Prissy moaned, licking her slippery fingers as if she were licking off the most delicious icing.

Watching her, Stan groaned hoarsely. "You're killing me, babe."

"Oh, is that what I'm doing?" Her eyes glimmered with naughty mischief as she leaned forward and flicked her tongue over the swollen head of his penis.

Stan jerked, electric jolts shooting down his spine. "Little witch," he whispered.

Prissy gave him a smile of such carnal sensuality, he nearly came right then and there.

As she took him deep into her hot mouth, Stan inhaled a sharp breath.

Closing his eyes, he moaned with ecstasy at the erotic sensations rampaging through his body. Cupping his heavy balls, Prissy licked and suckled him with deep, milking pulls that had his toes curling underwater.

When she pulled his cock halfway out of her mouth and sucked the plump head, heat ripped through his chest and shot out of his shaft, spurting down the back of Prissy's throat. Shuddering and swearing gutturally, he watched as she swallowed his seed with a hunger that sent aftershocks of raw pleasure ripping through him.

Prissy held his gaze as his shaft pulsed rhythmically inside her mouth. Only when his erection had softened did she slowly release him, a sultry smile teasing her lips.

"I love the way you taste," she whispered.

Stan groaned, sinking back into the water before his knees buckled under him. Prissy laughed softly as he pulled her back onto his lap and gave her a deep, lingering kiss.

"How is it possible," she murmured against his mouth, "that we've been married fifteen years, have five kids and *still* have sex like there's no tomorrow?"

Stan chuckled. "I don't know," he teased, sucking her lower lip, "but I *damn* sure ain't complaining. Are you?"

"Oh, no, far from it. A healthy sex life is a *very* important component of a successful marriage."

"Umm-hmm," Stan purred, reaching between her thighs, "I couldn't agree more."

"In fact—" Prissy broke off with a soft moan as he slipped his middle finger inside her warm, fleshy core.

"In fact?" he prompted, sensually stroking her.

She gave a low, husky laugh that tightened his groin. "I, um, lost my train of thought."

"Mmm. Too bad." Stan kissed her arched throat as he pushed a second finger into her, making her groan and writhe on his lap.

As his erection swelled against her shapely butt, she brought her lips to his ear and whispered, "I want you to take me from behind."

She'd barely completed the throaty command before Stan lifted her from his lap, set her down on her knees and knelt behind her. Bracing her hands on the edge of the Jacuzzi, Prissy parted her legs and bent slightly forward as he rubbed his engorged penis along her cleft. The erotic friction made them both shudder deeply with arousal.

Prissy looked over her shoulder at Stan, their hungry gazes locking as he slowly entered her. As her tight, succulent walls gripped his shaft, he groaned thickly and squeezed his eyes shut, already on the verge of exploding.

Trying like hell to pace himself, he began moving inside her with deep, measured thrusts that made her moan with pleasure.

Opening his heavy-lidded eyes, he reached around her body to cup her swaying breasts, brushing his thumbs across her distended nipples. She shivered hard and gyrated her hips to the rhythm of his long, thick strokes.

Soon their guttural cries and moans pierced the night as they rocked together under the silvery moonlight, the steamy water lapping at their joined bodies. Stan watched Prissy's face contort with ecstasy as he pumped in and out of her, his pelvis slapping against the lush roundness of her ass.

Heart thundering, sweat sheening his brow, he wound her hair around his fist and tugged her head back, then leaned down to bite the side of her neck.

Prissy cried out and shuddered against him.

When she retaliated by reaching between her legs and squeezing his swollen sac, he swore hoarsely as jolts of raw pleasure screamed down his spine.

Moments later they erupted violently together, gasping each other's names as Stan shot his seed into her convulsing womb.

After ejaculating for what seemed like hours, he collapsed against her, clasping her trembling body to his as their ragged pants filled the air.

Minutes passed before Prissy whispered, "Do you think the kids heard us?"

Stan chuckled, nipping her shoulder. "Guess we'll find out in the morning if they give us strange looks."

Prissy let out a soft, breathy laugh. "You don't know how hard it was for me to hold back my screams."

"I wish you hadn't," Stan murmured, caressing the delectable swell of her butt. "You know I love to hear you scream."

She grinned over her shoulder at him. "*That* definitely would have woken them up."

He smiled, brushing his lips over hers. "Let's go inside, sweetheart."

"Mmm, yeah. I'm starting to pucker."

Chuckling, Stan stood and climbed out of the Jacuzzi, then lifted Prissy out and set her down, enjoying the delicious slide of her wet, naked skin against his.

As they helped each other into their robes, Prissy smiled up at him. "Are you ready for bed?"

"Yeah"— Stan bent and swept her effortlessly into his arms —"but not for sleep."

Chapter 12

"Excuse me, beautiful. Is this seat taken?"

Prissy glanced up from the martini she'd been sipping to meet the interested gaze of an attractive, forty-something black man who'd joined her at the bar. Everything from his cheap suit to his flirtatious smile told her he was a lonely businessman on the prowl for a one-night stand.

Unfortunately for him, Prissy was a happily married woman who was still coming off the high of the explosively erotic sendoff her husband had given her last night. So cozying up to another man was the *last* thing on her mind.

"Is it okay if I sit here?" the stranger persisted.

Not wanting to be rude, Prissy murmured, "It's a free country."

His smile widened as he lowered himself onto the bar stool beside hers. The heavy musk of his cologne invaded her nostrils, making her want to sneeze. When the bartender materialized, the man ordered a gin on the rocks, then glanced at the martini that Prissy was nursing.

"Can I buy you another drink?" he offered.

"No, thank you," Prissy demurred. "I'm still working on this one."

After the bartender served the glass of gin and moved off, the man returned his attention to Prissy.

"My name's Torrance," he introduced himself.

Prissy shook his proffered hand. "Nice to meet you."

"The pleasure's all mine..." He trailed off pointedly, waiting for her to supply her name.

She hesitated. "Priscilla."

"Priscilla," he repeated, his dark eyes slowly roaming over her body to linger on her crossed legs. "Beautiful name for a beautiful woman."

Prissy chuckled softly. "Not that I don't appreciate the compliment—"

"I was being sincere."

"Maybe, but your sincerity is wasted on me."

"Why?" He nodded at the twinkling four-carat diamond ring on her left hand. "Because some lucky man had the privilege of meeting and marrying you before I could beat him to it?"

Prissy laughed, shaking her head at him. "Do you rehearse these pickup lines before you use them? Or have you had so much practice approaching women at bars that the lines just roll off your tongue?"

He smiled suggestively. "Well, since you've taken such an interest in my tongue—"

"*There* you are," a woman's familiar voice interrupted. "I've been looking all over for you."

Prissy glanced over her shoulder just as Celeste Wolf leaned down and kissed her on the cheek.

"Hey, baby." At the narrowed look Prissy gave her, Celeste winked, indicating that she should play along. "Have you been waiting for me very long?"

"Long enough," Prissy answered gamely. "But I know you're always worth the wait."

"Aww. Aren't you sweet?" Celeste stroked Prissy's cheek, then turned and raked the man with an amused look. "Who's your new friend?"

"He says his name's Torrance," Prissy drawled.

"Torrance, huh?" Celeste gave him another mocking once-over. "Looks more like a Dick to me."

Torrance laughed, seemingly unfazed by the insult. "Funny you should mention—" He broke off to watch as Prissy dipped two fingers inside her martini glass and retrieved the olive, then fed it to Celeste, who sighed with exaggerated pleasure.

Torrance looked from Prissy to Celeste, his tongue all but hanging to the floor. "Are you two...?" He trailed off, barely able to contain his excitement at the thought of the two women being lovers.

When they just smiled at each other, he asked hopefully, "Is there somewhere we could all go to get better acquainted?"

Celeste smirked at him, draping a possessive arm around Prissy's shoulders. "Sorry, sugar," she said, affecting a Southern drawl that was thicker than molasses. "Two's company, three's a crowd."

"But—"

"I don't think she stuttered, Torrance," Prissy said mildly.

Giving her and Celeste a look of patent regret, Torrance picked up his drink and moved off, no doubt to find a more willing conquest.

Prissy and Celeste looked at each other, then burst out laughing like two schoolgirls.

"Oh, Pris. It's *so* good to see you again." Celeste hugged Prissy tightly, then drew back to give her an admiring once-over. "Girl, you look *amazing!*"

"Thank you," Prissy said, not entirely immune to the flattery. "I've been trying like hell to stick to my diet and exercise regimen. I'm determined to fit into the gown I bought months ago for next Saturday's fireman's ball."

"Well, whatever you're doing is definitely working," Celeste declared. "Girl, you look like you're already back down to a size eight!"

"Um, not quite. But thanks for saying so." Prissy smiled at Celeste. "You look good, too."

But that was nothing new. For as long as Prissy had known her, Celeste had always been beautiful. At thirty-five she boasted a petite, slender figure, a flawless café au lait complexion and cinnamon-brown eyes. Like Prissy, she wore black heels with a fitted black dress. But unlike Prissy, Celeste hadn't needed to tuck in her stomach with a girdle.

Gently clasping Prissy's hands between hers, Celeste said earnestly, "Thank you so much for agreeing to meet me for dinner, Pris."

"You didn't give me much of a choice," Prissy said wryly. "You called my hotel room and threatened to crash my workshop tomorrow if I didn't have dinner with you."

Celeste grinned unabashedly. "Desperate times call for desperate measures."

Before Prissy could respond, the hostess appeared to escort them to a table tucked into a corner of the upscale downtown restaurant, which was reputedly one of the best in Rochester.

After Prissy and Celeste perused the leather-bound menus and ordered their entrées, they quietly regarded each other across the linen-covered table. Both knew they had a lot of ground to cover, but neither knew where to start.

It was Celeste who broke the silence. "How long will you be in town?"

"Just until Sunday when the conference ends."

Celeste smiled knowingly. "I'm sure you're eager to get back home to Stan and the boys."

"I am," Prissy admitted. "I miss them already."

As soon as she checked into her hotel room that afternoon, she'd called Stan to let him know that she'd arrived safely. After they chatted for a while, he'd passed the phone around to their sons. By the time Prissy finished talking to Mason—who'd promised to score a touchdown for her during his football game on Saturday—she'd been ready to grab her suitcase and catch the first flight back home. How pathetic was she?

"How's your mother doing?" Celeste asked.

Prissy sipped her martini that she'd brought from the bar. "I just spoke to her this morning. She's doing well."

Her widowed mother lived with Prissy's older brother, Theo, and his wife and twin daughters. "Everyone's coming to Coronado for Thanksgiving this year."

"Oh, that's wonderful," Celeste said warmly. "I know how much your mom and Theo miss seeing the boys every day. I thought they'd never forgive you for leaving Atlanta."

"I'm not sure they have," Prissy said wryly. "They fuss at me every chance they get."

"They mean well." Celeste's smile was tinged with sorrow. "I'm not sure where I'll be spending Thanksgiving. Grant invited me to accompany him to Vermont, but I don't think I'm ready to meet his family. It's...too soon."

Prissy said nothing.

An uncomfortable silence passed.

"So," Celeste ventured carefully, "how are things between you and Stan?"

Draping her linen napkin across her lap, Prissy said evenly, "Things are fine." No way was she telling Celeste the truth—that part of her still suspected Stan was having an affair, to the extent that she'd considered canceling her trip so he wouldn't be tempted to play while she was away.

"So I was right," Celeste continued. "Your fears about Stan were completely unfounded."

"Yes." Prissy forced a smile. "You were right."

"See? I told you that man loves you and would never cheat on you."

Prissy was spared from responding when the waiter materialized with their starter salads. As she and Celeste began eating, Prissy decided to steer the conversation in a different direction.

"Where are you and Grant staying?"

"Around the corner from the Mayo Clinic," Celeste answered. "They put him up in a beautiful two-bedroom condo with lakefront views."

"How nice." Prissy paused, then couldn't resist adding, "Sounds like quite an upgrade from the humble abode you recently vacated."

The edges of Celeste's mouth tightened. "*You* asked the question."

"I did," Prissy calmly acknowledged. "But I didn't expect you to embellish on a description of your love nest without an ounce of shame."

Celeste's nostrils flared. With forced composure, she speared a slice of cucumber and slid the fork into her mouth, chewing slowly and deliberately.

Prissy waited.

"I know you think I'm a horrible person for what I did to my family," Celeste said quietly, keeping her gaze trained on her plate. "Believe me, not a day goes by that I don't regret my actions. I wish things could have turned out differently."

"Do you?" Prissy countered cynically.

Celeste's eyes snapped to hers. "What do you mean?"

"Do you *really* wish things could have turned out differently? Or are you just saying what you think I want to hear? Because it seems to me that everything is working out pretty well for you so far. You're living in a lakefront condo on someone else's dime. You'll be getting your master's degree on someone else's dime. You quit your job, yet here you are wearing Chanel and treating me to dinner at a five-star restaurant you couldn't have stepped foot inside three months ago. You seem to be getting everything you ever wanted, Celeste. So forgive me if I have a hard time believing that you wish things could have turned out differently."

"*Are you serious*?" Celeste demanded, her eyes flashing with outraged disbelief. "Do you honestly think that losing my family has been a damn picnic for me? Marcus hates my guts! Every time I call the house, he refuses to speak to me, and Michael can't get off the phone with me fast enough! I love my children and I want custody of them, but I can't bear the thought of hurting Sterling any more than I already have, and I'm not even sure that Michael and Marcus would agree to live with me after what I did. I feel like a complete failure, the worst mother that ever walked the face of the earth. So don't you *dare* sit there and tell me that I'm enjoying the way my life has unraveled, because you have *no* fucking clue what you're talking about!"

"Oh, please!" Prissy hissed furiously. "Spare me your sob story, Celeste. You're not a damn martyr. *You're* responsible for the way your 'life has unraveled.' Not only did you cheat on Sterling, but then you had the audacity to allow Grant into your *home*, for God's sake! You weren't thinking about your husband and children. All you cared about was fulfilling your own selfish needs and desires. And you proved that once again when you decided to run off with Grant without giving a second thought to the children you *claim* to want!"

"What's that supposed to mean?" Celeste fired back, oblivious to the curious glances they were attracting from other diners. "I *do* want my boys, but I refuse to put Sterling through a bitter custody battle. *That* would be selfish. As for me running off with Grant, I told you we're only going to be here for four months. *If* we eventually get married and decide to relocate to Minnesota, it's not like I'd be committing a capital offense. As hard as it may be for you to accept, Priscilla, that's what people do when they get divorced. They move on with their lives. Deal with it."

Prissy had heard enough. Setting down her fork, she leaned across the table and said coldly and succinctly, "Sterling Wolf is a good man—the best thing that ever happened to you. He was there for you when Wendell died, and he manned up and did right by you when you got pregnant with Michael. For the sixteen years you were married, he was nothing but a wonderful husband and father. He may not be as rich or successful as Grant Rutherford, but he's ten times the man that Grant will *ever* be. Someday, after you've finished chasing *whatever* it is that you're chasing, you're going to wake up and realize what a horrible mistake you made by walking out on Sterling. And when that day comes, it will give me great pleasure to look you in the eye and say I told you so. Until then"— Prissy tossed her napkin down on the table and stood —"have a nice fucking life."

"Wait!" Celeste said urgently. "Please don't leave, Pris."

"I have *nothing* else to—"

"I'm pregnant."

Prissy gasped.

Even if she'd tried to walk away at that moment, her legs wouldn't have supported such an endeavor.

Reeling with shock, she dropped back into her chair and stared at Celeste. "*What* did you just say?" she whispered.

Celeste smiled weakly. "I think you heard me the first time."

"I couldn't have, because I thought I heard you say that you're *pregnant*."

"I am."

"But...how? You had your tubes tied after Marcus was born."

"I did," Celeste confirmed, her tone wry. "But apparently I've now joined the one percent of women who still manage to become pregnant after undergoing a tubal ligation."

"But you got your tubes tied ten years ago! I thought the chance of getting pregnant decreases every year after the procedure."

"That's true. But there are always exceptions." Celeste shook her head, her lips twisted into a bitterly sardonic smile. "As a nurse, I've seen my fair share of medical miracles. I just never thought I'd become one."

Prissy stared at her, at a loss for words.

Just then the waiter arrived with their meals. Prissy watched impatiently as the young man made a production of grinding black pepper over their steaming pasta before he gathered their salad plates and departed.

Neither woman touched her food.

"When did you find out?" Prissy asked.

Celeste hesitated. "A month after I moved out of the house. When I first noticed that my period was late, I just assumed it was from the stress of everything that had happened. Never in my wildest dreams did I think I could be pregnant after all these years. But then I started feeling really tired and nauseous. So I went to see my doctor and...well, the rest is history."

"Wait a minute." Prissy stared at Celeste, struck by a sudden realization. "Is there any chance that the baby is *Sterling's*?"

Celeste held her gaze for a long moment, then whispered, "Yes."

"Oh, my God."

Tears welled in Celeste's eyes. "Sterling and I made love the night after I slept with Grant at the hospital. So the baby could be either of theirs."

"Oh, my God," Prissy repeated, leaning back against her chair as she shook her head at Celeste. "What are you going to do?"

"I don't know." Celeste sniffled, swiping at the corners of her eyes with trembling fingers.

"I just thought of something," Prissy said. "Getting pregnant after a tubal ligation can lead to having an ectopic pregnancy, right?"

Celeste nodded.

"So is the baby...?"

Celeste hesitated for a long moment. "My doctor ran tests."

"And?"

"The baby appears to be normal."

The disappointment in her voice was unmistakable, and Prissy knew why. Ectopic pregnancies were so high-risk that they often had to be terminated to save the mother's life. Being forced to abort an unwanted child would have absolved Celeste of any responsibility.

"Does Grant know?" Prissy asked her.

"No."

"What?" Prissy was stunned. "Why haven't you told him?"

"I'm not ready." Celeste exhaled a deep, shuddering breath. "Grant doesn't want any children."

"*What?*"

"It's not that he doesn't like children," Celeste hastened to defend her lover. "He *does* like them. He just doesn't want any of his own. His career is really taking off. If we stay in Atlanta, he'll be promoted to head of the neurosurgical residency program, which means even greater responsibilities on top of his research studies and the numerous committees he serves on. And once I start school next fall, we'll *both* be too busy to raise a child."

So once again, the couple's needs and ambitions took precedence over the welfare of innocent children.

"What about Sterling?" Prissy demanded. "He has a right to know that you might be carrying another child of his."

Celeste grimaced. "I know."

"So when are you going to tell him?"

"I haven't decided."

Prissy's eyes narrowed warningly. "I hope you're not thinking of keeping this a secret from him."

"Of course not." But Celeste didn't look or sound too convincing.

Prissy frowned. "Celeste, you can't—"

"Damn it, Pris," she snapped, "stop telling me what I *can* and *can't* do! Everything's not as black and white as you like to believe! I love Sterling, God knows I do. But I was drowning in our marriage, drowning in misery and hopelessness. So I'm not going to sit here and pretend to be okay with this pregnancy. I'm *not* okay. I'm devastated. I don't want another baby—with Sterling, Grant, or anyone else. If that makes me even more of a monster in your eyes, then so be it."

Prissy had gone still. "What are you saying, Cel? What are you planning to do?"

The two women stared at each other as the word *abortion* hung in the air between them.

After a long, tense silence, Prissy sat forward in her chair. "Whatever you decide to do," she said in carefully measured tones, "please don't keep Sterling in the dark. You were married to him for sixteen years. He has a right to know that you might be pregnant with his third child. If the baby is his, he deserves to have a say in what happens to him or her."

"I agree." Celeste held Prissy's gaze. "I'll tell him when I'm ready."

"And when will that be?"

"I don't know. But I need you to promise me that you won't breathe a word of this to Sterling, Stanton *or* Mama Wolf."

"Damn it, Celeste—"

"I'm serious, Pris. Not a word to anyone."

Prissy scowled. "You know I don't like keeping secrets. And you're putting me in an impossible position by asking me to lie to my husband."

"I'm sorry, but you know as well as I do that if Stan finds out that I'm pregnant, he won't hesitate to tell Sterling. And that wouldn't be fair. It's *my* body and *my* baby. So the news should come from me, not anyone else." Celeste pinned Prissy with an intent look. "Do I have your word that you won't say anything until I'm ready?"

After wavering for several moments, Prissy heaved a resigned breath. "Fine. I won't tell anyone."

"Thank you." Celeste's expression softened with gratitude. "Even though you're angry at me and you don't approve of the recent decisions I've made, I'm glad you're here, Pris. I need your friendship now more than ever."

The naked vulnerability in her voice tugged at Prissy's heartstrings, making her feel guilty for the way she'd turned her back on Celeste after the divorce. Celeste had made a terrible mistake, but did that mean she deserved to be permanently banished from Prissy's life?

"Is everything all right?"

Prissy and Celeste glanced up to find the waiter hovering at their table with an anxious expression. "You haven't touched your meals," he said, "so I just wanted to make sure everything was okay."

Celeste looked meaningfully at Prissy. "Is everything okay?"

Prissy hesitated for a long moment, then nodded slowly. "Everything's fine."

Celeste smiled, visibly relieved.

But as Prissy picked up her fork to begin eating, she couldn't help feeling as though she'd just made a pact with the devil and condemned her soul to the fiery pits of hell.

Chapter 13

Thick clouds of smoke billowed from the roof of the small white clapboard house on Kedron Street.

Stan charged up the porch steps, adrenaline and fear pumping hard through his veins. He heard no wail of approaching sirens, no shouts from other firefighters arriving on the scene.

He was on his own.

After pausing to secure his helmet over his hood, he rammed his shoulder against the front door, forcing it open with a loud, splintering *crack!*

Barreling across the threshold, he was assaulted by the scorching blast of an inferno that knocked him backward. Gasping sharply, he dropped to his knees.

The living room was engulfed in thick black smoke. Flames danced up the walls and swept across the ceiling.

Breathing hard behind his oxygen mask, Stan lifted his head and peered through the curtain of smoke.

That was when he saw them.

Two bodies seated side by side on the old sofa. Unconscious, eyes closed, heads resting limply against each other's.

The moment Stan recognized the middle-aged couple, his heart rushed into his throat. Lunging to his feet, he forced his way through the acrid smoke, heedless of the searing flames and plaster falling from the ceiling.

Reaching the sofa, he crouched down before the couple, his panicked gaze shooting from one to the other.

"Mama!" he called out hoarsely. "Dad!"

Neither stirred.

Choking back blind terror, Stan reached toward his mother with the intent of tossing her over his shoulder and carrying her outside to safety.

But before he could grab her, she suddenly disintegrated to ashes.

He recoiled in shocked horror, watching as his father also turned into a charred corpse.

"NO!" Stan shouted, a sound of raw anguish. *"Please God, nooo!"*

Hearing a loud roar overhead, he looked up quickly.

The roof was collapsing!

As a fiery beam plummeted toward him, he opened his mouth and screamed—

Stan bolted upright in bed, lungs burning, chest heaving violently as he fought to catch his breath.

After several frantic seconds, he glanced down at himself. Instead of wearing his heavy turnout coat and bunker trousers, he had on black shorts and an old T-shirt dampened with clammy sweat. When he looked up at the dark ceiling and saw that it was very much intact, he exhaled a ragged breath and dragged trembling hands over his face.

Jesus.

He'd been dreaming about his dead parents again.

Grief and nausea churned in his stomach, curdling the digested remains of the chili he'd cooked for dinner.

He tossed the covers aside and swung his legs over the side of the bed, then stood and staggered into the bathroom. Twisting on the sink faucet, he splashed cold water onto his face.

Shivering uncontrollably, he gripped the edges of the counter and squeezed his eyes shut, trying to banish the horrific image of his parents' charred corpses. But it was seared into his conscience as indelibly as if someone had taken a branding iron to his brain.

It had been eighteen years since his parents died in a house fire. Stan and his older brother, Sterling, had been away that fateful summer, visiting their grandmother in Savannah. One devastating phone call from home had turned their lives upside down, and they'd never been the same again.

Swiping water from his face, Stan tossed aside the hand towel and trudged out of the bathroom. Since he knew he wouldn't be able to go back to sleep anytime soon—not without Prissy's warm body to curl up with—he left the bedroom and made his way through the dark, silent house to the kitchen.

Crossing to the refrigerator, he grabbed a frosty beer, popped the top and downed half the can in one swallow.

Still feeling disoriented, he stumbled over to the table and collapsed into the nearest chair.

For the past five months, he'd been tormented by nightmares. Vivid, harrowing nightmares that ended with him perishing in the same inferno that had claimed the lives of his parents.

Although some rational part of his brain told him there was no correlation between his dreams and reality, he couldn't shake the growing premonition that something terrible was going to happen to him.

And soon.

God help me, Stan thought bleakly, dropping his face into his open palm and closing his eyes. The nightmares had taken a devastating toll on his mind and body, leaving him mentally and physically drained.

"Dad?"

Startled, Stan jerked his head up to watch as Manning cautiously entered the kitchen, eyeing him worriedly.

"Are you okay, Dad?"

"I'm fine." Stan's voice was a hoarse rasp, as if he'd just battled a four-alarm fire without wearing an airpack. "What're you still doing up?"

"I couldn't sleep," Manning mumbled, joining him at the table.

Stan smiled wanly. "Miss your mom, huh?"

"No," Manning said swiftly.

At Stan's knowing look, a sheepish grin tugged at his son's mouth. "Maybe just a little," he admitted.

Stan chuckled. "Mama's boy."

Manning blushed. "Hey, I'm not used to her being gone. Even though she only goes out of town once or twice a year, it sucks when she's not here."

"I know." Stan took a long pull on his beer. "If it makes you feel any better, I miss her, too."

"I can tell." Manning regarded him sympathetically. "You seem kinda lost without her."

Stan chuckled quietly. "There's probably some truth to that."

Manning nodded slowly. "So you and Ma...you're okay?"

"Of course." Stan searched his son's face. "Why? Were you worried about us?"

"Nah. Not at all." Manning grinned, visibly relieved, then pushed back his chair and stood. "I think I'll have some more chili."

Stan cocked a brow at him. "It's after midnight."

The boy shrugged. "It's not like I have to get up for school in the morning. Besides, we're talking about your award-winning chili," he said, referring to Stan's first place victory at the fire department's annual chili cookoff that summer. "So I can eat it *anytime*."

"Hmm." Stan watched as his son shuffled to the refrigerator and opened the door. Raising his beer to his mouth, Stan ventured casually, "Is there something you wanna tell me about you and Caitlyn?"

Manning froze.

Calmly setting down his drink, Stan waited.

After several moments, Manning closed the fridge and turned with obvious reluctance to face Stan.

They stared at each other.

"Should I repeat the question?"

Manning swallowed nervously. "No."

"Then answer me."

The boy shifted from one bare foot to another. "I don't know what you want me to tell you," he mumbled.

"Why don't you start with the truth?" Stan suggested.

Manning dropped his gaze to the floor, then drew a deep breath as if to shore up his courage. "The other night, Caitlyn came to my room—"

"She climbed up the ladder?"

Manning paused a beat. "The trellis."

"What?"

"Caitlyn says it's called a trellis."

"I don't give a damn *what* she called it. What the hell was she doing sneaking up to your room in the middle of the night?"

When Manning looked at him as if the answer should be obvious, Stan scowled. "Damn it, Manny. Didn't we just talk about this? What part of 'you're not ready to start having sex' did you not understand?"

"What was I supposed to do, Dad?" the boy countered, spreading his hands in a helpless gesture. "She was there...in my room...naked."

Stan swore under his breath, scrubbing a hand over his face. "I knew that girl was trouble. Did you at least use a condom?"

"Of course."

"You'd better have," Stan growled. "The *last* thing you need is to become a father at fourteen." At the stricken look Manning gave him, Stan shook his head in angry disbelief. "That didn't even occur to you, did it? While you were getting it on with Caitlyn—with me and your mother *right* downstairs—not once did you stop to consider the ramifications of what you were doing, did you?"

When Manning's eyes shifted guiltily away, Stan snorted in disgust. "So much for all those talks we've had."

"I'm sorry, Dad."

"You should be. I'm really disappointed in you, Manny. I expected better of you."

The boy, to his credit, looked suitably ashamed. "Are you gonna tell Ma?"

Stan scowled blackly. "I don't know."

Although he hated the thought of keeping such a secret from Prissy, he knew she'd be heartbroken if she found out that her baby boy had lost his virginity.

Shaking his head, Stan downed the rest of his beer, then shoved to his feet and stalked to the trash bin to throw away the empty can.

As he approached Manning, the kid looked ready to bolt.

Stan frowned. "Look, son, I haven't forgotten what it was like to be your age. Your body's changing, your hormones are running amok and you're horny as hell. Which is *exactly* why you have no business becoming sexually active. You're not mature enough to understand what you're getting yourself into. And you need to realize that women aren't as casual about sex as men are. They get emotionally attached after sleeping with a guy. So while *you* might be ready to move on by next week, I guarantee you that Caitlyn will feel differently."

Manning looked skeptical. "But she's a junior, and she can have any dude at school she wants."

"Yeah, and the dude she wants is *you*."

Manning said nothing, his brows furrowed as he absorbed his father's words.

As Stan observed him, he was suddenly reminded that Manning was the same age he'd been when his parents died. In that moment, he tried to imagine not being there to watch Manning graduate from high school, land his first job out of college, get married and become a father. The thought of missing all of those milestones was so inconceivable that it nearly brought him to his knees with despair.

"I need you to make wise choices, son," Stan said, his voice laced with sudden urgency. "I need you to be responsible."

"I know," Manning mumbled.

"No, I don't think you really do." Stan reached out and gripped the boy's shoulder. "If anything happens to me, *you'll* become the man of the house. So you know what that means? It means you'll need to man up, like your name says, and take care of your mother and your younger brothers. Do you understand that?"

"What're you talking about, Dad?" Manning whispered, staring at him. "What's gonna happen to you?"

Seeing the stricken expression on his son's face, Stan realized that he'd frightened him, which was the last thing he'd intended to do.

Overcome with emotion, he hauled Manning roughly into his arms. "I love you," he choked out hoarsely. "Love you so damn much, son."

"I love you too, Dad," Manning whispered.

Stan clung to him for as long as he could, then kissed the top of the boy's head and drew away, blinking back tears that were mirrored in Manning's eyes.

Mustering a shaky smile, Stan patted his son's cheek and said gruffly, "See what happens when your mom's not around? I get all girly and sentimental."

Manning grinned crookedly.

At the sound of approaching footsteps, they glanced around just as Montana, Magnum, Maddox and Mason appeared in the doorway.

Stan eyed them expectantly. "What's up, fellas?"

The brothers exchanged uncomfortable glances.

"Couldn't sleep," Monty explained.

"Wind's blowing too hard," Magnum muttered.

"Not really tired," Maddox added.

Only Mason was brave enough to confess the truth. "I miss Ma," he complained.

The others looked at one another, then burst out laughing.

Chapter 14

"When are you going to tell your wife about us?"

Stan was lying on his back with his eyes closed, hands folded over his stomach, long legs stretched out on the plush leather sofa. He'd been so deep in thought that he didn't hear the question at first. When the words gradually registered, he opened his eyes and glanced over at the woman who'd spoken.

She sat across from him in a comfy armchair, a yellow notepad resting on her lap. Her dark hair was secured into a bun, and she wore gold-rimmed eyeglasses that made her appear studious without detracting from her good looks.

Stan eyed her quizzically. "Us?"

Dr. Gilliard cleared her throat, uncrossing and recrossing her long, shapely legs.

Is it just me, Stan wondered, *or are her skirts getting shorter?*

Frowning at the thought, he shifted his gaze to the oriental rug that covered the polished wooden floor of the cozy office.

"Let me rephrase the question. When are you going to tell your wife that you've been seeing a therapist about your nightmares?"

Stan's frown deepened, guilt gnawing at his insides as he turned his head to stare up at the ceiling. "I haven't decided."

"Well, how much longer do you think you can keep our sessions a secret from her?" the doctor pressed.

Stan sighed heavily. "I don't know."

When the nightmares first began, he'd had no intention of telling anyone. But late one night at the firehouse, he'd surfaced from a dream shouting for his parents, which had awakened the other firefighters on duty. He'd apologized for the commotion and assured them that he was okay, then jokingly told them to go back to sleep so they could resume dreaming about *Playboy* centerfolds. After the men's drowsy laughter died down and they rolled over on their cots, Stan had gotten up and crept downstairs to the kitchen. He was soon joined by his concerned captain, Fisher Sullivan, who'd asked him about the nightmare.

Over steaming cups of strong black coffee, Stan had opened up to Sullivan, who'd encouraged him to make an appointment with the department psychologist. Stan had resisted the idea for another two months, hoping the nightmares would simply go away. But they hadn't.

So there he was stretched out on the proverbial shrink's couch, counting down the minutes until the hourlong session ended.

"I know how difficult it is for men to seek mental health counseling," Dr. Gilliard spoke in that calm, soothing tone that lulled her patients into confiding their deepest, darkest secrets. "As you know, many of my clients are firefighters and cops. And all of them, without exception, have admitted to me that they think seeing a therapist is a sign of weakness, like it's somehow unmanly to seek professional help. *You* had that misconception when you first started coming to me, remember? You were worried about what your comrades would think if they found out you were in therapy, and you were concerned that it would hurt your chances at being promoted to captain."

"Yeah, I remember," Stan grunted.

"It took two full sessions before you felt comfortable enough to open up to me about the nightmares you'd been having. But that was three months ago. I think we've made a lot of progress since then, wouldn't you agree?"

"Sure." Stan knew that the sooner Dr. Gilliard gave him a clean bill of health, the sooner he could appease his captain and end the counseling sessions.

It wasn't that he didn't appreciate the good doctor's efforts to probe his psyche in order to diagnose what ailed him. He *was* appreciative, because he knew how important it was for him to talk to someone about the nightmares that plagued him. But after three months under Dr. Gilliard's care, the bad dreams hadn't gone away or lessened in frequency. So it was only natural that he'd begun to question whether he was wasting his time, and hers.

Dr. Gilliard flipped to a clean sheet on her notepad. Somehow she always managed to fill several pages during their sessions, although she seemed to do more talking than Stan. "I'd like to explore your reasons for not divulging to your wife that you're in therapy. I know you've told me that you don't want to worry or upset her, but I think it goes much deeper than that."

Stan exhaled a deep, ragged breath. "Believe me, I'm not proud of keeping this from Prissy. I hate lying to her about *anything.*"

"Then why do it?" Dr. Gilliard paused for a moment. "It's not as if you're having an affair."

Stan grimaced as Prissy's angry words echoed through his mind. *Who paged you...I know you're lying to me...I don't know what's going on with you...*

Until that night, it hadn't occurred to him that she might think he was cheating on her. But even now that he knew of her suspicions, he *still* wasn't ready to confide the truth to her. Because he honestly didn't know which would be worse for her: believing that he was unfaithful, or facing the very real possibility that his days with her were numbered.

"Stan?" Dr. Gilliard prompted gently. "Why are you so reluctant to tell your wife about the nightmares?"

Stan stared at the ceiling for several moments before answering, "When Prissy was ten years old, her father was killed in a machinery accident at the textile factory where he worked. The family was devastated, especially Prissy's mother. She fell into such a deep depression that Prissy and her older brother more or less became the adults, having to look after her and themselves. Being forced to grow up so fast changed them in ways they never could have imagined.

"About six months after Prissy and I got married, I told her that I wanted to become a firefighter because of what had happened to my parents. We'd talked about it when we were dating, but she'd always thought—maybe hoped—that I wasn't serious. She wasn't crazy about the idea. Given the dangerous nature of firefighting, she was understandably worried for my safety."

"Because of what happened to her father," Dr. Gilliard surmised.

Stan nodded, his mind traveling back to the early years of his marriage. He'd often come home from the firehouse to find his young wife waiting at the front door with Montana perched on her hip and Manning huddled at her side, his small hand tightly clutching hers. Prissy's eyes would be filled with anxiety because she'd heard about the blaze that Stan and his unit had put down during their shift. She'd ask him a bunch of questions about the fire until, sensing her distress, Manning or Montana—or both— would start crying. As Prissy tended to Manny, Stan would take Monty from her arms and gently rock the baby to sleep, giving his wife a chance to calm her overwrought nerves.

"How did her lack of support affect your marriage?" Dr. Gilliard asked, pulling Stan back to the present.

He frowned. "Lack of support?"

"Well, yes. She didn't want you to become a firefighter, even though she knew how important it was to you in the aftermath of losing your parents. I imagine her reaction must have been very difficult for you."

Stan shook his head. "I didn't see it that way. She genuinely admired my reasons for wanting to become a firefighter, and she knew I'd be good at it. But she was scared for me. She didn't want our boys growing up without their father, and she didn't want to end up a widow like her mother. I understood where she was coming from. So I never thought she was being unsupportive."

Out of the corner of his eye, Stan saw Dr. Gilliard making notations on her pad. After several moments, she asked quietly, "Have you ever thought of quitting?"

Stan was silent, pondering her question even though he already knew the answer.

But how could he explain to her what it was like to crawl down a pitch-black hallway with searing waves of heat pushing him to the floor? How could he articulate the thoughts that raced through his mind as he instinctively groped his way through the darkness, doing a primary search for victims even as he prayed that they had already escaped? How could he verbalize the emotions that swept through him—a double-edged cocktail of dread and relief—when he discovered a body among the smoke and flames? How could he describe the adrenaline-fueled sense of urgency that pumped through his veins as he hefted the victim over his shoulder and began the painstakingly perilous journey toward safety? How could mere words adequately capture the sheer exhilaration he felt upon reaching the exit and hearing the victim inhale that first ragged lungful of clean air?

Firefighting, and saving lives, were in Stan's blood. He couldn't imagine doing anything else. So he answered Dr. Gilliard the only way he could. "No."

"You've never thought of finding another line of work?" she confirmed.

"No."

The doctor jotted more notes. "Since you've been putting out fires for fourteen years, I assume Prissy has accepted your job by now."

"She has." Stan paused. "I think what really helped is that she bonded with the wives of the other firefighters. They formed a support group that helped them encourage one another. Thankfully she's been able to find a similar network here as well."

"That's good."

"It is." Stan smiled softly. "Now don't get me wrong. She still watches the news and worries whenever there's a major fire, and she still expects a phone call from me the moment I get back to the fire station. But after all these years, I think she's finally at peace with what I do for a living."

"So you don't want to rock the boat."

"Exactly. If I tell her about the nightmares—which always end with me dying—then we'll be back to square one. I can't put Prissy through that, not after I've spent the past fourteen years assuring her that nothing's gonna happen to me."

"In all likelihood, Stan, nothing *is* going to happen to you."

When Stan was silent, Dr. Gilliard continued pragmatically, "You and your brother suffered a devastating tragedy. Not only did you lose your parents, but then *you* had the terrible misfortune of seeing the autopsy photos."

Stan grimaced, remembering the day the arson investigator had showed up to speak to Mama Wolf about the fire, which had been caused by a gas leak. When the two adults stepped into the kitchen for privacy, Stan had stolen a peek at the contents of the envelope the investigator had unwittingly left on the coffee table. He'd been horrified by the gruesome pictures of his parents, who were charred beyond recognition. For a long time afterward, he couldn't get the shockingly grisly images out of his mind, no matter how hard he'd tried.

To this day, Prissy was the only one he'd ever told about the autopsy photos. And now Dr. Gilliard.

"Much of the fodder for our dreams comes from past or present experiences," the doctor calmly explained. "I believe that the nightmares you've been having are a symptom of posttraumatic stress disorder. They began when your parents died, then they stopped after a while."

"Yeah," Stan muttered, "but I never saw myself dying in *those* dreams."

"You weren't a firefighter back then. Now that you risk your life on a regular basis, it's only natural that you've become more conscious of your own mortality."

Stan was silent. He wished like hell that he could accept the doctor's reasoned explanation, but the nightmares were too intense—too ominous—to be dismissed.

"How are things at work?" Dr. Gilliard probed. "Have the dreams begun to affect your performance on the job?"

"You mean, have I found myself hesitating before rushing into a burning building? Or have I been making mental mistakes that could endanger the safety of my crew?" Stan shook his head grimly. "No, thank God."

"That's good." Pause. "What about your performance...in other areas?"

"Other areas?"

"Yes." Dr. Gilliard met Stan's inquisitive gaze. "People who suffer from traumatic nightmares experience a host of physiological symptoms. Since you haven't been sleeping well for months, it wouldn't be abnormal for you to experience, for example, a decreased sex drive."

"Is that right?" Stan couldn't stop a slow, wolfish grin from spreading across his face at the memory of the erotic interlude he and Prissy had shared in the Jacuzzi two nights ago.

Observing his satisfied grin, Dr. Gilliard noted wryly, "So I take it you've got no complaints in that department?"

"No, ma'am," he drawled. "No complaints whatsoever."

"I see." The doctor smiled brightly. "Well, that's good to hear."

"Indeed."

Just then Stan's watch beeped. As he silenced the alarm, Dr. Gilliard raised a brow at him.

"Sorry," he said sheepishly. "I promised Manning that I'd take him to a matinee this afternoon before his brothers get home from school, so I'll have to cut out fifteen minutes early today."

"Is this the same Manning who's supposed to be on punishment for getting suspended from school?"

"Yeah." Stan sat up and swung his booted feet to the floor. "I took his brothers to the movies on Tuesday, so I kinda owe the kid."

"Lucky him."

Ignoring the note of disapproval in Dr. Gilliard's voice, Stan asked, "Have you found a new receptionist yet?"

"Not yet. I've interviewed a few candidates and hope to make a decision soon. In the meantime, I'm afraid you're stuck scheduling appointments through me."

Stan nodded, not entirely comfortable with the arrangement. "That reminds me. When you paged me the other day—"

"I'm so sorry about that," Dr. Gilliard interrupted with an embarrassed grimace. "I actually thought I was paging someone else, but I must have dialed the wrong number. I apologize if I caused you any trouble."

Talk about an understatement, Stan mused grimly. Aloud he merely said, "No harm done."

"Great." Dr. Gilliard watched as he rose from the sofa and crossed to the coat rack to retrieve his battered leather jacket. "By the way, I really like that sweater you're wearing. That shade of green looks amazing on you."

"Thanks," Stan said, glancing down at himself. "Prissy bought this for me."

"Really?" Dr. Gilliard smiled. "So she has good taste in clothes *and* men."

Stan chuckled, watching as the doctor stood and came toward him. "Thanks for the talk," he told her.

"You don't have to thank me, Stan. I always enjoy our sessions. Besides," she added with a wink, "your insurance company compensates me just fine."

He laughed. "I'm sure they do. See you next month."

"Actually," Dr. Gilliard blurted as he opened the door to leave, "I'll see you at the fireman's ball on Saturday night."

He turned back to her. "You'll be there?"

"Of course." She smiled teasingly. "I consider it my professional duty to observe how my patients behave in social settings."

Stan grinned. "In that case, I'll try to be on my best behavior."

Dr. Gilliard laughed, casually laying a hand on his arm.

"All kidding aside," Stan said ruefully, "since Prissy doesn't know that I've been coming to you, I hope you'll understand that I can't introduce you to her."

"Of course I understand," Dr. Gilliard assured him. "Doctor–patient confidentiality is very important to me, Stan."

He flashed her a grateful smile, then turned and walked out, never suspecting that she hurried to the window to watch him saunter to his truck. Never suspecting that long after he'd driven out of sight, she stood there plotting ways to lure him away from his wife.

Chapter 15

Golden ribbons of sunlight washed over Stan's dark, powerful body as he rose above Prissy, midnight eyes boring into hers, face taut with passion as he thrust into her. His shaft was rock-hard and throbbing, driving inside her with deep, penetrating strokes that sent waves of white-hot ecstasy crashing through her.

"Oh, baby," she panted breathlessly. "Right there, honey...ohhh, yes...*yesss!*"

She ran her hands down his strong back and dug her fingernails into the flexing muscles of his round butt, making him shudder and groan. His firm, sweaty stomach slapped against hers as he picked up the tempo, banging the headboard against the wall with the ferocity of his thrusts.

Prissy *loved* it when he took her like this. Rough, raw, no finesse. No mercy. And with their kids out of the house that morning, she had no shame or inhibitions. So she moaned wantonly and shouted encouragements to her husband, reveling in the way her dirty talk fueled his lust and hunger.

"You feel so good, sweetheart," he groaned raggedly. "*So* fucking good."

"So do you," Prissy moaned, intoxicated by the animalistic sounds of lovemaking that echoed around the room, as heady as the carnal musk of their bodies that filled her senses.

As she watched, Stan lowered his mouth to her bouncing breasts, sucking her swollen nipples until she arched off the bed with a broken cry.

She tightened her slick thighs around his waist and frantically rocked her hips against him, matching his relentless rhythm until she erupted in an orgasm that tore a rapturous scream from her throat.

As her feminine muscles clenched fiercely around Stan's engorged shaft, he swore savagely and wrapped her legs around his upper torso, giving him a deeper angle of penetration as he plunged harder and faster. Moments later he came with a hot burst of semen that exploded inside Prissy's body.

He hung over her for several moments, chest heaving, muscled arms shaking as he supported his own weight.

Slowly easing her legs from around his chest—but keeping his thick shaft wedged inside her—Prissy curved her arms around his neck and brought his head down to hers for a deep, sensual kiss.

"I missed you," Stan confessed in a husky whisper.

"Mmmm," Prissy purred languorously. "I can tell."

He chuckled, sucking her bottom lip before trailing lazy kisses to her throat. "Did you miss me?"

"Hmm, let me think—"

When he bit the sensitive side of her neck, she threw back her head and laughed. "Just kidding! Just kidding!"

"Tell me you missed me," Stan commanded softly.

Prissy smiled. "I missed you, sweetheart. Do you even have to ask?"

He smiled into her eyes, tenderly brushing damp tendrils of hair off her face. "The boys and I took a vote, and we unanimously decided that you're not allowed to go out of town anymore."

"Is that so?" Prissy teased, nibbling his goateed chin. "Well, I think the school board might have something to say about that."

"Too damn bad," Stan growled.

Prissy laughed.

God knows she was in no hurry to leave on another business trip. She'd missed her family terribly, and her journey home had been long and stressful thanks to a violent thunderstorm that had delayed her flight three hours. By the time she'd arrived in Denver, she was beyond exhausted. But her fatigue had taken a backseat to the pure joy she'd felt when she saw her husband and sons waiting for her. They'd surrounded her, greeting her with rib-crushing bear hugs as other travelers looked on with envious smiles. As Manning grabbed her luggage and Stan clasped her hand, the others took turns vying for her attention, updating her on their weekend activities.

Prissy had been further delighted to return home to an immaculate house and a fragrant, home-cooked meal. After dinner, Stan had drawn her a hot bubble bath. When she fell asleep in the tub, he'd carried her to bed and spooned her for the rest of the night.

The next morning, the boys had served her breakfast in bed and kept her company until it was time for them to leave for school. When Stan returned from dropping off Manning, he'd wasted no time climbing back into bed with Prissy and having his wicked way with her.

What a homecoming, she mused now, cuddling closer to her husband's warm, damp body. Since she'd taken the day off to rest and it was Stan's last vacation day, they both wanted to make the most of their time together.

Which might not involve leaving the bed.

"So," Prissy drawled, lazily rubbing the sole of her foot along Stan's hard, muscular calf, "let's recap what I missed over the weekend. Mason led his team to victory by scoring three touchdowns, Maddox's loose tooth finally came out, Magnum beat you fair and square at poker, Monty finished his book report on your ancestor Bishop Wolf, and Manny was called on to bless the offering at church. Anything else I missed?"

"Nah," Stan murmured, gently nipping at her breast. "That pretty much covers it."

"Are you sure?"

He hesitated for a fraction of a second before lifting his dark head to meet her gaze. "I'm sure."

Prissy searched his face. Although his expression betrayed nothing, she couldn't shake the feeling that he was keeping something from her.

"Any particular reason you decided to tack on two more weeks to Manny's punishment? Especially when *you're* the one who told me to go easy on him?"

Stan shrugged a shoulder. "I thought it over some more, and I decided that being grounded for a month, instead of two weeks, would make more of a statement."

Prissy nodded slowly. "That's a good point."

Before she could comment further, Stan turned the tables on her. "So, did you see her before you left?"

Prissy didn't have to ask whom he was referring to. Since Thursday night she'd been hoping and praying that he wouldn't bring up Celeste, but she should have known better.

Several beats passed before she gave a small, defeated sigh. "Yes," she admitted. "I saw her."

Stan stared at her in surprise. "I thought you weren't going to."

"I wasn't. But she called my hotel room and threatened to make a scene at my workshop if I didn't agree to have dinner with her."

"Typical," Stan muttered with a snort of disgust.

Prissy said nothing.

"So what'd she have to say for herself?"

"Not much," Prissy lied, ignoring a sharp pang of guilt at the thought of Celeste's shocking confession. "We had dinner at a nice restaurant. The next afternoon, after the conference sessions had ended for the day, she took me shopping and sightseeing."

"Did you see that fucking bastard?" Stan growled.

"Grant?" Prissy shook her head. "I refused to see him *or* the condo where they're staying."

Stan scowled, muttering a savage oath under his breath.

Not for the first time, Prissy marveled at the personality differences between Stan and his brother. Where Sterling was calm, even-tempered and longsuffering, Stan could be brash, broodingly intense and downright ruthless when provoked. There was little doubt in Prissy's mind that Stan would have killed Grant Rutherford with his bare hands if he'd been in Sterling's shoes.

"When is she gonna tell Sterl that she's in Minnesota?" Stan demanded.

"When she's ready." As Stan opened his mouth to protest, Prissy pressed a finger to his lips, silencing him. "We agreed not to interfere. Remember?"

"I know, but—"

"No 'buts,' honey. We had an agreement."

Stan clenched his jaw tightly, his eyes glittering with anger and frustration. After several tense moments, he growled, "I'm giving her two weeks to tell Sterl that she's in Minnesota."

Prissy frowned. "But—"

"*Two weeks*, Pris. My brother and nephews are more important to me than that damn woman's need for secrecy."

Stan's harsh tone and feral expression brooked no argument.

After studying him for a few moments, Prissy relented with a deep sigh. "I'll call and let her know."

Stan nodded curtly.

Prissy reached up, using her thumb to smooth the furrow between his brows. "You keep scowling like that," she murmured, "and your face is going to freeze into a permanent scowl."

Stan stared at her, the edges of his mouth twitching in amused recognition of the warning she often gave the boys when they were sulking.

"Uh-oh," Prissy intoned, running her fingertip over his soft, full lips. "Is that a smile trying to wiggle free?"

He eyed her silently for a long moment. Then, without warning, he rolled away and pulled her on top of him.

Prissy laughed, blowing her disheveled hair out of her eyes. "Thanks," she teased. "You *were* getting kinda heavy."

Stan's answering smile was distracted as he settled back against the soft mound of pillows and regarded her from beneath his thick black lashes. Sensing a shift in his mood, Prissy waited for him to speak.

Several seconds passed.

"Would you tell me if you were unhappy being married to me?"

Caught off guard by the question, Prissy stared down at him. "Where'd *that* come from?"

He didn't answer.

And then she understood. "Ohhh, I see. This is about what happened between Sterling and Celeste, isn't it?"

Stan gazed at her. "We were eighteen years old when we got married, Pris. We were crazy in love, but we knew nothing about the real world—buying a house, paying bills, raising a family. We'd never been on our own before, and then eleven months after we got hitched, along came Manny. You spent practically the first ten years of our marriage with child, or nursing a child."

"And I don't regret a single moment of that," Prissy said earnestly. "I love each and every one of my precious babies. I *love* being the mother of your children, Stanton."

His eyes probed hers. "You were one of the smartest kids at school, the class valedictorian. You could have gone to any college you wanted and become anything you wanted."

Prissy smiled softly. "The last time I checked, having a family didn't prevent me from earning a Ph.D. And *you* helped make that possible by adjusting your schedule at work and taking care of the boys so that I could study and attend school." She gazed wonderingly at Stan. "I couldn't have accomplished *half* of what I've accomplished without you by my side."

As his expression softened, he caught her hand and brought it to his mouth, kissing her knuckles so tenderly that her throat constricted. "I love you," he said huskily.

"I love you too, sweetheart," Prissy whispered feelingly. "I could never regret marrying you. You're the only man I've ever loved, the only man I've ever wanted. So you don't *ever* have to worry about me walking out on you and our children. I'm not going anywhere."

Sitting up, Stan cradled her cheek in his hand and kissed her—a deep, soul-shaking kiss that melted her from the inside out.

As they slowly drew apart, Prissy searched his glittering dark eyes. "Now it's my turn to ask the question."

"What question?"

She paused. "Would *you* tell me if you were unhappy being married to me?"

"That's not even a possibility," he said quietly, unequivocally. "You're the best thing that ever happened to me, Priscilla. I don't know what I'd ever do without you in my life."

Her heart soared. When he gazed at her like that and spoke with such love and devotion, her fears and misgivings dissolved. How could they not?

Leaning back against the pillows, Stan let his hands roam up her thighs, kneading and caressing her as he murmured, "What do you wanna do today, wife?"

Prissy smiled almost shyly. "Whatever you want. Doesn't matter to me."

"I thought we could have lunch at the Black Kettle," he suggested, referencing the town's only Native American restaurant, which had been named after a Cheyenne tribal chief who'd sacrificed his life to broker peace between Colorado's white settlers and the Cheyenne people during the 1800s. The quaint, popular café was owned and operated by the family of one of Manning's school friends.

"Mmm." Prissy's mouth watered at the thought of feasting on Indian fry bread stuffed with spicy chicken, black beans, cheese, red onions and salsa. "I'd *love* to have lunch there, but I promised myself I'd be good this week. I need to be able to squeeze into my dress for Saturday's ball."

"You will." Gently grasping her hips, Stan eased her over his shaft so he could rub the blunt head against the tender folds of her sex.

Prissy shivered at the delicious sensation. "I will?"

"Umm-hmm. And I'll help you."

She licked her lips. "How?"

His eyes glinted wickedly. "By helping you burn off as many calories as possible."

"How you gonna do that?" she purred.

Sliding into her wetness, he proceeded to show her just how.

After several more rounds of steamy lovemaking—which culminated in the shower—Stan and Prissy got dressed and ventured out for an early lunch at the Black Kettle, where they were greeted ceremoniously by members of the Navarro family, who ran the restaurant.

Since it was a balmy autumn day, Stan and Prissy decided to dine on the terrace to enjoy the breathtaking mountain views. When their fragrant meals were served, they sat close together, eating from each other's plates and sipping from a large margarita glass for two.

After their plates had been discreetly cleared, they lingered to savor the beautiful, postcard-perfect scenery. Talking and laughing softly between stolen kisses, they made plans to go on a cruise next August to celebrate their sixteenth wedding anniversary. This, of course, led them to begin reminiscing about the special ways they'd commemorated the occasion over the years.

Even when money had been tight, they'd always made a big deal of their anniversary, leaving the kids with Sterling and Celeste or Prissy's mother so that they could spend a romantic night at a hotel or enjoy an intimate candlelight dinner at home. And whenever their anniversary fell during the first week of school, Stan always had roses delivered to Prissy at work, making her the envy of her fellow teachers.

After leaving the Black Kettle that afternoon, they headed to one of their favorite parks and strolled hand in hand along the scenic lake. Not since the night in the Jacuzzi had Prissy felt so relaxed and utterly satiated. The look of lazy contentment on Stan's face told her he felt the same way.

With two hours left until their sons got out of school, they decided to go bowling.

When they arrived, the bowling alley was nearly empty, so they pretty much had the place to themselves.

While Prissy was an average bowler, Stan was a master, throwing multiple strikes in a row with the skilled ease of a professional. Whenever their family had gone bowling with Sterling, Celeste, Michael and Marcus back in Atlanta, all the boys had vigorously lobbied to be on Stan's team, because any team anchored by Stan usually won.

Over the next hour, Prissy laughed, groaned protestingly and thumped her head on the table as her husband made quick work of her, sailing to victory after two embarrassingly lopsided games. When she taunted him and talked trash in a pathetic attempt to throw him off his game, he merely laughed and pointed to the scorecard.

When he began their third match by knocking down nine pins, Prissy decided it was time to employ another strategy.

While Stan was waiting for his ball to be queued up, she unfastened the top four buttons of her fitted sweater, revealing enough cleavage to tantalize and distract without getting herself arrested for indecent exposure.

When Stan looked at her, she undid her ponytail and shook her hair loose, then combed her fingers through the thick, relaxed strands. As Stan watched her, she leaned across the table and plucked a cherry Tootsie Pop from the bowl of leftover Halloween candy. She unwrapped the lollipop and began licking it slowly and provocatively.

Stan was riveted.

"Better go before you forfeit your turn, baby," she warned silkily.

He swallowed hard and nodded, then turned away. Prissy watched as he rolled the ball down the lane and narrowly—uncharacteristically—missed the spare pin.

When he turned and shot her an accusing look, she sighed dramatically. "Better luck next time."

Stan scowled.

Smothering a triumphant grin, Prissy got up and started toward him, hips swaying as she sucked the Tootsie Pop. Stan's dark eyes glittered with hunger as he stared at her mouth and the plump swell of her cleavage.

As they approached each other, she slid the lollipop out of her mouth and gave it one last flick of her tongue, then held it out to Stan. "Could you hold this for me?"

"With pleasure." As he eased the glistening lollipop between his lips, her nipples hardened. Ignoring her body's traitorous reaction, she gave him a sultry smile and swatted him on the backside as she strolled past.

After picking up her ball, she took her sweet time perfecting her stance at the line and targeting her desired arrow. Stealing a glance over her shoulder, she saw that Stan was staring fixedly at her ass.

Hiding a satisfied smile, Prissy turned back, leaned forward and wiggled her butt before releasing the ball. It traveled down the middle of the lane and struck eight pins with a satisfying *thwack!*

Prissy cheered and pumped her fist. Her luck was changing already.

Or so she thought.

The next time she rolled the ball, she came up empty.

"Damn," she grumbled.

As Stan sauntered past her, he leaned down and taunted softly, "Better luck next time."

Prissy sucked her teeth, glaring at him. "Can I have my lollipop back?"

"Nah," he drawled. "It's mine now."

She couldn't help but laugh.

As he prepared to take his turn, she sidled over to him in flagrant disregard of bowling etiquette. Just as he was about to release the ball, she leaned close and whispered in his ear, "That's okay. I'll find something better to suck on later."

He jerked and lost his aim, pitching the ball down the gutter.

Prissy threw back her head and laughed.

Stan scowled, snatching the lollipop out of his mouth and jabbing it at her. "That was real dirty."

She shrugged, grinning impenitently as she sashayed back to her chair. "It's not my fault you have lousy concentration."

"*Lousy concentration?*"

"Yup."

Chuckling and shaking his head, Stan picked up his ball and returned to his starting position on the lane. "I got your lousy concentration *right* here."

Of course he retaliated with—what else?—a strike.

Prissy glared at him as he made an exaggerated show of buffing his nails on his shirtfront as he swaggered over to her and sat down.

"You know," she said imperiously, "it's rather ungentlemanly of you to gloat while beating me with absolutely no regard for my feelings."

"Oh?" His eyes glinted with amused challenge. "And is it unladylike of *you* to gloat for days whenever you beat me at tennis?"

That shut her up.

"That's what I thought," Stan said with a laugh, polishing off the lollipop and discarding the stick. "Your turn, woman."

When Prissy's next roll resulted in a split, she groaned loudly with frustration. "Aw, man, I can *never* get those."

Stan tsk-tsked. "Not with that attitude," he chided, recording her score on the card.

Prissy eyed him plaintively. "Can you help me, baby?"

"What?" He laughed. "Hell, nah, I can't help you."

She pouted. "Why not?"

"Because you're my opponent. Why would I help you improve your score and cut into my lead, especially after you just tried to sabotage me?" He shook his head, a broad grin sweeping across his handsome face. "Sorry. No can do."

"Come on, Stanny," she wheedled, using her pet nickname for him. "Just show me how to pick up the spare."

Leaning back against his chair, Stan deliberately folded his arms across his broad chest, stretched out his long legs and crossed his booted feet at the ankles. "Nope."

Prissy batted her lashes and pouted her lips, doing her best impersonation of a temptress in distress. "Pretty please?" she cooed. "With lots of sugar and chocolate drizzled on top?"

Stan looked at her, lips quirking as he valiantly fought the tug of a grin.

"Please, baby? *Pleeeaaase*?"

Heaving an exaggerated sigh of exasperation, he stood and sauntered over to her.

Prissy smiled at him as he positioned himself behind her, the heat of his big body instantly penetrating hers.

"Okay, wife," he drawled, the deep, velvety timbre of his voice making her shiver. "You wanna hit the number three pin so your ball will deflect into the number ten pin. So you need to aim for the seventh arrow to your right."

Prissy nodded, heat sizzling through her veins as he adjusted her feet on the floor and gently guided her arm through the swinging motion.

"Like that," he murmured. "See?"

"Mmm." Some naughty impulse made her lean back, pressing her backside into his groin. His breath quickened and his hand tightened on her hip, pulling her closer. Her clit pulsed and tingled at the feel of his hard, heavy shaft nestled between her butt cheeks.

A wicked smile curved her mouth. "How do I get my ball to hook like yours does?"

"It's all in the wrist and follow through." Stan's voice was rough with arousal as he nuzzled the sensitive skin behind her ear, sending delicious shivers through her. "If you don't hold and release the ball properly, you won't get enough spin on it."

"Hmm." Prissy turned, holding out her nine-pounder to him. "Show me."

"I can't, babe. My fingers won't fit inside your holes."

They looked at each other, then burst out laughing like a couple of dirty-minded adolescents.

When their mirth subsided, Stan pointedly cleared his throat before continuing, "Anyway, you only wanna hook the ball on your first throw. To pick up the spare, it's best to throw a straight ball 'cause if you spin it too much you won't hit the pins." He guided Prissy through the swinging motion again, then stepped back with obvious reluctance. "Now try it."

She took a deep breath, then moved into position, aimed for the seventh arrow and released the ball. She and Stan watched as it rolled down the lane and knocked over the spare pins.

"*YES!*" Squealing triumphantly, Prissy jumped up and down, then turned and leaped into Stan's arms. He laughed, lifting her off the floor as she threw her legs around his waist and smooched him on the lips.

When Stan sank his hands into her hair and deepened the kiss, Prissy purred softly. Their tongues met, doing a sensual tango inside each other's mouths until they were interrupted by a series of wolf whistles.

They broke apart and glanced around, encountering the amused stares of a group of senior citizens watching them from several lanes away. One of the old men winked at Stan and growled, "Go get 'em, tiger."

Prissy blushed as Stan laughed. Kissing the tip of her nose, he murmured, "Let's go home."

She smiled shyly. "Good idea."

After returning their rented shoes and paying for their games, they raced back to the truck, hopped inside, and began kissing and necking like a pair of horny teenagers.

As the windows fogged up, Stan grabbed Prissy and dragged her across the console and onto his lap. The steely ridge of his erection against her belly jolted her back to sanity.

Stan groaned protestingly as she broke their fevered kiss and scuttled back to her seat, giggling breathlessly as she glanced around the near-empty parking lot.

"We're gonna mess around and get ourselves arrested," she panted.

Stan grinned wolfishly. "I can't think of a better reason to go to jail, can you?"

She laughed. "The kids will be let out of school soon, so we'd better get going."

"Good idea," Stan agreed, twisting the key in the ignition. "If we hurry back, we'll have time for a quickie before they get home."

Again Prissy laughed, shivering with arousal.

As they rode home holding hands and exchanging heated looks, she almost convinced herself that nothing could ever come between them.

Chapter 16

After school that day, Manning and his friends were walking out to their buses when he saw Taylor standing alone beneath a large sycamore tree that graced the front lawn of the building.

"I'll catch up with you fellas tomorrow," Manning told his comrades, who'd been laughing uproariously at some joke about a detested science teacher.

"How long will you be grounded?" Yuma Navarro asked Manning.

He made a pained face. "A month."

"A *month*?"

"At least."

His friends' sympathetic groans followed him as he wove through the noisy crowd of students heading toward the buses along the curb. As he neared Taylor, he saw that she wore headphones and was listening to a Walkman tucked into the front pocket of her camouflage jacket.

When Manning reached her, he tapped her lightly on the shoulder.

She jumped, glancing sharply around. When she saw Manning standing there, her face lit up with one of those smiles that sucker-punched him right in the gut.

Removing her headphones, she said shyly, "Hey, Manning."

He smiled. "Hey, yourself. I didn't mean to scare you."

"That's okay."

He pointed to her Walkman. "What're you listening to?"

She blushed. "You're gonna laugh if I tell you."

"No, I won't. Try me."

She hesitated, tugging her bottom lip between her teeth. "I was listening to Ella Fitzgerald."

"Hey, that's cool, Tay. My brother likes her, too. You should hear him play 'Lullaby of Birdland.' "

"Ooh, that's one of my favorite Ella Fitzgerald songs!" Taylor enthused.

"Monty's, too. My mom says he inherited her father's love for jazz, which is why Grandpa named Ma's brother after his favorite jazz musician, Thelonious Monk."

"Your uncle is named after Thelonious Monk?"

"Yeah. My grandfather heard him play at some jazz club in New York during the forties. Grandpa was so blown away by his music that he insisted on naming his firstborn after him."

Taylor grinned broadly. "How cool is *that*?"

Manning chuckled. "My uncle didn't always think so," he drawled, glancing back toward the idling school buses. He was relieved to see that his own bus was running late, because he wasn't ready to part company with Taylor yet. For reasons he couldn't begin to explain, he'd found himself thinking more about her—and their kiss—than the hot, sweaty sex he'd had with Caitlyn.

That morning in precalculus, he'd sat behind Taylor and playfully tugged on her ponytail when Mr. Langenkamp's back was turned. Giggling softly, she'd tucked her hair into her hooded sweatshirt, only to have him pluck it free again. They'd kept at this little game until one of their classmates—a snooty senior—rolled her eyes and muttered in disgust, "Stupid freshmen."

It was all Manning and Taylor could do to keep from bursting into laughter.

"Why aren't you getting on your bus?" he asked her now.

Taylor beamed. "I'm waiting for my dad to pick me up. He got back from his business trip yesterday, so he's taking me and my brother ice skating."

"That sounds like fun." Manning smiled at her. "Are you a good skater?"

"Sure." She grinned wryly. "I'm no Dorothy Hamill, but I can make it around the rink without falling on my butt. Hey, why don't you come with us?"

"Ice skating?" Manning said dubiously.

"Yeah. I told my dad all about you and how you stood up for me, and now he wants to meet you."

Manning was undeniably flattered. "I'd love to meet your pops, but I can't go skating with you today."

"Why not?"

He gave her a pointed look. "I'm grounded, remember?"

"Oh, God, that's right. How could I forget?" Taylor bit her lip, her eyes filled with fresh guilt. "I'm really sorry for—"

Her apology was interrupted by the sound of her name being called.

Manning and Taylor glanced around to see her friend Janelle—*former* friend—standing several yards away with the two cheerleaders she'd been with last week when she snubbed Taylor in the hallway. Today Janelle was all sunshine and smiles as she waved at Taylor.

"You're still coming to my sleepover on Friday, aren't you?" she called out cheerfully.

"Um, sure," Taylor called back halfheartedly.

"Awesome!" Janelle smiled harder at Taylor, silently communicating a message that finally prompted Taylor to mutter under her breath, "Oh, yeah, I almost forgot."

As Manning watched, she dug into the back pocket of her jeans and pulled out a pink slip of paper, which she reluctantly handed to him.

He gave her a puzzled look. "What's this?"

Her eyes lowered to the ground. "It's Janelle's phone number. She asked me to give it to you."

Manning arched a brow at her, then glanced over at Janelle. She smiled flirtatiously at him and fluttered her fingers in a wave.

"She wants you to call her," Taylor mumbled.

"Yeah?" Holding Janelle's gaze, Manning brought the piece of paper to his nose. It smelled sweet, like bubble gum lip gloss or something just as girly.

As Janelle stared expectantly at him, Manning smiled. As her smile widened in response, he slowly and deliberately balled up the paper in his hand.

Taylor gasped. "*Manning!*"

He laughed, watching as Janelle's face reddened with humiliation while her friends burst into hysterical giggles.

As Manning dropped the wad of paper in Taylor's slack palm, she darted a mortified glance at Janelle, then hissed, "Why'd you do that? You totally embarrassed her, and now she's gonna uninvite me to her sleepover!"

Manning grinned unabashedly. "Aw, you didn't wanna go anyway."

"That's not the point," Taylor protested, even as her lips twitched with suppressed laughter. "She's gonna think I told you something bad about her."

"Who cares?"

"Manning," Taylor said in exasperation.

Again he laughed. "Okay, okay. If she says something to you, just tell her she's not my type."

"Oh, really?" Taylor gave him a teasing look. "And what *is* your type, Manning?"

He smiled, tucking a stray strand of hair behind her ear. "Well, now that you mention it—"

"Yoo-hoo! Manning!"

Inwardly groaning at yet another interruption, Manning followed the direction of the voice to the designated pickup area of the parking lot. Caitlyn was waving at him from her flashy red Camaro. With the top down, the sun on her face and a gentle breeze blowing through her long hair, she could have been shooting a scene for a movie.

Manning acknowledged her with a smile and a nod, then returned his attention to Taylor.

She raised a brow at him. "Friend of yours?"

He scratched his ear. "Um, well—"

He was interrupted by the sudden blast of a horn. When he looked back at Caitlyn's car, she smiled and crooked her finger at him. "Come here."

He felt a quick surge of annoyance. Glancing around, he saw that several other students had turned to stare at him and Caitlyn, their eyes filled with curiosity and speculation.

"Manning." Caitlyn's tone had grown impatient. "Come here."

Before he could respond, Taylor interjected grimly, "You should probably go talk to her."

Manning looked at Taylor, wondering why he felt the sudden need to apologize. "I'll be right back."

"Sure." Taylor stepped away from him and slipped on her headphones.

Feeling dismissed—and not liking it one damn bit—Manning turned and stalked over to Caitlyn's car. By the time he reached her, *she* had the nerve to look pissed.

As he crouched down beside her door, she demanded, "Were you trying to ignore me?"

Manning scowled. "No. But aren't *you* the one who told me you didn't want anyone at school to know that you went all the way with a freshman?"

She sniffed. "I changed my mind. All my friends think you're totally hot, so it doesn't matter how young you are." She looked him up and down, her hazel eyes gleaming with possessive satisfaction. "Get in."

"Nah, I'm taking the bus home."

"No, you're not. I'm giving you a ride home."

Manning's temper flared. "Yo, I'm not your little bitch, alright? Stop telling me what to do."

Caitlyn's eyes widened with wounded disbelief. "What's wrong with you? Do you seriously expect me to believe that you'd rather take the cheese bus home than catch a ride with *me*?"

Manning clenched his jaw. It *did* sound crazy.

When he didn't respond, Caitlyn looked over his shoulder, her lip curling scornfully. "Like, oh my God. Please don't tell me you're ditching me for that...that *thing*."

"Don't."

Caitlyn hesitated at the low, deadly warning in his voice. "Don't what?"

"Don't call her that. Her name's Taylor."

Caitlyn eyed him incredulously. "You think I give a shit what her name is? Look at her, Manning. She's, like, a total disaster! Look at her clothes, and those *heinous* shoes. Where the hell does she shop? At a thrift store for circus freaks?" She cast another disparaging glance at Taylor, then let out a shriek of laughter.

Manning had heard enough.

As he moved to get up, Caitlyn grabbed his arm. "Wait, Manning, don't go."

"Yo, I ain't got time for this petty bullshit," he snarled.

"I'm sorry," Caitlyn said contritely. "I didn't mean to make fun of your little friend. I know you stood up for her because you felt sorry for her, and that was really admirable of you. But, sweetie, no one's expecting you to become her best friend now. You've already done more than enough for her. You've made her the envy of practically every girl at school because you chivalrously protected her, and now all the other little nerds look up to her, too." Caitlyn smirked. "She might even get herself a dweeby boyfriend out of the deal."

Manning glared at her for a moment. "I have to go. My bus is here."

Caitlyn glanced across the parking lot, watching as the buses began to depart. "No, it's not. Ms. Shirley probably has another 'flat tire.' " She made air quotes around the last two words, alluding to the rumor that the bus driver was a closet drunk who was sometimes late because she was hung over. But Manning's mother had already looked into the rumor and proved that it wasn't true. After personally meeting with Ms. Shirley—who took care of her elderly father—Mom had urged Manning to speak up for the bus driver whenever possible so that her good name and reputation wouldn't be ruined by malicious lies.

Not that kids like Caitlyn were interested in the truth.

Caitlyn sighed, gently stroking Manning's cheek. "I'm so glad I don't have to ride the cheese bus anymore. And *you* don't have to, either, if you play your cards right."

His eyes narrowed. "What's that supposed to mean?"

"It means that I can give you a ride every day if you want." She smiled wickedly. "And not just in my car, either."

Manning swallowed, feeling his body react to her provocative words. Even though she'd pissed him off, his hormones couldn't ignore how sexy she looked in her tight pink sweater and micro-miniskirt. No dude in his right mind would turn down what she was offering.

Sensing his weakening resolve, Caitlyn leaned out the car and whispered seductively in his ear, "Let me take you home, baby. My parents are at work, so we can have the house all to ourselves. We can do it anywhere you like, and we can get as loud and freaky as we want."

Manning shuddered, closing his eyes as his father's warning echoed through his mind. *The girl may be beautiful, but she's trouble with a capital T....*

"I can't," Manning mumbled as Caitlyn nibbled his earlobe. "I'm supposed to go straight home."

"Just call and tell your parents that you have to stay after school to make up work or something, and let them know that

I'll give you a ride home because I have to stay, too." She took Manning's hand and slowly guided it between her parted legs. When his fingertips encountered the warm silk of her panties, he jerked free of her grasp and stood up.

"I have to go."

Caitlyn heaved a sigh, shaking her head in exasperation. "If you'd rather go home and jerk off to relieve that"— His face heated as she pointed to the telltale bulge in his crotch —"it's *your* loss."

"Believe me," Manning muttered darkly, "I know."

As he started backing away, Caitlyn called out, "By the way, I tried to sneak up to your room the other night."

Manning stopped, staring at her. "You did?"

She nodded, smirking. "I didn't get very far though. When I stepped into the backyard, I could hear your mom and dad getting busy in the Jacuzzi."

"You were *spying* on my parents?"

"Not really. I couldn't see them, but judging by the sounds your mom was making, your dad was *definitely* handling his business." Caitlyn grinned, her eyes glinting wickedly as she looked Manning up and down. "Guess the apple doesn't fall far from the tree."

He frowned, shaking his head at her. "You're crazy, you know that? Stay out of my backyard."

She winked and blew him a kiss.

As she drove off, Manning saw Taylor approaching a blue Pontiac Bonneville that had just pulled up at the end of the row of cars.

"Taylor," he called, starting toward her.

She glanced up.

Their eyes met and held.

Without a word, Taylor ducked inside the car and slammed the door.

As the Pontiac rolled past, she stared straight ahead.

Manning stood there watching the departing vehicle until his bus arrived.

Then, walking over on leaden legs, he climbed aboard the noisy bus, flopped into an empty seat near the back and stared out the window, glumly wondering when his life had gotten so damn complicated.

Chapter 17

"Tell the truth, Lieutenant Wolf. You've never seen a more spotless bowl in your life, have you?"

"Hmm," Stan murmured, inspecting the sparkling white toilet bowl that Jake Easton had just finished scrubbing. "I must admit, rookie. It's pretty damn spotless. Smells good in here, too."

Jake grinned, his broad chest puffed out with pride. He'd been up since four-thirty a.m. doing his morning housework detail.

As he and Stan left the immaculate bathroom, Jake—eager to please—rattled off the list of other chores he'd completed. "I put up the flag, opened the gates, made a pot of coffee, emptied the dishwasher, cleaned my equipment—"

Stan half listened as they headed past the sleeping quarters, where the other firefighters on duty were beginning to stir in their cots.

Stan's muscles were sore and his eyes were gritty from the restless night he'd had. His unit had been out on a late emergency call last night, rescuing four people who'd been trapped inside their vehicles following a head-on collision. Racing against the clock, the fire crew had used axes and the Jaws of Life to pry back the roofs of both vehicles in order to extricate the injured occupants.

By the time the firefighters cleared the crash scene and returned to the station, they'd all been exhausted. But Stan was too wired to sleep. He'd tossed and turned for hours before lapsing into a fitful dream state haunted by dark, disturbing images he couldn't decipher. He'd awakened abruptly but quietly, no scream tearing from his throat to disturb the others, thank God.

"I've already been on the floor to inventory the apparatus," Jake was saying. "And as soon as Cooper arrives for his shift, we'll practice throwing ladders and timing how fast we can put on our SCBA gear."

"Good." Stan nodded approvingly, pleased that Jake understood the importance of performing the daily drills. The kid was a good firefighter—bright, conscientious, respectful, and a team player. He took pride in his work, whether he was washing the station rig or loading hose after a job. Because he rarely complained about doing the least desirable chores—like cleaning the toilets—the senior firefighters liked him enough to spare him the worst of their pranks, which was saying a lot for the wise guys of Engine Company 8.

Stan, who'd taken Jake under his wing from day one, knew that the kid had a promising career ahead of him.

As they neared the kitchen, Jake announced, "By the way, I asked Lara Dominguez to be my date for the ball tomorrow night, and she said yes."

"Hey, that's great, rookie." Stan paused, frowning. "Wait a minute. Who's Lara Dominguez?"

Jake laughed. "Your kid's first grade teacher."

"Oh. Right." Stan grinned ruefully. "Sorry. I only know her as Miss Dominguez."

"That's funny," Jake said, following him into the kitchen, "because when I was talking to her after the presentation last week, she kept referring to you by your first name."

"Really?" Stan crossed to the cupboard and removed a misshapen ceramic mug that Maddox had made for him in Boy Scouts. It was black with crooked white lettering that read WORLD'S AWESOMEST DAD.

"I didn't realize she and I were on a first-name basis," Stan mused, pouring hot black coffee into the mug. "I've only met her twice since the school year started."

"Well, you obviously made quite an impression on her," Jake teased, nimbly straddling a chair at the oversize table. "After you and Mason left that day, she couldn't stop raving about you and your 'wonderful, educational' presentation. No mention of how *I* totally rocked as Sparky the Fire Dog."

Stan grinned, sipping his coffee. "Well, she agreed to go out with you, so you obviously did something right."

"That's true." Jake flashed a cocksure grin. "You know the ladies can't resist a smokin' hot firefighter."

Stan snorted. "Yeah, okay."

After a moment, Jake's grin wavered with uncertainty. "Wait a minute. What if she only agreed to go to the ball so she can see *you*? I mean, what if she secretly has the hots for you, lieutenant, and she spends the whole evening asking questions about you?"

Stan frowned, raising his mug to his mouth. "You're talking crazy, kid. Miss Dominguez doesn't have the hots for me."

"Maybe you're right." Jake's blue eyes glinted with sudden mischief. "But if she corners you and propositions you, could you at least find out if she'd be interested in a threesome?"

Stan choked, spewing out a mouthful of coffee.

Jake burst out laughing. "Sorry, boss! I couldn't resist."

Stan scowled, grabbing a paper towel and dabbing dark splotches of coffee from his CFD T-shirt. "That shit wasn't funny, rookie."

"Sorry." Jake wiped tears of mirth from the corners of his eyes. "I think I've been hanging around the fellas too long."

"Probably. But say some shit like that to me again, kid, and your ass will be permanently sporting the Sparky costume. Ya dig?"

Jake sobered at once. "Yes, sir. I'm sorry. I was way out of line. I know you're a happily married man and you would never cheat on your wife."

"Damn right I wouldn't." Stan swept an impatient glance around the kitchen. "Now where the hell is the newspaper?"

"I'll get it for you." Jake shot up from his chair and beat a hasty retreat.

Moments later, some of the other firefighters began filing into the kitchen, and breakfast was soon under way.

As the senior officer on the shift, Stan sat at the head of the large table as the men scarfed down their food while laughing and exchanging rowdy banter. Their language was profane, and more than a few of their jokes were vulgar.

At one point someone demanded with mock indignation, "You kiss your mother with that mouth?"

"No, I kiss *yours*," came the retort, which set off another round of raucous laughter that included Stan's.

There was nothing like the camaraderie between a group of men who lived together on a twenty-four-hour shift. The ritual of trading insults was as innate to them as sharing meals, swapping stories, sliding down poles and racing off to put out fires.

When the alarm sounded halfway through breakfast, no one took another sip of coffee or forked up another bite of eggs. No one bemoaned the unfairness of having to respond to another emergency right before their shift was supposed to end.

The men sprang into action, rushing out to the large garage where the fire engine and rescue and ladder trucks were parked. With practiced speed and efficiency, they donned their turnout gear, snapped suspenders into place, shoved feet into boots and grabbed their heavy coats and helmets.

When the nature of the emergency was announced—a house fire on South Yosemite Street—Stan's heart rate kicked into overdrive.

A small, ominous voice whispered, *Is today the day?*

He allowed himself a moment—no more than a few seconds—to kiss the miniature photo of his wife and children that he'd begun wearing in a locket around his neck. And then he stuffed the chain back inside his gear, hopped into the rig beside the driver and shouted above the wailing siren, "Let's haul ass!"

Several hours later, he was in his own truck and headed home. He was weary to the bone but grateful, as always, to be alive.

His unit had arrived at the scene to discover thick black smoke and flames shooting from the roof of a large two-story house situated on a quiet, tree-lined street. The fire had started when lightning from an early-morning thunderstorm struck the home, igniting a fiery blaze that had taken over two hours to extinguish. When all was said and done, the roof and the upper level of the house were destroyed. But thankfully the homeowners, along with their beloved Golden Retriever, had gotten out safely as soon as the fire began.

By the time Stan returned to the station and completed his incident report, then called the hospital for an update on the status of last night's accident victims, it was late afternoon.

After checking in with Prissy, he left the station and swung by the high school to pick up Manning, who'd surprised Stan and Prissy when he announced that he would be staying after school three days a week to help with math tutoring.

On the way home, father and son caught each other up on the other's day. Once Manning heard about the fire, he was full of questions, reminding Stan of those halcyon days back in Atlanta when he'd taken his sons to work, delighting them with tours of the firehouse and rides on the rescue truck. With the engine roaring, lights flashing and siren blaring, the boys had been in seventh heaven.

As they neared their neighborhood, Stan asked conversationally, "So how's Taylor doing?"

A shadow crossed Manning's face before he turned to stare out the window. "She's okay," he mumbled.

Puzzled by the sudden change in Manning's demeanor, Stan prodded, "She's tutoring math too, right?"

"Uh-huh."

Stan studied the boy's brooding profile. "Everything all right?"

Heavy pause. "Yeah."

"Doesn't sound like it."

After another pause, Manning blew out a harsh breath and blurted, "She has a boyfriend."

"Really?" Stan was surprised. "When did that happen?"

"This week," Manning grumbled, his thick brows furrowed with displeasure. "He's in the band. They have two classes together."

"Is that so? Well, good for Taylor…right?"

Manning's scowl deepened. "She doesn't even like him."

Stan gave his son a sidelong glance. "How do you know?"

"I just do."

Stan hid a knowing smile, amused at the realization that Manning was jealous of Taylor's new relationship. Maybe Prissy had been on to something after all.

Moments later they entered their development and headed up a hilly road flanked by live oaks, perfectly manicured lawns and custom homes with curved driveways.

As Stan turned onto their street, he saw Caitlyn washing her Camaro in front of her house. Although it was barely sixty degrees outside, she wore a wet tank top and a pair of skimpy denim cutoffs that rode up her butt as she bent forward, slowly running the soapy sponge over the hood of her car.

As if sensing the approach of Stan's truck, she tossed her long hair back and glanced over her shoulder, giving father and son a sultry smile.

"Whoa," Manning breathed, craning his neck to stare after her as they passed her house. "*Dammmmnnn.*"

Scowling, Stan reached over and slapped the back of his son's head.

Manning jerked around, grinning sheepishly as he hunched down in his seat. "Sorry, Dad, but Caitlyn's—"

"Too damn fast," Stan groused, shaking his head in angry disbelief. "If she were *my* daughter, there's no way in *hell* I'd let her outside looking like that."

Manning's grin widened. "Then I guess it's a good thing you only have sons, huh?"

When Stan shot him a dark look, the boy laughed.

Reaching their house at the end of the cul de sac, Stan swung into the driveway beside the family van.

As he cut the ignition, Manning sighed heavily. "Dad?"

"Yeah?"

"Is it wrong to be attracted to more than one girl at the same time?"

Stan chuckled. "Of course not. Hell, you can be attracted to every female you pass on the street. But—" He broke off to watch as Prissy opened the front door and waved at them, then folded her arms against the brisk temperature as she waited for them to come inside.

"But?" Manning prompted.

Stan smiled softly. "But, ultimately, only one will steal your heart."

Chapter 18

Coronado's annual fireman's ball was held at the historic Oxford Hotel in downtown Denver. Proceeds from the gala went toward funding scholarships at local high schools, sponsoring Little League teams and purchasing new equipment for the area firehouses.

That Saturday evening, the hotel's grand ballroom had been transformed into a winter wonderland. The floor was covered with white carpeting, a canopy of paper snowflakes and twinkling lights hung from the ceiling, and silver tree branches festooned with icicles and glass votive candles served as table centerpieces. As the elegantly dressed guests milled about, the live band serenaded them with Kool and the Gang's "Celebration."

Standing at the entrance to the ballroom, Prissy beamed with satisfaction as she surveyed the festive scene. As a member of the planning committee—which was composed mostly of other firefighters' wives—she'd helped choose the theme for this year's ball. Yesterday evening after work, she and the other women had carpooled to the hotel to decorate the ballroom, laughing and chatting companionably as they worked late into the night. Prissy was beyond pleased with the fruits of their labor.

"Everything looks absolutely beautiful, doesn't it, Stan?"

"Definitely. You and the ladies did a wonderful job." But Stan's admiring gaze was on *her* instead of the dazzling scenery. Leaning close to her, he murmured in her ear, "I can't wait to get you home and out of that dress."

Prissy blushed as a shiver of pleasure raced down her spine. She smiled demurely, giving him a look beneath her darkly mascaraed lashes. "We just got here, and you're already talking about going home?"

"Hell, yeah," he growled softly. "You would be too if you were seeing what I'm seeing."

Prissy's flesh heated as his dark, glittering gaze took another slow tour of her body. He'd been devouring her like that ever since she'd emerged from their bedroom in her evening gown—a white mermaid ensemble with a fitted bodice that accentuated her voluptuous curves before the skirt flared dramatically at the knees. To complete the glamorous look, she'd asked her stylist to arrange her hair into an elegant upsweep that showcased the sleek column of her throat and drew attention to the diamond choker she wore, which Stan had given to her for their fifteenth anniversary in August.

As she'd surveyed her reflection in the mirror, inspecting herself from every angle, she'd felt a deep sense of pride and satisfaction. After months of dieting and getting up at the crack of dawn to exercise, her hard work and discipline had paid off. She looked good, but more important, she *felt* good.

And that was *before* she'd ventured out to the living room, where Stan and the boys had been reclining in front of the television. At Prissy's appearance, Stan had gotten slowly to his feet, staring at her with an awestruck expression that reminded her of the way he'd looked at her on prom night and on their wedding day. As she'd turned in a circle to model her gown, the boys had whistled boisterously and showered her with compliments while Stan merely continued to stare. It was only when their sons began laughing and teasing him that he'd snapped out of his trance long enough to declare Prissy the most breathtakingly beautiful woman he'd ever seen.

She hadn't stopped blushing since.

Of course, *she* wasn't the only one who cleaned up nicely.

Stan was devastatingly handsome in his navy blue dress uniform, which was adorned with his rank insignia and the service medals he'd earned over the course of his career. As he stood beside Prissy—tall, dark and dashingly powerful—she had to fight the overwhelming urge to drag him somewhere private so she could peel off his uniform, layer by layer, like she was unwrapping a decadent chocolate bar.

"You keep looking at me like that," Stan warned huskily, "and we'll be seeing no parts of this ball."

Prissy smiled as her belly quivered. "Later," she promised.

"You'd better believe it." Stan winked at her, then tucked her arm through his and led her through the arched doorway.

The grand ballroom was filled with fire department employees and representatives, city officials, local businessmen, civic and union leaders, and people from all walks of the community who'd come out to have a good time while supporting worthy causes.

As Stan and Prissy began moving through the crowd, they were intercepted by their friends, Kelvin and Roxanne Wimbush.

As Stan and Kelvin exchanged brotherly handshakes, their wives hugged like they hadn't just seen each other last night at the decorating party. As they drew apart, Roxanne swept an admiring glance over Prissy and Stan and exclaimed, "You two look like the belle and beau of the ball!"

Prissy laughed, cheeks flushing. "Oh, girl, hush."

"I'm serious," Roxanne insisted. "You both look stunning. And, girl, you are wearing the *hell* out of that gown. Isn't she, Kel?"

"She certainly is," her husband agreed, dark eyes glinting with frank male appreciation as he looked Prissy over.

Stan bumped him hard on the shoulder. "Watch it now."

Kelvin, Roxanne and Prissy laughed.

The Wimbushes were the first couple Stan and Prissy had befriended when they moved to Coronado. They'd met them at the fire department's Labor Day picnic, and had hit it off right away. Stan and Kelvin worked at the same fire station but on different shifts. The couple's daughter was in Magnum's fifth grade class while their son played on Mason's football team. The two families often got together for dinner, cookouts and fun outings at amusement parks.

Kelvin was an attractive brown-skinned man with the sturdy, athletic build of a pro running back while Roxanne was plump and petite, with skin the color of caramel, a dimpled smile and a vivacious personality that always kept things lively.

For the ball that evening, all the firefighters' wives had decided to wear white to complement their husbands' navy blues. So Roxanne was elegantly attired in a flowing white gown that she'd accentuated with a spray of miniature white roses in her coiffed hair.

"You look beautiful," Prissy told her.

Roxanne beamed. "Why, thank you, hon. I feel like a fairy princess in an enchanted wonderland." Her brown eyes twinkled. "Ever since we got here, people have been coming up to me to rave about how spectacular the place looks, saying that this is the classiest fireman's ball we've ever had. So I've been telling the other ladies that we ought to pat ourselves on the back."

"We'll do it for you," Kelvin humorously offered.

Roxanne and Prissy laughed as their husbands obligingly patted their backs.

When the playful moment passed, Kelvin said, "We were on our way to the cash bar to get some drinks. You two want anything?"

"Not at the moment," Stan and Prissy declined.

"Okay. See you at the table." Kelvin and Roxanne smiled before moving off.

As Stan and Prissy headed across the ballroom, they were frequently stopped and drawn into conversation with his colleagues and their spouses. In the two short years Stan had been with the CFD, he'd earned the respect of his peers and proved himself to be a worthy member of this brotherhood of firefighters.

As he and Prissy mixed and mingled, Prissy couldn't help noticing the way women reacted to Stan, smiling flirtatiously at him and playfully cajoling Prissy to allow him to pose for the firefighter's beefcake calendar. Even when Stan and Prissy moved on, the women's admiring stares tracked him around the room. Prissy couldn't really fault any of them. Without an ounce of shame or conceit, she could honestly say that her husband was the most scrumptious man at the ball. And that was saying *a lot*, considering the plethora of other good-looking firefighters in attendance tonight.

Shortly after eight, the emcee for the evening approached the podium and cheerfully asked everyone to be seated so the festivities could begin. After a few opening remarks by Fire Chief Ellis Buckner, dinner was under way.

Prissy and the other members of the planning committee had wanted to strike a happy medium between "macho man" fare and gourmet cuisine. So they'd chosen a menu of beef tenderloin, braised chicken marsala, scalloped potatoes, lemon herb pasta and sautéed vegetables.

Over the next hour, Stan and Prissy laughed and conversed with everyone at their table, which included Kelvin and

Roxanne, Captain Sullivan and his wife Judith, two other firefighters and their spouses, as well as Mr. and Mrs. Campbell, an older black couple who'd lost their home to a fire earlier that year.

When Stan had enlisted the support of his colleagues to hold a fundraiser to help the displaced couple, the Campbells were overwhelmed with gratitude. They'd lovingly adopted him into their family, and the bond that developed between Stan and Mr. Campbell poignantly illustrated the void that Stan's father's death had left in his life. When the couple's home was rebuilt that fall, they'd invited Stan and Prissy to be the guests of honor at their housewarming dinner. It was only fitting that they be Stan's special guests at tonight's ball.

Prissy was pleased that everyone seemed to be having a wonderful time. The food was delicious, the live music was enjoyable and the jovial emcee kept the crowd entertained with good-humored jokes about firefighters and paramedics.

But shortly after dessert was served, Prissy felt an uncomfortable prickling sensation, as if she were being watched.

When she glanced around, her gaze collided with a pair of sultry dark eyes that belonged to a strikingly beautiful woman seated at the next table. The woman was staring at Prissy, her eyes gleaming with such animosity that Prissy was taken aback.

As she frowned, the woman suddenly blinked and plastered on a smile, as if she were sliding a mask back into place. When Prissy didn't return her smile, the woman averted her gaze to her attractive male companion.

Prissy watched her, eyes narrowed speculatively.

After several moments, she turned to Stan, who'd been laughing and bantering with Mr. Campbell beside him. When Stan paused to take a sip of his drink, Prissy leaned over and murmured to him, "Honey?"

"Yeah, babe?"

"Do we know that woman sitting at the next table?"

"What woman?"

"The light-skinned one in the sequined red gown. The Jayne Kennedy lookalike."

Something inscrutable flashed across Stan's face, disappearing so swiftly Prissy could have imagined it. As she watched, he slowly set down his glass and glanced toward the table she'd indicated.

After a few moments, he answered casually, "I think that's Dr. Gilliard."

"Who's Dr. Gilliard?"

Stan hesitated for a fraction of a second. "She's the department psychologist. I've seen her around headquarters once or twice, but I don't know her personally." Again he paused, meeting Prissy's gaze. "Why do you ask?"

"She was glaring at me just now."

"*Glaring?*"

Prissy nodded. "Like I stole something of hers."

Flicking another glance at the woman, Stan gave a low chuckle. "I'm sure she wasn't glaring at you, babe."

Prissy bristled at his mildly patronizing tone. "You think I don't know when someone's giving me the evil eye?"

Instead of answering, Stan helped himself to a forkful of her tiramisu, then winked at her before resuming his conversation with Mr. Campbell.

Prissy frowned as a strange unease settled over her.

Seated to her left, Roxanne was saying, "I'll be so glad when my kids are old enough to stay home by themselves so I don't have to go through the hassle of finding a reliable babysitter."

"Me, too," one of the other wives commiserated. "You won't believe some of the disastrous experiences we've had with sitters."

"Oh, I can imagine. We've got a couple horror stories of our own." Roxanne sent Prissy an envious look. "You're so lucky that Manning is old enough to watch his younger brothers."

Prissy smiled. "When he turned fourteen, we figured he was ready to handle the responsibility. But that doesn't mean I wasn't tempted to accept when our neighbor's teenage daughter offered to babysit for me tonight."

Overhearing her comment, Stan turned to stare at Prissy. "Which daughter?"

She met his alert gaze. "Caitlyn, from down the street. While you were out this afternoon, Caitlyn came by and offered to watch the boys tonight. She said she's trying to earn some extra money for the holidays, so she figured she'd offer her babysitting services to parents in the neighborhood."

"That was nice of her," Roxanne said.

Prissy nodded. "She seems like a nice girl, even though I'm not too crazy about the way she dresses," she added wryly. "But her mother tells me that she's an honor roll student, and she wants to become an attorney like her father and has already been accepted into Yale."

"Impressive," one of the other women remarked. "Sounds like an ideal babysitter to *me*."

Prissy smiled. "I know. But I told her that we're trying to show Manning that we trust him, so—" She broke off as Stan suddenly wiped his mouth with his napkin, dropped it onto the table and stood. She eyed him curiously. "Where are you going?"

"To call and check up on the kids."

"Oh, I can—"

"No, stay and finish your dessert." He gave her shoulder a gentle squeeze. "I'll be right back."

The women watched him leave, then sighed and looked pointedly at their husbands. Exchanging guilty glances with one another, the men mumbled dutifully, "Guess we'd better make some phone calls, too."

"Could you, please?" their wives chorused sweetly.

As the men excused themselves from the table—leaving only Mr. Campbell behind—the women dissolved into laughter.

After dinner, the raffle and silent auction winners were announced, followed by brief speeches from the mayor, the fire chief and other department brass. And then it was time to present the outstanding service awards to the individuals who'd gone above and beyond over the past year.

Awards were given in the categories of Rookie of the Year, Paramedic of the Year, Unit of the Year, and Distinguished Service to retiring members of the department.

Fire Chief Buckner took to the podium to present the final award of the evening. "Last but certainly not least," he announced in his booming, authoritative voice, "the recipient of the Firefighter of the Year award was chosen by his peers for his exemplary leadership, his commitment to mentoring other firefighters, his compassionate outreach to the community, and for serving bravely and honorably in the finest tradition of the

Coronado Fire Department. Without further ado, it gives me great pleasure to present the Firefighter of the Year award to Lieutenant Stanton Wolf."

As the ballroom erupted into thunderous applause, Stan looked stunned.

Bursting with pride and elation, Prissy cupped his face between her hands and smooched him on the lips. "You won, baby!" she cried excitedly. "You won!"

He grinned broadly at her as Kelvin and Roxanne clapped him on the back while Mr. and Mrs. Campbell beamed like proud parents and urged, "Go on up there and get your award, Stanton."

As he stood and strode to the podium, the rowdy members of Engine Company 8 drummed their fists on their tables and chanted, "Wolf...Wolf...Wolf...Wolf!"

After shaking hands with the mayor, the fire chief and other dignitaries standing on the stage, Stan accepted his shiny plaque and stepped to the podium amid a flurry of flashing camera bulbs. He appeared slightly dazed as he looked out into the audience.

"Wow," he began, his deep baritone pouring through the microphone.

An outbreak of lusty feminine whistles sent laughter sweeping over the crowd. But Prissy was too busy gazing at her husband to mind.

When the noise died down, Stan chuckled softly and continued, "As many of you know I'm from Atlanta, where we're often celebrated for our Southern hospitality. But since moving here and joining the Coronado Fire Department, I've learned that the gift of hospitality isn't just a Southern thing. Thank you for graciously welcoming me and my family into your community, and for allowing me to be a part of this extraordinary family of firefighters."

The crowd applauded with warm appreciation as he paused to contemplate the plaque in his hand before holding it up. "There's no greater honor than being recognized by your peers, so I'd like to thank each and every one of you for bestowing this tremendous honor upon me. You know, anyone who's ever been assigned to double company firehouses can tell you all about the friendly rivalry between engine and truck guys. We like to play pranks on one another and joke about who really has the most important job. *Engine,*" he coughed into his hand, drawing a hearty round of laughter, guffaws and whistles of agreement.

Stan smiled quietly. "But at the end of the day, we all respect and appreciate the job everyone does, and we all know and understand that it takes teamwork to ensure successful rescue operations. No man is an island unto himself, so I humbly accept this award on behalf of all the dedicated men and women who strap on their boots every day and put their lives on the line. And I proudly share this recognition with my comrades at Engine Company 8—"

He paused, grinning crookedly as the men—and Dora—saluted him with a rowdy chorus of howls that drew more laughter.

As the audience settled down again, Stan continued soberly, "Firefighters are often hailed as heroes, but throughout my career, I've met so many people whose courage in the face of extreme adversity *personifies* heroism. People like the Campbells, who lost their home but not their ability to see the silver lining in the storm they'd weathered. I'm moved and inspired by them. And I'm eternally grateful to my beautiful wife, Priscilla, who's always been there for me, who's given me fifteen of the best years of my life, and who blessed me with five of the most amazing children any man could ever ask for." His achingly tender gaze held Prissy's. "Thank you for making our home a refuge from life's storms. I love you, baby."

I love you, too, Prissy mouthed back, her heart overflowing with pride and adulation as she gazed at him.

"I consider it an honor and a privilege to serve the good people of this community," Stan concluded, once again addressing the room at large. "God willing—" He paused, his voice hitching with emotion. After another moment he continued huskily, "God willing, serving you is a privilege I will enjoy for many more years to come. Thank you all, and God bless."

The crowd began cheering and clapping as Stan moved away from the podium. Suddenly he reconsidered and stepped back to the microphone. "One more thing," he added. "For those of you who live in the Coronado School District, please come out on

Tuesday to vote yes on the bond proposal. Our schoolchildren need your support." He winked. "Thank you kindly."

The audience laughed, then collectively surged to their feet and saluted him with a rousing standing ovation as he strode back to his table, where Prissy awaited him with tears shimmering in her eyes.

He handed his plaque to Mr. Campbell, then captured Prissy's face between his hands and lowered his mouth to hers as a roar of cheers and applause erupted from the crowd.

Half an hour later, they were still stealing tender kisses as they swayed together on the dance floor beneath a twinkling canopy of lights and paper snowflakes. Lost in their own private world, they were completely oblivious to the other couples slow dancing around them to the Gap Band's "Yearning for Your Love."

"I'm so proud of you," Prissy murmured, her arms wreathed around Stan's neck as his big hands encircled her waist, holding her closer than close.

He smiled lazily. "You know I couldn't leave that stage without putting in a plug for the bond election."

Prissy smiled. "That was wonderful of you, and very much appreciated. But you know that's not what I was talking about. I'm so proud of you for winning the award tonight, and for everything you've accomplished in your career. But most of all, sweetheart, I'm proud of the absolutely amazing man you are. I must be the luckiest woman in the world to have you in my life."

His expression softened. "*I'm* definitely the lucky one, Pris," he said huskily. "And I meant every word I said in my speech."

"I know," she whispered. "Why do you think I consider myself so damn lucky?"

Stan gazed wonderingly at her. "I love you so much."

"I love you too, darling. With all my heart."

They shared another deep, stirring kiss.

As they slowly drew apart, Prissy sighed with blissful contentment. "Every time we dance together at a formal affair, I'm reminded of our prom night."

"Me, too."

They gazed into each other's eyes, awash with memories of that magical night when their lives had forever changed. The details were embedded in Prissy's memory as vividly as if their prom had been held yesterday. After she and Stan were crowned prom king and queen, they'd taken to the floor to dance to Percy Sledge's "When a Man Loves a Woman." When the romantic ballad ended, Stan had shocked Prissy—as well as their friends, classmates and teachers—by suddenly dropping to one knee and proposing.

Stunned, she'd gasped and clapped a trembling hand over her mouth. As Stan gazed earnestly at her and literally professed his undying love, tears had flooded her eyes.

Without thinking she'd blurted, "*Yes, I'll marry you!*"

Because even at the age of eighteen, she'd known that she wanted to spend the rest of her life with Stanton Wolf.

As husband and wife smiled nostalgically at the memory, Stan lowered his head to hers, and their lips met and clung. They simply couldn't get enough of each other.

"Get a room, you two," Kelvin and Roxanne teased as they waltzed by.

Stan and Prissy laughed.

"You know," Stan drawled, eyes glinting, "that's not a bad idea. We *are* at a hotel."

"What about the kids?"

"They can fend for themselves for one night."

Prissy laughed, shaking her head at him. "I don't think so."

"Come on, baby," he cajoled silkily, his powerful thighs rubbing hers as he turned her slowly in a circle. "Just think about it. We can check into a room, take a hot shower together and make love until sunrise."

"Mmmm." Prissy arched her head back and closed her eyes as he ran his warm lips along her throat, nuzzling the sweet spot he'd made his own years ago. "That *does* sound tempting—"

"See?"

"—but I don't think I'm ready to leave the kids alone overnight. And judging by how eager you were to check up on them earlier, I don't think *you're* ready, either."

Stan groaned softly, then sighed. "No," he conceded. "I'm not."

Prissy grinned at him. When it came to their family, Stan was as overprotective as she was. And she loved that about him.

"Look on the bright side," she purred, nibbling his lower lip. "Thanks to you being such a kickass firefighter, we have a wonderful, relaxing week at a ski lodge to look forward to."

"Mmm," Stan rumbled with pleasure. "That's true."

As the winner of the Firefighter of the Year award, he would have his name added to the permanent plaque on display at the main fire hall and would receive a check for $1,000, a paid week off and a complimentary stay at an upscale ski resort nestled in the Rocky Mountains. He and Prissy had already decided to take the kids, along with her older brother and his family, her mother and Mama Wolf, who would be visiting for Thanksgiving.

"Maybe we should just go by ourselves," Stan murmured, gently rubbing his nose against Prissy's. "It'd be more romantic if we were alone."

"True," she smilingly agreed, "but we've been promising to take the kids skiing ever since we moved here, so they'd be awfully disappointed if we went without them. And the cabin sleeps fifteen, so we'd feel guilty if it were just the two of us there."

"Speak for yourself."

Prissy chuckled, kissing the strong bridge of his nose. "Don't worry, baby. I'll make sure we get some privacy during that weekend, even if we have to lock everyone out of the cabin for a few hours so we can feast on each other."

A wicked gleam filled Stan's eyes. "Is that a promise?"

"Absolutely."

"In that case," he drawled, "let the countdown to the feast begin."

Chapter 19

Erin Gilliard was seething with fury.

If she were any hotter under the collar, she'd burst into flames and would need help from the roomful of firefighters. But there was only one firefighter she'd want to be rescued by, and *he* hadn't spared her so much as a passing glance all night.

How can Stan completely ignore me like this? she wondered with mounting frustration. How could he just pretend that she didn't exist when he'd spent the past three months confessing some of his deepest, darkest secrets to her? Telling her things he hadn't even told his own wife?

After everything he and Erin had shared, didn't she at least deserve some gesture of acknowledgment? A private smile? A wink?

Something?

Apparently not.

For the past hour, she'd sat at her table simmering with jealousy as she watched Stan and Prissy dance together, their bodies flowing from one song to another. Even when the music changed to something faster and they began grooving rhythmically together, Stan couldn't resist curving an arm around Prissy's waist and pulling her closer, so that by the end of the song they were right back in each other's arms, kissing like they were the only two people in the damn world.

Erin silently fumed as she stared at the couple. Prissy's head was resting on Stan's shoulder and her eyes were closed in an expression of dreamy euphoria that drove daggers of envy through Erin's heart.

Stan looked like every woman's fantasy in his navy blue dress uniform. When he'd first entered the ballroom that evening, Erin knew she wasn't the only female who'd nearly swooned at the sight of him.

She grudgingly acknowledged that Prissy—what the hell kind of nickname was that anyway?—looked lovely in her slinky white mermaid gown, though it was obvious that she battled with her weight. She couldn't hold a candle to Erin, whose breathtaking beauty turned heads everywhere she went. From the moment she'd arrived at the ball tonight, men had been ogling her and flirting shamelessly with her.

But once again, she remained invisible to the only man whose attention she craved.

It isn't fair, Erin raged.

She should have been seated at that table with the other firefighters' wives—laughing, gossiping, commiserating about wayward children and whatever else mothers commiserated about when they got together.

She should have been wearing white like the others, instead of being dressed like the outsider who hadn't gotten the memo.

She should have been the lucky recipient of Stan's adoring gaze and that powerfully moving tribute that had sent a wave of sentimental sighs sweeping over the ballroom. *She* was the only one who truly understood why he'd gotten choked up at the end of his speech.

So it should have been *her* in his arms right now, looking like the most sublimely contented woman on earth.

Instead she sat practically alone at her table, feeling as miserable and unwanted as a scorned lover. To add insult to unspeakable injury, she'd been abandoned by her date, a handsome surgeon who'd been paged by the hospital where he worked. He'd apologized profusely before dashing off, leaving Erin to make small talk with an over-perfumed woman who was three sheets to the wind.

She'd jumped at the chance to escape her inebriated companion when an attractive businessman came over and asked her to dance. But when he boldly propositioned her for sex halfway through the song, she'd told him off and marched back to her table, where she was forced to sit and watch as Stan and Prissy—along with a group of their friends—laughingly boogied to the Commodores' "Brick House." The dance between Stan and Prissy was playful yet sexually charged, with Stan singing the chorus to Prissy and rocking his hips against her shapely backside while she grinned over her shoulder at him.

It was more than Erin could bear.

She'd worked hard to get where she was, and she'd always prided herself on being a consummate professional. So she knew it was downright unethical to become involved with a patient. She could lose her practice. Her license. Her reputation.

She could lose everything.

And none of that mattered.

Because ever since she met Stanton Wolf, she'd been forced to reevaluate the things she'd once held so dear—her medical degree, her thriving career, her luxury condo.

She'd give it all up in a heartbeat if she could have Stan.

She wanted him to leave his wife and marry *her*. She wanted to make passionate, back-clawing love to him every night. She wanted to bear his children, maybe give him the daughter that Prissy never had.

She wanted him like no other man she'd ever wanted before.

So she had to do something.

Since Stan refused to tell his wife about her, she had no choice but to force his hand.

Making a split-second decision, she got up and strode purposefully across the room to Deputy Fire Chief Hugh Van Dorn, a recently divorced man who had a weakness for Jim Beam whiskey and pretty women. He was seated at a table with one of the firefighters' union bosses. The two men were laughing companionably and swigging beers as they watched the partygoers on the dance floor.

Erin sidled up to the table and greeted the pair, whose eyes widened with appreciation as they roved over her sequined body. She smiled coquettishly and batted her long lashes, then— injecting enough saccharine into her voice to give herself a mouthful of cavities—she asked Van Dorn to dance.

He was on his feet before she could complete the invitation, his pale face flushing with delight at being the object of a beautiful woman's attention.

He led her out to the dance floor and folded her into his beefy arms as some syrupy tune by Barry Manilow began playing. Erin forced herself to smile and laugh on cue at Van Dorn's flirtatious platitudes as he twirled her around the dance floor. Though he wasn't a bad dancer, he was nowhere near as smooth and confident as Stan.

Erin waited two songs before she made her move.

"You and your colleagues must be so proud of Lieutenant Wolf," she warmly remarked.

"Of course," Van Dorn agreed, smiling affably. "Wolf is a good man, a real asset to the department. Everyone speaks very highly of him."

Erin smiled. "Have you had an opportunity to dance with his lovely wife yet?"

"Can't say I've had the pleasure."

"Really?" Erin tsk-tsked, shaking her head at him. "You firefighters may know plenty about saving lives, but you're woefully clueless when it comes to observing social customs."

The deputy chief's blue eyes twinkled with mirth. "Is that so?"

"Yes. Stan Wolf is the man of the hour. As one of his superiors, it's proper etiquette for you to ask his wife to dance."

"Oh?" Van Dorn grinned. "I didn't realize that."

Erin gave him a lofty smile. "Aren't you glad I enlightened you?"

He laughed. "Certainly."

As Air Supply's "All Out of Love" began playing, they made their way over to Stan and Prissy, who were once again swaying gently together. When Van Dorn tapped Stan on the shoulder, he opened his eyes and lifted his head from the top of Prissy's. He looked surprised to see the deputy chief and Erin standing there.

"How's it going, sir?"

"It's going well, lieutenant. Mind if I cut in?" Van Dorn inquired.

Stan hesitated for a moment, dividing a wary glance between his superior and Erin.

Van Dorn chuckled good-naturedly. "Come on, Wolf. You've been monopolizing your beautiful wife all night. Let someone else have a turn." He smiled charmingly at Prissy. "That is, if Mrs. Wolf doesn't mind?"

Prissy looked at Erin, then smiled graciously at Van Dorn. "I don't mind at all."

A muscle clenched in Stan's jaw as he reluctantly relinquished his wife to the deputy chief, then took Erin into his arms. The moment her breasts made contact with the hard, muscular wall of his chest, her nipples tightened and her heart began racing like that of a schoolgirl who'd gotten to dance with her secret crush.

Giddy with nerves and excitement, she slid her arms around Stan's neck and stared up at him. He was so tall, no less than six foot five, and his shoulders were so massive she felt as if she were standing at the bottom of a mountain. A mountain she wanted desperately to climb.

She smiled at him. "Congratulations on being named Firefighter of the Year. It's a well-deserved honor."

"Thanks," he murmured. But he was staring over her head at Prissy and Van Dorn, who were smiling and chatting companionably as they danced several feet away.

"I really enjoyed your speech." *Except the part where you paid homage to your wife.* "I could tell you were speaking from your heart."

"Hmm," came Stan's noncommittal reply. His jaw was tight, and beneath his crisp uniform, his muscles were rigid with tension. He held Erin loosely, leaving more daylight between them than she would have preferred.

But it didn't matter. After the long, torturous months she'd spent fantasizing about him, just *being* this close to him had her pulse hammering, her body humming and her loins throbbing with need. She wanted more than anything to press herself against him and rub her pelvis against his groin to see if he was as aroused as she was.

But she dared not.

As an uncomfortable silence stretched between them, she saw one of Stan's company comrades—Jake Easton, if memory served—drift by with his beautiful young date. When Stan and Prissy had been dancing together, Jake had grinned slyly and given the couple a thumbs up every time he'd waltzed past them. Now he eyed Stan and Erin with barely concealed curiosity.

Ignoring the young firefighter, Erin refocused her attention on her brooding dance partner.

Stan didn't wear cologne on the days he was on duty. So when he came to her office, she could only detect a hint of soap or a freshly laundered shirt underlaid by warm male skin. But tonight he wore something subtle and woodsy. Potently masculine.

As her mouth watered, she smiled up at him. "You dance remarkably well."

He spared her a brief glance. "Thanks."

Swallowing a sharp pang of disappointment that he hadn't returned the compliment, she lowered her gaze to his full, sexy lips framed by a manicured goatee. She was so tempted to lay her head on his shoulder and close her eyes with dreamy ecstasy, as Prissy had done. But she knew she couldn't do that. People were watching them, so she had to keep up appearances. And the rigid tension in Stan's body warned her that he wouldn't welcome such a blatant gesture of intimacy.

So she contented herself with simply being in his arms, which was more than enough for now. Of course, she'd be even happier if she could get him to stop staring at his damn wife and focus on *her*.

Trying to capture his attention, she remarked conversationally, "Everything looks really—"

Suddenly those obsidian eyes snapped to hers, impaling her with the piercing directness of a high-powered laser. "Why did you do this?" he demanded.

Caught off guard by the question—and the harsh accusation blazing in his eyes—she stumbled over her feet.

Stan smoothly righted her without missing a step.

"W-What do you mean?" she stammered weakly. "Do what?"

"I told you I couldn't introduce you to my wife."

"I know," Erin mumbled.

"So you should have kept your damn distance."

She blinked rapidly, dismayed to feel tears welling in her eyes. As he looked away again she ducked her head, fighting shame and a crushing humiliation that was like nothing she'd ever experienced before.

The moment the song was over, Stan released her and stepped back.

As they regarded each other, he smiled smoothly and sketched a gallant bow, no doubt for the benefit of anyone watching them. But only *she* saw the steely glint in his eyes, the unyielding set of his jaw.

"Enjoy the rest of your evening," he said, deceptively mild.

She summoned a shaky smile. "Same to you."

He inclined his head, then turned and sauntered away from her without a backward glance.

She watched as he retrieved his wife from Van Dorn's clutches, possessively cupping her elbow and leading her away.

Suddenly Prissy looked over her shoulder at Erin.

Their eyes met and held.

A range of emotions flickered across Prissy's face—suspicion, anger, fear, uncertainty—before she glanced away and kept walking.

And for the first time that evening, Erin felt a glimmer of hope.

Because even though Stan had coldly rebuffed her, she'd accomplished her mission.

She'd forced his hand.

Chapter 20

Even if Stan and Prissy had wanted to stay and party into the wee hours of the night—which he didn't—fate had other plans.

Shortly after they returned to their empty table, his pager went off. When he checked the display screen and saw their home number, he felt a jolt of alarm, because he'd instructed Manning to page him in case of an emergency.

Prissy stared alertly at him. "What is it? Is it the kids?"

He nodded, rising quickly from his chair as Prissy jumped to her feet, her eyes filled with instinctive panic. Stan took her hand, and together they hurried from the ballroom to use the courtesy phone in the hotel lobby.

Although Stan was used to responding to emergencies, it was different when the emergency was your own. So he didn't argue when Prissy insisted on being the one to call home and speak to Manning.

He stood beside her, hands jammed into his pockets as he anxiously waited to find out what was going on.

"Manny, this is Mom. Is everything okay?"

Stan stared at Prissy as she listened to their son's response.

After several moments, he watched some of the tension ebb from her body as she exhaled a shaky breath.

"Okay," she told Manning. "Give him some ginger ale to help calm his stomach, and make him lie down. We're on our way home, okay, baby?"

As soon as she hung up the phone, Stan asked with concern, "Who's sick?"

"Maddox. Manny says he threw up twice and he's running a fever."

Stan nodded grimly, remembering that Maddox had seemed quieter than usual before he and Prissy left home that evening. "Come on, babe, let's go."

They returned to the ballroom long enough to say good night to their friends and stop by the coat check before they departed.

A tense, heavy silence hung between them on the ride home.

Prissy stared out the window, her hands folded tightly in her lap. Stan told himself that she was just worried about Maddox, but he knew there was more to her silence.

And he knew that sooner, rather than later, he'd have to answer the hard questions he'd been avoiding for months.

He could thank Dr. Gilliard for that.

Damn her, he thought darkly.

What the hell had she been thinking tonight? Why had she come anywhere near him after he'd specifically told her that he didn't want to introduce her to his wife?

Stan frowned, stealing another glance at Prissy. Her stony profile yielded no clue to her inner thoughts.

He wished like hell that he hadn't lied to her about not knowing Dr. Gilliard, but he'd been completely blindsided when, out of the blue, she'd turned to him and asked him about the doctor. Before dinner he'd caught a glimpse of Dr. Gilliard seated at the next table, and he'd been slightly unnerved by her proximity. But he'd figured that she wouldn't do anything to blow his cover, so he'd forgotten all about her until Prissy pointed her out to him.

He'd automatically dismissed Prissy's assertion that Dr. Gilliard was glaring at her because he couldn't fathom why on earth his therapist would glare at his wife. He didn't want to speculate on the possible reasons, nor did he want to examine Dr. Gilliard's motives for not keeping her distance tonight.

He was afraid of what he might uncover if he went digging beneath the surface.

And at the moment, he had far more pressing matters to worry about.

Three hours later, Stan stood in the doorway of the blue-and-white-striped bedroom shared by Maddox and Mason.

Prissy and Maddox had fallen asleep on the boy's narrow, wood-framed bed. Maddox's head was tucked beneath her chin, his wiry body curled against hers as they slept peacefully. Prissy still wore her white ball gown because Maddox had been throwing up when she and Stan arrived home, so her only concern had been tending to their sick child.

While Stan kept the others preoccupied, Prissy gave Maddox some children's Tylenol and bathed him in lukewarm water to help bring down his high fever. After dressing him in his pajamas, she'd asked Stan to bring Maddox a popsicle. When he arrived, Prissy had tucked their son into bed and was reading *The Lion, The Witch and The Wardrobe* to him.

Stan sat at the bedside and listened, as enchanted by the sound of Prissy's soft, animated voice as Maddox. By the time the boy finished his popsicle, he was struggling to keep his heavy eyelids open. Long after he drifted off to sleep, Stan and Prissy sat and watched him, his deep, even breaths the only sound between them.

After a while, Stan had gotten up to take Maddox's soiled clothes downstairs to the washing machine. After sending the others to bed—Manning had graciously offered to sleep in the basement so that Mason could have his bed in case Maddox was contagious—Stan had returned to the boys' room to find Prissy fast asleep.

As he stood in the doorway gazing at mother and child, a fierce wave of protective tenderness washed over him. His family meant the world to him. He couldn't bear the thought of being removed from their lives. It was unimaginable.

Swallowing a hard knot of emotion, he walked over to the bed and leaned down to press a tender kiss to his son's warm forehead.

Feel better, champ, he silently mouthed.

Then, moving carefully so as to not waken the boy, Stan lifted Prissy into his arms, switched off the bedside lamp and strode from the room.

As he carried Prissy down the staircase, her eyes slowly opened and focused on his face above hers. His heart thudded as he met her gaze.

She didn't speak, and neither did he.

Reaching their bedroom, he closed the door and carried Prissy over to the bed. He set her down gently, then knelt before her. He knew she was exhausted. She'd stayed late at the office nearly every night this week gearing up for the bond election, and then she'd been out past midnight helping to decorate the hotel ballroom. In all likelihood, she'd spend the rest of the weekend nursing Maddox back to health while Stan was at work.

Holding her gaze, he reached under her silk gown and began peeling off one thigh-high stocking. Prissy closed her eyes as if she were in pain.

As he slowly rolled the sheer nylon down her smooth leg, she stopped him.

"I can take it from here," she murmured.

Stan hesitated, then nodded and reluctantly moved back.

She finished removing the stockings, then slid off the bed and started across the room.

Stan sat on the floor with his back to the bed and watched as she went through the motions of undressing by unzipping her gown from the back and dragging it down her body. After draping the dress over a chaise lounge, she reached up and painstakingly unpinned her hair, letting the thick black tresses tumble about her face and shoulders. When she stood in her strapless lace bra and panties, Stan's groin heated, and he lamented that their evening would not end with passionate lovemaking, as he'd hoped.

He stared at Prissy as she unhooked her bra, then crossed to the cherry dresser and opened the top drawer. Instead of reaching for one of his CFD T-shirts that she'd long ago confiscated, she chose a long cotton nightshirt.

Stan hung his head, suffering the subtle sting of her rejection.

When she'd finished changing, she reached up to remove her diamond choker. But her fingers were trembling, and she fumbled with the clasp until Stan got up and walked over to help her.

He didn't release the catch right away, stealing a few moments to inhale the sweet fragrance of her hair and her warm, silky skin.

When he lingered too long, she reached back impatiently. "I'll do it."

"No," he murmured. "I got it."

Slowly he slid the necklace off, letting his knuckles skim the nape of her neck. She shivered at his touch, then reluctantly turned to accept the choker from his hand.

They stared at each other.

"Baby—" he began.

She abruptly stepped past him, crossing the room to return the necklace to her jewelry chest.

Pushing out a deep breath, Stan unbuttoned his shirt cuffs and tugged the shirttail out of his waistband as Prissy padded into the bathroom to brush her teeth and wrap her hair in a satin scarf.

When she emerged a few minutes later, Stan was perched on the edge of the bed with his hands clasped between his legs, debating how to tell her that he'd come to believe he was going to die in a fire, and so strong was this premonition that he'd recently taken out a second life insurance policy to doubly ensure that she and their children would never want for anything long after he was gone.

Prissy walked over to the bed and sat down to perform her nightly ritual of moisturizing her feet with cocoa butter. Before she could open the jar of cream, Stan picked it up and set it down on her nightstand.

As she stared at him, he sank to his haunches in front of her, bringing himself to eye level with her.

"Pris." His voice was low, husky with suppressed emotion. "I need to talk to you."

She raised a weary hand. "Please," she murmured. "Not tonight."

He swallowed tightly. "It's important."

She shook her head. "I'm tired, Stanton. And you must be, too."

"That doesn't mat—"

"We had a wonderful time at the ball. You won a well-deserved award. So let's just savor that for tonight, okay? Besides, you have to be up early for work, and I need to get some rest so I can take care of Maddox tomorrow."

Her words sent a sharp jab of guilt through Stan. He knew how exhausted she was, so the last thing he wanted to do was burden her. But he couldn't allow the chasm between them to grow any wider than it already had.

So he had to get through to her. "Pris—"

She made a strangled sound of frustration. "Damn it, Stanton! I can't deal with anything else right now! The bond election is only a few days away, and I still have a lot of work and campaigning to do. When I come home from the polling station on Tuesday night, we can talk then. Whatever you have to say, I'll listen. But I can't—" Her voice broke, catching in her throat.

Fighting back tears, she eyed him almost piteously. "I can't deal with anything else until after Tuesday. All right, baby? *Please?*"

Stan held her gaze for several moments, then relented with a nod. "All right."

"Thank you," she whispered.

As she rose from the bed and sidestepped him, he slowly rubbed his hands over his face and exhaled a ragged breath.

"I'm going to sleep in the boys' room in case Maddox wakes up in the middle of the night and needs me," Prissy announced quietly.

Stan stood and turned to face her.

She'd paused at the door with her hand on the knob, head bent as she stared blindly at the floor. She looked like she wanted to say more.

Stan waited tensely.

After a prolonged silence, she whispered, "Good night."

His heart twisted painfully. "Good night, sweetheart."

Without another word, she opened the door and walked out.

Chapter 21

"How's my grandbaby doing?" Dinah Kirkland asked her daughter late Tuesday afternoon. "Is he feeling better?"

"Yes," Prissy answered, cradling the phone between her ear and shoulder as she quickly scrawled her signature across the bottom of the form her secretary had brought to her. She handed the signed document back to Gayle, who pointed at her watch.

Prissy held up a hand and mouthed, *Five more minutes.*

Gayle nodded and strode briskly from the office.

"Prissy?" Dinah prompted. "Are you there?"

"Sorry, Mama. Today's the bond election, so things have been really hectic around here, and I need to head back to the polling station soon." She exhaled a deep, weary breath. "Yes, Maddox is feeling much better. He stayed home from school yesterday with Stan, who took him to the pediatrician. Apparently there's been some sort of stomach virus going around. But Maddox's fever is gone and he's not experiencing any more nausea or diarrhea, so I think we're out of the woods."

"Oh, that's good. You know how I worry about my babies."

"I know, Mama."

Prissy knew what was coming next, so she could only shake her head to herself when her mother sighed and lamented, "If you hadn't moved all the way across the country, I could have helped you take care of Maddox while he was sick."

"I know, Mama," Prissy murmured.

"Doesn't make any sense for you to be out there with no family," Dinah fussed. "And it's not right that your brother and I only get to see the boys a few times a year. It's not fair to *them*, either."

Prissy sighed, striving for patience. "Mama, this really isn't a good—"

"I know, I know. Believe it or not, I didn't call to lecture you. I wanted to see how you're doing, and I also wanted to tell you how happy I was to hear about Stan receiving the Firefighter of the Year award. How wonderful!"

"Yes," Prissy murmured. "It *is* wonderful. I'm very proud of him."

"I can't believe neither of you told me! I only found out when I called the house yesterday to check up on Maddox, and all he could talk about was the award his daddy had just won. Stan hadn't mentioned a *word* when we were on the phone."

"You know how modest he's always been," Prissy reminded her.

"I know." There was a smile in Dinah's voice. "Remember how proud we all were five years ago when he and his unit received the Medal of Valor for rescuing those families from that burning high-rise? I thought you and Mama Wolf would *never* stop weeping at the ceremony."

A quiet, reminiscent smile curved Prissy's mouth. "I remember."

"Of course you do. It was one of the proudest moments of your life." Dinah's voice softened. "Aren't you glad you didn't succeed in talking him out of becoming a firefighter?"

Prissy's smile faded. "I never tried to do that."

"Oh, but you wanted to," her mother countered mildly. "I'll never forget the day you showed up at Theo's house and told us that Stan wanted to become a firefighter. You were practically in tears, even though he'd already told you in high school that he wanted to fight fires for a living. When he landed that good-paying construction job after graduation, you just assumed that he'd forgotten about joining the fire department. But you knew, deep down inside, that he was meant to be a firefighter. And that scared you to death."

Prissy said nothing. She couldn't deny the truth of her mother's words.

Dinah continued, "You tried to convince me and Theo that you were only concerned because Stan wouldn't make as much money as a firefighter as he would doing construction, and that was a problem because you both wanted a big family. But your brother and I knew what was really bothering you. You were terrified that something would happen to him."

Prissy swallowed with difficulty. She remembered the fear that had gripped her every time Stan left home for work, leaving her to wonder whether she'd seen him for the last time. She remembered the many nights she'd spent tossing and turning in bed, or pacing up and down the floors until dawn. She remembered the panic attacks she'd suffered every time she'd turned on the television and heard about a fire raging somewhere nearby. And she remembered the overwhelming relief that had flooded her when he would finally walk through the front door—slightly battered and exhausted, but safe and sound.

Since Saturday night, she'd found herself reliving those dark days when she'd been tormented by fears of losing Stan. It had taken years for her to conquer her demons and make peace with his dangerous occupation.

Now, after all this time, it shook her to realize that she might lose him after all.

Not to a deadly inferno, but to a woman.

Prissy leaned back in her chair and closed her eyes, haunted by the image of Stan holding that beautiful woman in his arms at the ball. To the casual observer, he may have appeared bored or detached as he and Dr. Gilliard danced together. But Prissy had detected what others had likely missed.

Stan had been angry. Seethingly angry.

And the way he'd kept staring at Prissy had reminded her of a man who was desperate to keep his two worlds—one inhabited by his wife, the other by his mistress—from colliding.

Even as she'd told herself not to jump to conclusions, she couldn't shake the feeling that something was going on between her husband and Dr. Gilliard. Something that would tilt her world on its axis, never to be righted again.

Which was why she'd panicked when Stan had tried to talk to her that night. She'd looked into his somber eyes and imagined him uttering the words she most dreaded to hear.

I've met someone else, and I'm leaving you.

She'd imagined him relaying the sordid details of his affair, causing her to burst into tears and scream hysterically at him. She'd imagined kicking him out of the house, sending him straight into the arms of his mistress. Worst of all, she'd imagined having to break the devastating news to their children—with Thanksgiving right around the corner—that she and their father were splitting up, just as their aunt and uncle had done.

Was it any wonder she hadn't been ready to hear what Stan had to say?

"Prissy?"

Pulled out of her painful reverie, Prissy opened her eyes and tiredly rubbed the bridge of her nose. "Sorry, Mama. What were you saying?"

"Well, I was just telling you that I'm glad you've learned that history doesn't have to repeat itself. Just because your father died on the job doesn't mean the same thing will happen to Stan."

"I know." Prissy swiveled toward the window, gazing out at the scenic view of the Rocky Mountains as she relived the fun, romantic day that she and Stan had eaten lunch at the Black Kettle and gone bowling together. A lifetime ago, it seemed.

She sighed. "Can I ask you a question, Mama?"

"Of course, dear."

Prissy hesitated for a moment, choosing her words carefully. "If you'd been given a choice, would you have wanted to know that Daddy was going to die?"

Her mother was silent for so long that Prissy wondered whether they'd gotten disconnected. She was about to say something when Dinah finally spoke, low and haltingly. "I never told you or your brother this..."

As her voice trailed off, Prissy instinctively tensed. "Told us what?"

"There was a woman...She attended our church, but you were probably too young to remember her. She was beautiful and, well, I thought your father might be attracted to her. He'd never given me any reason to suspect that he would be unfaithful, but there was something about this woman that I just didn't trust. Your father was one of the church deacons, and whenever this woman needed help carrying something heavy to her car or repairing things around her house, she always sought out your father. As the months went by, I became more and more convinced that something was going on between them. So one morning I confronted your father, just asked him outright if he was having an affair with that woman. He adamantly denied it, but I didn't believe him. We got into a terrible argument before he stormed off to go to work." She paused for a long moment. "The next time I saw him was when I had to identify his body at the morgue."

Stricken, Prissy gasped.

"Oh, Mama," she whispered, her heart constricting with compassion. "Why didn't you ever tell me any of this?"

"Because I was ashamed," Dinah admitted, her voice heavy with sorrow and regret. "And I didn't want to plant any seeds of doubt in your mind concerning your father. After his funeral, the woman came to see me. She admitted to me that she'd been enamored of your father for a long time, but she knew he would never return her feelings because he loved me and was committed to our family. Before she left, she handed me a small photograph that your father had given to her shortly after she'd confessed her feelings to him. It was an old photo of me. He'd told her that every time she thought of him, or was tempted to hope that they could ever be together, looking at my picture would help bring her back to reality."

"Oh, Daddy." Prissy swallowed hard, her throat tightening with raw emotion. "That's why you never fully recovered from losing him, isn't it, Mama? You blamed yourself because your last words to him were angry, hurtful accusations."

"That's right," Dinah said mournfully. "Not a day goes by that I don't regret arguing with your father that morning. So when you ask me whether I would have wanted to know that he was going to die, my answer is yes, but only because I would have done things differently had I known that our days together were numbered. I wouldn't have wasted so much time being consumed with jealousy and suspicion. I wouldn't have assumed that his occasional silences and mood swings meant he was cheating on me. If I'd had the gift of foresight, baby, I would have spent every waking minute showing your father how much I loved and appreciated him, and how happy and grateful I was to be sharing my life with him."

Prissy gazed out the window, her vision blurred by hot tears. "But what if he really *had* been cheating, Mama? How would you have known unless you came right out and asked him?"

"I suppose I *wouldn't* have known," her mother conceded. "Short of catching him in the act, how does any woman ever know for sure that her man has been unfaithful? If you ask him and he lies, what then?"

"You at least have to ask," Prissy insisted, swiping at her watery eyes. "The alternative is to bury your head in the sand because you're too much of a coward to face the possible truth."

Dinah was silent, no doubt sensing that they were no longer talking about her and her late husband.

After several moments, she said with quiet gravity, "I suppose my advice to any woman would be to make damn certain you know what you're talking about before you accuse a man of infidelity. And you'd better know in your heart of hearts that you're ready to deal with whatever the outcome may be. Because as I learned the hard way, you can't unring a bell once it has been rung."

Chapter 22

"This is Heather McNulty reporting to you live from the Coronado Central Fire Station on Braun Road, the polling station for today's special bond election. I'm joined by Coronado School District Superintendent Priscilla Wolf." The attractive brunette turned and smiled at Prissy, who stood beside her in front of the redbrick firehouse. "Dr. Wolf, I know you've been actively campaigning for the passage of the $17.4 million bond initiative ever since it was unanimously approved by the school board back in May. Now that Election Day is finally here, what would you like to say to any of our viewers who may be on the fence about voting in favor of the proposed bond? What can you tell anyone who may not be familiar with what's at stake here?"

Prissy smiled warmly at the reporter. "Well, Heather, anyone who has lived here for a while can attest to the fact that Coronado is a growing community. Over the past five years, the district's enrollment has more than doubled, creating a need to build more schools in which to educate our students. The proposed $17.4 million bond will help the district build a new junior high school and renovate existing schools by adding several classrooms to Coronado High and Cedar Creek Junior High. Additionally, the bond funds will be used to help the district maintain our current infrastructure by replacing roofs, boilers and waterlines, and upgrading parking lots, technology systems and fire alarms."

"Speaking of fire alarms," the reporter teasingly interrupted, "I understand that your husband was named Coronado's Firefighter of the Year at Saturday's ball, and at the end of his acceptance speech, he petitioned attendees to vote yes on the bond initiative. Did you put him up to that?"

Prissy laughed. "I wish I could take credit, but no, he did that all on his own."

Heather grinned broadly. "Good man."

"Yes." Prissy smiled. "He is."

"So getting back to the matter at hand," Heather continued, "you've made a strong case for why the $17.4 million bond funds are necessary. But what do you say to residents who are worried about paying higher taxes if the bond proposal passes?"

"I'm so glad you asked, Heather. Let me take this opportunity to remind or inform viewers of the school board's stated pledge that no tax rate increase will occur if voters approve the bond proposal. Let me repeat that, because it's very important. The current tax rate will *not* change if the bond initiative is approved."

"Sounds wonderful, but skeptics may be wondering how the school board can make such a promise?"

"Well, first of all, new homes and businesses are broadening the tax base in Coronado County. So that means that others who move into the county, as well as businesses that grow, will help share the load of the bond debt in years to come. Second, the funds will be issued over a period of five years, which spreads out the debt and ensures that taxpayers won't be overburdened."

Heather nodded approvingly. "Makes perfect sense to me. Okay, Dr. Wolf, I'm going to ask you to put on your prognosticator hat. Since the certified election results won't be available until tomorrow morning, what's your sense of the way things are going?"

Prissy smiled. "Well, I've been in and out of here all day, and I'm really pleased with the turnout we've had," she said, gesturing to the steady flow of people filing into the fire station. "I've had the pleasure of speaking to many citizens who understand the important goals we're trying to achieve through this bond initiative. I'd like to encourage everyone who hasn't already voted to come out tonight and cast your ballot. The passage of this bond will support our school district's academic progress and foster a better learning environment for our youth, who are our future leaders. So please come out tonight and show them your support."

When she'd finished her earnest plea to viewers, Heather turned to the camera and said, "Well, folks, you heard it here from Superintendent Wolf. Your votes will determine the outcome of this crucial bond election, so come on down and exercise your civic duty—and enjoy some delicious refreshments while you're at it. The polls will be open until eight, so you still have time to get here." She flashed her sunny reporter's smile.

"Reporting to you live from the Coronado Central Fire Station on Braun Road, I'm Heather McNulty for KDCI News."

After signing off and removing the microphone clipped to her lapel, Heather smiled warmly at Prissy and shook her hand. "Thank you so much for taking the time to talk to me, Dr. Wolf. I just want to say what a pleasure it is to meet you. I grew up in this county and graduated from Coronado High School, and since you took over as superintendent, I've heard nothing but great things about the improvements you've already made, and the work you're doing for the school district and the community. Thanks for your vision and leadership."

Prissy smiled, touched by the reporter's heartfelt words. "Thank you so much, Heather. I really appreciate hearing that."

Heather grinned. "I always strive to be objective in my reporting, but I'm sure it was pretty obvious that I support the bond proposal. So on that note, I'm heading inside to enthusiastically cast my yes vote."

Prissy beamed with pleasure. "Wonderful. Thank you, Heather."

As they headed inside the building together, Prissy was soon detained by several school board members who exuberantly congratulated her for all the hard work and effort she'd put into campaigning for the bond election. She was all but promised a raise if the $17.4 million bond proposal passed.

After conversing with the board members for a while, Prissy continued moving through the crowd, greeting school administrators, teachers, parents, neighbors and people from all walks of the community who'd come out to vote.

She made her way to a table near the back of the hall, where Gayle and Roxanne were serving refreshments that had been generously donated by the wives of the firefighters whose husbands were assigned to this station, which had been chosen because it was the largest in town.

When Prissy reached the refreshment table, she saw that it was laden with even more food than before—homemade cakes, cookies, pumpkin pies and banana bread, as well as coffee, hot apple cider and hot chocolate.

Gayle beamed at her. "Isn't this a great turnout?"

"Yes," Prissy smilingly agreed, turning to watch as more people streamed through the main doors and were directed to the area that had been cordoned off for the voting booths. "It's a wonderful turnout."

"It sure is," Roxanne pronounced, surveying the crowd. "I have to admit that I had my doubts when you first told me that you'd persuaded the school board to schedule the bond election for the week before Thanksgiving. Since most folks would have just voted in the presidential election two weeks earlier"— She rolled her eyes at the reminder of Ronald Reagan's recent landslide victory —"I just figured they'd be less inclined to come out to the polls again so soon. But, boy, was I wrong. Holding the election this week was a stroke of genius, Prissy. Your bond issues didn't get lost in the shuffle of national politics, and since people feel more relaxed and charitable around the holidays, they're more likely to vote in favor of the initiative." She grinned at Prissy. "Brilliant strategy, woman."

"It was also her idea to serve refreshments and bring Sparky the Fire Dog for the kids." Gayle gestured around the crowded hall. "These people look like they're at a holiday social instead of a polling station. I'm betting that some folks who might have shown up to vote against the bond probably took one look at this festive atmosphere, saw the children playing with Sparky the Fire Dog, and changed their votes to yes." Gayle grinned proudly. "Is my boss awesome or what?"

Prissy laughed, shaking her head at the two women. "Thanks for the accolades, but if you ladies heap any more praise on me, my head's gonna get so inflated that I'll float up, up, up and away from here."

Gayle and Roxanne laughed.

For the next half hour, Prissy helped serve refreshments while chatting with voters and answering more questions. When Sparky the Fire Dog wandered over—Jake had graciously consented to don the costume on his day off—Prissy posed for pictures with him, then snapped photos of him with grinning children and their parents.

About the time she was feeling totally relaxed, she looked up and saw Stan sauntering through the entrance.

Her heart lurched.

Since he'd just gotten off from a late shift, he still wore his blue uniform and black boots, and he had a toothpick dangling lazily from a corner of his mouth.

Pulse thudding, Prissy watched as his dark gaze scanned the crowd before homing in on her with that unerring focus that always stole her breath.

When their eyes connected, his expression softened, one corner of his mouth lifting in a small smile.

Prissy smiled back.

Following the direction of her gaze, Gayle whistled appreciatively. "About time a hot firefighter showed up here."

"Hey!" Jake protested, his voice muffled behind the humongous dog head he wore. "What am I? Chopped liver?"

Gayle raked him with an amused glance. "You're dressed like an overgrown Dalmatian."

"Which means I've got an even bigger tongue," he quipped suggestively.

"Hey, hey, none of that!" Prissy laughingly protested.

"Yes," Roxanne humorously scolded, "have you forgotten that there are children around?"

Jake chuckled sheepishly. "Sorry."

"Mmm," Gayle hummed, eyeing him with newfound interest.

Prissy watched as Stan made his way through the crowd, smiling, shaking hands and briefly conversing with different people who stopped him. When he finally reached the refreshment table, he exchanged friendly greetings with everyone before leaning down to press a soft kiss to Prissy's mouth.

"Hey, hey, none of that," Jake teased, mimicking Prissy's admonition to him.

Drawing away from his wife, Stan narrowed his eyes at Jake. "Don't you have some children to entertain, rookie?"

Everyone laughed as Jake made an exaggerated show of hanging his big floppy-eared head and shuffling off to do as he'd been told.

As a group of people wandered over to help themselves to refreshments, Stan and Prissy stepped away from the table to have some privacy.

They stood without speaking for several moments, Stan's eyes roaming across Prissy's face in a way that reminded her that they hadn't seen much of each other over the past two days. She'd worked late yesterday evening. By the time she came

home, Stan had to leave for his night shift, giving her a quick
update on Maddox's improving condition before he'd headed
out the door. Prissy had slept poorly for the second night in a
row, her thoughts veering erratically between the bond election
and the shaky state of her marriage.

"How was your day?" she and Stan asked each other at the
same time.

"You first," Prissy prompted softly.

"My day was uneventful." His eyes glinted with humor. "I'm
sure yours was anything *but* that."

Prissy smiled faintly. "I've been busy."

"I know that's an understatement." Stan glanced around the
crowded room. "Looks like a great turnout."

She nodded. "Let's hope that translates into the right votes."

"I'm sure it will, but if you'd like, I can go stand at the door,
fold my arms across my chest and stare down anyone who even
looks like they might not be on our side."

Prissy laughed, envisioning how easily her six-foot-five, two-
hundred-forty-pound husband could intimidate any voter with
just a scowl.

"Um, yeah, that won't be necessary," she said teasingly.
"Besides, I've already heard from a number of people who
showed up tonight because of the announcement you made. So
you've done more than enough to help the cause, Lieutenant
Wolf."

Stan grinned, giving her a lazy salute. "Glad to be of service,
ma'am."

Prissy chuckled, enjoying their playful banter more than
anything she'd experienced in days. Stan must have felt the same
way, because his expression softened and he murmured, "I've
missed you."

Prissy's throat tightened. "I've missed you, too," she
whispered.

They stared at each other.

Stan said, "I hope we can—"

Suddenly they were interrupted by school board president
Boyd Dewhurst, who was accompanied by a news reporter who
wanted to interview Prissy outside for the late evening
broadcast.

"Sure," she consented with a bright smile, then glanced apologetically at Stan. "I'll see you later."

He smiled faintly. "Take your time. I'll be here."

Prissy was halfway across the room with her boss and the reporter when she saw a beautiful, long-haired woman emerge from one of the voting booths.

With a start, Prissy realized it was the woman from the ball. Dr. Gilliard.

As she stared, the doctor was joined by a handsome older couple who could have been her parents. The threesome started toward the main doors, laughing and chatting companionably.

Suddenly Dr. Gilliard glanced around and met Prissy's gaze.

They stared at each other.

After several seconds, the doctor's gaze shifted past Prissy.

When Prissy glanced over her shoulder, she saw what—*who*—had caught the other woman's attention. Wearing an infectiously boyish grin, Stan was crouched down talking to a group of beaming children while their equally captivated mothers looked on.

As a wave of possessive pride washed over Prissy, she turned back to arch a brow at Dr. Gilliard.

The woman met her gaze, the barest hint of a smile curving her mouth.

As the fine hairs lifted on the back of Prissy's neck, Dr. Gilliard briefly inclined her head, then turned and left with the older couple.

"Isn't that right, Dr. Wolf?"

Belatedly realizing that her boss and the reporter had been conversing the entire time, Prissy plastered on a smile and smoothly concurred, "That's right, Dr. Dewhurst. I couldn't agree more."

By ten o'clock, the fire station was mostly deserted.

All the votes had been counted and collected by the county election officials, who would publicly announce the results tomorrow. The poll workers and volunteers had left, along with the school board members who'd hung around to make speeches and celebratory toasts once the polls officially closed. At Prissy's adamant insistence, Roxanne had gone home to make sure her husband had put the kids to bed, while Gayle and Jake had departed together, walking so close that the sides of their legs brushed.

Only Stan and Prissy remained behind to finish cleaning up. When she told him to go home and check on the boys, he flatly refused, insisting that he'd promised to lock up the firehouse, and there was no way in hell he'd leave her there alone at that time of night.

As they worked in silence, a heavy thunderstorm swept through the area, causing the overhead lights to flicker intermittently.

As Prissy tossed leftover refreshments into the last of the trash bags, she stole covert glances at her husband, who was cleaning the black-and-white linoleum floor with a dust mop. One of the advantages of being married to a firefighter was that he wasn't averse to doing domestic work. Stan and his crew members, like firefighters everywhere, took great pride in keeping their fire station spotless.

"So," Prissy began very casually, "did you see Dr. Gilliard?"

Stan glanced up sharply from his task. "What?"

"I said," Prissy repeated coolly, "did you see Dr. Gilliard? She was here tonight. With her parents, I think."

"Yeah?" Stan's voice was neutral. "I didn't see her."

"Hmm."

He frowned at her. "What?"

"Nothing," Prissy said with feigned nonchalance. "I'm just wondering whether we're going to keep running into her everywhere. First the ball, now here."

"She lives in Coronado, Pris," Stan pointed out dryly. "It's a small community."

"I know that," Prissy said irritably. "I was just making an observation."

Stan said nothing, quietly pushing the dust mop across the floor.

As Prissy watched him, her mother's sage warnings ran through her mind. *Make damn certain you know what you're talking about before you accuse a man of infidelity....You can't unring a bell once it has been rung....*

She turned away from the table and bent down, her movements sharp and jerky as she tied up the plastic trash bag. "I think Dr. Gilliard is attracted to you."

There was a pause.

"I don't think so," Stan said flatly.

Prissy gave a derisive snort. "Typical."

"What's that supposed to mean?"

"You *never* think any woman is attracted to you, Stan. No matter how many of them throw themselves at you, you're always completely clueless. It's ridiculous. It's as if you've never looked in a damn mirror."

"I'm a married man," he bit out tersely.

"*So what!* For goodness' sake, Stan! Just because we're married doesn't mean other people can't find us attractive and want to sleep with us." She paused, then some perverse instinct made her volunteer, "I met a good-looking businessman while I was in Rochester. I was having a drink at the bar, and he sat down next to me and started flirting. So men might use a more direct approach than women, but..." She trailed off pointedly.

Dead silence.

The next sound she heard was the dust mop clattering to the floor, and then suddenly Stan was upon her, the heat of his body scorching her as he hauled her up and against him.

"What is this?" he demanded roughly against her ear. "You trying to start an argument with me? Or are you trying to have me ripping that city apart to find the bold motherfucker who stepped to my wife?"

"Of c-course not," Prissy stammered, nervously licking her lips. "I'm just suggesting—"

"What, you think you're leaving me or something?" Stan growled, sending fiery shivers through her. "You think I'd ever let you go anywhere? *Huh?* You must be out of your damn mind."

Prissy trembled hard, feeling like a child who'd accidentally ignited an inferno after playing with matches. "Stan—"

He whipped her around, framing her face between his hands as his obsidian eyes blazed into hers. "There's no one else," he said fiercely. "When we get home tonight, we're gonna sit down and talk about everything, I promise you that. But for now, I need you to know and believe me when I tell you that there's no one else. There hasn't *been* anyone else since the day I met you and lost my heart."

"*Oh, God,*" Prissy whimpered as tears flooded her eyes. She shook her head at him. "I'm so confused, baby. I want to bel—"

He crushed his mouth to hers. When she instinctively resisted, he tightened his arms around her, holding her imprisoned against the hard wall of his chest as he kissed her fiercely and possessively, demanding her surrender.

Prissy moaned helplessly and sucked his tongue, feeling her body melt even as she wrestled with her anger and fears.

With a supreme effort she managed to break free and stumble backward, panting sharply for breath.

Stan stared at her, dark eyes smoldering, nostrils flaring.

Without warning he lunged forward, picked her up and tossed her over his shoulder in a fireman's carry.

"*Stanton!*" Prissy gasped. "What do you think you're doing?"

He carried her across the hall and past the kitchen area to the metal pole that stretched up to the second floor of the fire station. He set Prissy down on her feet, then sank to his haunches in front of her.

Before she could react or protest, he spun her around and quickly unzipped her black skirt, then dragged it down her thighs and over her stiletto boots.

Prissy stared over her shoulder at him, trembling uncontrollably with desire as he seized the waistband of her black panties and eased the scrap of silk down her legs.

"Step out," he roughly commanded, and she obeyed without question.

His eyes glittered with possessive satisfaction as he tenderly caressed her round bottom, the scrape of his callused palms sending delicious chills through her. When he gently slapped her butt cheek, she whimpered and grabbed the pole, wantonly parting her legs wider.

Leaning forward, Stan kissed the small of her back, then slowly ran his hot tongue down the cleft of her bottom, making her shiver and groan as jolts of sensation rushed to her loins. When he reached the underside of her butt, he paused, deliberately drawing out her torture as his mouth hovered at her fleshy lips.

He raised his eyes to hers. "You're mine, wife," he told her, the ferocity of his dark gaze rocking her to the core. "No other man will *ever* lay claim to you. You belong to me, and I belong to you. Do you understand?"

Prissy nodded quickly and squeezed her eyes shut, her pulse pounding right into cardiac arrest levels.

When he stroked his tongue over her labia, she shuddered violently and arched backward, convinced that he would kill her with ecstasy before this night was over.

Without warning he spun her back around and pushed her against the pole. As their heated gazes locked, he hooked her booted leg over his left shoulder and lowered his mouth to her throbbing sex.

She cried out, frantically reaching above her to grab the pole for purchase.

"*Baby...*" she mewled as Stan licked the plump folds of her sex, tasting and teasing her until her breath came in short gasps and her hips twisted and writhed against his tormenting mouth. When he drew back the hood of her clit and sucked her between his lips, she came with a hoarse, primal scream.

As her knees buckled Stan caught her. Surging from the floor, he lifted her into his arms and slanted his mouth over hers, sharing her erotic taste with her. She groaned with mindless pleasure as he palmed her ass cheeks and ground his huge erection against her.

As moisture dripped from her aching sex, she attacked Stan's uniform shirt, too impatient to bother unfastening the buttons. He let out a dark, rumbling laugh as she yanked the shirt open, sending buttons flying in every direction. Together they tugged off his white undershirt and cast it aside, then made quick work of shedding the rest of each other's clothes.

When Prissy stood in nothing more than her black stiletto boots, Stan made a guttural sound of masculine appreciation before hoisting her into his arms. She locked her legs around his waist, her pussy full and throbbing with anticipation.

They stared into each other's eyes as he thrust into her, stretching her as he sank all the way inside her wetness. His husky groan of pleasure joined hers as he began rocking her against the pole, imprisoning her between the warm metal and his hard, muscular body. She held on to his impossibly wide shoulders and let her head fall back as his lips raked over her exposed throat.

She was burning up, so hot that she swore the furnace must be on full blast. She arched against Stan as his scorching mouth lowered to her bouncing breasts and sucked her nipples, sending spasms of pleasure tearing through her loins.

She tightened her damp thighs around his hips, feeling his stomach and butt muscles clench and unclench as he pumped into her, the force of his powerful thrusts moving her up and down the pole.

She moaned his name, searing flames licking at her body as she sought to quench the blazing inferno that was raging through her.

Lifting his head from her breasts, Stan stared into her eyes, the feral intensity of his gaze making her tremble from the inside out. "I need you so damn much, baby," he confessed in an achingly raw voice. "You can't ever leave me. *Ever.*"

Tears scalded Prissy's eyes. "I won't," she promised fervently. "I *swear* I won't."

His nostrils flared with emotion. Slanting his mouth over hers, he kissed her with savage tenderness as he drove deeper into her, his steely shaft stroking every part of her. Their bodies made wet slapping sounds as sweat slickened their skin, salty beads rolling between their joined genitals and dripping onto the floor.

Prissy gripped Stan's muscular shoulders and clawed at his back as waves of pleasure soared through her, so blisteringly intense it was almost unbearable.

"*Stan...*" she whimpered helplessly. "*Oh, baby...!*"

As the scorching ache within her erupted, she threw back her head and sobbed in ecstasy, tears spilling from her eyes. Stan exploded at the same time with an exultant shout of her name, his hips pumping furiously as he ejaculated inside her.

They clung desperately to each other, her breasts heaving against his chest, their bodies shuddering from the violent aftershocks of orgasm.

When a sharp clap of thunder suddenly shook the building, Prissy smiled through her tears and joked, "Talk about moving heaven and earth."

They shared a soft, breathless laugh.

"Mmm," Prissy purred after a few moments, nibbling Stan's jaw. "What a naughty boy you are, Lieutenant Wolf, debauching your wife at the firehouse. And not even your own firehouse, at that."

He chuckled lazily. "I'm just wondering why we never did this sooner."

"Mmm. Good question. We'll have to make up for lost time."

Stan gave a husky laugh. "One thing's for damn sure," he drawled. "After tonight, I'll never look at another pole the same way again."

Prissy grinned impishly. "Me, neither."

Stan kissed her ear, her closed eyelids, her mouth and her arched throat, murmuring tender words of love.

Enveloped in his strong arms, their bodies intimately joined, Prissy felt a profoundly powerful sense of completion wash over her.

Right then and there she vowed not to let anything—or anyone—come between her and her husband ever again.

Hours later, as they lay in the darkness of their bedroom with streaks of lightning forking across the night sky outside the window, Stan whispered softly, "Pris?"

She didn't respond.

"Pris? You awake?"

She mumbled incoherently, snuggling closer to him beneath the heavy covers.

"Baby?"

"Hmm?"

"We were supposed to talk," he reminded her. "I know it's late—"

She laid her fingers over his mouth. "Sleep," she whispered.

Stan smiled. "Okay," he acquiesced, gently kissing her soft fingertips. "We'll talk another time."

Long after Prissy drifted back to sleep, he lay awake watching her quietly.

No matter how painful or difficult it was, he would tell her about the nightmares.

He would tell her everything.

But first he had to take care of some unfinished business.

Chapter 23

An hour after Prissy arrived at work the next morning, she received the phone call from her boss that she—and everyone else in the office—had been anxiously anticipating. Dr. Dewhurst informed her that the citizens of Coronado had overwhelmingly voted to pass the $17.4 million bond proposal.

Prissy accepted her boss's hearty accolades and congratulations, then hung up the phone and squealed with triumphant elation.

Seconds later the door burst open and Gayle rushed into her office holding a bottle of champagne and two wineglasses. "We heard you squeal out here. Looks like it's celebration time!"

"Yes! Oh, my God, Gayle. The bond proposal passed!" Unable to contain her excitement, Prissy jumped out of her chair, and she and Gayle hugged and celebrated the good news with a happy dance around the room.

Doubling over with breathless laughter, they dropped into the visitor chairs across from Prissy's desk and sighed contentedly. "The others are on their phones calling everyone they know," Gayle informed Prissy, "but you know they're gonna be rushing in here any minute to congratulate you. In the meantime"— She uncorked the bottle of champagne with a soft *whoosh* —"let's get this party started!"

Prissy grinned broadly, watching as Gayle poured champagne into the two wineglasses and handed her one. "I see you came prepared this morning."

"Oh, no, boss lady. I've had this stuff in my desk for months. I've been saving it for this special day." Gayle smiled, her eyes twinkling with warm admiration as she held up her champagne flute. "I'd like to propose a toast to the hardest working, most dedicated and brilliant superintendent that the Coronado School District has ever had."

"Oh, Gayle," Prissy guffawed, flushing with embarrassment. "You're giving me *way* too much credit. I couldn't have accomplished anything without the hard work and support you gave me every step of the way—setting up my meetings with the various community organizations, preparing my presentation materials, keeping me on schedule, running interference for me with parents and teachers, staying late whenever I needed you to, and the list goes on and on. You've been the best right-hand woman I could have ever asked for."

Gayle's expression softened with gratitude. "Thank you, Dr. Wolf."

"Thank *you*." Smiling, Prissy held up her glass. "A toast to you, and to the good people of Coronado who put our children's needs and best interests above everything else."

"Hear, hear," Gayle heartily agreed.

They clinked glasses and sipped.

"Now that the bond proposal has passed," Gayle said, "I know you've got your work cut out for you with getting the construction projects under way."

"Yes." Prissy sighed. "The next several months—heck, years—are going to be *very* busy. But right now I'm just looking forward to having next week off to relax and spend time with my family."

"Amen. I can't *wait* to go home and see my family."

Prissy smiled warmly. "I'm sure they can't wait to see you, either."

Several years ago, Gayle had left behind the only home she'd ever known and immigrated to the United States to attend school. After receiving her bachelor's degree, she'd landed a job with the Coronado School District, serving as secretary to the previous superintendent. From the moment Prissy came on board, she and Gayle had bonded. Prissy could talk to Gayle for hours, whether she was sharing humorous anecdotes about her childhood in Ocho Rios or venting her frustration over the asinine behavior of one of her graduate school professors. And every time Gayle made Prissy some jerk chicken, plantains, and rice and peas—which Prissy had craved throughout her first pregnancy—she wanted to give Gayle a raise. Which she deserved anyway.

As much as Prissy dreaded the thought of losing her invaluable secretary once she earned her master's degree in education administration, Prissy intended to do everything in her power to ensure that Gayle secured the position of her choice within the school district.

She gave Gayle a teasing sidelong glance. "You know I've been craving jerk chicken lately. Will you bring some back for me?"

Gayle laughed. "I'll bring you *anything* you want. But wait a minute." A speculative gleam entered her dark eyes. "You used the word 'craving.' You and Mr. Wolf aren't expecting, are you?"

"Girl, no!" Prissy exclaimed with a laugh. "I had my tubes tied, burned and thrown out the window after Mason was born! Good Lord, I already have *five* children. How many more do I need?"

Gayle grinned impishly. "About five more."

"*Five?*"

"Yes. I have some nieces back home who will make excellent wives for your sons someday."

Prissy could only laugh and shake her head.

"By the way," Gayle said, "I felt really guilty about ditching you last night. I hope you and Stan weren't stuck at the fire station too long."

Prissy smiled demurely, her cheeks heating at the memory of their explosively erotic encounter against the fireman's pole. "That's okay," she murmured, sipping her champagne. "I don't mind being stuck anywhere with Stan."

Observing her intimate smile, Gayle let out a shriek of wicked laughter. "I bet you don't mind being stuck *to* him, either!"

Prissy laughed, nearly choking on her wine. Dabbing at the corners of her mouth, she grinned slyly at her secretary. "Which reminds me, I couldn't help but notice that you and Jake left the station together last night. Something you'd like to share?"

Gayle guffawed, waving a dismissive hand. "You know I'm not interested in no white boys."

"Umm-hmm. But?"

"Well," Gayle conceded, her eyes twinkling with mischief, "he *is* kinda cute. And there was something rather endearing about him in that Sparky costume."

Prissy grinned. "Lucky Jake. Good things happen to him when he's dressed as an overgrown Dalmatian. That's how he met my son's teacher, Miss Dominguez. Whatever happened between them anyway? The last time I saw them together, they were dancing and having a good time at the fireman's ball."

"I don't think it worked out. He told me she might be interested in someone else." Gayle shrugged. "Anyway, he's taking me to dinner on Friday. I'm giving him *one* date to impress me."

"Uh-oh. He'd better leave the Dalmatian costume at home, then."

"Yeah." Gayle grinned lasciviously. "But he can bring the long tongue."

The two women were still howling with laughter when the rest of the staff poured into the office to celebrate the bond passage.

When Gayle left to answer the phones, then returned a few minutes later carrying a beautiful floral arrangement that had just been delivered, Prissy's face lit up with pleasure. Even before she read the card aloud, she knew who had sent the flowers.

Congratulations, sweetheart. I've always known you could accomplish anything you set your heart and mind to. Those voters never stood a chance. When you've finished celebrating there, I'll be here waiting for you. Champagne...candles...clothing optional. Love Always, Your Biggest Fan

Prissy gave a dreamy sigh and fanned her watery eyes as her staff members traded soft, sentimental smiles.

Dabbing tears from the corners of her own eyes, Gayle sniffled and smiled at the only male staff member. Pointing to the card clutched to Prissy's heart, she declared, "Now *that* is how you love a woman."

Everyone laughed and nodded vigorously in agreement.

Half an hour later, Prissy strode past Gayle's desk, car keys in hand, briefcase swinging at her side.

Gayle gave her a broad, knowing grin. "I guess I don't have to ask where *you're* going."

Prissy grinned. "If anyone calls looking for me, you can reach me at home." She winked. "Or not."

Gayle laughed. "Don't worry, boss lady. I got your back."

Prissy smiled gratefully. "And that's why you're the best, Gayle. Simply the best."

And then she sailed out the door and went home to her husband, where the celebrating continued for the rest of the day, and long into the night.

Chapter 24

Sprawled on the sofa with his long legs stretched out before him, Manning broodingly watched a rerun of *Good Times*. It was one of his favorite shows, but halfway through the episode, he'd barely cracked a smile. Not even the sight of Thelma in a short skirt could cheer him up.

He'd been moping around the house for the past two and a half weeks. And who could really blame him? First he'd gotten suspended from school for fighting, then he'd gotten busted when his dad found out that he'd had sex with Caitlyn. Dad had grounded him for another two weeks and had taken away his phone privileges, so Manning wouldn't even be able to shoot the breeze with his friends or Mike during the Thanksgiving break, which had officially begun today.

As if that weren't bad enough, Taylor had been ignoring him ever since she'd started going out with that loser, Henry Rhodes. Henry carried Taylor's books and walked her to all her classes like a lovesick puppy. Whenever Manning passed them in the hallway and smiled at Taylor, Henry's face would get all twisted up into a frown.

Punk ass, Manning thought darkly. If he weren't already in so much trouble, he'd have gladly given that chump something to *really* frown about.

As the closing credits rolled at the end of *Good Times*, Manning grabbed the remote control and began surfing channels, though he didn't feel like watching anything else.

His parents had left him in charge while they went out to run errands. As soon as they walked out the door, he'd threatened bodily harm to his brothers if any of them even *thought* about getting sick. As he'd skulked off toward the basement, he'd heard them grumbling about his foul mood, which had given him a perverse twinge of satisfaction. When he'd paused to glower at them, they'd scampered off to the backyard, wisely deciding to stay out of his way.

Manning heaved a frustrated sigh, slumping deeper into the sofa cushions.

Minutes later he heard the basement door open, followed by the lazy thud of footsteps coming down the stairs.

"Well, ain't *this* a sorry sight to behold," drawled an amused voice.

Manning whipped his head around. His eyes widened with shock at the sight of his cousin, Michael, standing there.

Manning shot to his feet. "*Mike?*"

Michael grinned crookedly. "In the flesh."

Overcome with excitement, Manning strode over to his cousin, and they exchanged a hearty backslapping hug.

As they laughingly drew apart, Manning was embarrassed to feel tears pricking his eyelids. His parents, standing nearby, smiled softly at each other.

Manning grinned at Michael, who could have been his twin except that he was two years older and an inch taller. "What're you doing here, man? I didn't even know you were coming!"

"You weren't supposed to," Michael said with a laugh, patting Manning's cheek. "Your parents wanted to surprise you."

"Really?" Manning beamed at his mom and dad, then glanced around expectantly. "Where's Uncle Sterling and Marcus?"

Mom answered warmly, "Marcus ran to the backyard to surprise the boys. Your uncle couldn't get off from work until Tuesday, so he'll be flying down with Mama Wolf, Uncle Theo and the gang, and Quentin and his mother."

Manning's eyes widened. "You mean *Q's* coming for Thanksgiving, too?" he exclaimed.

Michael grinned broadly. "Yup."

Manning whooped with excitement. Things were suddenly looking *way* up.

Leaning close, Michael took a whiff of Manning, then reared back flapping his hand in front of his nose. "Yo, man, have you taken a shower today?"

"Um, yeah." When Manning cautiously sniffed at his underarms, Michael grinned mischievously.

"Gotcha."

They both laughed, then slung their arms around each other's necks and headed upstairs to join the others in the backyard.

That evening they went to a new all-you-can-eat buffet, where they feasted on juicy steaks, barbecue chicken, pork ribs, macaroni and cheese, mashed potatoes, cinnamon apples and hot, buttery rolls. The desserts were good, but they left everyone hankering for the mouthwatering cakes and pies baked by Mama Wolf, who couldn't get there soon enough.

During the lively meal, Manning noticed other diners staring and smiling at them. One white woman could be seen counting the number of heads at their long table. When she wandered over and asked Mom and Dad whether all seven boys were theirs, they told her yes. The awestruck woman gushed over how young Mom and Dad were, and how wonderful Mom looked to be a mother of seven. Before she and her husband left the restaurant, they asked to pose for a picture with the Wolf Pack. When Mom graciously agreed, the couple was so excited you'd have thought they'd just met the famous Jackson family.

After dinner, they all went to the movies. Even though it was after eleven when they returned home, Mom and Dad allowed everyone to stay up late since they were on vacation. While the boys played video games, Michael and Manning took turns shooting baskets at the indoor basketball hoop.

"I can't get over this basement," Michael marveled, draining shots with the natural ease he'd honed as an All-American power forward for his high school basketball team. "It's like you've got your own arcade down here."

"I know." Manning swept an appreciative glance around. "It's my favorite part of the house."

"No kidding. The whole house is amazing, for real."

Manning shrugged dispassionately. "I guess."

Michael raised a brow. "*You guess?*"

"Yeah. I mean, don't get me wrong, Mike. The house is nice, and I definitely like having my own room. But"— again Manning shrugged —"I really miss Atlanta."

Michael passed him the basketball. "Is that why you were looking so miserable earlier?"

"That's part of the reason," Manning mumbled.

Michael watched as he sank a series of shots. "On the way back from the airport, your dad told me you were grounded. But he said he'd let you tell me why."

Manning glanced across the room to make sure that the others—especially Mason—weren't eavesdropping. Thankfully the boys were absorbed in the video game, laughing boisterously and taunting one another.

Turning back to Michael, Manning gave him the rundown on his fight with Rory Kerrigan and his three-day suspension from school.

When he'd finished his account, Michael clapped him consolingly on the back. "Sucks that you got in trouble, but you did the right thing. That asshole had it coming."

"Most definitely," Manning agreed.

"Has he tried to step to you since then?"

Manning snorted. "I wish he would."

He and Michael laughed.

As Manning resumed shooting the ball, Michael said slyly, "So you like Taylor, huh?"

Startled, Manning stared at him. "I never said that."

Michael chuckled. "You didn't have to. I could tell by the way you were talking about her."

An embarrassed flush heated Manning's face. "I hardly said anything about her," he mumbled, setting down the basketball. "And she's not even my type."

"Then how come you were kissing her?"

Manning whipped his head around to see Mason smirking gleefully at him from across the room.

"Kissing who?" the others wanted to know.

"That weird-looking girl who came over to our house," Mason replied. "I saw Manny kissing her. *Eeeuuuwww!*"

Manning blushed harder as the others howled with laughter. Glaring accusingly at Mason, he growled, "I thought you promised not to tell anyone."

Mason shrugged, lifting his palms in a helpless gesture. "You were mean to us today."

"Now we know why," Montana joked. "Taylor probably dumped him!"

This set off another round of laughter that had Michael grinning and shaking his head sympathetically at Manning. "Dontcha just love little brothers?"

Manning scowled. "At least *you* only have one."

"One is more than enough." But Michael's expression had softened as he watched Marcus wrestling playfully with Magnum. The ten-year-old cousins were like two peas in a pod, so close that they'd probably end up rooming together in college.

"It's good to see Little Man laughing again," Michael said quietly. "It's been a while."

Manning sobered at the reminder of the painful ordeal Michael and Marcus had recently gone through with their parents. As he watched, Marcus smacked Magnum upside the head with a pillow, then burst out laughing.

Manning smiled softly. "This week will be good for him."

"Yeah," Michael murmured. "For both of us."

Hearing the husky catch to his cousin's voice, Manning reached out and squeezed his shoulder.

Neither spoke for several moments.

"You're lucky," Michael said quietly. "Uncle Stan and Aunt Prissy really love each other. When they're together, they're like...like high school sweethearts."

Manning smiled a little. "They were."

"I know. And it shows."

Manning thought of the tension he'd sensed between his parents over the past few months. Whatever had been troubling them seemed to have passed. Thank God, because he honestly didn't know *what* he'd do if they ever got divorced.

"I know you miss Atlanta," Michael continued solemnly. "I probably would, too. But if I could turn back time and keep my family together, I'd do it in a heartbeat—even if we had to move to Timbuktu."

He and Manning shared a quiet chuckle.

Sobering after another moment, Michael gently grasped his cousin's shoulder. "You have a lot to be grateful for, Manny. This beautiful house, your loving parents, even your little brothers— who look up to you whether you realize it or not. You've got it made. So the next time you're tempted to feel sorry for yourself, stop and count your blessings instead."

Manning nodded slowly, thoroughly humbled by his cousin's heartfelt words. He knew Michael was right. He'd been wearing a chip on his shoulder for the past two years. It was time for him to stop sulking and start appreciating everything he had. Starting now.

Watching his expression turn to one of acceptance, Michael grinned with satisfaction. "Now that we've had shrink time," he teased, "I think I'll give you a good old-fashioned butt whupping for old times' sake. Does that half court in the backyard have lights?"

"Yeah," Manning said slowly, "but it's almost midnight. And it's, like, fifty degrees outside."

"Chicken?" Michael challenged.

Manning laughed. "Hell, no! I've gotten used to Colorado winters, so while *you're* standing there shivering in your long johns, I'll be raining threes on your head."

Michael laughed as they headed upstairs to suit up in sweats. "You can take the boy out of Atlanta—"

"—but you can't take Atlanta out of the boy." Manning grinned. "And don't you forget it."

"I won't." Michael sent him a meaningful look. "And neither should you."

Chapter 25

After church the next afternoon, Stan took his sons to the barber shop, which had opened on Sunday to accommodate clients who would be traveling out of town for Thanksgiving. Michael and Marcus, who'd gotten fresh haircuts before leaving Atlanta, had opted to stay at the house with Prissy until the others returned.

While the boys entertained themselves in the basement, Prissy started dinner and washed linens and towels in preparation for the arrival of more houseguests on Tuesday. She had just carried a fresh load of laundry into her bedroom when the telephone rang.

Setting the basket down on her bed, she grabbed the phone from her nightstand and answered, "Hello?"

"Pris?" came Celeste's subdued voice.

"Oh, hey, girl." Prissy smiled ruefully. "I'm glad you called, because I've been meaning to get in touch with you—"

"The baby's gone, Pris."

Prissy froze with shock, thinking she'd heard wrong. "What did you say?"

"My baby...It's gone."

"Oh, my God," Prissy breathed. Struck by a sudden horrible suspicion, she demanded accusingly, "*What did you do?*"

When she heard muffled little sobs on the other end, she realized that Celeste was crying. "I had...a miscarriage," she choked out.

"Oh, God." Stunned, Prissy sank weakly onto the bed. "I'm so sorry, Cel. Are you okay?"

"No! I'm *not* okay! I...I lost my baby. A baby I didn't even *want*. Oh, God, Pris. I didn't want her, so God took her from me!"

As Celeste began sobbing harder, tears welled in Prissy's eyes, blurring her vision. "I'm so sorry, honey," was all she could say.

"She was a girl, Pris," Celeste whimpered.

"How do you know?" Prissy whispered hoarsely. "It was too early to tell, wasn't it?"

"Yes, but I *know* in my heart she was a girl. She *felt* like a girl to me. And now...now she's gone. And it's all my fault!"

"Shhh," Prissy soothed. "Don't say that. It's not your fault."

"Yes, it is! I didn't want her, Pris! *You* know that. I was devastated when I found out that I was pregnant, and I thought about getting rid of the baby just about every day. So God decided I didn't deserve her, and He took her away from me!"

Celeste's anguished wails tore at Prissy's aching heart. "Where are you, honey?"

It took several moments before Celeste could compose herself enough to choke out a fragmented response. "I'm at...the condo. Grant went...to the store...to pick up some things...for me."

"You shouldn't be alone, sweetie. Not at a time like this." Prissy stared up at the ceiling through a sheen of tears. "When...when did this happen?"

"Yesterday morning. I came back from the hospital last night. I've been in bed ever since." Celeste inhaled a deep, shuddering breath and released it slowly. "I...I wanted to surprise Grant. I'd bought a beautiful painting of an old farmhouse in Vermont...I knew it would remind him of his childhood. I was trying to hang it on the wall when I felt a sharp pain in my back and stomach. I dropped the painting and fell to my knees. I-I knew something was terribly wrong. By the time I crawled to the bathroom, there was so much blood...So much blood, Pris."

Prissy was silent as tears rolled down her face, one after another.

"Grant came home and found me lying on the bathroom floor, bawling my eyes out. He was so scared he turned white as a ghost. He took me to the hospital—" Celeste broke off with another choked sob.

Prissy waited for her to continue. Somehow she knew the worst was yet to come.

"The baby wasn't Grant's," Celeste confessed.

Prissy's grip tightened on the phone. "How do you know?"

"He had a vasectomy four years ago. He doesn't want any children, but he told me that his thinking at the time was that if he ever met someone he loved enough to marry, he'd be willing to get the vasectomy reversed."

"Dear God." Prissy brought trembling fingers to her mouth, stunned by the import of Celeste's revelation. "So the baby was Sterling's."

"Yes." Celeste was weeping again, and so was Prissy.

Minutes passed without either of them speaking. The raw outpouring of grief was too much.

Celeste was the first to finally regain her composure.

"About eleven years ago," she whispered brokenly, "I was going to ask Sterling for a divorce. We'd been unhappy for a while, and I just thought it was time for us to go our separate ways. And then I found out I was pregnant with Marcus. No way could I leave Sterling after that."

While Prissy was still reeling from this new revelation, Celeste continued in a low, haunted voice, "Every time I think I'm done with Sterling Wolf, something else happens to keep me tied to him. Once again I tried to leave him, and once again I wound up pregnant. That *has* to mean something, doesn't it, Pris?"

Prissy shook her head sorrowfully. "I don't know, Celeste."

Celeste sighed. "Maybe we *are* meant to be together. Maybe when it's all said and done, time will reveal that Sterling and I are truly soul mates."

"Maybe," Prissy murmured.

A long, mournful silence passed between the two women.

"You know," Celeste said reflectively, "we used to say that if we ever had a girl, we'd name her Savannah because some of our happiest times together were at Mama Wolf's house. This summer when we were driving home from there, do you know what Michael said? He was staring out the window, and all of a sudden he cheerfully announced that if he had a daughter someday, he would name her Savannah because it was one of his favorite places in the whole world. Sterling and I just looked at each other and smiled."

Prissy smiled, too.

"Why don't you come here for Thanksgiving, Celeste?" she gently cajoled. "Michael and Marcus are already here, and everyone else is coming on Tuesday. You need to be around family right now."

"I know, and I'd love nothing more than to spend the holiday with my boys. But I can't come. I...I can't be around Sterling right now. It's too painful."

Prissy nodded with sympathetic understanding. "Are you going to tell him...about the baby?"

After a prolonged silence, Celeste answered quietly, "There's no point now, is there? If I tell him that I miscarried our third child, he's going to be as devastated as I am. Why hurt him any more than I already have?"

Prissy closed her eyes on a heavy sigh. "You have a point, but aren't you tired of keeping secrets, Celeste?"

"Yes," she admitted sadly. "But this is one I'm willing to take to my grave to spare Sterling any more pain."

Prissy nodded slowly, accepting her decision. "I won't tell a soul, either," she promised.

"Thank you, Pris," Celeste whispered. "For everything."

Prissy swallowed tightly. "Get some rest, sweetie, and I'll check up on you tomorrow."

"All right. And Pris?"

"Hmm?"

"Will you kiss my boys for me?"

Prissy had already intended to do just that. She smiled softly. "I sure will."

After she hung up the phone, she padded to the bathroom to rinse her face and blow her nose. When she felt sufficiently composed enough to face her nephews, she ventured downstairs to the basement.

Michael and Marcus were playing with the pinball machine, their boyish laughter blending with the noisy *ping-ping-ping* sounds radiating from the flashing contraption. Although Prissy had told them to change when they all returned from church, the two brothers still wore their white dress shirts, which were untucked from their dark pants with the sleeves rolled to their elbows.

For several moments Prissy just stood on the stairs watching them, these beloved boys who looked so much like her own that she could have given birth to them.

Marcus was the first to glance up and notice her. "Hey, Aunt Prissy! Are they back yet?"

She smiled indulgently. "No, baby, not yet. There're six of them, so it usually takes a while."

"Yeah. That's why me and Mike decided not to go with them." Marcus made a disgruntled face. "It takes *forever* at the barber shop."

Prissy laughed. "You should try coming to the hair salon with me one day," she teased, descending the rest of the stairs.

"No way," Marcus said with a vigorous shake of his head. "My mom used to—" He broke off abruptly, his expression darkening with pain and anger. After shooting a glance at Michael, he returned his attention to the pinball machine, but with far less enthusiasm than before.

Prissy's heart broke.

She looked at Michael, who'd been studying her with that keenly perceptive gaze that always reminded her of his father's and Stan's. "Is everything okay, Aunt Prissy?" he asked in concern.

She nodded quickly, even as tears crowded her throat. "If my eyes look a little red," she lied, "it's from chopping onions for dinner."

Michael nodded, though he didn't look entirely convinced. "What're you making?"

"Oh, nothing fancy. Just a pot roast with garlic mashed potatoes and honey-glazed green beans."

"Sounds good," Michael said approvingly.

"I think you might enjoy it." Prissy smiled fondly at him. "Your father tells me you've been cooking for him and Marcus."

Michael shrugged dismissively. "Dad works long hours, so...." He trailed off with another shrug of his shoulder.

Prissy wasn't at all fooled by his attempt to downplay the way he'd been taking care of his broken family. "Your dad says whenever you come home from a tough practice, or if your basketball team loses, you march straight to the kitchen and start cooking up a storm to work off your anger and frustration. He says by the time you're finished, the kitchen looks like a disaster area, but you've made enough food to last for two weeks."

Michael fought a smile, looking embarrassed. "Dad tends to exaggerate."

"No, he doesn't," Marcus interjected without glancing up from the pinball machine. "You *do* cook like that. And his food's pretty good, Aunt Prissy."

"I bet it is," she agreed, affectionately rubbing both of their backs as she stood between them. "I still remember the delicious omelet he made for us over the summer at Mama Wolf's house. Best omelet I've ever had. Maybe one day you can become a chef, Michael."

"Nah." He shook his head. "I'm gonna be an engineer."

Prissy smiled softly. "Well, whatever you decide to be, I know that your parents will be very proud of you. Of both of you," she added, turning to Marcus. "They love you both very much, and your happiness means more to them than anything else."

When her nephews said nothing, she thought of the family experiences they would never again share with their parents, the memories they would never make. And she thought of the brother or sister they would never get to meet and bond with.

Suddenly the tears she'd been struggling to contain broke free and began streaming down her face.

Marcus eyed her worriedly. "Why are you crying, Aunt Prissy?"

"Because I love you and your brother so much," she whispered achingly, tenderly kissing their foreheads. "And I hope you know that I will always be here for you, no matter what. If there's anything I can do for you, *anything* at all, you pick up the phone and call me. Will you promise me that?"

The two brothers looked at each other, eyes bright with unshed tears, nostrils flaring with suppressed emotion. As proud and vulnerable as wounded eagles trying to soar above the darkest storm clouds.

Without a word they turned to Prissy, Marcus wrapping his arms tightly around her waist while Michael drew his arms around her shoulders. She closed her eyes, her heart expanding as she savored the precious connection.

She wasn't their mother, and she would never try to be. But from that day forward, she vowed to do her damnedest to ensure that Michael and Marcus would never lack the warmth of a mother's love.

Chapter 26

"Stan," Dr. Gilliard breathed, greeting him with a smile of undisguised pleasure as she opened the door to her office. "It's wonderful to see you again. Please come in."

"Thanks for agreeing to see me on such short notice," Stan said, entering the room. "I hope I'm not throwing off your schedule."

"Not at all. I had a cancellation, so I'm all yours for however long you need me."

"Uh, well, actually—" He broke off as Dr. Gilliard peeled his jacket off his shoulders and hung it on the coat rack. When he looked at her, she smiled warmly and gestured to the sofa.

"Please have a seat," she invited.

Stan hesitated, then walked over to the sofa and sat down. He'd come there to tell her that he didn't need her services anymore. On the way to her office, he'd rehearsed what he would say. But now that he was here, he felt awkward. Out of his element.

How exactly does one break up with one's therapist?

Dr. Gilliard sat in her armchair and slowly crossed her legs. Today she had on a cream cashmere sweater dress and wore her long hair down. Her glasses, which had been missing at the ball, were back in place.

"So," she began conversationally, "do you have any special plans for Thanksgiving?"

"Yeah. We've got family coming from out of town, and on Wednesday evening we're driving up to the mountains to spend Thanksgiving weekend at a ski lodge."

"Oh, wow, that sounds wonderful." Dr. Gilliard smiled brightly. "That should be really fun for everyone."

"Definitely. We're all looking forward to it, especially the kids." Stan paused, then asked politely, "What about you? Got any special plans?"

"Oh, nothing as exciting or romantic as a ski trip," the doctor said with a dismissive wave of her hand. "I'm just having dinner at my parents' house."

Stan nodded.

"I'd love for you to meet them."

Stan's brows shot up. "Your *parents*?"

Dr. Gilliard had the mortified look of someone who just realized she'd unintentionally spoken aloud. "Well, um, my father is retired military, and he and my mother are, um, really active in the community. So I just thought they'd both be, uh, honored to meet Coronado's Firefighter of the Year."

As she muddled her way through the convoluted explanation, Stan stared at her, eyes narrowed speculatively.

Dropping her gaze, Dr. Gilliard became absorbed in removing a speck of lint from her dress.

Stan regarded her in silence for another moment, then frowned. "Listen, I would have preferred to do this over the phone, but I thought I owed you the courtesy of telling you in person—"

Her eyes snapped to his face. "Telling me what?"

He met her gaze. "I won't be continuing our therapy sessions."

She looked stricken. "What do you mean?"

Stan frowned. He thought he'd spoken plainly enough. "I don't think—"

"Is this because of what happened at the ball? Because I'm really sorry about that. Van Dorn insisted on dancing with your wife, and I didn't know how to talk him out of it."

Stan grimaced. "This isn't about that, although dancing with you *did* put me in an awkward position. But that's not why I'm ending our sessions."

"Then why?"

Stan hesitated for a moment, then opted for complete honesty. "I've been coming to you for over three months now, and while I appreciate the time you've taken to help me, I'm no closer to understanding or overcoming my nightmares than I was when I first began seeing you."

Dr. Gilliard looked stung. "Three months isn't *nearly* enough time to determine that therapy isn't working for you, Stan. It takes some of my clients *years* to make any sort of breakthrough. You just have to be patient."

He shook his head grimly. "I think we've made all the progress we're going to make."

"I disagree."

Stan frowned. "Listen—"

"We haven't even tried hypnotherapy," Dr. Gilliard blurted, an edge of desperation to her voice.

"Hypnotherapy?" Stan repeated skeptically. "You want to *hypnotize* me?"

"I know it may sound farfetched, but hypnotherapy has been clinically proven to provide medical and therapeutic benefits. I've used hypnotic regression to successfully treat several patients who suffered from depression. By regressing them to their childhood, we were able to uncover traumatic memories of sexual and physical abuse."

Stan scowled blackly. "I wasn't abused. My parents loved me and my brother, and they took damn good care of us till the day they died."

"I'm not suggesting that you were abused, Stan," Dr. Gilliard hastened to assure him. "I'm merely offering an alternative method of treatment that we haven't explored yet."

Stan eyed her dubiously. "I don't think I can be hypnotized."

"We won't know unless we try. Look, I know you've told me that the nightmares haven't affected your job performance, but how much longer will that hold true? As a consultant to the police and fire departments, it's my professional duty to ensure that my clients—be they cops or firefighters—don't pose a threat to themselves or others. You're up for a promotion to captain. At this point, I'm not sure how comfortable I'd be signing off on a psych evaluation for you."

Stan's eyes narrowed on hers. "Are you suggesting that I'm not *fit* to serve as captain?" he said through gritted teeth.

"Of course not! God, I would *never* suggest anything like that! Everyone knows you're *more* than qualified to be promoted." Dr. Gilliard sat forward in her chair, eyeing him intently. "I know what's at stake for you, Stan, so I want to do everything in my power to help you. Let me try the hypnotherapy. Let's see if we can get to the root cause of your nightmares."

Stan wavered, a muscle throbbing in his jaw.

"Just give it a chance," Dr. Gilliard gently implored. "If you still believe we're wasting each other's time, then I'll respect your wishes to discontinue therapy. Deal?"

Stan regarded her silently for several moments, then relented with a brusque nod.

"Wonderful." Dr. Gilliard beamed with pleasure, then smoothly uncrossed her legs and glided to her feet. "I'm going to close the blinds to make it a little less bright in here. I want you to lay back on the sofa and try to relax."

Stan reluctantly complied as she strode to the window. After a few seconds, the room was plunged into soft shadows. Closing his eyes, Stan listened to the doctor's quiet footfalls moving across the oriental rug as she returned to her chair and sat down.

"You're not relaxing, Stan," she murmured chidingly.

"How do you know?"

"I can feel your tension from all the way over here. You're thinking too hard. I want you to empty your mind of everything but this moment. What normally relaxes you?"

A soft smile touched his lips. "Prissy's hands."

Dr. Gilliard paused. "Oh?"

"Yeah. She gives the most amazing massages. Whenever I come home really stressed, she lays my head on her lap and massages my scalp, then turns me over and rubs my shoulders and back and—"

"I get the picture."

Stan grinned sheepishly. "Sorry."

Dr. Gilliard muttered something under her breath.

Stan opened his eyes and glanced over at her. "What was that?"

"Nothing." The doctor forced a bright smile. "Since your wife isn't here to, ah, relax you, let's try a different approach, shall we?"

Stan nodded, turning away.

"I want you to look up at that small water stain on the ceiling. Can you see it?"

"Yeah."

"Good. I want you to stare at that stain and let your breathing become slow and deep. Let your body begin to unwind, starting with the muscles in your feet and toes. Let your thighs relax, Stan. Let all that negative tension flow out of your— What is it? What's wrong?"

Stan was frowning. "The building manager should really get that water stain taken care of."

Dr. Gilliard made a strangled sound of exasperation.

"Sorry," Stan said abashedly. "I used to be in construction, so—"

"Never mind," the doctor snapped. "Don't focus on the ceiling. Close your eyes instead, okay?"

His lips twitched. "Okay."

As he obligingly lowered his eyelids, he heard Dr. Gilliard inhale a deep breath, clearly striving for patience.

After several moments, she began speaking again. But the soothing cadence of her voice didn't lull Stan into a trancelike state. Instead he found himself tuning her out, her words fading into the background as his mind began wandering.

He thought of his family members who would be arriving in town tomorrow. He and Prissy would pick up Mama Wolf from the airport since her flight from Savannah arrived first. Later that afternoon, Prissy's brother would bring home the Atlanta crew in the van he'd already rented from the airport. Stan couldn't wait to see everyone, especially his grandmother and Sterling. And he still needed to pack for the ski trip—

"...that's it, Stan," Dr. Gilliard encouraged, her tranquil voice penetrating his thoughts. She sounded closer than before. "You're doing really great."

He frowned. "Actually, I don't think this is— *What the fuck?*" he burst out suddenly, his eyes snapping open to find Dr. Gilliard straddling him. He bolted upright so violently that she lost her balance and tumbled backward, landing in an ignominious heap on the floor.

Catching a glimpse of red panties, Stan exclaimed, "*Shit!*" and quickly covered his eyes. Keeping them tightly closed, he swung his feet to the floor and demanded furiously, "What the hell do you think you're doing?"

"I-I'm sorry," Dr. Gilliard stammered. "I don't know what came over me."

"You must have lost your damn mind!"

"I, well, um—" She broke off with a heavy sigh. "You can open your eyes now."

Cautiously cracking one eye open, then the other, Stan saw that the doctor had composed herself and now sat on the floor with her legs neatly folded beneath her.

He glared at her in outraged disbelief. "Care to tell me what the hell just happened here?"

"I think you know."

"The hell I do!"

She gazed up at him. "I'm in love with you, Stan."

"*WHAT!*"

"Believe me, I didn't want this to happen," she said earnestly. "I've never crossed the line with a patient, never even been tempted to. But then you came along and changed all that. I can't stop thinking about you, Stan. You're the most amazing man I've ever met, and I'd give anything—"

He held up a hand to halt her impassioned declaration. "Stop right there. Are you *crazy*? Have you completely forgotten that I'm *married*?"

"Of course not," she mumbled, her resentful gaze flicking to the gold wedding band on his left hand.

Stan clenched his jaw. "You need to understand something. I love my wife—"

She flinched. "I know you do. I can tell by the way you talk about her, and I saw it with my own two eyes at the ball. But loving your wife doesn't mean you can't have feelings for me. You must feel *something*, Stan, or you wouldn't have gone to the trouble of coming here today when you could have just spoken to me over the phone."

"Like I said," Stan bit out, "I thought I owed you the courtesy of a face to face conversation. Believe me, I'm regretting that now!"

"Don't," she urged, her sultry eyes locked onto his. "I'm glad you came today, Stan. After that night at the ball, I was afraid I might never see you again. And that would have been unthinkable. Because I love you, Stan, and I want to make you happy."

He shook his head in disbelief. "I *am* happy—with my wife!"

"But I can make you happier."

And with that, she threw herself into his arms.

Prissy stared out the window at the nondescript office building she'd been parked outside for the past five minutes.

She'd been on her way home from running errands that afternoon when she'd passed Stan's truck on the road. Some instinct had compelled her to turn around and follow him at what she hoped was a safe distance. When he'd turned into the parking lot of a small medical center, she was puzzled. He hadn't mentioned having a doctor's appointment today, and his physician's office was on the other side of town.

So what is he doing here? Prissy wondered for the umpteenth time since her arrival.

She felt like a fool—a paranoid wife who'd sunk to stalking her husband around town to catch him in the act of cheating. Which made no sense. She'd genuinely believed Stan when he swore to her that he wasn't having an affair. She trusted him, so she had no reason to be spying on him like this.

She should start the car and leave right now.

But something kept her rooted to the spot.

And then, suddenly, she saw movement in an upper window that faced the parking lot. A woman had appeared.

But not just *any* woman.

Dr. Gilliard, Prissy realized with a jolt.

As she watched, the doctor peered outside for a moment, then suddenly drew the blinds closed.

Prissy's stomach lurched, and a cold sweat broke out on her skin.

Not wasting another second, she flung her door open and lunged from her minivan.

Her tan trench coat flapped in the wind as she hurried toward the building and entered the lobby. Crossing to the building directory, she scanned the board until she found the entry she was looking for.

DR. ERIN GILLIARD, PSY.D., LPCC, SUITE 529

Pivoting on her heel, Prissy strode to the elevator and impatiently pressed the call button. As she waited for the cab to arrive, she paced back and forth, her boot heels clicking sharply against the linoleum floor, her mind racing at warp speed. She couldn't fathom any reason that Stan would be secretly seeing a psychologist. But if he wasn't being treated by Dr. Gilliard...the alternative explanation was unbearable.

When the elevator finally arrived minutes later, Prissy boarded quickly, then had to grit her teeth and wait with forced patience as an elderly couple followed her into the cab, moving slower than molasses. On the second floor, they disembarked at the same maddening snail's pace.

When the cab stopped on the third level to admit a passenger who'd mistakenly thought the elevator had been going down, Prissy wanted to scream with frustration.

It seemed an agonizing eternity before she finally reached the fifth floor. The moment the elevator doors opened she leaped out, then followed the numbered sign to Dr. Gilliard's office.

Stepping into the suite, she saw that the tastefully furnished reception area was empty.

Relieved that she didn't have to deal with a gatekeeper receptionist, Prissy started down the narrow corridor, her heart thundering against her ribs.

Reaching a closed door near the end of the hallway, she paused, momentarily paralyzed by fear and dread as she wondered what she would encounter on the other side.

What if Stan's not even here? her conscience challenged. *What if Dr. Gilliard is with another patient, and you make a fool of yourself by barging into her office?*

Hearing voices from within the room—one of which *definitely* belonged to her husband—Prissy burst through the door.

She gasped, stunned at the sight of Dr. Gilliard kneeling between Stan's legs with her arms wrapped tightly around his neck.

Prissy didn't think, just reacted.

Marching furiously across the shadowy room, she snatched a handful of Dr. Gilliard's long hair, making her screech in pain. Viciously tightening her grip, Prissy dragged the woman away from Stan and flung her to the floor like a cheap ragdoll.

As Stan jumped up from the sofa and reached for Prissy, her mother's voice ran through her mind. *Short of catching him in the act...*

"WHAT THE HELL IS GOING ON HERE?" she screamed, her chest heaving as she divided an outraged glance between her husband and the doctor, who had scrambled to her feet and was tugging down her dress.

Stan gently grasped Prissy's arms. "Let me explain—"

"You'd better talk fast because *somebody's* about to get hurt up in here!"

Out of the corner of her eye, she saw Dr. Gilliard take a discreet step away from her. Turning her head, Prissy snarled at the red-faced woman.

"Baby," Stan tried again, "it's not what you think—"

"No? Then what the hell was she doing all over you, Stanton? And why the hell is it so dark in here?"

Scowling ferociously, Stan barked at Dr. Gilliard, "Open those damn blinds!"

She obeyed without hesitation.

As daylight flooded the small room, Stan took Prissy's face between his hands, his dark eyes boring intently into hers. "Baby, listen to me," he said urgently. "Despite what you just saw here, I swear to you that there's *nothing* going on between me and Dr. Gilliard."

"But you lied to me!" Prissy cried accusingly. "You told me you didn't know her personally!"

"I know." Stan looked pained. "I shouldn't have lied to you, honey, but it was the wrong time and place to share the truth with you. As I told you that night, Dr. Gilliard is a psychologist. What I didn't tell you is that she's been counseling me for the past three months because I've been having nightmares."

It was the last thing Prissy had expected him to say. Stunned, she stared at him. "Nightmares?"

"Yes," he croaked.

Choking back an instinctive surge of fear, she whispered, "What kind of nightmares?"

Stan closed his eyes in an expression of raw anguish that heightened Prissy's alarm. "I've been having nightmares about the fire that killed my parents."

Prissy's heart instantly melted with compassion. "Oh, sweetheart," she gently consoled, reaching up and tenderly stroking his cheek. "I'm so sorry. Why didn't you tell me?"

He shook his head. "I didn't want you to know, didn't want you to worry." When he opened his eyes, they were haunted. "You see, the dreams aren't just about my mom and dad."

Prissy searched his face. "What do you mean?"

Stan swallowed tightly, holding her gaze. "At the end of the dreams...I die in the same fire that killed my parents."

The blood drained from Prissy's head. Her mind flashed back to the years she'd spent being tormented by fears of him dying on the job, leaving her a young widow like her mother had been.

Watching the play of emotions across her face, Stan shook his head grimly. "That's why I didn't tell you about the nightmares. I knew they'd only upset you. And to be totally honest with you, they've scared the hell out of me, too. Which is why I've been seeing a shrink."

A combination of guilt, shame and regret swept through Prissy at the realization that her husband had been suffering in silence because he'd been afraid to awaken her inner demons. At a time when he'd needed her the most, she'd utterly failed him.

Tears welled in her eyes. "That's why you started sleeping on the sofa," she whispered. "You didn't want me to be there when you woke up from the nightmares."

He nodded, nostrils flaring. "I know I shouldn't have kept this from you for so long," he said, his voice husky with raw emotion. "I honestly thought it was for the best, but I now realize that I caused you more pain and confusion than I ever intended. Can you forgive me?"

Could *she* forgive *him*?

"Listen to me." Prissy tenderly cradled his face between her hands, nearly undone by the tears shining in his eyes. "You mean *everything* to me, Stanton Wolf," she fervently declared. "The next time you have a nightmare, I'll be right there to kiss you, hold you in my arms and rock you gently back to sleep. I swear to you that you will *never* have to suffer through another nightmare alone."

"*Oh, God.*" Overcome with emotion, Stan hauled her into his arms, clasping her tightly to him as he rubbed his jaw against her hair. "I love you more than life itself, sweetheart."

"I love you, too," she whispered achingly as she clung to him, her wet cheek pressed against his broad chest, absorbing the heat and strength that radiated through the soft fabric of his sweater. He was alive, vibrantly alive, and he wasn't going anywhere if she had anything to say about it!

As he lifted her into his arms, she wrapped her arms around his neck and locked her legs around his waist. With a ragged groan of satisfied relief, he crushed his mouth to hers in a breathtakingly fierce kiss that shook her down to her soul.

"Come on, baby," he murmured against her mouth. "Let's go home."

She gave a teary smile. "Thought you'd never ask."

As Stan began carrying her from the room, she caught a glimpse of Dr. Gilliard, whose presence had been heretofore forgotten. The woman looked so devastated that Prissy almost felt sorry for her. But then she remembered the shocking scene she'd interrupted minutes ago, and she realized that the good doctor wouldn't have felt an ounce of pity for her if *she* were the one being carried out of the room by Stan.

As Prissy and Stan reached the door, she murmured, "Hold on a moment, baby."

He stopped, albeit with obvious reluctance.

Meeting the other woman's wounded gaze over Stan's shoulder, Prissy said with quiet composure, "I don't doubt that you're good at what you do, Dr. Gilliard. And I'm sure you've helped many of your patients overcome their personal issues."

Dr. Gilliard's chin lifted a proud notch. "I have."

"And that's why I'm not going to report your inappropriate behavior." Prissy's tone turned steely to match her stare. "But know this. If you *ever* come anywhere near my husband again, I will personally see to it that you never practice medicine again. Do we understand each other, Dr. Gilliard?"

The woman's face reddened with humiliation, even as a trace of grudging respect flickered in her eyes. Coolly inclining her head, she murmured, "I understand you perfectly, Dr. Wolf."

"Good." Prissy held her gaze a moment longer, then gently nipped Stan's earlobe and whispered, "Take me home, husband."

His eyes glinted at her. "With pleasure, wife."

As soon as they pulled into their driveway twenty minutes later, Stan hopped out of his truck and came around to help Prissy from the minivan. Without a word passing between them, he swept her into his arms and strode purposefully up the walk toward the house. She clung to his neck as he unlocked the front door and carried her across the threshold, where the sounds of boisterous laughter and banter drifted from the kitchen.

"Michael," Stan called out.

Instantly the noise evaporated.

Moments later Michael emerged from the kitchen trailed by the others. "Hey, Aunt Prissy and Uncle Stan. You called me?"

"Yeah." Stan tossed his car keys to his nephew, who caught them nimbly. "Take everyone to the pizzeria around the corner, then you boys go bowling or something."

Michael looked stunned. "You're letting me drive your truck?"

"You have your license, don't you?"

"Yes, sir. Had it since my sixteenth birthday in June."

"I know. I was one of the first people you called, remember?" Stan smiled. "Anyway, your dad tells me you're a very good driver, and he lets you use his car on the weekends."

"Yup." Michael grinned broadly.

Without setting Prissy down—the strength and dexterity of firefighters never ceased to amaze her—Stan fished out four large bills from his wallet and handed the money to his nephew. "You fellas get whatever you want."

"*Cool!*" the others exclaimed, celebrating their bounty with cheers and high fives.

"I can't *wait* till I get my license," Manning said enviously.

As the rowdy pack began charging toward the front door, Stan said sternly, "Michael."

He turned back. "Yes, sir?"

Stan jabbed a warning finger at him. "No speeding and no joy rides, or your behind is mine."

Michael gulped visibly. "Yes, sir."

"Don't forget your coats, fellas," Prissy reminded them.

"Yes, ma'am," they parroted.

As the boys retrieved their coats from the mud room and headed out the door, Maddox could be heard speculating curiously, "What do you think Mom and Dad are gonna do while we're gone?"

"Believe me," Manning warned, "you don't wanna know."

As Michael and Montana erupted into knowing laughter, the younger ones exchanged bewildered glances and shrugged.

The door had barely closed behind them before Stan carried Prissy into their bedroom and kicked the door resoundingly shut. They hurriedly undressed each other and tumbled across the bed, where they spent the rest of the night making love with the tender ferocity of reborn lovers.

Chapter 27

Evangeline Wolf was a spry-looking woman in her sixties with cocoa brown skin and a short natural that had turned completely white over the years. Her dark eyes were keenly intuitive, and her soft face was etched with strength and character.

Although she was a Wolf by marriage, not birth, she was the relative that everyone flocked to at family reunions, weddings and funerals. She was the benevolent matriarch that everyone sought out for recipes, or remedies for various ailments, or advice on everything from disciplining children to forgiving wayward husbands. She was the keeper of the family's history and genealogy. If anyone wanted to trace the large clan's ancestral origins back to West Africa, Evangeline was the one to consult.

She'd survived the death of her husband, and then the tragic death of her only son Michael Josiah, for whom Michael and Manning had been christened—Michael claiming their grandfather's first name, Manning his middle name.

After Sterling and Stan lost their parents, Evangeline had locked up her Savannah home and moved to Atlanta to take care of her orphaned grandchildren until they both graduated from high school. They owed her their lives, though she wouldn't hear of such a thing, insisting that she'd only done "what needed to be done."

But her protestations fell on deaf ears, because they all knew that Evangeline was the cornerstone of the Wolf Pack, adored and revered by everyone from the eldest to the youngest member of the family.

Before Stan and Prissy left for the airport on Tuesday morning, the boys had begged to accompany them to pick up Mama Wolf. But Stan and Prissy had made them stay behind and clean up their rooms to make their great-grandmother proud. Subconsciously, Stan had wanted an opportunity to speak privately to Mama Wolf before they returned home. Because he'd known, even before she stepped off the plane, that he'd end up baring his soul to her, as he'd done last night with Prissy.

Sure enough, Evangeline had taken one look into his eyes, cupped his face between her hands and gently clucked her tongue. "Something's troubling your soul, precious. What is it?"

So on the way home from the airport, Stan told her about the nightmares he'd been having, and the devastating toll they'd taken on his psyche and his marriage. Mama Wolf listened quietly and compassionately, interrupting once or twice to ask for clarification, sometimes patting his cheek consolingly or reaching into the backseat to squeeze Prissy's hand when Stan grimly described the fiasco with Dr. Gilliard.

When they arrived home, Mama Wolf received nothing short of a hero's welcome from her great-grandsons, who erupted from the house and had her surrounded before she'd even stepped one foot out of the truck. Michael and Marcus, who saw her more frequently—especially since the divorce— greeted her just as ecstatically as the others. Stan and Prissy could only laugh and shake their heads as the boys ushered their beaming great-grandmother into the house, chattering excitedly at her the whole time.

After Mama Wolf generously doled out gifts—she always brought them gifts—and visited with them for a while, she told them that she needed to have grownup time with Stan and Prissy. After the boys dutifully made themselves scarce, Evangeline summoned the adults into the living room, where she awaited them on the silk-upholstered armchair with a small box resting on her lap.

As Stan and Prissy sat together on the sofa and joined hands, he had a pleasant flashback to the premarital counseling sessions Mama Wolf had given them, which had always been filled with an abundance of warm laughter.

"Precious heart," Evangeline addressed Stan now, "thank you for telling me what you've been going through these past several months. I wish you'd confided in me when the nightmares first began so we could have had this talk much sooner, but I know you and your brother have always needed to work things out in your own time."

Stan nodded, pushing out a long, deep breath. "Believe me, Mama, I regret keeping this bottled up inside me for so long, but

I honestly didn't want to worry any of you, especially Prissy and the kids."

When his wife gently squeezed his fingers, he paused and brought her hand to his mouth, tenderly kissing her knuckles as he gazed into her misty eyes. "I've been so terrified that these nightmares were a bad omen about the future. I just couldn't bear the thought of not being in your lives anymore." He looked at his grandmother. "*All* of you."

Evangeline's expression gentled with compassion. "I truly wish I had a simple explanation for you, baby. Only God knows why some folks are more susceptible to having dreams than others. How is it that two people can experience the same traumatic event, but only one ends up suffering from posttraumatic stress disorder? No one knows the answer to that question. But what I *will* tell you is that those nightmares are *not* prophetic, so you can just lay those fears to rest right now."

Easier said than done, Stan thought grimly.

As if she'd read his mind, Evangeline said, "I know that the dreams are terrifying, and they seem so realistic that it's easy to believe you're witnessing the future. But I don't believe it works that way, Stanton." She paused, pursing her lips for a moment. "You say that the nightmares began about five months ago. I think we can all make the connection to Manning's birthday."

Stan and Prissy nodded, staring at each other. "We talked about that last night," Prissy said quietly.

Evangeline nodded. "The nightmares were likely triggered by your son turning fourteen, which is the same age Stanton was when his beloved parents died."

"That's right," Stan murmured, wondering why he and Dr. Gilliard had never explored this line of reasoning, which now seemed so obvious to him. "Ever since Manny turned fourteen, I've been subconsciously fearing that history will repeat itself. I know it seems irrational...."

"Not for someone who's suffering from PTSD," Prissy gently interjected. "I'm no psychologist, but I'm sure we can all agree that when it comes to trigger mechanisms, we can pretty much throw out our definitions of rational versus irrational."

"That's very true," Evangeline concurred. "And speaking of trigger mechanisms, Stanton, that reminds me of something else I've been thinking. The frequency of your nightmares, and where you are when you have them. Do you remember whether you were at home or at the fire station the first time you had one of the dreams?"

Stan didn't have to think long. "I was at the firehouse," he said grimly. "I remember, because I woke up my crew when I called out in my sleep."

"Had you had an eventful night?" Evangeline probed.

"Not that particular shift," Stan answered. "But some other nights when we'd put down fires or responded to other stressful emergencies, I'd have nightmares afterward." He frowned, beginning to understand where this line of questioning was headed. "Are you suggesting that my job is not only physically dangerous, but it's also hazardous to my psyche?"

When Evangeline and Prissy shared an uneasy glance, his frown deepened.

"When was the last time you had one of the nightmares at home?" Evangeline gently prodded.

"About three weeks ago." Struck by a sudden realization, Stan stared at Prissy. "When you were out of town."

She squeezed his hand, then looked askance at Evangeline, who nodded as if she'd just had her theory confirmed.

"I believe that home is your safe haven, Stanton," she stated. "It's where you feel most at peace. And you have more control over your home environment than your work environment. You can't predict when and where a fire is going to take place, but you've established a comfortable routine at home. So you know when you're going to have dinner together as a family, you know when you'll be needed to help the kids with their homework, and you know when it's time for you to relax and unwind with Prissy. Anything that upsets that balance—"

"Like me going out of town," Prissy interjected, playfully bumping Stan's shoulder.

Evangeline chuckled. "Exactly. Your absence from his safe haven throws him off."

Stan grinned at Prissy. "Didn't I tell you that you can't go on any more business trips, woman?"

"Um, I'll have to get back to you on that."

Everyone laughed.

Sobering after several moments, Evangeline asked Stan, "How often do you have the nightmares at home?"

"Not often," he admitted. Come to think of it, he could probably count on one hand the number of times he'd actually awakened from a nightmare under his own roof.

"But you slept on the sofa just to be sure," Prissy surmised.

"Yeah," he said grimly. "The nightmares are so damn unpredictable. I didn't want to take any chances."

"And now you know that was the wrong solution," Evangeline gently admonished. "When a husband and wife begin sleeping apart, you open the door to temptation. Satan was using that woman—Dr. Gilliard—to prey on your vulnerable state of mind in order to lure you away from your wife. If you'd been a different type of man, Stanton, we might have been having an entirely different conversation right now."

When Stan and Prissy scowled at the reminder of his therapist's thwarted seduction attempt, Evangeline laughed and shook her head. "Oh, to have been a fly on the wall when my Prissy burst into that room. I know what you saw must have been a terrible shock to you, baby, but you handled yourself admirably. May all my great-grandsons be fortunate enough to find such strong, feisty women who know how to stay and fight for their men instead of assuming the worst."

"Amen," Stan agreed, smiling affectionately at his firecracker of a wife.

Evangeline watched them with a quiet smile of satisfaction. After Celeste's devastating defection from the family, her heart couldn't have handled losing another beloved granddaughter, or watching any more of her babies suffer.

She sighed, the sound drawing the young couple's gaze back to her. She smiled at them. "So now that we've analyzed the nightmares—or at least *attempted* to—I'd like to share the contents of this box that I brought from home."

Stan chuckled softly. "I've been wondering what's inside that box on your lap."

"Me, too," Prissy admitted.

Evangeline's smile deepened. "Well, for the past year, I've been working on a book that chronicles the life and military service of your ancestor Bishop Wolf, who, as you both know, proudly served our country as a Buffalo Soldier in the Tenth Cavalry."

Stan and Prissy stared at her in surprise. "You're writing a book, Mama Wolf?" they exclaimed.

"I am."

"That's *wonderful!*"

"Yes, it is." Evangeline's dark eyes glowed with pride. "I couldn't have been more thrilled when Montana called to tell me that he was writing a book report on Bishop Wolf. I told him about my own project and swore him to secrecy because I wanted to surprise all of you once the book is published next fall. But in light of everything you've shared with me today, I now understand why the Lord led me to bring these letters on my trip this week."

Stan and Prissy eyed her curiously. "What letters?"

"Letters from Bishop Wolf to his wife, Sadie." Evangeline opened the small box on her lap and carefully removed a stack of envelopes that were yellowed with age and bundled with frayed ribbons. She smiled tenderly at Stan. "I think it's time for me to share these with you."

Stan swallowed hard, then sat forward and reverently accepted the stack of letters from his grandmother. When he looked down at the bold, masculine handwriting scrawled across the stamped envelope on top of the pile, he was almost afraid to handle the fragile bundle a second longer.

He and Prissy exchanged awestruck looks, then stared at Evangeline. "Shouldn't these letters be preserved in a museum somewhere?" Stan asked wonderingly.

Evangeline smiled. "They will be soon enough. During Black History Month in February, the Georgia Historical Society in Savannah will be featuring Lieutenant Bishop Wolf and the Tenth Cavalry in an exhibit on Buffalo Soldiers. After that, a selection of Bishop's letters and other artifacts will be permanently on display at the Georgia Museum of Natural History."

"Wow," Stan whispered, thoroughly awed and humbled to be holding such an important piece of his family's history. His legacy. A key to the past.

"As I've explained to all of you over the years, Bishop Wolf was an educated man who'd gained his freedom long before he enlisted in the army. So he already knew how to read and write. And he wrote exceptionally well, as you will see for yourself."

Evangeline paused. "But what I never shared with you is that he was tormented by nightmares of dying on the battlefield."

Stunned, Stan stared at her. "Really?"

Evangeline nodded. "He was convinced that he wouldn't make it back home to his family. Which is understandable, since many of his fellow troopers *didn't* return home. As the nightmares increased over time, he became more and more consumed with the growing certainty that he was going to lose his life in battle."

Stan frowned. "But...he didn't."

"That's right. He didn't." Evangeline smiled, her eyes gleaming with the preternatural wisdom of an ancient sage— though, of course, she was anything *but* ancient. "Despite the terrible nightmares that plagued him as a soldier, Bishop Wolf lived to the ripe old age of ninety-three and fathered seven children."

Just then a shiver passed through Stan, as if he'd briefly encountered a spirit from beyond the grave.

Evangeline quietly observed his reaction. "Like you, Bishop was a lieutenant. A leader of men. And like you with firefighting, he knew the risks involved when he enlisted in the army, but that didn't stop him from wanting to serve. And though he was tormented by visions of his own death, he fought bravely and heroically in every battle."

Stan swallowed tightly as he stared down at the stack of letters in his hands, unable to dismiss the uncanny parallels between himself and his distant forefather.

"I can't tell you when your nightmares are going to end, precious heart," Evangeline continued with tender solemnity. "But I believe that reading your ancestor's letters will bring you some peace and comfort, and show you that sometimes history repeating itself can be a blessing in disguise."

***

Over the next two hours, Stan and Prissy sequestered themselves in their room, cuddled in bed and read Bishop Wolf's letters together.

Although his black regiment had fought in a surprising number of battles—including the famous 1898 battle on San

Juan Heights, Cuba, for which he'd earned the Medal of Honor—Bishop Wolf didn't dwell on the fury and bloodshed of warfare, nor did he share many details of the nightmares that plagued him.

But when he *did* speak of dying on the battlefield, Stan felt his fear and despair as acutely as if they were his own. Because he could relate all too well.

As he read his ancestor's letters aloud, it was like being transported back in time. The prose was so aesthetically powerful that Stan could almost smell the smoke rising from the soldiers' campfire, could almost taste the cold hash and beans they'd consumed for dinner.

Curled against Stan with her head resting on his chest, Prissy listened raptly as he read from one of Bishop's early letters to his wife, Sadie.

On tomorrow we continue advancing to the West. We have been making slow progress because many of the horses we were given are sickly and crippled. Negro regiments are not deemed worthy enough to receive the finest mounts. But the troopers are learning to take good care of the horses, some even better than they care for themselves. And speaking of my men, you may be amused to know that they have taken to calling themselves the Wolf Pack—

Stan paused to share a delighted grin with Prissy.

"So the nickname goes back even *that* far," she marveled.

"Long live the Wolf Pack," Stan proudly declared before he continued reading, picking up right where he'd left off.

—and the younger ones like to howl at the moon until they have to be hushed. You see, when long stretches of time pass with no other signs of civilization, some of the men tend to let their guard down, which none of us can afford to do. Because the Indians are stealth as wraiths, and they have been known to lie in wait to ambush an unsuspecting cavalry.

My dearest Sadie, I would never wish to burden your serene spirit with dire predictions of my own demise, but as we march deeper into enemy territory, I feel it is my solemn duty as your husband to share with you a matter that has weighed heavy on my heart and soul. For nearly a year now, I have been besieged by the most horrific dreams of my death, the details of which I will spare you. As it is I fear that I have already written too much, and if these revelations should cause you even a moment's pain and suffering, please know that this was the very outcome I most wished to avoid.

Whenever I awaken from these night terrors, I immediately reach for your photograph and hold it up to the moonlight. I stare at your beautiful image, and I long for the day that we will be reunited.

If I should fall at the hands of the enemy, I will remain forever grateful for the time we had together. In a world that has been more cruel than kind to our people, you have always been my refuge. Thank you for the precious gift of your love. And thank you for raising our beloved young sons to walk tall and proud, and to hold their heads high as free men should.

Until we meet again I am,

Eternally yours,
Lt. Bishop M. Wolf
10th Cavalry Reg.

By the time Stan finished reading the letter, his vision was blurred by tears. Meeting Prissy's luminous gaze, he saw that she, too, had been deeply affected by his ancestor's poignantly moving words.

"Oh, Stanton," she whispered as he carefully returned the letter to the envelope. "That was one of the most beautiful things I've ever heard."

Stan nodded in agreement and swallowed hard, then swallowed again when the knot in his throat wouldn't dissolve.

Prissy smiled softly through her tears. "Sometimes I forgot that the letters weren't addressed to me. He called Sadie his 'refuge.' You called me the same thing during your acceptance speech at the fireman's ball. Do you remember?"

Stan nodded. "It's true," he murmured, gently brushing her hair off her forehead. "You *are* my refuge."

"Oh, baby." Prissy gazed wonderingly at him. "I don't know what I'd ever do without you."

"I'm hoping you'll never have to find out," Stan told her
quietly.

Prissy searched his face intently. "Mama Wolf thought the
letters would make you feel better. Do you?"

Stan nodded. "I do. Since opening up to you yesterday, I've
felt like a huge weight has been lifted from my shoulders. And
then talking to Mama Wolf today and reading these incredible
letters with you..." He shook his head slowly. "Call me crazy, but
right now I'm feeling pretty damn lucky."

As Prissy's expression softened, she reached up and lovingly
cradled his cheek in her hand. "He would have been so proud of
you."

"Think so?"

"I *know* so."

Stan smiled quietly. "I'm proud to have descended from such
a great man. I look forward to reading Mama Wolf's book and
learning even more about him."

Prissy smiled. "Me, too."

Stan gently stroked her hair. "I love you, sweetheart."

"Don't ever stop," she whispered.

"I won't." He shook his head at her. "I couldn't even if I
tried."

As their lips met in a tender kiss, Stan remembered that
Mama Wolf had prayed over him and Prissy earlier, humbly
petitioning the Lord to heal Stan's troubled spirit and deliver
him from the traumatic nightmares.

Stan felt confident that God had been listening.

Chapter 28

"Well, little brother," Sterling Wolf mused, "looks like we've both been keeping secrets from each other."

Leaning against the balustrade that wrapped around the wide front porch, Stan ruefully regarded his brother. "Looks that way, doesn't it?"

Sterling nodded, rocking gently on the porch swing. "I never told you that Celeste and I were having problems, and *you* didn't tell me about the horrible nightmares you'd been having."

"I know." Stan sighed, suffering a fresh pang of guilt. "I didn't want you to worry about me."

"I know. And I *would* have worried," Sterling admitted matter of factly. "But I still wish you'd confided in me. That's what brothers are for."

Stan hung his head. "Damn, Sterl, I'm already in the doghouse with Prissy and Mama Wolf," he half joked. "You gonna put me there, too?"

Sterling chuckled, stretching out his long legs. "Since it's almost Thanksgiving, I'll cut you some slack."

"Thanks." Stan grinned, lazily swigging from a bottle of beer.

It was just after noon on Wednesday. After everyone enjoyed a hearty breakfast, Prissy's brother had taken his mother, wife, daughters and Mama Wolf to a local shopping center to pick up some items they needed for the ski trip. While the boys stampeded downstairs to the basement to entertain themselves, Prissy and Georgina Reddick had curled up on the living room sofa to play catch up. That left Stan and Sterling, who'd grabbed two frosted beers and headed outside to the porch to do some catching up of their own.

"This is a really beautiful neighborhood, Stan," Sterling remarked, surveying the quiet, picturesque street. He gestured to the house behind him. "Beautiful home, too."

"Thanks, Sterl." Stan paused a beat. "Coronado's a really nice community. Great parks and lakes. Great fire and police departments. Great schools. It's a wonderful place to raise kids, you know."

Sterling chuckled wryly. "Are you finished?"

Stan blinked innocently. "Finished what?"

"Your not-so-subtle sales pitch."

"I wasn't giving a sales—" Stan broke off, grinning at the knowing look his brother gave him. "Okay, maybe I *was* trying to sell you on moving here. But you have to admit it's not such a bad idea. The Wolf Pack would be together again."

Sterling chuckled softly, shaking his head. "You know I'm not leaving Atlanta. The boys and I have our whole lives there, and Michael will be graduating from high school in another year. And I'm a homicide detective. Don't seem like there's enough crime in Coronado to keep me busy."

Stan chuckled. "That's probably true."

"As for the other thing you said, the Wolf Pack will always be together right here"— Sterling patted his heart —"where it counts."

Stan nodded slowly. "I'll drink to that," he said, leaning over and clinking his bottle against Sterling's. Smiling at each other, they drank their beer.

After a few moments, Stan sighed. "But truth be told, as much as we're really starting to enjoy Coronado, Prissy and I have already decided that we'll be moving back to Atlanta in another five years or so."

"Really?" Sterling raised a surprised brow. "What prompted *that* decision?"

Stan shrugged a shoulder. "We miss being near family. Miss being there to watch Michael, Marcus and Prissy's nieces grow up. Prissy misses bonding with her mom and Theo. And hell, Sterl, I guess I miss seeing *your* ugly mug every day."

Sterling grinned teasingly. "Considering that folks often mistake us for twins, if *I'm* ugly, what does that make you?"

"Damn," Stan muttered. "Walked right into that one."

The two brothers laughed.

Sobering after a few moments, Stan said quietly, "At the end of the day, there's no place like home."

Sterling's expression softened, and he nodded. "Can't argue with that."

Stan smiled. Turning his face toward the gray winter sky, he inhaled a deep lungful of cold air and let it out slowly, watching as his warm breath gusted a silvery plume.

"Supposed to start snowing tonight," he idly announced.

"I heard. Think we should head out earlier for the cabin?"

"Nah. The resort's only an hour away. We'll be fine."

"I don't know," Sterling muttered dubiously. "Don't wanna get stranded in no damn mountains."

Stan grinned. "We're not gonna get stranded, Sterl. Stop being such a city slicker."

Sterling took umbrage. "Who you calling a city slicker? Need I remind you that *I'm* the one who organizes our camping and fishing trips every year?"

"Yeah, yeah, yeah," Stan teased, walking over and joining his brother on the swing. "Everyone knows you're the great outdoorsman."

Sterling grinned broadly. "Damn straight."

A companionable silence lapsed between them as they sipped their beers, their long legs gently pushing the swing back and forth.

"Thank you," Sterling said quietly.

Stan shot him a puzzled look. "For what?"

"For buying the plane tickets for Michael and Marcus."

"Aw, come on, Sterl," Stan muttered, waving off his brother's gratitude. "Cut that out."

Sterling ignored him. "You know my money's been extra tight lately, so I really appreciate the way you and Prissy came through for my boys."

"It was Prissy's idea, and you know you can't say no to that woman."

A quiet, knowing smile touched Sterling's mouth. "Well, *whoever's* idea it was, it was a godsend. I haven't seen Michael and Marcus this happy since..." He trailed off, unable to finish.

But he didn't have to. Stan knew what had been left unsaid.

A heavy silence descended between the two men.

After several moments, Stan took a swig of his beer and wiped his mouth with the back of his hand. "Anyway," he said gruffly, "having Michael and Marcus here this week was like an early Christmas present to my boys. You should have seen the way Manny lit up when Mike surprised him. The boy got so damn choked up he had his poor mama in tears."

Sterling gave Stan an amused sidelong glance. "And what about you?"

Stan grinned sheepishly. "I'm embarrassed to admit that I got a bit misty-eyed, too."

Sterling laughed, shaking his head at Stan. "You always were a big ol' softie beneath the tough guy exterior."

"I don't know what you're talking about," Stan grumbled, shifting uncomfortably on the swing. "And if I *am* getting soft in my old age, it's Prissy's damn fault."

"Uh-huh. I'll be sure to tell her you said that."

"Go ahead. She knows it's true."

"Well, I don't know about all that. What I *do* know," Sterling drawled, dark eyes twinkling with amusement, "is that your wife's got you wrapped around her pretty little finger."

Stan smiled softly, not even bothering to deny it.

"Which is as it should be," Sterling added almost to himself.

Stan's smile faded as a wave of guilt swept through him. It didn't seem right for him to be so deliriously contented and in love with his wife when his brother was still reeling from the painful destruction of his own marriage. Next to their late father, Sterling Wolf was the kindest, most honorable man Stan had ever known. If anyone deserved to be happy, it was Sterling.

Stan clenched his jaw, his gut tightening with the familiar anger and resentment he'd been harboring—rightfully so— toward Celeste. Striving to maintain his composure, he asked evenly, "When was the last time you spoke to her?"

Sterling didn't have to ask whom he was referring to. As pain tightened his features, Stan regretted bringing Celeste up, though the specter of her treachery had been looming over them all since the divorce.

"I spoke to her on Sunday," Sterling answered in a low voice. "She called to tell me that she's in Minnesota with Grant, who's working on some research project for the Mayo Clinic."

Stan's jaw hardened, but he said nothing.

Sterling's keen gaze searched his face. "You already knew, didn't you?"

Stan hesitated, then nodded reluctantly. "She called Prissy a few weeks ago. She wanted them to have dinner together while Prissy was in Rochester for her leadership conference."

"Did they get together?"

"Yeah." Stan grimaced. "I'm sorry, Sterl. I really wanted to tell you, but Prissy promised to let Celeste tell you herself when she was ready."

Sterling nodded slowly. "Prissy did the right thing. It was better coming from Celeste. It was still painful and shocking to hear, but...well, she's the mother of my children, and nothing will ever change that. So we have to keep the lines of communication open between us, no matter how difficult it may be."

Stan nodded, conceding the truth of his brother's words. "Did you work out an arrangement with her?"

"Yeah. She's going to fly home every other weekend—on Grant's dime—and stay at his penthouse so she can spend time with Michael and Marcus. My only stipulation was that she not take the boys over there under any circumstances. They've been traumatized enough, and God only knows what Marcus would do if he ever stepped foot inside his mother's love nest."

"Probably the same thing *I'd* do," Stan muttered darkly. "Set that motherfucker on fire."

Sterling choked out a laugh, shooting him a reproachful look. "Now what kind of talk is that coming from Coronado's Firefighter of the Year?"

Stan shook his head grimly. One word from his brother, and he'd have gladly wiped Grant Rutherford off the face of the earth.

"You're a better man than me, Sterl. That's all I have to say."

"Yeah?" A small, humorless smile twisted Sterling's mouth. "You think I haven't fantasized about retaliating against Grant for taking my wife and hurting my boys? You think I've never found myself parked outside his apartment building—my Glock in one hand, my badge in the other—wrestling with the temptation to bust down his fucking door and pump him full of lead? I'm a cop, so you know there are a number of other ways I could do him real dirty. But what good would any of that do? And if I wind up in the state penitentiary, where would that leave Michael and Marcus? Abandoned by their mother *and* father, that's where. Then what would become of them? What kind of future would they have?"

Sterling shook his head, looking grim and resolute. "Sometimes being a man means swallowing your pride and walking away from the fight you lost long before you ever entered the ring. Grant Rutherford didn't force himself on Celeste. She'd been unhappy with me for years, and she wanted something else. She made her choice, so I have to respect that and find a way to move on."

When he'd finished speaking, Stan could only stare at him. He didn't know whether to applaud Sterling for the dark, violent urges he'd confessed to having, or haul him roughly into his arms and assure him that everything would be okay. Either way, he'd never been prouder of his brother than he was at that moment—and that was saying a lot considering how much he'd always looked up to Sterl.

Observing his awestruck expression, Sterling chuckled and warned gruffly, "Now don't you go getting all sentimental on me, boy."

"As if," Stan mumbled as he glanced away and swallowed hard, trying to clear the lump of emotion that was clogging his throat.

"Well," Sterling drawled after a minute, lazily pushing to his feet. "Guess we'd better get to that poker game we promised the boys. Besides, my fingers and toes are starting to grow numb. It's cold as hell out here."

Stan grinned at him. "Wuss."

Sterling jabbed one of those numb fingers at him. "Just for that, I'm gonna take great pleasure in totally annihilating you at poker."

Stan laughed. "What else is new?"

When the two brothers reentered the house, Prissy and Georgina were curled up on the living room sofa while a cozy fire crackled in the hearth. They were holding mugs of hot chocolate and pealing with hysterical laughter.

"Uh-oh," Stan intoned, trading amused glances with his brother. "Why do I feel like we just stepped into a sorority house?"

Sterling grinned, hanging up their coats in the mud room. "Well, considering that Prissy is a Delta and Georgie is an AKA, your observation isn't *too* far off the mark."

Overhearing their exchange, Prissy and Georgina wiped tears of mirth from their eyes and sighed.

"Don't mind us," Prissy told the approaching men. "We were just enjoying an old private joke."

"Sounds intriguing," Stan drawled. "Care to share?"

"No," the two women blurted, then looked at each other and dissolved into fresh giggles that had Stan and Sterling shaking their heads and chuckling.

"Women and their secrets."

"Yup. What can you do?"

Prissy smiled at her darkly handsome husband and brother-in-law, and felt a renewed appreciation for the wondrous gift of black manhood.

"I hope you fellas are heading downstairs to play poker with the boys," she said.

"Yes, ma'am," they confirmed.

"Good, because Magnum wandered up here not too long ago, wanting to know when you two would be ready. I told him not to disturb your bonding session, but he's really eager to get the game under way." Her smile turned teasing. "Seems he's feeling his oats after beating his daddy—"

"*What?*" Sterling exclaimed, staring at Stan. "You let that boy beat you at poker?"

Stan scowled. "I had a lot on my mind that day."

Sterling guffawed, giving him a look of grave disappointment. "After everything I've taught you, you got beat by an upstart who's gonna boast and brag till the cows come home. Just for that, I'm *really* gonna have to show you no mercy today."

"You hear that?" Stan complained to Prissy. "See how he treats me, baby?"

Prissy laughed, shaking her head. "Please go easy on him, Sterl, or he won't be much company over the next few days. You know how he sulks."

Sterling's bark of laughter drowned out Stan's exclamations of protest.

Affectionately tweaking Prissy's nose, Sterling promised, "Just for you I'll show him some mercy."

She smiled sweetly. "Thank you, Sterl."

"Don't thank him too soon," Stan grumbled. "He's been known to pull a bait and switch, 'cause once he's seated at that poker table, he becomes a different person. Think Jekyll and Hyde."

As everyone laughed, Stan crouched down behind the sofa to smile into Prissy's eyes. "I need a good luck kiss."

She smiled. "Is that so?"

"Umm-hmm."

Prissy kissed the tip of his cold nose, then his soft mouth. "There. I gave you two. How's that?"

"Wonderful."

"Good. Now go and conquer."

He grinned. "Aye, milady."

As he got to his feet, Georgina smiled at Sterling. "I'd wish *you* good luck, but everyone knows you don't need it."

He winked at her, then gently squeezed her shoulder as he and Stan headed from the room.

Something about the brief yet intimate gesture had Prissy's eyes narrowing in speculation. Her radar went on full alert as she watched Georgina's gaze follow Sterling out of the room.

When he was gone, Georgina smiled privately and lowered her head to sip from her mug of hot chocolate.

Prissy stared at her. "What was *that*?"

Georgina met her gaze. "What?"

"That little smile. And the shoulder squeeze from Sterling. And the way you watched him leave the room just now..." Prissy trailed off, watching as Georgina blushed furiously. "Oh, my God," she breathed with dawning comprehension. "Did something happen between you and *Sterling*?"

As the other woman dropped her gaze to her cup, Prissy gasped in shock. "*Georgie!*"

"Shhh!" Georgina darted a nervous glance beyond the foyer to the closed basement door. "I don't want anyone to hear what we're talking about, especially Quentin."

Prissy waved a dismissive hand. "Girl, please. They're not gonna hear a thing with all that noise they're making down there. And the way they blast that television, it's a miracle none of them have gone deaf." Prissy scooped up both of their mugs and set them down on the small table beside her, then turned back to her longtime friend. "Now tell me what happened between you and Sterling."

Georgina blew out a deep breath and dazedly shook her head. With her smooth honey complexion, patrician features and long curly hair, she was a dead ringer for Lonette McKee, that pretty young actress from the movie *Sparkle*.

"I don't even know where to start," Georgina confessed in a husky voice. "I still can't believe what we did."

"What did you do?" Prissy whispered.

Georgina met her wide-eyed gaze, then sighed. "Let me start from the beginning. I sent Quentin to spend this past weekend with his daddy's family since he won't be there for Thanksgiving. They were *not* too happy about that, I might add. His aunts and grandmother gave me a real tongue-lashing for taking Quentin away for Thanksgiving, even though when Fraser was alive, we spent every holiday with his family. You know, since my parents cut me off years ago."

Prissy nodded sympathetically. "I remember."

Georgina hailed from a proud old Southern family of doctors and lawyers who'd expected her to marry someone of the same social standing. But when she met and fell in love with a cocky amateur boxer who didn't have a penny to his name, her family was appalled. When Georgina defied their wishes and married Fraser Reddick, her parents had disinherited and disowned her. Since then, nothing—not Quentin's birth or the tragic death of his father—had mended the rift between Georgina and her relatives. Prissy thought it would be poetic justice if Quentin— who was overprotective of Georgina—grew up to become a successful doctor or lawyer who'd reject his mother's family if they ever sought to make amends with him.

"Anyway," Georgina continued, "I know how much Fraser's kinfolk love to dote on Quentin. He looks and acts so much like his daddy that sometimes it feels like Fraser never left us. But the Reddicks shouldn't make me feel guilty for choosing to spend the holidays somewhere else for a change. And it wasn't just my choice. When I told Junebug that you'd invited us to accompany Sterling and the boys here for Thanksgiving, he was *so* excited. And that was even before I told him about the ski trip."

Prissy smiled softly. "You know you and Quentin have always been like family. We're so glad you both came."

"Me, too." Georgina sighed heavily. "And the timing couldn't have been better. I needed to get away from Atlanta for a few days. This past Sunday was Fraser's birthday. He would have been thirty-five."

"Oh, Georgie." Prissy reached over, gently grasping her friend's hands in hers. "I'm so sorry. I forgot to call—"

"Oh, girl, don't worry about it," Georgina said dismissively. "You can't be expected to remember every date. You always send a beautiful card on our wedding anniversary and the anniversary of his passing. And remember how you and Celeste would come over and drag me out of bed, take me out to lunch and treat me to a massage?"

A soft, reminiscent smile curved Prissy's lips. "I remember."

She remembered, too, how shocked and devastated everyone had been when Fraser—a police officer—was killed in the line of duty three years ago. She remembered going home the night of his funeral, getting down on her knees and thanking God that it wasn't *her* husband who'd been put into the ground that day. And she remembered Celeste's guilty confession to her that she'd gone home and whispered the same prayer.

Georgina continued quietly, "Quentin called me from his aunt's house on Sunday evening. They'd just finished cutting the birthday cake in Fraser's memory, and Quentin wanted to call and make sure I was okay. I assured him that I was, we chatted for a few minutes, and then I hung up the phone and cried myself to sleep. When I woke up, Sterling was at the front door. He'd stopped by on his way home from work to check up on me. But the moment I saw him, I could tell something was wrong. But he wouldn't tell me at first. He was more concerned about me."

"Typical Sterling," Prissy murmured fondly.

"Yes." Georgina smiled softly. "Always putting others above himself. We sat and talked for a while, and he told me that the fellas at the station had commemorated Fraser's birthday with some special ritual that involved gathering around a circle and toasting one another with Fraser's favorite brand of beer." She laughed ruefully. "I know I'm not explaining it right, but it was very touching."

Prissy smiled gently. "I'm sure it was."

Georgina gazed down at their joined hands. "I was moved to tears, Prissy. After Sterling comforted me, I turned the tables on him and asked him what was wrong. I had to keep prodding until he finally opened up and shared the conversation he'd had with Celeste that afternoon."

Prissy held her breath, wondering if Celeste had changed her mind and told Sterling about her miscarriage.

Georgina's somber gaze returned to hers. "She told him that she and Grant would be spending the next three months in Minnesota, and if Grant changed his mind about accepting the surgeon position at the Mayo Clinic, she planned to relocate with him." Georgina shook her head slowly. "Sterling was *so* hurt and devastated, Pris. He admitted to me that *that* was the moment he realized that his marriage was truly over. Before then, even despite their divorce being finalized, he'd been secretly hoping that there was still a chance for them to work things out. But Celeste's decision to move away with Grant dashed the last of his hopes. So it was *my* turn to console *him*." Georgina's expression softened. "One moment we were embracing, the next moment we were kissing desperately and undressing each other."

"Oh, my God." Prissy was stunned. "You and Sterling..."

"I know. I never would have imagined something like that happening between us. But it did. Oh, Prissy, he was *so* passionate. So tender and giving. Lord have mercy, I'm getting flushed just *thinking* about what an amazing lover he was." Georgina sighed, laying a hand over her heart as tears shimmered in her eyes. "He's the first man I've slept with since...."

"Since Fraser died," Prissy finished softly.

Georgina nodded. "It wasn't screwing, like we were just using each other to exorcise demons. We made *love*, Pris, and afterward we held each other tight and let our tears fall together."

As moisture filled her own eyes, Prissy gently squeezed Georgina's hands. "It sounds incredible."

"It was. We were two lonely, hurting souls who turned to each other in our time of need, and we shared a poignantly beautiful experience that I will never, *ever* forget."

"Oh, Georgie." Prissy's voice softened as she searched her friend's face. "Are you in love with Sterling?"

Georgina choked out a soft, teary laugh and shook her head. "You know Fraser is the only man I will ever love. But let me tell you. Sterling Wolf could steal *any* woman's heart, and if I'd met him before Fraser, I never would have wanted for anyone else. Men like Sterling—and your Stanton—represent what every man should be. Strong, dependable, unselfish, fiercely protective and loyal. True gentlemen through and through. Every woman should be lucky enough to have a husband like Sterling."

"One did," Prissy murmured sadly, "and she walked out on him."

Georgina shook her head. "I hate to say this about someone we both consider a dear friend, but Celeste is out of her fucking mind."

This startled a laugh out of Prissy. "*Georgina Reddick!* Since when do you use that kind of language?"

Georgina grinned unabashedly. "Sometimes profanity conveys what mere words cannot. I know Celeste had her reasons for doing what she did, but I truly believe she loves Sterling, and someday she's going to regret her decision to leave him and those precious boys."

"I know," Prissy murmured, swallowing a lump of sorrow at the thought of Celeste's lost baby. "I told her the same thing."

"Unfortunately for her, by the time she realizes her mistake, it may be too late."

"You think Sterling is going to remarry?"

"Oh, definitely. Some smart, lucky woman is gonna snatch up that Wolf."

Prissy smiled quietly. She hoped her friend was right. Sterling had so much love to give. He deserved to find someone who would appreciate all he had to offer.

She slanted Georgina a sidelong glance. "What about you? Do you think *you'll* ever remarry?"

Before Georgina could respond, the basement door burst open, and out ran Quentin and Montana.

As they laughingly raced toward the kitchen, Georgina called out, "Quentin Fraser Reddick! What have I told you about running in the house?"

"Both of you should know better," Prissy added admonishingly.

"Sorry, Ma, but Dad told us to hurry up with getting more snacks!"

As Montana continued to the kitchen, Quentin reversed direction and sauntered over to the living room. His golden skin was flushed from his sprint up the stairs, and his hazel eyes were bright with irrepressible laughter.

He was such a handsome boy, Prissy mused fondly. He and Michael had been best friends practically from birth, vigorously kicking inside their mother's wombs every time Celeste and Georgina were together. They'd been born three weeks apart and had been inseparable ever since.

Reaching the sofa, Quentin leaned down and kissed Georgina's forehead. "Hey, Ma."

"Hey, Junebug." She smiled, affectionately cupping his cheek. "Who's winning the game?"

He groaned. "You know who. Uncle Sterling."

Georgina and Prissy laughed.

"Uncle Stan's doing pretty good, too," Quentin informed Prissy.

"Whew," she said, making an exaggerated show of wiping her forehead. "*That's* a relief."

Quentin grinned at her.

"We're leaving for the cabin after dinner," Georgina reminded her son, "so make sure you have all your things together."

"Yes, ma'am."

"Q," Montana called from the kitchen, "I need your help carrying all the snacks!"

"Chill, dude. I'm coming." Quentin smiled at his mother and Prissy. "Gotta go."

And then he was off again, calling over his shoulder, "Thanks for inviting us this week, Aunt Prissy. This is the coolest vacation ever!"

Prissy and Georgina laughed, watching as he and Monty headed back downstairs with armfuls of sodas and bags of chips.

Alone once again, Prissy grinned conspiratorially at Georgina. "I just have one question. Are you and Sterling gonna be sneaking into each other's rooms for some hanky panky late at night?"

Georgina chuckled, her cheeks flushing as she shook her head. "Considering that I'm rooming with Mama Wolf, sneaking around might be a bit of a challenge. Not that we'd even try something like that." She sighed, a bit wistfully. "What Sterling and I shared was truly special, but we don't intend to start sleeping together. Sterling still loves Celeste, and I'm still mourning Fraser. So this isn't the right time for us to become involved."

Prissy gently searched Georgina's face. "So that night...was a one-time thing?"

Georgina hesitated, then nodded. "Yes."

"Are you sure?" Prissy prodded, suddenly feeling naughty. "Because the ski lodge we're staying at is supposed to be *very* romantic. And since the resort offers so many fun activities in addition to skiing, the kids won't always be around. And my mother and Mama Wolf have already planned their itinerary, which mostly consists of hitting the local town to spend hours browsing the little shops, stocking up on souvenirs and sightseeing. So that leaves...well, the three couples. By the time we're done enjoying the great outdoors, relaxing in the spa, cuddling around a fire, sipping hot toddies..." Prissy trailed off with a dramatic sigh. "No one would blame you and Sterling for succumbing to the romantic ambiance."

Georgina glowered at her. "That is *not* fair. I thought you were my friend."

Prissy laughed. "I am. Which is why I consider it my duty to warn you what you'll be up against."

"Thanks," Georgina said dryly. "I'll consider myself forewarned."

"Good." Prissy bit her lip, then couldn't resist prodding teasingly, "So no more hanky panky, Georgie?"

"No more." Georgina paused, her eyes glimmering with sudden mischief. "Well...I guess I won't completely rule out anything until we get there."

At that, the two women burst out laughing.

Chapter 29

After Uncle Sterling demolished everyone at poker, the boys headed outside to take out their frustration on the football field, which doubled as the front yard. Manning had just caught Marcus's deep spiral when he saw Taylor riding toward the house on her brother's old bicycle.

He froze, so shocked to see her that he didn't notice Magnum bearing down on him until it was too late.

"*Oof!*" he grunted as Magnum plowed into him, knocking him to the ground hard enough to make his teeth snap together and remind him why his brother's football teammates had nicknamed him "Bruiser." Manning had four years, thirty pounds and six inches on his younger brother, so at any given time he could beat the shit out of Magnum without breaking a sweat. But on the football field—which was Magnum's turf—the kid was a force to be reckoned with. So was Mason, for that matter.

Manning groaned hoarsely, clutching the ball to his chest.

"You okay, Manny?" Magnum asked worriedly. "I didn't mean to tackle you so hard. Well, okay, maybe I did. But I wasn't trying to hurt you, I swear. How come you were just standing there?"

Slowly opening his eyes, Manning saw seven—or was it eight?—concerned faces peering down at him.

"You okay, Manny?" Michael asked, waving a hand in front of his eyes.

"Man, you got *hammered*," Mason observed sympathetically.

"Shut up, Mason," Marcus snapped.

"Well, he did!"

"Nice going, Bruiser," Monty grumbled to Magnum. "If Manny has a concussion, we won't be able to go on our trip. If that happens, Ma's gonna *kill* you."

"She'll have to get in line behind me," Quentin retorted.

"And me," Maddox added.

Suddenly Taylor was shoving her way through the crowd to kneel down beside Manning. "Are you okay?" she asked, peering anxiously into his face.

He smiled dreamily. "Taylor?"

She nodded quickly. "I'm so sorry. It's all my fault. I didn't mean to distract you."

"It's okay." His eyes slowly roamed over her face, cataloguing her windswept dark hair and small, rimless eyeglasses. "Hey. You have new glasses."

She smiled shyly. "Yeah. I got them yesterday."

"I like them. They're nice."

A pretty flush stole across her cheeks. "Thank you, Manning."

"You're welcome."

She reached down and gently removed a clump of grass from his hair.

He smiled at her. "Thank you."

She smiled back. "You're welcome."

"Aw, he's okay," the younger ones muttered, sounding both relieved and disgusted as they moved back.

Taylor helped Manning sit up. As Michael pulled him to his feet, Quentin slung an arm around his neck and murmured in his ear, "Yo, dawg, she's kinda cute. She got a sister?"

Manning snorted, shoving him away. "No, she doesn't."

"Then you'd better watch your back." Quentin winked.

Manning just shook his head and laughed, because everyone knew Quentin Reddick's cardinal rules when it came to girls. No leftovers. No poaching.

Manning tossed the ball to Magnum and winked at him. "No hard feelings."

His brother flashed a relieved grin, then scampered off to rejoin the others.

Manning turned to Taylor, so happy to see her that he could barely keep a goofy grin off his face. Swiping at his runny nose with his shirt sleeve, he asked her, "What're you doing here, shorty?"

She smiled. "Well, for starters, I came to wish you a Happy Thanksgiving."

"Thanks. Same to you. Are you staying in town?"

"No, I'm going to Washington, D.C. to spend Thanksgiving with my mother. We're leaving tonight."

"Hey, that's great, Taylor," Manning said warmly. He knew how much she missed her mom, who'd given her the necklace with the violin charm that she wore every day. "I know she'll be happy to see you and your little brother."

Taylor beamed. "I think so, too."

Now that he could see them better, Manning realized that her eyes were even prettier than he'd suspected. So was her face, for that matter. He also noticed that her shoulder-length hair had been cut into layers, and she'd replaced the camouflage army jacket with a fur-trimmed belted coat that she wore with dark jeans and flat brown suede boots.

"You look different," Manning remarked.

Taylor chuckled wryly. "I know. My aunt took me shopping and to the hair salon yesterday. She said my mom would think Dad was neglecting me if I showed up looking like a ragamuffin. I guess I didn't realize how bad my clothes might look to some people."

Manning just smiled, wisely deciding not to touch that with a twenty-foot pole.

Taylor gestured across the large front yard, where the others had resumed playing football without him. "I see you've got some relatives in town, although the light-skinned one doesn't look like any of you."

"Quentin? Yeah, he's not related. But he definitely belongs in the Wolf Pack." Manning smiled. "I'll introduce you to him and my cousins when they take a break. Come on. Let's go sit on the porch before we get hit with the ball or something."

Taylor giggled. "Good idea."

As they started across the lawn together, Manning said conversationally, "We're going on a ski trip for Thanksgiving. We're leaving tonight, too."

"Oh, that sounds wonderful, Manning," Taylor enthused. "How fun and exciting! Do you know how to ski?"

He laughed. "No. I'm from Atlanta, remember?"

She gave him an amused glance. "Meaning what? People from Atlanta can't learn how to ski?"

"I guess some do. Not anyone *I* know, though." He grinned. "Needless to say, we'll all be sticking to the beginner slopes."

Taylor chuckled as they climbed onto the porch and perched on the railing, their backs facing the front yard.

"I'm playing the violin again," Taylor announced.

Manning shot her a surprised look. "Really?"

"Yeah. For the past two weeks now." She smiled quietly. "I'd forgotten how much I enjoyed playing."

"That's awesome, Taylor," Manning said warmly. "I'm proud of you."

"Thank you, Manning. Will you come to my Christmas recital?"

"Of course. I wouldn't miss it for the world." Struck by a sudden thought, he frowned. "I guess Henry will be there, too, since he's probably the one who talked you into playing again, him being in the band and all."

"Actually," Taylor countered softly, "it was you."

"*Me?*"

She nodded. "Do you remember the night I came over and we did our math homework in your kitchen?"

"Of course I remember." That was the night they'd shared their first kiss, which he'd been reliving in his mind ever since.

"When I told you that I'd stopped playing the violin, you encouraged me to pick it back up again. You told me, and I quote, 'If you're good at it, and it's something you enjoy doing, you shouldn't give it up.' After that night, I couldn't stop thinking about what you'd said. So I went to my dad and told him I wanted to start playing the violin again, and he couldn't have been happier." Smiling softly, Taylor reached over and laid her small hand over Manning's. "Thank you."

Manning swallowed tightly, his insides melting. "You're welcome," he whispered.

As they gazed at each other, he turned his hand over and linked his fingers through hers.

A minute passed while he worked up the nerve to ask one burning question: "Are you still going out with Henry?"

Taylor hesitated, then shook her head. "No."

"No?"

"No."

A huge wave of relief swept through Manning. Trying to play it cool, he said casually, "So what happened?"

Taylor grimaced. "I broke up with him."

This just keeps getting better and better. "Why'd you do that?"

She shrugged, glancing away. "He was too...too..."

"Clingy?" Manning offered. "Possessive?"

She laughed ruefully. "Yes, to both. But he was really nice and thoughtful," she hastened to add. "And he played the clarinet well."

Manning nodded. "He just wasn't right for you."

Her eyes met his. "Exactly."

Manning couldn't keep from smiling.

"Come on," he said, taking her hand and standing up.

"Where are we going?"

"I want you to meet Mama Wolf."

He took her inside the house and led her toward the noisy kitchen.

His parents' good friends, Kelvin and Roxanne Wimbush, had stopped by to visit the family before they left for the cabin. Also present were the Campbells, an older couple who'd become like doting godparents to Manning and his brothers.

While all the men were downstairs watching basketball, the women had congregated in the kitchen and were laughing and chattering animatedly as they put the finishing touches on dinner.

When Manning and Taylor appeared in the doorway, a hushed silence swept over the kitchen. Mom beamed with pleasure as Manning went around the room and introduced Taylor to Grandma Kirkland, Aunt Winnie, Aunt Georgina, Mrs. Campbell, Mrs. Wimbush, and his twin cousins Maya and Zora—named after Maya Angelou and Zora Neale Hurston.

When he came to Mama Wolf, Taylor smiled shyly and stepped forward with her hand outstretched. "Hello, Mrs. Wolf."

"Hey, baby." Mama Wolf clasped both of Taylor's hands between hers and gave her one of those warm, welcoming smiles that always made people feel like she'd known them from birth. "You can call me Mama Wolf."

Taylor couldn't have looked more honored than if she'd just been granted permission to call the Queen of England by her first name. Manning half expected her to bow and curtsy to his great-grandmother.

Taylor said earnestly, "I had the pleasure of eating some of your pound cake, and it was the most delicious thing I've ever tasted. I told Manning I'd tell you that if I ever got the chance to meet you."

Mama Wolf beamed with delight. "Why, thank you so much, baby. I'm glad you enjoyed the cake." She winked at Manning. "I like her already."

Everyone laughed.

"Would you like to stay for dinner, Taylor?" Mama Wolf invited. "There's more than enough for everyone, and the Campbells and Wimbushes have agreed to join us as well."

Taylor smiled. "Thank you for the kind invitation, Mama Wolf, but I'm afraid I can't stay. I'm going out of town for Thanksgiving—"

"Are you going to visit your mother, baby?" Mom inquired hopefully.

"Yes, ma'am, and we're leaving tonight. So I just stopped by to see Manning—"

The women exchanged soft, knowing smiles that made Taylor blush.

"—and, of course, I wanted to wish the rest of the family a Happy Thanksgiving as well," she hastened to add.

"That was very sweet of you, Taylor," Mama Wolf said, giving her a warm hug. "I'm glad I had the pleasure of making your acquaintance."

"Me, too," Taylor said sincerely.

Drawing back, Mama Wolf smiled at Taylor. "The next time I send one of my care packages, I'll be sure to include a pound cake for you and your family."

Taylor beamed. "We'd like that very much."

"Good." Mama Wolf winked.

Taylor smiled, then waved around the room. "It was nice meeting all of you."

"Same to you, Taylor," they chorused cheerfully. "Have a safe trip and a wonderful Thanksgiving."

"And don't be a stranger!" Mom urged.

Taylor glanced sideways at Manning. "I won't," she promised.

Moments after they left the kitchen, they overheard Mom boasting proudly, "*That*, ladies, was my future daughter-in-law. Mark my words."

Manning blushed hard as he and Taylor grinned shyly at each other.

As they reached the foyer, he steered her gently into the mud room, away from prying eyes and ears.

When they stood facing each other, he confessed, "I like you, Taylor."

She smiled winsomely. "I like you too, Manning."

"No, I mean. I like you, *like* you."

Her smile deepened. "I meant the same thing."

His heart leaped into his throat. Nervously licking his lips, he said, "Would you—"

"I owe you an apology," she blurted.

He blinked. "For what?"

"For the way I've treated you the past two and a half weeks. I haven't been a very good friend to you, and that was wrong of me, especially after the way you stood up for me and wound up getting in so much trouble. There's no excuse for my childish behavior, but I'd like to explain where I was coming from. That day after school when you left me and went to Caitlyn's car, I was really hurt. And I was insanely jealous of her because I knew I could never be as beautiful or popular as she is." Taylor bit her lip, her eyes lowering to the floor as she whispered, "I didn't think someone like you could ever be interested in someone like me."

"Are you kidding?" Putting his finger beneath her chin, Manning coaxed her gaze up to meet his. "That day in precalculus, when Mr. Langenkamp made me get up and solve the problem on the chalkboard, you gave me this smile...I'll never forget it. It made me wonder how the heck it took me two months into the school year to see you. I mean *really* see you. You're beautiful, Tay, and that three-second kiss we had meant more to me than...than anything I did with Caitlyn."

A soft, tremulous smile curved Taylor's lips. "You mean that?"

"I do," he said fervently.

Her face glowed with pleasure.

Damn, Manning marveled, *she's gorgeous.*

"What were you going to ask me before I interrupted you?" Taylor asked softly.

"Oh." Manning gulped a nervous breath, then took the plunge. "Would you go out with me?"

She closed her eyes for a moment, a dreamy smile hovering on her lips.

He waited anxiously.

"Yes," she said simply.

"Yes?"

She nodded slowly, opening her eyes. "Yes, I'd love to go out with you."

Manning's heart soared. He caught both of her hands and held them, grinning so hard his cheeks hurt.

Taylor grinned back at him. "Are you happy?"

"*Very.*"

"Me, too."

They stood there holding hands and cheesing at each other until Taylor's expression suddenly turned serious.

"What is it?" Manning asked her.

She hesitated. "If we're going to be together, you need to know something up front. I'm not putting out like Caitlyn. I'm saving myself for marriage, or at least until I know for sure that I'm ready to give myself to someone. My body is a temple, and any guy who wants to worship has to pay his dues first. So if you're looking for a girl like Caitlyn, then...we can just be friends."

A slow, satisfied smile spread across Manning's face.

"What?" Taylor asked nervously.

"I like you even more now."

She blushed, looking relieved. "I'm glad you're not disappointed."

Manning shook his head. "Nah."

His father had always told him to look for girls who respected themselves and had high standards. As much as Manning had enjoyed having sex with Caitlyn, the experience had left him feeling empty afterward, which was weird. He'd always assumed that whenever he lost his virginity, he'd be bursting at the seams to brag to Michael and Quentin that he'd joined their ranks. But ever since the fellas had gotten here, he hadn't uttered a word about Caitlyn.

So maybe Dad was right, Manning conceded. Maybe he *hadn't* been ready to start having sex after all. Or maybe Caitlyn hadn't been the right girl to lose his virginity to.

Both were probably true.

"Well," Taylor said apologetically, breaking into his thoughts, "I should get going so we won't miss our flight."

"Okay," Manning said. "I'll walk you outside."

As they started from the mud room, Taylor suddenly turned, threw her arms around his neck and crushed her mouth to his, shocking him with one of the sweetest, hottest, most thrilling kisses he'd ever had.

His head was still spinning when she pulled back and grinned at him. "I've been wanting to do that ever since we were interrupted that night."

Manning could only manage a grin that was as wobbly as his knees.

When they stepped out the front door, they saw that a light sprinkling of white flakes had begun falling from the sky.

"It's snowing," Taylor breathed.

Manning smiled, enjoying the delighted wonder on her face. Wanting to prolong their time together, he blurted, "Wait right here."

Taylor gave him a puzzled look. "Where are you going?"

"I'm gonna ask my dad for his car keys so my cousin can give you a ride home."

When he reached the basement, he found his father, Uncle Sterling, Uncle Theo, Mr. Campbell and Mr. Wimbush bantering and laughing raucously as they watched basketball on television.

"Hey, Dad," Manning said, raising his voice to be heard above the cacophony, "can Mike use your truck so we can take Taylor home?"

Sending a lazy glance in his direction, Dad dug his keys out of his pocket and tossed them to Manning.

"Thanks, Dad!"

As Manning raced back up the stairs, he heard Uncle Sterling inquire curiously, "Who's Taylor?"

Dad chuckled. "My future daughter-in-law, if Prissy has anything to say about it."

Manning was still grinning as he passed Maya and Zora on his way to the front door. The thirteen-year-old sisters always seemed to be huddled together—giggling, whispering and sharing secrets. They annoyed the hell out of Manning, but they looked so much like his mother that he sometimes gave them a pass for being such brats.

Sometimes.

As he deliberately shoved his way between them, they stumbled apart and sputtered protestingly, "Manny! Why'd you do that?"

He grinned unrepentantly. "You're identical twins, not Siamese."

After trading aggrieved looks with each other, they smirked at him and began chanting tauntingly, *"Manny has a girlfriend...Manny has a girlfriend..."*

"Damn straight," he smugly confirmed before heading out the door, where Taylor stood at the porch railing catching snowflakes on her tongue. She turned at Manning's appearance and smiled when he held up the car keys. He looked forward to the day when he'd be able to take her out on dates alone.

As the others ended their football game and began walking toward the house, Manning tossed the keys to Michael. "We're taking Taylor home, alright?"

Michael raised a brow, then grinned and wagged his head. "I'm beginning to think y'all only invited me here to be your chauffeur," he grumbled good-naturedly.

Everyone laughed.

As the younger ones ambled into the house to wash up for dinner, Manning, Michael and Quentin loaded Taylor's bike into the back of the truck. They had just finished and slammed the rear door when a sugary voice cooed, "Hey, Manning."

Turning around, he groaned inwardly at the sight of Caitlyn standing there, looking like a snow bunny in a white coat, white leggings and furry white boots. When Michael and Quentin turned to face her, her eyes widened with the unabashed delight of a kid who'd suddenly found herself in a candy store.

"Well, well, well," she purred as Michael and Quentin looked her up and down appreciatively. "What do we have here? More fine gifts from Atlanta?"

As Manning quickly made the introductions, he kept one eye on Taylor inside the truck, hoping and praying that she wouldn't turn around and see Caitlyn. He remembered all too well what had happened the *last* time Caitlyn intruded upon them.

After shaking hands with Michael and Quentin, Caitlyn looked at Manning and licked her lips, as if she were envisioning a foursome. It wouldn't have surprised him to know that she got down like that.

"You live around here, beautiful?" Quentin asked her.

"Just down the street, Hazel Eyes," she purred, her own hazel eyes twinkling invitingly. "You could be there in two minutes."

"That's probably about how long it'd take him," Michael quipped, which made Manning laugh as Quentin scowled at the double meaning.

Dividing an appreciative glance between them, Caitlyn murmured, "If you fellas don't have any plans—"

"Actually," Manning interrupted, "we were just heading out."

"Oh? Where?"

"We're taking Taylor home."

"*Taylor?*" Caitlyn looked inside the truck, saw Taylor waiting in the backseat and frowned with displeasure. "What's *she* doing here? I thought she was dating that band dork."

"She was." Manning smiled. "And now she's dating me."

"*What!*" Caitlyn exclaimed with shocked outrage. "You can't be serious, Manning. *Her?* She's—"

"My girlfriend, and I'm not gonna let you disrespect her like you did before." Not wanting to embarrass her in front of Michael and Quentin, Manning softened his tone. "Look, Caitlyn, you're cool and all. But I'm not interested in you like that. Never really was, to be honest with you. I've been crushing on Taylor for some time now, and thankfully she feels the same."

"But—"

"*HEY!*"

Everyone turned to stare as Taylor stepped from the truck and rounded the rear fender, her eyes narrowed menacingly on Caitlyn. "He said he's not interested," she snarled. "So back the hell off."

Manning's jaw dropped as Caitlyn's face flushed beet red.

As Michael and Quentin exchanged incredulous glances, Taylor tucked her small hand into Manning's and smiled ever so sweetly. "Can we go now?"

Smothering an amused grin, Manning nodded. "Absolutely."

He held the back door open for her, then ducked into the truck behind her.

Lips twitching with suppressed laughter, Michael nodded to Caitlyn and murmured, "Nice meeting you," before climbing behind the wheel and starting the engine.

Caitlyn turned hopefully to Quentin.

"So you and Manny, huh?" At her stiff nod, he shook his head lamentingly. "Too bad. We could have had something special."

"Could have?"

"Yeah. See, Manny's like a brother to me, so messing with you would force me to break one of my rules, which I simply can't do." Quentin gave her one last admiring once-over, then wagged his head with a look of genuine regret. "Damn shame."

Caitlyn stood there looking dumbfounded as he hopped into the passenger seat, then winked and waved farewell as Michael backed out of the driveway. When the two best friends grinned at each other, Manning knew that they'd get a good laugh over this episode for many years to come.

But none of that mattered right now.

All that mattered to him was Taylor.

On the way to her house, they held hands and smiled at each other like they were the only two people in the truck.

And when Michael and Quentin began crooning the sappy lyrics to "Puppy Love," Manning and Taylor could only laugh and secretly agree in their hearts.

Chapter 30

Nestled deep in the Rocky Mountains, the picturesque ski lodge was perched high on a bluff that overlooked rolling hills blanketed in sparkling snow. The day after Thanksgiving, the mountains would be filled with skiers zipping and swerving down the steep slopes.

But for today, the whitewashed landscape was stunningly beautiful and serene.

Inside the luxurious cabin, a cozy fire roared in the twenty-foot fireplace, and the sounds of festive holiday cheer permeated every room, along with the fragrant aromas wafting from the large kitchen, where dinner preparations were under way.

Mama Wolf bustled about with pots and pans, rattling off orders like an army general. The other occupants of the room—Dinah, Georgina, Winnie, Maya and Zora—obeyed the family matriarch's commands without hesitation, and the result of the women's combined efforts promised to be a Thanksgiving feast to rival all others.

Surveying the harmonious scene from where she stood at the picture windows in the living room, Prissy smiled contentedly. She'd been helping with dinner preparations when the appealing sounds of rowdy male laughter had lured her to the windows that overlooked the sprawling front lawn, where the menfolk's smash-mouth football game had evolved into an equally competitive snowball fight.

As Prissy watched with quiet amusement, Manning nailed Magnum squarely in the chest with a huge snowball, drawing roars of laughter and sympathetic groans from the others. Grinning triumphantly, Manning pointed at his brother's stunned face and declared smugly, "Payback for yesterday."

Taking pity on his younger son, Stan sauntered over and draped a consoling arm around Magnum's shoulders. As their heads bent conspiratorially together, Manning eyed them with a wary grin, bracing himself for any retaliatory sneak attacks. Meanwhile, Michael and Marcus snuck up behind Sterling and playfully tackled him to the snowy ground. Sterling bellowed with laughter as he wrestled with his sons, a sight that warmed Prissy's heart and brought a tender smile to her face.

Lifting her gaze to the bright blue sky, she imagined that somewhere up in heaven, Bishop Wolf was looking down upon his descendants and beaming with pride.

"Beautiful sight to behold, aren't they?"

Prissy turned to watch as she was joined by her mother, an attractive mocha-toned woman in her late fifties who was dressed comfortably in a burgundy cowlneck sweater and gray slacks that flattered her shapely figure.

Prissy grinned teasingly at her. "Uh-oh. Did Mama Wolf send you over here to get me?"

Dinah chuckled. "Actually, she gave me permission to come over here and *join* you. Wasn't that generous of her?"

Prissy laughed. "You know Mama Wolf doesn't play around when it comes to her Thanksgiving and Christmas dinners. I always feel privileged just to be allowed in the kitchen with her, since everyone knows she can whip up a feast in her sleep."

"I know. I always learn something new when I cook with her." Smiling, Dinah draped an arm affectionately around her daughter's shoulders as they stared out the windows, watching as Mason chased after Theo, his gleeful shrieks ringing through the air as he misfired snowballs at his retreating uncle.

Prissy smiled at her tall, ruggedly handsome brother, who was presently bundled up from head to toe like the others. "Theo's looking more and more like Daddy every day, isn't he, Mama?"

"He is," Dinah agreed with a soft, poignant smile. "I was just telling him that the other day. And the girls are looking more and more like you."

"I know." Prissy grinned. "Winnie was just complaining to me about that, saying how unfair it is that *she's* the one who had to carry the twins, eat for three and endure labor for over twenty-four hours. She said the *least* God could have done was allow her daughters to look like her. I told her not to be too mad at God, because the girls' resemblance to me was His way of compensating me for never having any daughters of my own."

Dinah smiled. "That should make her feel better."

"I think it did." Prissy chuckled wryly. "After reminding me that Maya and Zora would be spending their spring break with us, she joked that I'd be cured of pining for a daughter after a week of dealing with the girls' temper tantrums and dramatic outbursts."

Prissy and Dinah laughed.

As their mirth subsided, they resumed watching the snowball battle being waged outside.

Resting her head against her mother's shoulder, Prissy sighed contentedly and declared, "I love Thanksgiving."

"As you should," Dinah murmured. "You have a lot to be thankful for."

"I know." Prissy smiled quietly, reflecting on the conversation they'd had earlier that morning when they went for a walk along the scenic trail near the cabin. Prissy had bared her soul, telling her mother everything that had transpired between her and Stan over the past several months.

At the end of their conversation, as they'd headed back to the cabin, Dinah had stopped and cradled Prissy's face between her gloved hands. "Nothing will ever come between you and Stan, darling, because you belong together," she'd gently pronounced. "We all remember that the day you met him was supposed to be your last day at the high school because I'd decided to transfer you to the girls' preparatory academy, which was a better school. But then you crossed paths with Stanton on your way to class, and everything changed. I'll never forget the way you came home floating on cloud nine, and you told me that you wanted to stay at the high school because you might have just met the man of your dreams."

Prissy had grinned ruefully at her mother. "I was only sixteen. What did I know?"

Dinah had turned and gestured toward the cabin, where Stan had just stepped out onto the wide porch, his hands wrapped around a mug of coffee as he quietly contemplated the scenic mountain view.

"Apparently," Dinah said with an intuitive smile, "you knew plenty."

As a cold gust of wind intruded upon Prissy's reverie, she glanced around to watch as the menfolk spilled into the cabin—laughing, stamping snow from their boots and removing gloves, knit caps and heavy coats before making a beeline to the fireplace to warm themselves by the crackling fire.

Even as Stan bantered and joked with the others, his dark eyes sought Prissy out. Her heart somersaulted when their gazes connected and he sent her one of those lazy, crooked smiles meant just for her. Even after all these years, she marveled that Stanton Wolf could still make her heart somersault.

As they stared across the room at each other, she thought of the way things had unfolded over the past few days. They'd weathered the storm together, had survived the perilous flames of the inferno that had threatened to engulf them. As a result, their marriage was even stronger now than it had been before. Although only God knew what the coming years would bring, they both knew in their hearts that their love could—and would—withstand the test of time.

Prissy smiled softly and blew Stan a kiss, which he pretended to catch before winking at her.

As she and her mother returned to the kitchen to finish helping with dinner, Quentin turned on the big-screen television, and the men gathered around to watch the Chicago Bears take on the Detroit Lions.

After removing a large pan of macaroni and cheese from the oven and setting it down on the counter, Prissy couldn't resist sneaking another peek at one of Mama Wolf's picture-perfect turkeys. After admiring the beautifully roasted bird, Prissy tucked the foil shield back into place just as Evangeline appeared beside her, affectionately drawing an arm around her waist.

"Happy Thanksgiving, baby."

Prissy smiled warmly, kissing Evangeline's soft cheek. "Happy Thanksgiving to you, too, Mama Wolf. I'm so glad all of you could make it to Colorado this year."

"Oh, I wouldn't have missed being here for the world. Holidays just aren't the same without the whole family being together."

"I agree," Prissy said, naturally thinking of Celeste, who was spending Thanksgiving with Grant's family in Vermont. She'd called yesterday to speak to Michael and Marcus, and then she'd chatted briefly with Prissy. Although they hadn't mentioned the miscarriage, Prissy could hear a trace of lingering sorrow and regret in Celeste's voice. She hoped, in time, that Celeste would make peace with everything that had happened between her and Sterling. She hoped time would heal everyone's wounds.

"It's beautiful up here in the mountains," Evangeline remarked, her voice breaking into Prissy's melancholic musings.

She smiled. "It is, isn't it?"

"Umm-hmm." Evangeline swept an approving glance around the large, luxuriously furnished cabin. "Everyone is definitely going to enjoy their stay here."

"I think so, too. And I hope you don't mind rooming with Georgina. Since there are only five bedrooms, I had to pair everyone up in a way that made the most sense." So Theo and Winnie were obviously sharing a room, her mother was bunking with Maya and Zora, Sterling was sleeping alone, and the eight boys were camping out on air mattresses spread across the enormous living room.

"Oh, no, baby," Evangeline assured Prissy. "I don't mind rooming with Georgina at all. You know I've always liked her. She's a lovely young woman, and Quentin adores her the way your boys adore you. You're both wonderful mothers."

Prissy gave her a grateful smile. "Thank you, Mama Wolf."

Although Evangeline had taken great pains not to criticize Celeste, Prissy knew that she'd been angered and devastated by Celeste's betrayal. Evangeline was fiercely protective of her Wolf Pack, so she didn't look too kindly upon anyone who dared to hurt them—especially someone she'd lovingly and unreservedly welcomed into the fold.

"In fact," Evangeline added thoughtfully, "I think I'm going to enjoy getting to know Georgina better this weekend."

Prissy followed the direction of Evangeline's gaze to where Georgina had wandered into the living room to catch some of the football game. She stood directly behind Sterling, who sat flanked by Stan and Theo on the plush sectional. When the Bears scored a touchdown, Georgina cheered and excitedly grabbed Sterling's shoulder, something she'd done before on numerous occasions. But now that Prissy knew what had recently transpired between the two old friends, Georgina's innocent gesture took on greater significance.

As she and Evangeline watched, Sterling glanced over his shoulder at Georgina, smiled and gave her hand a gentle squeeze.

It was all Prissy could do to keep a poker face as Evangeline turned and looked at her, brows raised, a speculative gleam in those eyes that never missed anything.

Prissy was more than relieved when Theo wandered into the kitchen to get cold beers for him, Sterling and Stan. After kissing his wife's cheek and retrieving the drinks from the refrigerator, he set them down on the counter and impulsively grabbed Prissy, hoisting her into the air and spinning her around as he'd done when she was a little girl.

Prissy squealed with laughter, making Maya and Zora giggle hysterically as they watched from nearby.

As Theo set Prissy down and affectionately tweaked her nose, she grinned up at him. "What was *that* for?"

He grinned, shrugging a broad shoulder. "I don't know. Just felt like doing that for old times' sake."

Prissy smiled warmly at her older brother. Five years apart, she and Theo shared a special bond forged by the tragedy that had forced them to grow up sooner than they'd wanted to. After their father died, Theo had become the man of the house, taking care of all the things their dad used to while Prissy cooked, cleaned and looked after their grief-stricken mother.

Before proposing to Prissy on prom night, Stan had gone to Theo to ask his blessing. Although Theo had always liked and respected Stan, he was concerned that they were too young to get married, and he didn't like the idea of his brainy, ambitious baby sister postponing college to start a family. After he and Stan had a long man-to-man talk—the details of which remained confidential to this day—Theo had given Stan his blessing. Months later he gave Prissy away at her wedding, his broad chest puffed out with pride as he'd escorted her down the aisle, where Stan awaited her with tears shining in his eyes.

"Winnie says you booked our reservations at the spa tomorrow evening after dinner," Theo said, interrupting Prissy's reverie.

"Yup." She smiled. "I figure after a day of falling on our butts on the ski slopes, we'll need some pampering."

"Then how come only the grownups get to go to the spa?" Maya and Zora wanted to know.

Prissy grinned at her petulant nieces. "Because we're old, and falling on our butts takes more of a toll on our bodies than yours." When Winnie snickered, Prissy added sweetly, "And because spa treatments are a luxury you can't appreciate until you're a grownup."

"Not *all* the grownups are going to the spa," Dinah quickly interjected, seeking to pacify her pouting granddaughters. "It's a couples' thing," she added, winking at Prissy.

"Oh?" Evangeline shot another speculative glance toward the living room, where Georgina was now perched on the back of the sectional as she and Sterling laughed and quietly conversed.

After exchanging a look with Prissy that said, *I know you know more than you're letting on*, Evangeline stopped what she was doing and wandered from the kitchen to investigate the matter on her own.

"Everything sure smells good in here," Theo heartily declared, rubbing his flat abdomen. "Sure can't wait to sink my teeth into some delicious turkey and trimmings. Hint, hint."

Prissy laughed. "Oh, be quiet. Folks who don't help out in the kitchen don't get to rush the cooks."

"Especially when one of those cooks is Mama Wolf," Dinah added. "Besides, it's barely two o'clock, and we had a late breakfast."

"That's right," Prissy said, "so go sit down somewhere, Thelonious."

He looked affronted. "Winnie," he said, addressing his wife, "you gonna just stand there and let them talk to me like this?"

The voluptuous, mahogany-toned beauty laughed and shook her head at her husband. "Considering that your mother and sister are the only other women you ever listen to, I need to keep them as allies. So, yeah, baby, you're on your own."

Everyone laughed as Theo pretended to scowl before scooping up his beers and stalking off.

When Dinah, Winnie, Maya and Zora headed out to the living room a few minutes later, Prissy remained behind to keep an eye on the candied yams baking in the oven.

The harmonious cacophony of animated voices and laughter was pure music to her ears. With the fire crackling in the hearth, the men gathered around the blaring television and the younger boys tussling on the floor, the festive scene reminded Prissy of a Norman Rockwell painting come vibrantly to life. Standing there watching everyone, she felt deliriously content, and blessed beyond measure.

Sighing softly to herself, she turned back to the oven to remove Mama Wolf's candied yams. Lifting the pan to her nose, she inhaled deeply, savoring the hot, mouthwatering aroma of brown sugar and cinnamon that wafted up from the steaming casserole. Clearing space on the crowded countertop, she set down the yams and plucked off the oven mitts she wore.

"Pris." The deep, smoky rumble of Stan's voice near her ear skirted along her nerve endings and settled low in her belly. As he stood close behind her, she let her eyes drift closed, enjoying his intoxicating body heat.

"I came to collect on the feast you promised me," he whispered in her ear.

Prissy smiled demurely. "Dinner will be ready in an hour," she said, pretending to misunderstand him.

"Nice try, woman, but you know I'm not talking about food."

Opening her eyes, Prissy tipped her head back to look up at him. "As I recall, we were supposed to lock everyone out of the cabin before we, ah, commenced our feast. Surely you don't intend to put everyone out on *Thanksgiving*?"

Stan's mouth twitched. "That won't be necessary."

"Good. Because—"

"Come with me, wife," he growled softly.

Anticipation thrummed through her veins, quickening her pulse. "Right now?"

Stan nodded, already taking her hand and starting from the kitchen.

As they moved past the living room, Georgina glanced up and grinned knowingly. "Now I wonder where *those* two are headed."

Sterling chuckled. "To work on baby number six."

Prissy blushed self-consciously as the adults laughed while Manning groaned and complained, "Aw, man, not again."

"We're only going to talk," Prissy insisted. "We need to, er, finalize the itinerary for the weekend. Y'all know I'm a planner."

This was met with dubious laughter and guffaws.

Stan didn't miss a step, his strides long and purposeful as he led Prissy up the winding staircase and past the loft and the other four bedrooms before they reached the elegantly rustic master suite.

Stan ushered Prissy inside, then closed the door behind them and pinned her against it with the solid weight of his body.

Her lips parted on a soft gasp. "Stan—"

Before she could complete the thought, much less the sentence, Stan dipped his head and captured her mouth in an urgent, mind-blowing kiss that left her knees quaking and her loins throbbing.

"I've been trying to keep my distance," he whispered raggedly, "but I couldn't wait another second to get you alone."

Delicious shivers raced through her as he deftly began unbuttoning the long flannel shirt she wore over black leggings.

"Stan," she said breathlessly, batting his hands away, "what are you doing?"

"What does it look like? Getting ready to make love to my beautiful wife."

"You were *serious*?"

"Hell, yeah."

"But everyone's downstairs!"

He chuckled, low and sexy. "This is what they think we're doing up here anyway. So we might as well."

"But what if—"

He slanted his mouth over hers, sucking her bottom lip and twining his tongue around hers with a carnal sensuality that sent molten heat curling through her veins.

She moaned softly in surrender, sliding her arms around his neck. As the kiss deepened, his body settled more firmly against hers. When he lifted her from the floor, she wrapped her legs around his waist.

As he leaned down to nuzzle her arched throat, Prissy sighed languorously. "The cabin is absolutely *wonderful*, Lieutenant Wolf. I'm so glad it was one of your prizes."

Stan lifted his head and gazed down at her, his dark eyes sweeping over her face with searing tenderness. "Your love is the only prize I could ever want or need," he said huskily.

Prissy's heart melted as she gazed into his eyes. "You have it, sweetheart. And you always will."

"Good." He kissed her softly. "And now..."

Prissy's lashes fluttered closed, lips curving in a naughty smile. "Let the feast begin."

Giving a low howl of satisfaction, Stan locked the door and loosened her last button....

*****

Dear Cherished Reader,

I hope you have enjoyed the journey of Stan and Prissy Wolf, who were first introduced in *Treacherous*. Like the prequel, *Inferno* was originally intended to be a novella, but as I delved into the storyline and characters, I came to the realization that confining this family saga to the length of a novella was simply impossible. And so the pen continued to flow. (I know I don't actually write novels with a pen anymore, but it sounded so much better than saying "the keyboard continued to flow.")

I explored many serious themes in *Inferno*, including the reality of underage sex. I hope it was clear to everyone that I was *not* attempting to justify or advocate sex between minors. My objective was to showcase Manning's growth as a character and shed a realistic light on teen sexuality, which I take very seriously as an overprotective mother of a fifteen-year-old daughter. So please, *please* don't send me angry emails about this particular element of the story.

You will definitely be hearing more from Stan and Prissy, who, of course, will have *plenty* to say about the women who will one day steal their sons' hearts.

As for Sterling and Celeste, many of you have asked me whether I will continue the saga between the divorced couple. The answer is a resounding *yes*. As you just witnessed in *Inferno*, there are still some unresolved issues and secrets between Sterling and Celeste. So look for more drama to unfold in future Wolf Pack novels.

I hope you enjoyed your brief introduction to Stan's ancestor, Lieutenant Bishop Wolf. I thoroughly enjoyed conducting research for that portion of the story, and you will definitely hear more about Bishop in future Wolf Pack novels. You see, I've always been fascinated with the history and legacy of African-American soldiers who bravely served our country at a time when they were still enslaved. One of my favorite movies is *Glory*, which featured the 54th Regiment Massachusetts

Volunteer Infantry that courageously fought in the Civil War. One of my favorite songs is "Buffalo Soldier" by the legendary Robert Nesta "Bob" Marley. And one of my favorite historical romance authors is the wonderfully prolific Beverly Jenkins. Who knows? Maybe someday I'll be brave enough to try my hand at writing a historical romance.

Finally, I know that *Inferno* was promised to you months ago. Thank you for your patience, and I truly hope you came away feeling that the novel was worth the wait. And thank you so much for buying my self-published works. Your support enables me to write the longer, more complex stories that I most enjoy.

On that note, please turn the page for a sneak peek at Manning and Taylor's upcoming novel, *Seducing the Wolf.* And be sure to check out *Treacherous*, which is included as a bonus in this print edition of *Inferno.*

As always, I love to hear from readers. Please share your thoughts with me at author@maureen-smith.com.

Until next time, happy reading!

Blessings galore,

Maureen Smith

Coming Next from Maureen Smith

As Manning Wolf knows all too well, you never forget your first crush. Decades ago he lost his heart to sweet, brainy Taylor Chastain. When painful circumstances forced them to go their separate ways, Manning went on to become a wealthy, successful entrepreneur who can have any woman he wants. He's got the world at his feet, but something's still missing....

And then suddenly, unexpectedly, Taylor is back—a sexy, confident, stunningly beautiful woman who takes Manning's breath away. He swears that fate has smiled upon him...until he finds out that Taylor is soon to be engaged to another man. Manning must convince her that they belong together, or risk losing her forever. But as their rekindled attraction ignites into a scorching affair, he can only wonder... who's seducing whom?

Seducing the Wolf

Coming in 2013

Can't Get Enough of the Wolf Pack? Be Sure to Check Out These Other Titles!

Recipe for Temptation (June 2010)
Tempt Me at Midnight (December 2010)
Treacherous (March 2011)
Taming the Wolf (July 2011)

And Stay Tuned for the Continuation of the Series Starting in 2013

Seducing the Wolf (Manning)
Tempting the Wolf (Montana)
Bedding the Wolf (Magnum)
Enticing the Wolf (Maddox)
Chasing the Wolf (Mason)

ABOUT THE AUTHOR

Maureen Smith is the author of nineteen novels and two novellas. She received a B.A. in English with a minor in creative writing from the University of Maryland. She is a former freelance writer whose articles were featured in various print and online publications. Since the release of her debut novel in 2002, Maureen has been nominated for six *RT BOOKreviews* Reviewers' Choice Awards and numerous Emma Awards, and has won the *Romance in Color* Reviewers' Choice Awards for New Author of the Year and Romantic Suspense of the Year. Her novel, *Secret Agent Seduction*, won the 2010 Emma Award for Romantic Suspense of the Year. In 2011, she won the *RT BOOKreviews* Reviewers' Choice Award for *Recipe for Temptation* for Best Kimani Series Romance. She also received the Emma Award for Steamy Romance of the Year for *Recipe for Temptation*, Romantic Suspense of the Year for *Like No One Else*, and Author of the Year.

Maureen lives in San Antonio, TX with her husband, two children, and two adorable miniature schnauzers. She loves to hear from readers and can be reached at author@maureen-smith.com. Please visit her Web site at www.maureen-smith.com for news about her upcoming releases.

Please enjoy

TREACHEROUS

Chapter 1

July 1980

"Are we almost there?" Marcus Wolf asked anxiously.

Sprawled beside his brother in the backseat of the family's old Volvo, Michael warned, "If you ask that question *one* more time, I'm gonna shove my foot up your—"

"Michael!" his mother scolded, whipping around in her seat to glare at him. "That's no way to talk to your brother."

"Sorry, Ma," Michael grumbled, "but he's getting on my nerves. It's only been ten minutes since he asked if we were almost at Mama Wolf's house."

"So what?" Marcus retorted. "I wasn't talking to *you.* Anyway, you're just in a bad mood 'cause Kiara likes Quentin instead of you."

"*What?*" Michael sputtered indignantly. "Boy, you don't know what you're talking about!"

"Yes, I do."

"No, you—"

"That's enough!" Celeste interjected sharply. "What's gotten into you two? You've been bickering ever since we left home, and I'm getting sick and tired of it. I don't want to hear another word out of either of you until we get to your great-grandmother's house. Do you understand me?"

"Yes, ma'am," the brothers mumbled.

"Good." Celeste turned around in her seat, wearily pinching the bridge of her nose between her thumb and forefinger. "Great," she muttered under her breath. "Now I've got a headache."

Sterling reached over and gently cradled her cheek in his hand. "You can lie down and rest when we get there."

She snorted. "How am I supposed to do that with your brother's five sons stampeding through the house?"

Sterling chuckled. "Maybe they'll already be asleep by the time we arrive. It's gonna be pretty late."

"Not *that* late. Besides, you know those boys never go to sleep, especially when they're waiting for Michael and Marcus to get there." She sighed, leaning back against the headrest and closing her eyes. "It's going to be a madhouse. *Nobody's* getting any sleep tonight."

Sterling grinned. "I wasn't planning to," he said suggestively, for her ears only. "And neither should you."

A ghost of a smile curved Celeste's lips. "If you think we're doing *that* in a houseful of people, think again."

Sterling's grin widened. "We'll see about that."

Celeste just shook her head.

She was a beautiful, petite woman with shoulder-length black hair, a café au lait complexion, and eyes the color of cinnamon. She kept herself in great shape by making use of her exercise tapes and the treadmill she'd bought from one of her coworkers. Since she was a health-conscious nurse, she often tried to prepare nutritious meals for the family. But it was hard to keep the cabinets stocked with all-natural foods on a tight budget, which frustrated her—along with many other things about her life.

As silence lapsed between them, Sterling glanced in the rearview mirror at their two sons. They sat at opposite ends of the backseat, as far apart as they could get without being in separate cars. Both had their arms crossed as they stared broodingly out the window. Watching them, Sterling felt a sharp pang of guilt. Michael and Marcus looked forward to this trip every summer, but so far it was getting off to a rocky start. First they'd had to stew in rush hour traffic on their way out of Atlanta because Celeste hadn't gotten off from work on time. Once they were on the interstate, they'd gotten a flat and had to pull over to the side of the road. While Michael assisted Sterling with changing the tire, Celeste had insisted that she and Marcus keep a safe distance from the disabled car, which Marcus hadn't appreciated.

"Why can't *I* help change the tire?" he'd complained. "I'm ten years old, but you guys still treat me like a baby."

"That's because you *are* a baby," Michael had retorted, tossing a grease-stained rag at his brother's scowling face.

They'd been at each other's throats ever since.

It was unusual for Michael and Marcus not to get along. Although they were six years apart, they were closer than any two brothers could be. They played basketball together, shared secrets, and always looked out for each other. So Sterling knew there was more to their bickering than Michael moping over a girl, or Marcus feeling slighted over a flat tire. His instincts told him that the boys were reacting to the tension they sensed between their parents.

Things had been strained between Sterling and Celeste for the past several months. Between her pulling double shifts at the hospital and him working overtime on tough homicide cases, they'd become the proverbial ships passing in the night. If they weren't discussing one of their children or arguing over an unpaid bill, they didn't have much to say to each other. Which was why this trip couldn't have come at a better time. Something about being in the country—breathing in the fresh air, relaxing on the porch after dinner, going for leisurely walks—had a therapeutic effect on everyone. No matter what was happening before they left home, the family always returned from Savannah feeling well rested and rejuvenated.

For the next five days, Sterling wanted Celeste to forget about their mounting debt, the demands of her job, the declining state of their neighborhood—all the things that depressed her. He wanted her to let her hair down and relax. If they could just spend some quality time together, he reasoned, then maybe they could mend what was broken in their relationship.

Because something was definitely broken. And had been for a while.

He glanced over at Celeste. She was staring out the window, lost in thought. It was as if she were there in body, but not in spirit.

Sterling knew that she'd been reluctant to go on vacation. A few days ago she'd told him that things were busy at work, and she hated leaving the other nurses short-handed. But he'd overrode her objections, telling her that the hospital could survive without her for a week, just as his homicide investigations would be waiting for him when he got back. She hadn't put up any more protests, but now as he watched her, Sterling wondered whether she resented him for making her come on the trip. She'd spoken very little to him since they left home, and she'd been uncharacteristically testy with Michael and Marcus.

But Sterling wasn't going to apologize for insisting that she accompany them to Savannah. They needed this time together as a family, and he and Celeste needed to reconnect as husband and wife. Because they were drifting apart, and if something didn't change soon, he honestly didn't know how much longer their marriage could survive.

Night had fallen by the time they arrived at Sterling's grandmother's house. The large Queen Anne, with its decorative roof and rounded turrets, had been in his family for generations. He and his younger brother, Stanton, had been coming there every summer since they were born. After their parents died one August while Sterling and Stanton were visiting Savannah, Mama Wolf had unselfishly uprooted herself, moving to Atlanta to take care of her orphaned grandchildren until they both graduated from high school.

As Sterling pulled into the driveway behind Stan's rental van, a small figure burst from the house and dashed down the porch steps, announcing excitedly, "They're here! They're here!"

From the backseat, Michael and Marcus laughed. "He sounds like Tattoo from *Fantasy Island*," they joked.

Sterling and Celeste chuckled fondly as six-year-old Mason Wolf raced to the back of the Volvo and eagerly pressed his face to the glass, beaming at his older cousins.

Soon Stan and the rest of his sons emerged from the house and gathered on the wraparound porch. Broad grins wreathed their handsome faces, which were so strikingly similar there was no doubt that the same blood ran through their veins.

"About time you folks got here," Stan called out as Sterling and his family climbed out of the car. "You were supposed to be here hours ago."

"Better late than never," Sterling quipped, then scooped his youngest nephew into his arms and swung him around. "Boy, you're getting so big!"

"I know." Mason beamed with pride. "Dad says I'm gonna be as tall as Maddox pretty soon."

"I just bet you are." Grinning, Sterling kissed the top of the boy's head and set him down as they were joined by Stan, Manning, Montana, Magnum, and Maddox. They all exchanged hearty back slaps and hugs and affectionate banter.

Watching the boisterous reunion, Celeste smiled wryly and said, "I'm feeling outnumbered by all this testosterone. Where's your wife, Stan?"

He flashed his megawatt grin at her. "She and Mama Wolf walked down the street to deliver some food to Mrs. Abney. They hoped they'd be back before you guys arrived, but knowing how much Mrs. Abney likes to talk, they might be there for a while." He chuckled, nudging his brother. "Hey, Sterl, remember how we used to get stuck over at her house for hours, choking down her dry sugar cookies and listening to her childhood stories?"

"I remember." Sterling laughed, wagging his head. "Good ol' Mrs. Abney. Even back then she seemed ancient to us. This place wouldn't be the same without her."

"Sure wouldn't," Stan agreed.

Celeste smiled at them. "I need to use the bathroom, so I'll leave you fellas to your reminiscing." She glanced over at Michael and Marcus, who were roughhousing with their cousins. "Y'all bring our bags inside the house."

"Yes, ma'am," all seven boys chorused.

They retrieved the luggage from the trunk of the car and followed Celeste toward the house, laughing and chattering animatedly with one another.

"It sure is good to have the Wolf Pack together again," Sterling said, slinging an arm around his brother's shoulders. "It's gonna be a great week."

"Definitely." Stan was tall and broad-shouldered with smooth mahogany skin, a neatly trimmed goatee, piercing dark eyes, and strong, masculine features. He and Sterling looked so much alike that they were often mistaken for twins. But the similarities didn't end there. They'd both married right out of high school, became fathers shortly afterward, and pursued careers in public safety—Sterling as a police officer, Stanton as a firefighter.

Two years ago, Stan's family had relocated to a suburb of Denver after his wife, Priscilla, landed a job as a school superintendent. The move had been especially difficult on their children, who'd hated having to say goodbye to their cousins and leave Atlanta, the only home they'd ever known. They looked forward to these weeklong summer visits as much as Michael and Marcus did.

As Sterling and his brother started up the walk, he took in his surroundings. The pale blue house was shaded by large oaks draped with Spanish moss. The wraparound porch overlooked lush rose beds that perfumed the warm night air. Sterling breathed deeply, already feeling the stress and tension ebb from his body.

Once he stepped through the front door, he was enveloped by a familiar sense of homecoming, as if the old house had lovingly wrapped its arms around him. Everything was just as he remembered. The gleaming hardwood floors he and his brother used to slide across in their socks. The heavy antique furniture they'd had to polish as punishment for running indoors. The framed family portraits, which included sepia-toned images of Bishop Wolf, the ancestor who'd valorously served as a Buffalo Soldier during the 1800s.

Everything was right where it belonged, Sterling thought contentedly.

As the mouthwatering aroma of his grandmother's cooking filled his nostrils, a broad, satisfied grin stretched across his face.

There's no place like home.

Chapter 2

Celeste was hiding a secret.

A secret that had kept her awake many nights, wracked with guilt and despair.

A shameful secret that threatened to tear her family apart and change the course of their lives.

She'd done the unthinkable.

She'd fallen in love with another man.

But not just any man. Grant Rutherford, a handsome, brilliant neurosurgeon at the hospital where she worked. Just thinking about him brought a hot flush to her face and made her belly quiver.

Alone in the cozy guest room she and Sterling would share that week, Celeste sat down on the bed and let her troubled thoughts roam.

For the past several months, she'd felt as if she were leading a double life. On the surface she appeared to be a devoted wife and mother, one who packed her husband's lunches and rearranged her busy schedule to chaperone her son's field trips. But behind the facade of domestic tranquility, she was a woman consumed with forbidden feelings for another man. She constantly daydreamed about Grant, reliving the rare occasions when they were alone late at night, when the hospital was quiet and few others were around. Grant would follow her into the nurses' lounge, and after she'd poured each of them a cup of coffee, they'd stand close together, smiling and murmuring softly to each other. Her skin tingled whenever he touched her, brushing an errant strand of hair off her face or cupping her cheek in his palm. She'd stare into his mesmerizing green eyes and feel like she was drowning.

At home, she'd often be in the middle of folding laundry or cooking dinner when she found herself fantasizing about running her fingers through Grant's curly hair and feeling his warm lips against hers. She imagined his hands roaming over her, caressing her breasts, stroking between her thighs. The fantasies were so vivid that she'd lose track of what she was doing, refolding the same shirt or towel, sometimes burning the food she was cooking.

Celeste closed her eyes as a hot wave of shame swept over her. Although she and Grant hadn't slept together, that didn't make her behavior any less deplorable. Because she *wanted* to sleep with him, wanted it more than anything. But she knew that once she crossed that line, there'd be no turning back. Once she and Grant became lovers, that would spell the beginning of the end of her life with Sterling. And she wasn't ready for that.

She loved Sterling. He was a good husband—strong, caring, dependable, hardworking. And she couldn't have asked for a better father for Michael and Marcus, who worshipped the ground their dad walked on. Any woman would be lucky to have a man like Sterling Wolf.

Yet there she was, pining for another.

A sudden knock on the door made her jump. Pulse pounding, she turned and called out shakily, "Come in."

The door opened to reveal a spry-looking older woman with cocoa brown skin and a short natural that had turned completely white over the years.

Celeste rose to her feet, smiling warmly as her hostess bustled into the room. "Hello, Mama Wolf. How are you?"

"I'm just fine." Evangeline Wolf embraced Celeste, teasing her nostrils with the scent of cinnamon and roses before she pulled away and clasped both of Celeste's hands between hers. "I'm so sorry I wasn't here to welcome y'all when you arrived."

"That's okay," Celeste assured her. "Stanton told us you'd gone to visit Mrs. Abney. How's she doing?"

"Oh, she has her good days and bad. She can't get around much anymore, so that bothers her sometimes. But as long as she's got folks stopping by to see her, she'll be fine." Evangeline patted Celeste's hand. "Now what about you, dear? Sterl says you're not feeling well. What's wrong?"

Celeste felt a stab of guilt. "Nothing. I just needed to lay down for a while, that's all."

A hopeful gleam lit Evangeline's dark eyes. "You're not expecting, are you?"

"God, no," Celeste said with such vehemence that the old woman frowned at her.

"Children are a blessing from the Lord," Evangeline said chidingly. "Would it be so terrible if you *were* pregnant?"

Absolutely! "Of course not, Mama Wolf. It's just that, well, Sterling and I are done having kids. We're not exactly getting any younger."

"Nonsense," Evangeline scoffed. "You're only thirty-five. Women your age have babies all the time!"

"Not this woman." Celeste hesitated, then confided, "I had my tubes tied after Marcus was born."

Evangeline looked dismayed. "Please tell me you didn't!"

"I'm afraid I did."

Frowning deeply, Evangeline sank down on the edge of the bed. "That's really too bad."

Celeste gave her a knowing smile. "Your reaction wouldn't have anything to do with you wanting a great-granddaughter, would it?"

"Of course not." At Celeste's skeptical look, the old woman grinned sheepishly. "Well, maybe a little. Don't get me wrong. I love every last one of my rowdy, handsome boys. But it would have been nice to have a great-granddaughter to bond with." She sighed. "Sterling and Stanton are my only grands, and I just can't believe that they've got seven children between them, and not a girl in the bunch."

"I know what you mean," Celeste said consolingly, sitting beside Evangeline and putting an arm around her. "I would have enjoyed having a daughter. But the Lord gave me sons, and I wouldn't trade them for the world."

Evangeline smiled gently at her. "I know you wouldn't. You're a good mother, Celeste. The boys not only respect you, they adore you. They know you'd never do anything to hurt them."

Celeste held the other woman's gaze for a long moment, then glanced away guiltily. "No," she agreed in a low voice. "I wouldn't."

She could feel Evangeline studying her closely. "The devil's always trying to lead us into temptation. But we have to be strong and steadfast. That's the only way we can resist Satan's wiles."

Celeste's heart was pounding. She searched Evangeline's face, wondering if she'd somehow uncovered her shameful secret. How many times over the years had Sterling told her that his grandmother possessed an uncanny sixth sense about people? Had the old woman taken one look at Celeste tonight and discerned that she was hiding something?

Swallowing nervously, Celeste ventured, "Mama Wolf, is there something you're trying to tell me?"

Evangeline gave her a long, assessing look. "I know things haven't been easy for you and Sterling. You're both working so hard, doing the best you can to provide for your family. But I know it's been a struggle, living paycheck to paycheck. No, Sterling didn't tell me anything," she added when Celeste opened her mouth to protest. "He's too proud and stubborn to ask for help, even though he knows I'd do anything for him. Anyway, I know how much it bothers him not to be able to give you the kind of life you want—"

Celeste flushed. "I never said—"

"—and I also know that money problems can take a serious toll on even the strongest marriage." Evangeline paused. "I know you look around this big house filled with nice furniture and family heirlooms, and you assume that my late husband and I had it made. And maybe we did. We were more fortunate than most black folks we knew, and we understood that. But we *did* face many challenges in our marriage, things you probably wouldn't believe if I told you."

Her expression softened. "But we got through our problems because we loved each other, and we were committed to keeping the vows we'd made before God and our families."

Celeste dropped her gaze, rapidly blinking back tears.

Evangeline reached over and gently took her hand. "I want you to know that if you ever need anything, *anything* at all, I'm here for you. Do you believe me?"

Celeste nodded, not trusting her voice.

"Good." Evangeline leaned over and hugged her, then drew back and patted her knee. "I'm going to give you and Sterling some money before you leave."

Celeste shook her head. "That's okay, Mama Wolf—"

"Call it a loan, if that makes you feel better about accepting it. But you *will* accept it," Evangeline said implacably. "See, baby, the Lord laid it on my heart to bless you and your family. So the money is actually a gift from God. Surely you wouldn't refuse *Him*?"

"No," Celeste said meekly, "I guess not."

Evangeline smiled. "Good girl."

"But what about Sterling? You know he won't take any money from you, Mama Wolf."

"That's why we should keep this our little secret. Not that I condone lying to your husband, mind you. But sometimes a woman's gotta do what a woman's gotta do."

Evangeline and Celeste shared a quiet smile of understanding just as a knock sounded on the door.

They turned to see Priscilla Wolf poke her head into the room. She surveyed them for a moment, dark eyes twinkling in a pretty, mocha-toned face. "I don't mean to interrupt," she said wryly, "but part of the reason I always look forward to this trip is that I get to spend some time around other women. You know, since I'm always surrounded by—"

From downstairs came a loud exclamation of, "Ugh! Maddox farted!" which was followed by a raucous burst of male laughter.

Prissy sighed and shook her head. "See what I mean?"

Laughing, Celeste and Evangeline rose from the bed.

"Come on, girls," said the family matriarch, leading the way from the room. "Estrogen to the rescue."

Later that night, Celeste was awakened by the sound of Sterling creeping into their bedroom. He and Stan, along with the boys, had stayed up late playing poker and watching old blaxploitation films.

Celeste lay still, listening to the soft rustle of fabric as Sterling removed his T-shirt and jeans, then dropped them on the floor. The mattress dipped under his weight as he crawled into bed beside her, so close that she could feel the warmth of his breath on her nape.

She smiled in the moonlit darkness. "Who won?"

She felt him jerk in surprise. "I thought you were asleep."

"I was," she said wryly.

"Sorry, babe," came his sheepish reply. "Didn't mean to wake you."

"That's okay. I wasn't in a deep sleep anyway." Her mind had been racing all night, replaying her conversation with Mama Wolf. *The devil's always trying to lead us into temptation...They know you'd never do anything to hurt them...We got through our problems because we loved each other....*

Celeste had spent the entire evening covertly watching her husband, thinking of how handsome and virile he was, and calling herself all kinds of a damn fool for being tempted by another man.

"How're you feeling?" Sterling asked, interrupting her thoughts. "Headache gone?"

"Yes." She sighed. "I think I was just feeling a little stressed. But being here at your grandmother's house...Atlanta just seems so far away. And I think that's a good thing."

"I think so, too." Sterling folded her into his arms, pressing his body against her back. She cuddled closer, savoring his strength and warmth.

"So who won the poker match?" she asked.

Sterling chuckled. "I won, of course. But Michael came pretty damn close."

"Are you surprised? You taught him and Marcus everything you know about poker. It won't be long before they're beating you at your own game."

"In that case, I guess I'd better enjoy my dominance while it lasts."

"That's probably a good idea," Celeste smilingly agreed.

"So," Sterling murmured, kissing her bare shoulder, "what's my reward for winning tonight?"

Celeste shivered at the touch of his soft, warm lips. "Reward?"

"Yeah." He ran a hand over her hip, the heat of his skin penetrating her flimsy cotton nightgown. She marveled that after sixteen years of marriage, and despite the problems that plagued their relationship, Sterling could still turn her on like a switch.

"Since the fellas and I didn't play for money," he continued, gently caressing her bottom, "I was hoping to get my reward from *you*."

"Oh, really?" Celeste's hips were slowly undulating, grinding against the rigid bulge of his erection. "And who told you to expect a reward from me? *I* certainly don't remember promising you anything."

"Like I said," he drawled, his voice husky with arousal as he dragged her nightgown up her thigh, "I *hoped* you would."

"Well, you can *hope* all you—" She broke off with a soft gasp as he reached between her legs and touched her pulsing sex.

"Mmmm," he rumbled appreciatively. "I love it when you go to bed without any underwear."

Celeste groaned with pleasure as he stroked the slick, plump folds of her labia. Her thighs parted of their own accord, giving him better access even as she protested feebly, "I told you we can't do this in a houseful of people."

Sterling laughed softly, rubbing her clitoris. "You say that every summer, babe, and we *still* end up doing the nasty. If it makes you feel any better, Stan and Prissy are probably doing the same thing this very minute."

Celeste barely heard a word he'd said. Her heart was pounding as tremors of sensation raced through her body. When Sterling eased a long finger inside her, she closed her eyes and moaned his name—part encouragement, part rebuke.

"Just relax and enjoy this," he murmured coaxingly as he fingered her, ratcheting up her need. "You feel so damn good, honey. I've missed touching you like this."

"I've missed you, too," Celeste whispered, writhing against his hand as a delicious pressure swelled in her loins. "Make love to me, baby. *Please.*"

He was already sliding his finger out of her and yanking down his boxer shorts. She sat up halfway and tugged her nightgown over her head, then flung the garment to the floor. Sterling pulled her close and kissed between her shoulder blades, the soft rasp of his goatee making her shiver.

Keeping her on her side, he lifted up her leg and slid into her wetness. She cried out, arching backward as her body stretched to accommodate his thick, hard length.

He groaned hoarsely. "*So* damn good."

Celeste couldn't agree more. This had always been one of her favorite sexual positions with Sterling. As he began moving inside her, the friction of his shaft rubbing against her clitoris drove her out of her mind.

Looking over her shoulder, she met his gaze. His dark eyes glittered fiercely in the moonlight pouring through the window. He leaned down and kissed her, deeply and sensually. His mouth was flavored with whiskey and peach cobbler. Celeste sucked his tongue, savoring the taste and texture of him.

As they licked into each other's mouths, Sterling reached around her and cupped her swollen breasts, stroking her erect nipples. She broke the kiss, burying her face in her pillow to muffle a loud moan.

He spread her butt cheeks as his thrusts deepened, his hips slapping softly against her backside. They rocked back and forth together, their bodies moving in perfect synchrony. When they were connected like this, Celeste couldn't remember why she was so unhappy, why she felt trapped. All that mattered was the way Sterling made her feel, like she'd perish if she were ever deprived of the sheer pleasure of his lovemaking.

So when they came together, shuddering and whispering tender endearments to each other, leaving him for another man was the furthest thing from her mind.

Chapter 3

When Sterling strolled into the bright country kitchen the next morning, there was a small crowd gathered around the stove, where Michael was cooking an omelet.

Glancing up at Sterling's approach, Evangeline smiled warmly. "Good morning, baby. You're just in time for your son's demonstration."

Sterling chuckled, bending to kiss her soft cheek. "That boy showing off again?"

"You know it, Uncle Sterl," Manning drawled, lounging at a large cedar table that overlooked a sprawling backyard. Unlike everyone else, he apparently didn't need or want a front-row seat to his cousin's culinary theater. "That Negro thinks he's Julia Child or something."

"Shut up, Manny," Michael retorted. "You're just jealous 'cause you can't do this—" He grabbed the skillet handle and flipped the omelet into the air with a flourish to rival the skill of any professional chef. As the others oohed and aahed, Michael grinned cockily.

"How'd you do that, Mike?" his younger cousins marveled.

"I've asked him," Marcus grumbled, "and he won't teach me."

Michael chuckled. "Nothing to it. It's all in the wrist." He slid the picture-perfect omelet onto a plate, added a fork, then gallantly presented the dish to his great-grandmother.

Evangeline beamed with pleasure. "My goodness. This looks and smells wonderful, baby." She cut into the thick, fragrant omelet and ate a forkful. "Oh, that is *heavenly*, Michael. Where on earth did you learn how to make these?"

Snickering, Manning interjected, "I told you, Mama Wolf. He's been watching Julia Child's show."

"Ha ha. Very funny, clown." Michael jabbed a finger at his smirking cousin. "We'll see who's cracking jokes when I kick your sorry behind on the basketball court later. That is, if you don't chicken out on playing me."

Everyone laughed as Manning scowled, ducking his head at the memory of the drubbing he'd suffered during last summer's face-off with Michael. The cousins, who were two years apart, had a humorously adversarial relationship that reminded Sterling of the way he and Stanton had always competed with each other.

After shutting Manny up, Michael made a show of cracking his knuckles before returning to his cooking. "Who wants the next omelet?"

"I do!"

"No, me!"

"I was here first!"

As the boys began bickering and jockeying for position around the stove, Evangeline sighed and passed her plate to Sterling. "Here, baby. You finish this for me while I help Michael with breakfast. Don't want no riot breaking out." Unable to resist, she ate another bite of the omelet, then made an appreciative sound. "Absolutely delicious. He'll have to give me the recipe."

As Sterling chuckled at the thought of his grandmother needing a recipe from anyone—let alone a sixteen-year-old kid—Evangeline gave Manning a stern look. "Boy, make yourself useful and set the table."

"Yes, ma'am."

As he rose to do her bidding, Sterling claimed a chair at the table and enthusiastically dug into his omelet. He'd polished it off and was hankering for another one when Celeste entered the kitchen. Wearing a sleeveless yellow sundress and flat sandals, she looked so pretty and feminine that she took Sterling's breath away.

Meeting his rapt gaze, she blushed and smiled demurely. He knew she was remembering the steamy night of passion they'd shared. They'd made love into the wee hours before dawn, unable to get enough of each other. When he crept out of bed that morning, she'd been sleeping so soundly she didn't even hear him leave the room.

Pulling her shy gaze from Sterling's, Celeste glanced across the large kitchen to where Evangeline and Michael were getting breakfast ready. "Good morning, you two," she greeted them.

"Good morning, dear," Evangeline said warmly.

Michael glanced over his shoulder. "Hey, Ma."

Celeste smiled. "Hey, yourself. Do you two need help with anything?"

"No, baby," Evangeline answered, briskly stirring a pot of grits. "Michael and I have everything under control now that we shooed everyone out. So you just take a seat beside your husband and wait to be served."

"All right," Celeste agreed, walking over to the table.

Before she could sit down, Sterling reached out and caught her around the waist. She let out a surprised gasp as he pulled her onto his lap.

"What're you doing?" she whispered. "Not in front of—"

Sterling kissed her, silencing her protest.

Their lips clung for several long, pleasurable moments before Celeste drew away. Her cheeks were flushed as she glanced self-consciously at Evangeline and Michael, who were grinning at them.

"Don't mind us," Evangeline said gaily. "Just pretend we're not even here."

Sterling grinned wickedly. "In that case—"

"Oh, no, you don't," Celeste warned, jumping off his lap before he could steal another kiss. He laughed, watching as she settled into the chair beside him and primly crossed her legs. If they'd been alone, he would have slipped his hand under her dress, running his fingers up her thigh until he found her sweet spot. Just thinking about touching her there made him want to toss her over his shoulder and carry her back to bed.

"Good morning, everyone."

Sterling glanced toward the doorway, where Stan and Prissy had just appeared. Both wore sheepish grins and looked slightly disheveled, as if they'd dressed in a hurry.

Chuckling, Sterling leaned over and murmured in Celeste's ear, "I told you we weren't the only ones doing the nasty last night."

She took one look at the other couple, and dissolved into laughter.

After breakfast, the Wolf Pack descended upon downtown Savannah to enjoy a lazy afternoon of sightseeing. Although Sterling had practically grown up in Savannah, and had brought his family there every summer for the past sixteen years, he'd never lost his appreciation for the city's picturesque charm.

Spanish moss cascaded from majestic oaks that lined the historic streets. Horse-drawn carriages meandered past elegant old mansions adorned with lush gardens. Tourists gathered on verandas to sip mint juleps and watch passersby.

Strolling hand in hand with Celeste as they lagged behind the others, Sterling felt a deep sense of contentment wash over him. Although his life was far from perfect, he knew he had a lot to be grateful for. He had a beautiful wife and two amazing sons, a close-knit family, a career that he enjoyed, good friends, and excellent health. What more could a man ask for?

"You're doing it again."

Celeste's mildly amused voice pulled him out of his reverie. He glanced at her. "Doing what?"

"Looking like the cat that swallowed the canary."

Sterling chuckled. "Is that how I look?"

"Yup. You've been smiling so hard your cheeks must hurt." Her voice softened. "I don't think I've seen you this relaxed in ages."

He grinned. "We're on vacation. I'm *supposed* to be relaxed."

"I know." A small, whimsical smile touched her lips. "Maybe we shouldn't go back home."

"What?"

Celeste shrugged. "If being here makes you this happy, then maybe we should just stay."

"What? An extra week?"

She hesitated. "Permanently."

"*Permanently*?" Sterling laughed, shaking his head at her. "I think the heat must be getting to you, honey. You know we can't stay here."

She met his gaze directly. "Why not?"

"Are you serious? Because we—"

"Hey, Dad," Marcus interrupted excitedly. "Can I have a snow cone?"

Sterling glanced around, surprised to realize that they had reached Market Street, which comprised nine blocks of shops that sold unique gifts, souvenirs, artwork, homemade candy, and a wide selection of products manufactured in Savannah.

Marcus was eyeing him hopefully. "Can I?"

Sterling removed a crisp bill from his wallet and handed the money to his son. "Get one for everybody else, too."

"Cool! Thanks, Dad!"

Sterling and Celeste smiled, watching as Marcus dashed off to rejoin his cousins, who gave him high-fives when they saw the twenty-dollar bill he'd scored. A few yards away, Michael and Manning stood talking to two pretty, brown-skinned girls who could have been students at the local college.

"They're all growing up so fast," Celeste murmured, a wistful note in her voice. "I still remember each of them in diapers, cake smeared on their faces at their first birthday parties. It seems like only yesterday that Prissy was pregnant with Mason." She chuckled. "Remember how big she was? We all swore she was having twins."

Sterling laughed, his gaze wandering to where his brother and his wife, along with Mama Wolf, were admiring some African-American artwork. Evangeline had never met a painting she didn't want to buy, whether for herself or someone else. The pieces she'd given Sterling and Celeste over the years were among their most valuable possessions.

As they started across the square, a tinkling peal of laughter drew their attention to where Michael and Manning were still flirting with their female companions. One of the girls was resting her hand on Michael's arm and beaming at him, clearly charmed by whatever he was telling her.

Celeste's eyes narrowed. "Is it just me, or do those girls look old enough to be in college?"

"Nope, it's not just you."

When Sterling caught his brother's gaze, Stan raised a thick brow as if to say, *Are you seeing what I'm seeing?*

Sterling nodded.

They traded slow, conspiratorial grins.

Excusing themselves from their wives, they sauntered toward the small group. As they drew near, Michael could be heard saying, "So listen, baby, why don't you give me your number and I'll—*ow!*" He whipped his head around to glare at Manning, who had elbowed him sharply in the ribs. "What the hell's wrong with you?"

Following the direction of his cousin's alarmed gaze, Michael's eyes widened with dread at the sight of their approaching fathers.

"Gentlemen," Sterling greeted them, draping an arm around each boy's tense shoulder. "How's it going? Enjoying yourselves?"

"Yeah," they mumbled, eyes downcast.

"Yup," Sterling agreed, "it certainly looks like you are."

"Aren't you gonna introduce us to your lovely companions?" Stan drawled.

When Michael grudgingly made the introductions, the two girls smiled and offered friendly greetings to Sterling and Stan.

"Wow," the shorter one exclaimed. "All of you look *just* alike."

"Yeah, we get that all the time," Stan said, grinning affably. "Anyway, it's always good to see the boys making new friends. Savannah's such a beautiful city that we've even considered moving here. Hey, maybe the four of you would end up at the same high school."

The two friends giggled. "Oh, we're not in high school anymore. We're sophomores at Savannah State."

"Really?" Sterling and Stan echoed with identical expressions of exaggerated surprise. "You're both in college?"

"Yes." The taller girl glanced at Michael, who looked like he was ready for the ground to open up and swallow him whole. "Aren't you and your cousin in college?"

Before Michael could respond, Sterling guffawed. "Is that what he told you?"

"Well, yeah." The girl frowned. "He said they were both going into their second year at Morehouse."

The two fathers laughed.

"Sorry, ladies," Sterling said ruefully. "But Mike's only sixteen—"

"—and Manny's fourteen," Stan finished.

"*What?*" the girls exclaimed, looking the shamefaced cousins up and down. "But they're both so tall—"

"—and they look older than that!"

Stan grinned with relish. "Don't let the peach fuzz fool you. These boys are bona fide jailbait."

"Oh, hell no. Come on, Jessica, let's go." The two friends stomped off in an indignant huff.

Sterling and Stan burst out laughing as their sons groaned and hung their heads in abject humiliation.

"Was that really necessary?" Michael grumbled darkly. "We weren't doing anything wrong."

Sterling chuckled, affectionately palming the back of Michael's head. "Lying to a woman is never a good way to start off a relationship, son. Remember that."

"Yeah, sure," came the boy's surly response.

Sterling grinned, watching as his brother put Manning in a playful headlock, coaxing a reluctant grin out of him.

"All this walking's got me hungry," Sterling announced cheerfully. "Who's ready to eat?"

They went to one of their favorite home-style restaurants, where they dined on steaming platters of fresh seafood, fried chicken, black-eyed peas and collard greens, with generous helpings of pecan pie and banana pudding for dessert.

During the meal, everyone teased Michael and Manning about their thwarted attempt to pick up older women.

"It was *Mike's* idea to tell them we were in college," Manning said accusingly.

"They wouldn't have talked to us if they knew how old we were, dummy," Michael shot back.

"Are you kidding? Didn't you see the way they were checking us out?"

"Checking *me* out, you mean," Michael corrected, then laughed as Manning tossed a crab claw at him.

"No throwing food at the table," Prissy lightly scolded, then shook her head at the feuding pair. "I still can't believe those silly girls fell for your lie. Even if Mike *could* pass for a college freshman—"

Sterling snorted. "And that's a big *if.*"

"—there's no way anyone could believe that my Manny is in college. Not with this baby face," she cooed, cupping his cheek in her hand.

"Ma," Manning groaned in embarrassment.

Laughter swept around the table.

Marcus sighed dramatically, shaking his head at Michael. "My poor brother. This just hasn't been your week, has it? First you lost Kiara to your best friend—"

Michael scowled. "I told you—"

"Wait a minute," Manning laughingly interjected. "Who's Kiara?"

"A girl from the neighborhood he likes," Marcus said smugly. "Only problem is, *she* likes Quentin."

"How do you know?"

"Last week when Mike was at basketball camp, I saw Kiara and Quentin walking to the corner store together, holding hands. The next day I overheard Mike and Q arguing about her."

"Marcus," Celeste gently chided. "What have I always told you about eavesdropping?"

"I wasn't eavesdropping, Ma. They were loud."

"Well, well, well," Manning gleefully intoned, grinning at Michael. "Guess you're not the man after all."

Michael shrugged dismissively. "I'm not worried about Kiara. There's plenty more fish in the sea."

Celeste grimaced. "Darling, can we not refer to females as 'fish'?"

"Yes, please," Prissy agreed.

"Aw, leave the boy alone," Stan said. "He's right. Life's too short to be losing sleep over one girl. If she wants that light-skinned pretty boy, let her have him. And when Q breaks her little heart—'cause you know he will—that should teach her a lesson. Right, Sterl?"

Sterling took one look at his wife's indignant face, then Prissy's, and held up his hands in mock surrender. "I'm staying out of this."

Everyone laughed.

Chapter 4

After dinner, Sterling and Celeste opted to attend an open-air concert at Forsyth Park while the rest of the family went to see a movie.

After stopping at a boutique to buy a blanket, they strolled to the park, which was a long strip with open fields at one end and scenic gardens at the other. At the center was a massive cast-iron fountain that was one of Savannah's most iconic landmarks, as evidenced by the tourists snapping photographs and posing in front of the beautiful monument.

Sterling and Celeste weaved through the crowd until they found an ideal spot beneath a canopy of live oaks. They stretched out on their blanket and spent the next two hours listening to the symphony perform beneath the stars.

It was the most romantic evening they'd had in ages. When the concert was over and the crowd began to disperse, they lingered behind, wanting to prolong the experience. As they sat there cuddling underneath the trees, the silvery Spanish moss swayed in the gentle breeze, adding to the otherworldly romantic atmosphere.

Celeste sighed, a sound of utter contentment. Resting her head on Sterling's shoulder, she murmured, "This is so nice."

"Isn't it?" Sterling agreed, rubbing his cheek against her soft, fragrant hair.

"I'm glad we decided to come here instead of going to the movies."

"Me, too."

"Why don't we do things like this more often?"

Sterling felt a pang of guilt. "We should," he admitted. "I guess we need to make more of an effort."

"We really do." Celeste paused. "I meant what I said earlier."

"About?"

"About us staying here, not going home."

Sterling went still.

After several moments of silence, Celeste lifted her head to look at him. "Well?"

He shook his head at her. "I didn't think you were serious."

"Why not?"

"Why not?" Sterling echoed incredulously. "Because we both have jobs waiting for us. And the boys have their schools, their extracurricular activities, their friends."

"All of which they could find right here in Savannah," Celeste pointed out. "Just think about it, Sterl. We could move in with Mama Wolf until we find a place of our own. God knows she's got plenty of room, and I know she'd *love* having us there with her."

Taking Celeste's chin between his thumb and forefinger, Sterling searched her face. "What are you running from?"

"Nothing," she said quickly. Too quickly.

Sterling frowned, a strange unease stirring in his gut. "What's going on, honey?"

"Nothing." She swallowed visibly, dropping her gaze. "It's just that...well, I've been thinking that maybe we need a change of scenery. You know, like Stan and Prissy did."

"They moved because Prissy got a good job," Sterling reminded her. "And Stan and the boys hate Denver."

"That's because they haven't given it a chance."

"It's been two years, and they still want to come back home."

"Well, that's *their* problem," Celeste snapped.

A heavy silence fell between them. The relaxed, romantic mood they'd enjoyed all night was suddenly gone, and Sterling wasn't sure why.

"What's happening between us?" he asked quietly.

Celeste averted her gaze, staring off into the distance. Tears glistened in her eyes, heightening Sterling's alarm.

"Talk to me, honey," he prodded gently.

She hesitated another moment, then confided, "I always hoped that I'd be able to leave Atlanta someday. Wendell and I talked about it all the time. We planned to move away after we'd both graduated from college. We were going to start over someplace new. But after he died..." She trailed off, unable to finish.

But she didn't have to. Sterling knew what she'd been about to say. Even after all these years, the specter of Wendell Portman's ghost hung between them.

Celeste and Wendell had been high school sweethearts, the most admired couple among their peers. Celeste was a beautiful, popular cheerleader. The preacher's daughter every boy wanted to seduce. But she'd only had eyes for Wendell, the smart, ambitious class president who'd already secured a scholarship to Morehouse, while Celeste was bound for Spelman. Everyone had expected the couple to get married and live happily ever after. But just days after their high school graduation ceremony, tragedy struck. On his way home from visiting Celeste one night, Wendell's car was broadsided by a speeding drunk driver. He was killed on impact.

Shattered and grief-stricken, Celeste had sought solace from Sterling, whom she'd been friends with for many years. She'd showed up at his apartment while his grandmother and Stanton were attending bible study at church, a weekly ritual Sterling had avoided that evening by pretending to be sick. In hindsight, he realized that he'd played right into the devil's hands.

One moment he'd been consoling Celeste and wiping her tears. The next moment they were making sweet, passionate love like their lives depended on it. Four weeks later, Celeste came to him with the most devastating news. She was pregnant, but she didn't know whether the baby belonged to him or Wendell, whom she'd slept with two nights before he was killed.

Her revelation left Sterling reeling with shock. He was only eighteen, and had been looking forward to starting college that fall. Although he'd never had any lofty expectations of becoming rich or famous, he knew his prospects would diminish even more if he were saddled down with a family. He wasn't ready to tackle the responsibilities of fatherhood. But Celeste was pregnant and terrified, knowing she'd incur her father's wrath if she had a child out of wedlock. Her strict Baptist upbringing also ruled out abortion as an option.

She'd needed Sterling to be a man. So he'd done the only thing he could. He'd asked her to marry him. And thus began their rocky journey together.

Gently stroking Celeste's hair, Sterling murmured, "Are you feeling restless in Atlanta?"

She hesitated, then nodded against his chest. "I've been there all my life. From the time I was young, my father made it clear to me that Atlanta was my home, and that was where I belonged. Going to college somewhere else was never even a consideration—it was Spelman or nothing."

"I thought that was because your mother went to Spelman," Sterling interjected, "and he wanted to continue the family tradition."

"That was part of it, yes. But the main reason is that he wanted to keep me close by." Celeste sighed. "I know you always saw my father as this larger than life figure. A strict disciplinarian and a fire-and-brimstone preacher who struck fear in the hearts of his congregants—"

"And our children," Sterling added wryly. "Every time he was around, Michael and Marcus became perfect little angels."

Celeste grinned. "That's true. They knew Daddy would take his belt to their backsides the second they got out of line."

"Hell, *I* was scared of him," Sterling joked.

They both laughed.

Sobering after several moments, Celeste continued, "Yeah, Daddy could be very intimidating. But what most people didn't know is that he was also very vulnerable and needy. You remember how it was. When my mother first got sick, he started leaning on me, expecting me to take care of all the things she no longer could. Mom used to tell him to give me some space, because I had my own family and responsibilities to worry about. But once she passed away, I became my father's whole world." She grimaced, shaking her head. "I can remember getting off from work, picking up Michael from the babysitter, then rushing over to the church to type Daddy's sermons for him because that's what Mom used to do."

"I remember those days," Sterling murmured, thinking of how guilty he'd often felt for resenting her father's intrusion into their lives. It hadn't helped that the old man openly disapproved of their marriage, believing that Celeste could do better than Sterling.

"Those were some trying times, God rest Daddy's soul." Celeste sighed. "Anyway, to make a long story short, I think I'm ready for a change of scenery."

Sterling nodded slowly. "And how do you know you won't feel restless in Savannah?"

She hesitated, biting her lip. "I guess I *don't* know."

Sterling said nothing, continuing to stroke her hair.

After a prolonged silence, she let out a deep, resigned breath. "You're right. We can't just pack up our family and move here on a whim. I'm talking foolish."

"It wasn't foolish," Sterling countered mildly. "I understand where you're coming from, wanting to experience someplace different. But it's just not practical for us right now. And as much as the boys love spending every summer in Savannah, I don't necessarily think they'd want to live here. They'd miss home too much."

"I know. And so would you."

Sterling didn't deny it.

Celeste angled her head to smile wryly at him. "You know, I didn't need a paternity test to tell me that Michael is your son. He's just like you. They both are. If they ever decide to leave Atlanta, I know they'll find their way right back."

Sterling chuckled. "That's probably true."

As a sultry breeze wafted over them, Celeste sighed languorously. "I could stay out here all night, Sterl. Isn't this so romantic?"

"Very," he agreed. "Next time we visit, we'll leave the boys at Mama Wolf's house and spend a couple nights at one of those bed-and-breakfasts."

"Mmm, that's a *wonderful* idea."

Sterling grinned. "I get one every now and then. Speaking of which— Whoa, what're you doing?"

Celeste had reached down and started unzipping his jeans. At his startled question, she gave a low, naughty laugh. "What does it look like I'm doing?"

"It *looks* like you're trying to get us ar—" Sterling broke off as her warm fingers slipped inside his boxers and wrapped around his penis, which grew instantly hard.

"Oooh," Celeste crooned with wicked satisfaction, stroking him slowly. "Looks like *someone* wants some special attention."

Sterling groaned with pleasure, even as his eyes darted around the moonlit park to make sure no one was nearby.

"Relax, sweetheart," Celeste murmured, lowering her head to his lap. "No one's gonna see us."

"I'm not so sure about—" Sterling sucked in a sharp breath as she took him between her lips. His head fell back, eyes rolling closed in ecstasy.

As she slid her hot mouth up and down his length, he groaned raggedly. "This is crazy, woman. I used to arrest people for this kind of thing."

Celeste's soft, throaty laughter was the sexiest sound he'd ever heard. "No one's getting arrested tonight, Detective," she purred, swirling her tongue around the sensitized head of his shaft, "unless you brought a pair of handcuffs you wanna use on me."

Sterling swore hoarsely, his pulse kicking into overdrive. He'd always loved it when his wife talked dirty to him.

She began sucking him harder as his hips thrust upward, making love to her mouth until her low moans of pleasure joined his.

"Babe, I'm about to—"

As he tried to pull out of her, her lips clutched at him, not letting him go. He came violently, shuddering as he spent himself inside her mouth. She swallowed greedily, as if she were receiving nourishment from his body.

When she'd milked him dry, Sterling collapsed onto his back with a husky groan. Celeste snuggled against him, discreetly draping her sundress across his waist to conceal his open fly.

"That was..." Sterling trailed off, at a loss for words.

Celeste laughed softly. "That good, huh?"

"Hell, yeah."

"I told you no one would catch us." She motioned to the gently swaying canopy of moss. "It's like we're in our own little cocoon under here."

Sterling grinned. "I still say you're gonna get us arrested."

Celeste chuckled. "They can't arrest you," she said, propping her head in her hand as she smiled down at him. "They'd be violating some unwritten code of brotherhood."

"Maybe." Sterling smiled lazily, reaching up to slide his hand into her hair. He felt ten years younger, so buoyant and carefree he could have floated away at any moment. "We definitely need to do things like this more often."

"*Definitely.*" Celeste leaned down and nibbled on his earlobe, then traced the shell of his ear with her wicked tongue. It was enough to send a hot rush of blood straight to his groin.

As if sensing his body's reaction, she let her hand wander over him until she cupped his thickening erection. "Mmmm," she purred seductively. "I think you're ready for round two, Detective."

Pulse galloping, Sterling watched as she sat up and reached under her dress. Smiling like a naughty schoolgirl, she pulled off her panties and tossed them at his face. He caught the scrap of silk with a laugh, enjoying her playfulness.

"So you act all shy and virginal at my grandmother's house," he teased, propping himself up on his elbows, "but out in public, you become an exhibitionist."

Celeste gave a sultry laugh, squatting beside him to tug his jeans and boxers just past his hips. "You know what they say about preacher's kids."

"Umm-hmm," Sterling agreed as she straddled his thighs, her dress billowing around them. The feel of her hot, moist cleft against his skin sent a jolt of raw hunger through him. If he hadn't already gotten his second wind, *that* definitely would have done the trick.

He slid his hands beneath her dress and grasped the plump, curvaceous swell of her butt. Her skin felt like heated silk. As he caressed her bottom, she curved her arms around his neck and slowly undulated her hips.

Holding her smoky gaze, he leaned forward and captured her lower lip between his teeth, gently sucking it the way she liked. She shuddered with arousal, sliding her tongue into his mouth. They shared a long, deep, sensual kiss.

Pulling away, Sterling tugged down the bodice of her dress, humming appreciatively as her round, perky breasts spilled out over the top. He palmed them, rasping his thumbs over her nipples until they tightened. Lowering his head, he drew a dusky areola into his mouth. Celeste moaned as he laved and suckled her, first one nipple and then the other.

They stared into each other's eyes as she raised her hips, then guided his erection into the snug, wet clasp of her sex. As they both groaned with pleasure, Sterling began thrusting into her. She moved naturally with him, their bodies rising and falling as one under the moonlight. Whatever else their problems, they'd always known how to satisfy each other.

As the tempo of their lovemaking increased, sweat dampened their skin and pooled between their joined bodies. Sterling groaned as he plunged in and out of Celeste, watching as she threw back her head and cupped her bouncing breasts. The sight was so erotic that it blew his mind.

He felt her thighs begin to shake seconds before she whimpered, "I'm coming. Ohhh, Sterling...*baby*!"

Her back arched sharply as the orgasm tore through her. Moments later Sterling exploded, tightly gripping her butt as he spilled into her womb.

Celeste dropped her head onto his shoulder as they both panted harshly, trying to catch their breath.

They remained locked together for several minutes, the air thick and warm around them.

At length Celeste sighed deeply. "I'll never forget this night, Sterling."

"Neither will I," he said softly, then wondered if he'd only imagined the note of farewell in her voice.

Chapter 5

"Girl, I'm exhausted."

Celeste glanced up from the magazine she'd been perusing to watch as Prissy wrapped a beach towel around her dripping, swimsuit-clad body and flopped down on the lounge chair beside hers.

Celeste smiled at her. "No wonder you're exhausted. You've been swimming with the fellas all afternoon. If I didn't know better, I would think you were training for the Olympics."

"Not quite," Prissy said wryly, smoothing her wet dark hair off her face. "I'm just trying to lose some weight."

Celeste arched a surprised brow. "What for? You look great."

"Thanks, girl," Prissy said with a small, self-deprecating smile, "but we both know I could stand to lose a few pounds. I'm still carrying around some baby weight, and it's been six years since Mason was born."

Celeste gaped at her. "You're kidding, right? Prissy, you're the mother of five children. Not one, not two. *Five.* Do you know how many women would *kill* to have your figure after popping out that many babies?"

Lips pursed, Prissy unwrapped her beach towel and looked down at herself, critically assessing her gently rounded belly, flared hips, and thick, healthy thighs. She frowned. "I wish I could get rid of these damn stretch marks."

"Girl, please. Did you hear what I just said? You're a mother of five. Those stretch marks are your badge of honor."

Prissy snorted, shooting an envious glance at Celeste's smooth, slender thighs. "Easy for *you* to say. You don't have any stretch marks."

"I also don't have a bodacious booty that makes grown men act a damn fool whenever I walk by. You obviously didn't notice all the heads you turned when you strolled across the beach to get in the water. But your husband sure noticed," Celeste added with a chuckle. "Girl, one brotha was ogling you so hard, I thought Stan was gonna kill him."

Prissy laughed. "You're right. I completely missed all that. But it's nice for Stan to see how *I* feel sometimes, watching the way women throw themselves at him. It's ridiculous."

Celeste smiled ruefully. "I guess that's the price you pay for being married to a tall, dark, and handsome firefighter."

Prissy sighed, staring across the beach. "Tell me about it."

Celeste followed the direction of her sister-in-law's gaze to the water, where Stan, Sterling, and the boys were laughing and splashing in the frothy waves, their beautiful dark skin glistening in the sun.

That morning, the two families had packed a large picnic basket, donned their swimwear, and headed to Tybee Island, a scenic coastal town located twenty miles outside of Savannah. Only Mama Wolf had stayed behind, needing time to recover from yesterday's sightseeing excursion.

Once they arrived at the crowded beach, Celeste had pulled out a few magazines, stretched out on a lounge chair beneath an umbrella, and contented herself with relaxing in the shade while everyone else went swimming. After the steamy workout she and Sterling had given each other last night, she'd earned the right to be lazy.

"I think Stan's having an affair."

Startled out of her reverie, Celeste swung her head around to stare at Prissy. "*What* did you say?"

Meeting her stunned gaze, Prissy said quietly, "I think Stan's cheating on me."

Celeste gasped. "Why on earth would you think something like that?"

"It's the way he's been acting lately. Distracted, restless...unhappy." Her voice dropped to a trembling whisper. "I think there's someone else."

"Oh, honey," Celeste said soothingly, setting aside her *Jet* magazine and sitting up on the chair so that she could face her sister-in-law. "I'm sorry, but those aren't good enough reasons to assume your husband's cheating on you. Maybe he's just stressed out from work—"

"He's been putting out fires for fourteen years," Prissy interrupted. "By now he should be used to the pressures and dangers of the job. Besides, I know it's not that. He *loves* being a firefighter. He couldn't imagine doing anything else."

"All right, so maybe it's not work. Maybe something else is bothering him." Celeste hesitated, then gently confided, "Sterling told me that Stan and the boys aren't adjusting well to Denver. They want to move back home."

Prissy nodded, guilt flashing in her dark eyes. "I know they're not crazy about Denver. And I know, to some extent, they blame me for uprooting them the way I did. But I had no other choice. I couldn't pass up the opportunity to make *twice* what I was earning as a high school principal in Atlanta. And God knows it's impossible to support a family of seven on a fireman's salary."

She grimaced, hearing her own words. "That didn't come out right. I don't begrudge Stan's career choice. Ever since his parents died in that house fire when he was younger, he's wanted to become a firefighter, and he's damn good at it." She sighed. "It's just that...well, before he was promoted to lieutenant, I used to wish that rescuing people from burning buildings was a bit more lucrative."

Celeste nodded sympathetically. "You don't have to explain yourself to me. You know I understand better than anyone how difficult it is to raise a family on modest incomes. Sterling and I are just barely making ends meet." Her lips twisted ruefully. "Yesterday when he gave Marcus twenty dollars to buy some snow cones, I couldn't help wondering how far that would set us back."

"Oh, God," Prissy said, her eyes filling with concern. "I can't believe I'm over here whining about my problems when you and Sterling are going through such hard times. Do you need to borrow some—"

"Girl, no," Celeste said quickly, her face flushing with embarrassment. "I didn't tell you that to make you feel sorry for me. I just wanted you to know that I understand and respect your decision to accept the job in Denver. You did what was best for you and your family, and someday they'll realize that and thank you."

Prissy nodded slowly, gnawing her lower lip. "Are you sure you don't need some money?"

Celeste heaved a sigh, wishing she'd never opened her mouth. "Of course I need money," she admitted. "But I won't take any from you."

Prissy frowned. "Why not?"

"Well, let's see. You've got more mouths to feed than I do, you have to pay the mortgage on that nice big house of yours, and I know for a fact that the cost of living in Denver is much higher than you're used to. So, no, I won't take a dime from you. Besides," she added when Prissy opened her mouth to argue, "Mama Wolf already offered to loan us some money, and I accepted. But *please* don't tell Sterling. You know how proud he is."

"I won't say a word," Prissy promised. "But how are you going to explain the extra funds?"

"I'm telling him I got a bonus from the hospital. Anyway, let's get back to you and Stan. What I was saying is that you shouldn't jump to conclusions just because he's been acting differently. If he's still unhappy about living in Denver, couldn't *that* explain his behavior?"

"Maybe." But Prissy didn't look or sound convinced.

"Do you have any other reason to suspect he's having an affair?" Celeste prodded. "Has he been staying out later than usual? Lying about his whereabouts? Getting strange phone calls at all hours of the night?"

Prissy frowned, shaking her head. "No to all of the above."

"And you haven't found a woman's phone number in his pants pocket?"

"Of course not. He wouldn't be that careless." Prissy pushed out a long, deep breath. "Look, I don't have any proof that he's cheating on me. It's just a feeling I have. An instinct."

"An instinct," Celeste repeated skeptically.

"Yeah. You know, women's intuition." Prissy searched her face. "Don't you think you'd be able to sense something was wrong if Sterling was cheating on you?"

Celeste glanced away, her face heating with shame at the thought of her forbidden feelings for Grant Rutherford. She wished she could confide in her sister-in-law and get some advice, but that was out of the question. No one could know her guilty secret. Absolutely no one.

"Well?" Prissy prompted.

" 'Well' what?" Celeste mumbled.

"Don't you think your instincts would warn you if Sterling was cheating on you?"

"Sterling would never cheat on me," Celeste said with quiet certainty. "Just like Stan isn't cheating on you."

Prissy was silent.

When Celeste looked at her, tears were shimmering in the other woman's eyes.

"That man loves you," Celeste said gently. "Anyone can tell by the way he looks at you. *You* might think you need to lose weight, but whenever Stan sees you, it's obvious to me that he thinks you're the most beautiful woman in the world. He can't keep his hands off you, Pris. Every time I turn around he's touching your face, or running his fingers through your hair, or playfully swatting you on the ass." She smiled wryly. "Do those sound like the actions of an adulterer?"

But Prissy, staring off into the distance, seemed not to have heard her. "Maybe it's worse than an affair," she whispered.

Celeste frowned. "What do you mean?"

"Maybe he secretly resents me for being the breadwinner. Maybe he resents me for putting him and the boys on the backburner while I was getting my Ph.D. Maybe he resents the long hours I work, the endless meetings I have to attend, the numerous social functions he's forced to escort me to."

Celeste said nothing, contemplating her sister-in-law's words. She'd never suspected that Stan and Prissy's marriage was in trouble. They'd been together since high school and had always seemed like the perfect couple, so madly in love that nothing could ever come between them. Celeste couldn't conceive of Stan harboring animosity toward his wife, let alone cheating on her.

But wasn't *she* living proof that appearances could be deceiving?

Suppressing a grimace at the thought, Celeste reached over and laid a gentle hand on Prissy's arm. "I didn't know you and Stan were having problems. As often as we talk on the phone, you never mentioned any of this."

"I know," Prissy admitted glumly. "It's not that I didn't want to confide in you. Believe me, I did. But at the same time, I didn't want you worrying about me. And I guess I was hoping that things would eventually get better between me and Stan. But they haven't, and I don't know what I'm going to do."

Celeste rubbed her arm consolingly. "Well, the first thing you need to do is share your concerns with him. Give him a chance to tell you where he's coming from before you assume the worst of him. It sounds like you both have a lot to get off your chests. The sooner you talk, the better."

"I know." Prissy sniffled, dabbing tears from the corners of her eyes. "You're absolutely right."

"Of course I am." Celeste smiled softly. "You and Stan are going to pull through just fine."

Prissy gave her a watery smile. "Thanks for saying that."

"I mean it. Whatever happens, I know everything's going to work out."

If only she could say the same of her own marriage.

***

"Look at our boys, Sterl," Stan said. "Just *look* at 'em."

Sterling was already staring across the manicured front lawn, where their sons were engaged in a rough and tumble football game. They ran up and down the yard—shoving, blocking, catching passes, and tackling one another. All of them were fiercely competitive, from Michael down to Mason, who was holding his own against the older, bigger players.

"You're looking at the future starting lineup for the Atlanta Falcons," Stan declared, his broad chest puffed out with pride.

Sterling chuckled, sipping from a glass of lemonade. "Nothin' wrong with aiming for the stars."

"Damn straight." Stan rapped his knuckle on the arm of his chair.

It was the day before they were supposed to go home. After lunch, their wives had gone shopping with Mama Wolf while the boys raced outside to play football, heedless of the steamy temperature that gave even the moss-draped oaks the appearance of sweating. Declining their sons' invitation to join the game, Sterling and Stan had chosen to watch from the cool, relaxing shelter of the porch.

Sterling grinned. "Look at us, Stan. Sitting here in the shade, sipping lemonade and watching our kids play like a couple of old fogies."

Stan snorted. "Speak for yourself. *I* ain't no old fogie."

"You're only two years younger than me. If *I'm* old, so are you."

"Nothing old about this body," Stan boasted, dark eyes glinting wickedly. "If you don't believe me, just ask my wife."

Sterling laughed. "No, thanks. I don't need more of a mental picture than the one I've been getting every morning when you two show up late for breakfast."

Stan grinned. "Hey, what can I say? There's a reason three of my kids were conceived right here in this house. Something about being in Savannah brings out the freak in Prissy. It's incredible."

Sterling smiled to himself, savoring the memory of what he and Celeste had shared in Forsyth Park five nights ago. He knew he'd never see that park the same way again.

Catching his satisfied expression, Stan grinned slyly. "Looks like Savannah's been good to someone else, too."

Sterling's lips twitched. "True gentlemen never kiss and tell." He paused. "But, yeah, it's been a good week."

The two men laughed.

Sobering after several moments, Stan glanced sideways at Sterling. "So everything's all right between you and Celeste?"

"Oh, yeah. Most definitely." Wishing he felt as confident as he sounded, Sterling met his brother's steady gaze. "What about you and Prissy? Everything okay?"

A shadow crossed Stan's face, disappearing so swiftly Sterling might have imagined it. "Oh, yeah," Stan replied, nodding vigorously. "We're good. Most definitely."

An odd silence fell between the two men.

As if by mutual agreement, they returned their attention to the yard, where Marcus had just thrown a deep spiral to his wide receiver. Manning had barely caught the pass before he was tackled by Michael, who drove him into the ground. Taking umbrage, Manning bounded to his feet and charged at Michael. The two cousins shoved and shouted at each other until Marcus intervened, stepping between them to prevent one of their notorious brawls.

Stan chuckled, wagging his head. "Forget what I said about all of them playing for the Falcons. I think Marcus is gonna be a lawyer."

Sterling grinned. "I think you're right. He seems to be the only one who can talk Mike and Manny out of killing each other."

Laughing, they watched as their firstborn sons made up, slinging their arms around each other's shoulders as they sauntered back to their teammates.

Stan smiled quietly. "Nothing's ever gonna break up the Wolf Pack."

Sterling hesitated, then raised his glass to his brother's. "Long live the Wolf Pack."

Chapter 6

Celeste nosed her Volvo into the empty space in front of her home and cut off the ignition. Instead of climbing out of the car, she sat there staring out the window, dismally surveying the block of row houses made of brown and yellow brick. The facades of several homes were crumbling with decay, and the surrounding lawns were overgrown and choked with weeds. Though Sterling kept their own yard neatly groomed, and Celeste had planted pretty flowers in the window boxes, their efforts—along with those of a few other conscientious residents—were not enough to change the look of neglect that plagued the neighborhood.

Sitting there in her Volvo, Celeste was struck by an overwhelming urge to restart the car and get out of there. Just keep driving until she'd put this miserable place in her rearview mirror.

A sudden tap on the glass made her start violently.

Heart thumping, she whipped around to find her son's best friend, Quentin Reddick, standing at the window.

He flashed his trademark crooked smile. "How ya doing, Mrs. Wolf?"

Celeste smiled wanly. "Hello, Quentin."

He held the door open for her as she got out of the car. He was so tall that she had to stand on tiptoe to kiss his cheek.

"How's your mama doing?" she asked him.

"She's doing good. Working hard, keeping herself busy."

Celeste nodded understandingly.

Georgina Reddick's husband had been killed in the line of duty three years ago. The senseless tragedy had devastated her and Quentin, who'd been forced to grow up faster than most boys his age. He'd become his mother's rock, and she, in turn, became the center of his universe.

Celeste smiled, gently patting his cheek. "You tell her I said hello."

"Yes, ma'am, I sure will."

"Good. Now since you're here," Celeste said, rounding the fender to open the trunk, "you can help me carry the groceries into the house."

Quentin bowed gallantly. "Your wish is my command."

She laughed, shaking her head at him. With his golden complexion, hazel eyes, and devilish smile, Quentin was a natural-born heartbreaker. Celeste felt sorry for all the unsuspecting females who would fall prey to his irresistible charm in the future.

"Hey, man, stop flirting with my mom." Michael had emerged from the house, followed by Marcus.

Quentin grinned at his best friend. "What's up, man? How was the trip?"

"Not long enough. Hey, Ma. How was work?"

"Tiring." Celeste kissed Michael's cheek, then affectionately rubbed the back of Marcus's head. "You boys get the groceries so we can go inside. It's hot out here."

After they'd grabbed all the bags, Celeste closed the trunk and followed them up the walk. As soon as she entered the house, the appetizing aroma of garlic, oregano, and tomato sauce filled her nostrils.

"Mmm. Something smells delicious."

"I made spaghetti for dinner," Michael told her, leading the way to the small, utilitarian kitchen. "Garlic bread's in the oven."

"Oh, darling," Celeste said tenderly, overcome with gratitude. "What would I do without you?"

He shrugged, setting down his armload of grocery bags. "It's just spaghetti. No big deal."

"*Of course* it's a big deal," Celeste countered, smooching his cheek until he groaned with embarrassment.

"Ding Dongs!" Marcus exclaimed, waving the package of snacks in the air. "Thanks, Ma!"

She smiled indulgently at him.

"My mom's working late tonight," Quentin announced, giving Celeste one of those deceptively guileless Eddie Haskell grins he'd perfected over the years. "So can I stay for dinner?"

"No," Michael said flatly.

"Of course," Celeste replied at the same time.

Michael frowned. "Ma—"

She tsk-tsked him. "Don't be rude, baby. Girls will come and go, but Quentin will always be your best friend."

"That's right," Quentin averred, lazily sprawling in a chair at the small breakfast table in the corner. "Besides, I'm not even messing with Kiara anymore."

Michael glanced up from unpacking groceries, his eyes alight with interest. "Why not?"

Quentin sucked his teeth. "Man, that girl don't know what she wants. Every time we're together, all she talks about is you. Later for that."

Michael could barely keep a satisfied grin off his face. "I'm sorry to hear that."

Quentin snorted out a laugh. "Sure you are!"

Chuckling at the exchange, Celeste grabbed a stack of mail from the counter and left the kitchen.

By the time she reached her bedroom, her humor had evaporated.

Nestled between the junk mail and bills was a letter from the bank. With a sinking sense of dread, she closed her bedroom door and tore open the envelope. It was an overdraft notice. When she read the details of the transaction, she rushed over to her nightstand, snatched up the phone, and dialed Clayton University's admissions office.

When a clerk answered the phone, Celeste quickly explained her dilemma. "I applied for the master's in nursing program, but my application fee didn't go through. I just received the overdraft notice from my bank. Is there any way I can resubmit the payment? I have the money now."

"I'm sorry, ma'am," the clerk said sympathetically, "but the application deadline for the fall semester has passed."

"I know, but—"

"We have a limited number of spaces for the nursing program, and they've all been filled."

"I realize that," Celeste argued, "but it's not like I didn't turn in my application on time."

"Yes, but the fee is part of the application, and yours wasn't processed. I'm sorry. You're more than welcome to apply for the spring semester. The deadline is—"

"I know what the deadline is," Celeste interrupted, flopping down heavily on her bed. "Thanks for your time."

She hung up the phone, trembling with anger and frustration. She was still sitting there clutching the overdraft notice in her hand when Sterling walked through the door ten minutes later.

"Hey, baby," he greeted her.

She said nothing, watching sullenly as he crossed to the dresser to remove his shoulder holster, weapon, and badge. He wore dark trousers and a white broadcloth shirt with the sleeves rolled to his muscled forearms.

"What a long day," he muttered, unbuttoning his shirt. "Seems like all hell broke loose as soon as I stepped foot in the police station this morning. I definitely wouldn't have minded spending another week in Sav—" He broke off, catching Celeste's reflection in the mirror.

Frowning, he turned around. "What's wrong?"

Wordlessly she held out the crumpled overdraft notice.

Sterling hesitated, then walked over and took the paper from her. She watched his face as he scanned the contents. He didn't look surprised as he calmly handed the notice back to her.

"Why didn't you tell me that my check had bounced?" Celeste demanded.

"I didn't know," he said grimly. "I was hoping it wouldn't."

"You were *hoping?*"

He winced at her sharp tone. "Look, I tried to work your application fee into our budget, but other bills were a priority."

"Why didn't you tell me that?"

"By the time I remembered to, you'd already sent off the check. So I just crossed my fingers and hoped that the payment wouldn't be processed before our next pay day."

"Well, it was," Celeste snapped. "And since the check bounced, I have to wait until the spring semester to apply again!"

Sterling ran a weary hand down his face and blew out a ragged breath. "I'm sorry."

"Like hell you are," she spat bitterly, ripping the bank notice in half and tossing the pieces to the floor.

Sterling scowled at her. "What's that supposed to mean?"

She glared accusingly at him. "You knew how important this was to me. All I've wanted for the past five years is to get my master's degree so that I can move into another area of nursing and earn more money. But you've never supported that goal. So forgive me if I have a hard time believing that you're genuinely sorry about this latest setback."

He eyed her incredulously. "Are you suggesting that I let the check bounce on purpose?"

"*You* tell me!" she flung back.

Clenching his jaw, Sterling strode across the room and closed the door so that their sons wouldn't overhear them arguing. At that moment, Celeste was beyond caring.

Angrily folding her arms across her chest, she glowered at him as he walked back to the bed and sat down beside her. "Look, baby, I know how much you want to go back to school. And contrary to what you may believe, I *do* support that goal. But the reality is that graduate school is expensive, even if you qualify for financial aid. Hell, we're still paying off the loans we took out for your bachelor's degree. And there're other things to consider as well. Like how many hours you'd have to cut back at work in order to accommodate your class schedule, or how often you'd be available to pick up the boys from their different activities." He shook his head regretfully. "I'm sorry, Cel, but this just isn't a good time for grad school."

"It's *never* going to be a good time!" she cried shrilly, jumping up from the bed.

Sterling frowned at her. "That's not true."

"No?" she challenged, hands thrust on her hips. "So tell me, then. When *will* it be a good time? When Michael goes to Morehouse in two years? Or when it's Marcus's turn? How about when they've *both* graduated from college and are established in their own careers? Is *that* when it'll be a good time for me to go back to school, Sterling?"

"Of course not. I'm just asking you to be patient a little longer—"

"I've been patient long enough!" Celeste screeched.

Sterling scowled. "Damn it, woman, keep your voice down before—"

Something snapped inside Celeste, and she burst out hysterically, "I can't do this anymore, Sterling!"

He went very still, staring at her. "What are you saying?"

She gestured around their cramped bedroom, at the threadbare carpet and secondhand furniture and the cheap comforter draped across their bed. "This isn't the life I planned!"

"What do you want from me?" Sterling exploded, lunging to his feet so suddenly that Celeste jumped. "Do you want me to apologize for not giving you the life you always dreamed of? Fine, here goes. *I'm sorry* that we don't live in a mansion in Buckhead and drive expensive cars. *I'm sorry* that I can't whisk you around the world in a private jet, and keep you decked out in diamonds and furs and designer clothes. *I'm sorry* that I didn't finish college, and I make less than the doctors you fawn over at the hospital."

Celeste's face heated with guilt, even as she sputtered protestingly, "Don't you dare—"

"You think I like living paycheck to paycheck?" Sterling demanded, his dark eyes flashing with fury. "You think I enjoy holding you back from pursuing your professional goals? You think I *want* to raise our children in a neighborhood that's going to hell in a damn hand basket?"

"I don't know, Sterling!" Celeste shouted. "Sometimes you seem so accepting and complacent about our situation—"

"*Complacent?*" he thundered incredulously. "You think I'm complacent just because I don't wallow in self-pity and regret the way *you* do? Damn it, woman, I'm doing the best I can to take care of this family, but if that's not good enough for you, you can just go to hell."

Choking on tears of pain and outrage, Celeste shrieked, "*You* go to hell!"

Sterling regarded her stonily, a muscle throbbing in his rigid jaw.

And Celeste knew, right then and there, that they'd crossed a line from which there would be no turning back.

As if he'd made the same unsettling revelation, Sterling's expression softened. "Look, I don't want to—"

Suddenly his pager went off.

Swearing under his breath, he grabbed the device clipped to his waist and glared at the small screen. Without a word, he turned toward the nightstand and picked up the phone to make a call.

"This is Detective Wolf," he announced brusquely.

Trembling with nerves and raw emotion, Celeste walked over to the bed and gingerly perched on the edge, not facing Sterling.

After a brief conversation, he hung up the phone. "There's been a double homicide. I have to go."

Celeste nodded mutely, keeping her back to him.

He hesitated for a moment. "I don't know what time I'll be back, so—"

"I know the drill."

Sterling was silent. She could feel him watching her, willing her to turn around and face him, to assure him that the chasm between them could be bridged. But she didn't turn around. And she offered no such assurances.

Because she couldn't.

After an agonizing eternity, he stalked to the dresser and grabbed his weapon and badge. It was only when she heard the door close behind him that she lowered herself to the bed, curled into a fetal position, and unleashed the torrent of tears she'd kept dammed up for far too long.

It was after midnight by the time Sterling returned home.

Pausing in the foyer, he shrugged out of his sport coat and shoulder holster, then trudged into the kitchen and opened the refrigerator. Out wafted the fragrant aroma of Michael's spaghetti, reminding him that he'd missed dinner. He smiled slightly, eyeing the foil-covered plate his son had left for him. Normally he would have heated up the food and inhaled it while standing, regardless of the late hour. But tonight he didn't have an appetite, and it had nothing to do with the particularly gruesome crime scene he'd just left.

That evening, as he'd worked his way around the bedroom of a young couple who'd been brutally murdered as they slept, all Sterling could hear were the words Celeste had hurled at him earlier.

I can't do this anymore!

She'd stopped him cold in his tracks with that statement. Though they'd argued many times over the years—especially in recent months—tonight's confrontation had been different. Because tonight was the closest Celeste had ever come to asking Sterling for a divorce.

He was still reeling with shock.

Grabbing a cold beer from the refrigerator, he popped open the can and took a healthy swig as he left the kitchen. Instead of heading to his bedroom on the second floor, he made his way down a creaky flight of stairs to reach the basement.

Not surprisingly, both of his sons were still up watching television, the glow from the screen providing the room's only illumination. Michael was sprawled across the worn leather sofa, while Marcus lay on his stomach on the floor with his chin propped in his hands. They were watching *The Chinese Connection*, an old martial arts action film starring Bruce Lee. They'd seen it so many times they could recite nearly every line of dialogue, and sometimes when they were feeling playful after watching the movie, they'd test their karate moves on each other, arguing over who was the better fighter.

But there would be none of that tonight, Sterling concluded. One look at his sons' gloomy countenances, and he knew that they'd overheard the argument between him and Celeste.

Suppressing a heavy sigh of frustration, he advanced into the shadowy room. "Hey, fellas."

They glanced over at him. "Hey, Dad."

Michael sat up, swinging his long legs over the edge of the sofa to make room for his father as Marcus rolled over and leaned back on his elbows to regard Sterling.

He smiled, nodding toward the television. "I see you're watching one of your old favorites."

"Yeah," Michael grunted.

" 'This time you are eating paper,' " Sterling said in his best imitation of Bruce Lee's accented voice. " 'Next time it will be glass.' "

The familiar joke fell flat, coaxing only halfhearted smiles out of Michael and Marcus.

Sterling grimaced. "Tough crowd," he muttered, taking a sip of his beer.

"Sorry, Dad," they mumbled dispiritedly.

He chuckled. "No need to apologize. I probably need to come up with new material anyway."

Michael and Marcus exchanged troubled glances that undoubtedly had nothing to do with their father's lame voice impersonations.

Knowing he could no longer ignore the elephant in the room, Sterling blew out a deep, weary breath. "What's on your mind, boys?"

They shared another uneasy glance.

"Are you and Ma getting a divorce?" Marcus blurted.

When Sterling winced, Michael scowled at his brother. "Nice going, Little Man. *Real* subtle."

"What?" Marcus protested, taking umbrage. "Isn't that what we wanted to ask him?"

"Not like that," Michael growled.

"It's okay," Sterling intervened before an argument erupted. "You didn't say anything wrong, Marcus. You both have a right to know what's going on between me and your mother."

"We heard you fighting," Marcus whispered. "So did Quentin."

"I know," Sterling said grimly, "and I'm real sorry about that. We should have kept our voices down."

"You tried to, but Ma made you mad." Marcus frowned, nervously chewing on his thumbnail. "Why's she so sad all the time?"

"Because she thinks we're poor," Michael said bitterly. "She wants things we can't afford."

"Now hold on," Sterling interjected, putting a hand on Michael's rigid forearm. "I don't want this to turn into a gripe session about your mama. No matter what you may have heard tonight, or how upset you may be, she's still your mother. She loves you both, and she deserves your respect. Are we clear on that?"

"Yes, sir," they mumbled obediently.

"Good." Sterling paused, carefully choosing his next words. "There are things about me and your mother...things about our relationship that you boys are too young to understand. But just because we argue, that doesn't mean we don't love each other. We just see certain things differently, and there's nothing wrong with that."

When Michael and Marcus traded dubious looks, Sterling heaved a resigned sigh. His sons were too smart, too intuitive, to swallow the sugarcoated explanation he was trying to feed them.

Staring down at his can of beer, he decided to level with them. "Your mother and I are having problems. Serious problems. We're going to do everything we can to work through them because we love each other, and we love both of you, and we want to keep our family together. I wish I could wave a magic wand and make everything instantly better, but I can't. What I *can* tell you is that no matter what happens, we're all going to be okay because we're family, and nothing will ever change that."

When he'd finished speaking, his throat was tight, and the boys' eyes were bright with unshed tears. As if they sensed that life as they knew it was about to come to an end.

"I wish we could go back to Mama Wolf's house," Marcus said glumly.

"Me too, Dad," Michael agreed. "You and Ma were happier there."

Remembering Celeste's entreaty for them to move to Savannah, Sterling smiled at his sons and said quietly, "As your wise great-grandmother used to tell me and your uncle, 'Happiness doesn't come from where you lay your head. It comes from where you lay your heart.' "

Chapter 7

Celeste paused outside the open doorway at the end of the darkened hospital corridor. Her heart was drumming erratically, and her hands were damp with perspiration as she stared at the brass nameplate on the door.

DR. GRANT J. RUTHERFORD, M.D., NEUROSURGERY.

After not seeing him for over a week, she'd been secretly pleased to find herself on call with Grant that evening when the nurse regularly assigned to neurosurgery was unable to come in. Celeste had assisted Grant as he performed emergency surgery on a car accident victim who'd suffered massive head injuries. After the successful operation, he'd discreetly pulled Celeste aside and asked her to stop by his office before she went home. She hadn't asked him what he wanted. She didn't care.

After getting the patient transported to the post-anesthesia care unit, she'd hurried to the restroom to brush her teeth and freshen her lipstick before making her way to Grant's office.

Now, standing there in the silent corridor, she felt a moment's hesitation. At two in the morning, the hospital was practically deserted. She should have gone home after the surgery, like the anesthesiologists and scrub tech had done. She was a married woman, a mother of two. So she had no business being alone with the very same man whose mere existence threatened to destroy everything that mattered to her.

Go home, her conscience warned. *Go home to your family before it's too late.*

She closed her eyes and inhaled a deep, shaky breath.

And then she stepped into the open doorway.

Grant was seated behind a large cherry desk in the elegantly furnished office. He was munching on a chocolate bar as he scribbled on a tablet, dictating the operative notes he was required to submit after every surgical procedure. He'd exchanged his scrubs for a Harvard University sweatshirt and khaki pants. His curly black hair gleamed in the soft glow cast by the brass desk lamp. Celeste's fingers itched to plunge through the thick strands, to luxuriate in the silky texture.

Swallowing hard, she shifted nervously from one foot to another. Grant didn't look up from his writing. Assuming he hadn't noticed her, she opened her mouth to speak when he held up one finger, signaling that he'd be with her shortly.

She nodded, remaining in the doorway.

Lips twitching with humor, he crooked that same finger at her and gestured to the visitor's chair across from his desk.

Celeste hesitated, then moved forward on rubbery legs. Though Grant didn't watch her approach, the smile playing at the corners of his lips gave her the impression that he was counting every step that brought her closer. The moment she sat down, he silently mouthed, *Atta, girl.*

She blushed like an infatuated teenager.

As she waited for Grant to finish his task, her eyes strayed behind him to the wall of framed degrees, plaques, and certificates that documented his path to becoming one of the country's leading neurosurgeons. His precision with a scalpel often made Celeste wonder whether he'd been born with one in his hand. In addition to being a brilliant surgeon, he was also a researcher who served on numerous committees and was being groomed to head the hospital's neurosurgical residency program.

To say that the man was going places would be a colossal understatement, Celeste mused, staring at a framed photograph of his parents, an attractive, sixty-something biracial couple who lived in Vermont. Grant had told her all about them—educated, hardworking, pillars of the community. The kind of parents who'd demanded nothing but the best from their four children, all of whom became successful in their own right.

As Celeste's gaze returned to Grant, her stomach fluttered, as it frequently did when she looked at him. Though she'd always preferred dark-skinned men, she'd been attracted to Grant from the moment she saw him. He was incredibly handsome with golden-brown skin, piercing green eyes, and thick, curly hair. He wasn't tall, but he had a great, athletic body honed from the rigorous workouts he squeezed into his demanding schedule. The nurses flirted shamelessly with him, cornering him in the hallways to ask inane questions about medical procedure just so they'd have an excuse to talk to him. Celeste had employed a more subtle approach, treating him with such polite cordiality he'd had no choice but to notice her, and wonder why she was so different from the other women who fawned over him.

She watched now as he set down his pen and lifted those sexy eyes to hers. "Sorry about all the sign language," he said, smiling ruefully. "I didn't want to lose my train of thought."

"I understand." She smiled, watching as he finished his chocolate bar and discarded the gold wrapper in the wastebasket beside his desk. "So the rumors are true. You really *do* eat a candy bar before or after every surgery."

He grinned lazily. "Of course. Didn't you know that chocolate's an excellent brain food?"

"*Chocolate?*" Celeste repeated skeptically.

"Sure. See, the cacao bean has certain nutrients and antioxidants that can be beneficial to everything from brain and cardiovascular health to skin elasticity." His grin widened. "Mark my words, Celeste. In twenty years researchers will be claiming that cacao beans hold the key to longevity."

She laughed. "And all this time I thought chocolate was a guilty pleasure to be avoided as much as possible."

He shook his head. "Just goes to show."

"What?"

"Not all guilty pleasures are bad for you," he said softly.

Celeste stared at him, shivers of awareness snaking through her body. It was obvious that he was no longer talking about candy bars.

She smiled demurely. "Got any more of those guilty pleasures?"

"Chocolate?" His voice deepened suggestively. "Or did you have something else in mind?"

Her mouth went dry. "I, um, meant the chocolate."

Eyes glinting wickedly, he opened his desk drawer and removed another candy bar. Instead of passing it to her, he stood and walked around the desk. Celeste sat back as he knelt beside her chair and partially unwrapped the chocolate.

He held it out to her. "Why don't you try a bite first and see if you like it," he suggested.

Holding his gaze, Celeste leaned forward and opened her mouth. As her lips closed around the dark chocolate bar, Grant's eyes glittered in a way that made her pulse race.

"Mmm," she murmured, chewing slowly. "That's good. Very rich and exotic."

"It's imported from Belgium," Grant told her. "It has a high percentage of cacao."

She smiled. "So it's the good stuff."

"Absolutely," he said huskily, watching her mouth as he fed her another bite. "Nothing but the best."

"Um-hmm," she agreed.

When he bit into the chocolate bar, her nipples hardened and heat pooled between her thighs. She'd never realized that sharing candy with a man could be so tantalizing.

When Grant offered her another bite, she laughed softly and shook her head. "That's enough for now."

"You sure?"

She nodded. "It's so rich and decadent. I don't want to overdo it."

He chuckled, rewrapping the half-eaten candy bar. As he handed it to her, their fingers brushed. A current of pure sexual awareness quivered between them.

They stared at each other for several charged moments before Celeste glanced away, tucking the chocolate into her tote bag on the floor.

Grant remained kneeling by her chair. "Have you ever been to Belgium?"

She shook her head.

"It's a beautiful country. You should go sometime."

"Sure," she drawled. "Just as soon as I win the lottery."

Hearing the trace of cynicism in her voice, Grant searched her face. "You don't think you and your husband could set aside some money, maybe a little at a time—"

"No," Celeste said flatly. If she and Sterling couldn't even afford a fifty-dollar application fee, a trip to Europe was out of the question.

"That's too bad," Grant lamented. "You seem like a woman who'd enjoy traveling, seeing other parts of the world."

"I'm sure I would," Celeste retorted. "But since that's not an option for me, it doesn't make much sense for me to dwell on it, now does it?"

He looked taken aback by her harsh tone. "Celeste—"

She glanced impatiently at her watch. "Look, it's getting late. I should go."

He grabbed her wrist, detaining her as she started to rise from the chair. "Don't go," he said with gentle urgency.

"Grant—"

"I'm sorry. I didn't mean to offend you by prying into your personal affairs. Please forgive me."

Celeste wavered, staring into his earnest face. After another moment, she blew out a resigned breath and sank back against the chair, dragging a shaky hand through her hair.

"It's not your fault," she murmured. "I overreacted."

"No, I was out of line."

"Maybe you were," she conceded. "But I wouldn't have reacted that way if...well, if I wasn't dealing with some issues at home."

"I understand," Grant murmured, rubbing his thumb back and forth across her hand. "Do you want to talk about it?"

Celeste hesitated, torn between her loyalty to her husband and her overwhelming need to confide in someone.

After several moments of indecision, the loyalty instinct won.

"I appreciate the offer," she said ruefully, "but it'd probably be best if I kept my marital problems to myself."

Grant nodded. "I understand. But if you ever need a listening ear, just remember that I'm here for you."

"Thank you." She lowered her gaze to their joined hands, watching as his thumb stroked her knuckle in a slow, gentle caress that sent heat coursing through her veins. She swallowed tightly. "Grant—"

"The reason I asked you up here," he interrupted softly, "is that I wanted to thank you for your help tonight in the OR."

Her eyes lifted to his. "You don't have to thank me. I was just doing my job."

"And you do it very well. You're an outstanding nurse, Celeste. You're knowledgeable, well prepared, and you work great under pressure. I wish every nurse at this hospital was as skilled as you are."

Celeste warmed with pleasure. "Thank you, Grant. That really means a lot, coming from a surgeon of your caliber. I think you bring out the best in everyone who works with you."

He chuckled. "You don't have to flatter me just because—"

"I'm not flattering you," she said earnestly. "Everyone knows what an amazing surgeon you are. I've been a fan of yours ever since the day we shared a crowded elevator together. You didn't notice me standing in the corner, but *I* noticed you. You were talking to another doctor about the technological advances that were coming to MR imaging. The excitement and passion in your voice gave me goose bumps. The first time I got to be part of your surgical team was one of the most exciting days of my life."

By the time she'd finished gushing—there was no other word for it—Grant's expression had softened. He reached out, gently cradling her cheek in his hand. "You don't know how much it means to me to hear you say those things, Celeste."

She stared at him, her heart knocking against her rib cage. He was so close that she could count every strand of his thick, curly eyelashes. Every instinct screamed at her to get up and leave, to put an end to this dangerous mating dance before things went too far.

But she couldn't move.

Worse, she didn't want to.

"I've been trying so hard to resist my feelings for you," Grant confessed, low and husky. "But it's a losing battle. I want you, Celeste, and unless my instincts are totally wrong, you want me too."

She opened her mouth to offer a denial, but nothing came out.

Taking her silence as confirmation of her feelings, Grant leaned forward and slanted his mouth over hers.

Instant heat suffused her body. After only a slight hesitation, she wrapped her arms around his neck and parted her lips. His hot, velvety tongue stroked hers, making her shudder with need.

Deepening the kiss, Grant moved between her legs. When she felt the hard bulge of his erection, she wrenched her mouth free, gasping for breath.

Grant stared at her, chest heaving. "Celeste—"

"That was a mistake," she whispered hoarsely, fumbling for her tote bag on the floor. "I have to go."

"No, you don't. Please—"

Scraping back her chair, she lunged to her feet and started across the room on wobbly legs. She'd just reached the open doorway when Grant called out to her, "How long can we keep this up?"

She stopped in her tracks. Her heart was hammering so hard she thought she'd need a defibrillator at any moment.

"How long can we go on fighting our attraction to each other?" Grant continued, ragged frustration edging his voice. "Months? Years? How long, Celeste?"

She turned slowly to face him. He was gazing intently at her.

"I'm married," she whispered.

"Not happily," he countered. "If you were, you wouldn't be here."

Her face flamed. She couldn't even deny what he'd said, and they both knew it.

"Look," Grant murmured, taking a step toward her. "You don't have to make any decisions tonight. But these feelings we have for each other aren't going anywhere. The sooner we deal with them, the better off we'll both be."

Celeste's pulse was pounding. "And how do you propose we...deal with them?"

Grant said nothing, but the smoldering heat in his eyes left no doubt what he wanted from her.

An electric moment passed between them.

Holding his gaze, Celeste let her tote bag drop to the floor.

A heartbeat later Grant was there, shoving the door closed as he crushed his mouth to hers. She kissed him back with equal fervor, needing him more than her very next breath.

They staggered backward, landing against the door. She hooked her leg over his hip and wantonly ground against him, seeking to assuage the ache between her thighs.

His hands went to her blouse, hurriedly unfastening the small buttons before he gave up halfway and ripped the material from her body. Celeste hazily registered the sound of buttons scattering across the floor, but she was too far gone to care that she'd have to come up with an explanation later for the ruined garment.

Trembling with desire, she watched as Grant lifted his head and unclasped the front hook of her black satin bra. He swore softly as her breasts sprang free. She groaned as he cupped them in his warm hands, brushing his thumbs over her puckered nipples before pushing them together.

"You're so beautiful," he uttered before bending to pull her nipples into his mouth.

She cried out, her spine arching off the door as jolts of sensation shot through her. He sucked her areolas, the sensual stroke of his tongue deepening the burn between her thighs until she thought she'd explode.

He licked his way from her breasts to her quivering stomach, scorching her flesh. Panting with anticipation, Celeste watched as he squatted and unzipped her jeans, peeling them over her hips and down her legs, then off her feet as she stepped out of her clogs.

As he stared at her bare toes, she was glad that she'd taken the time to re-polish her nails yesterday.

"Even your feet are gorgeous," Grant murmured appreciatively.

She gave a husky laugh that melted into a moan as he reached between her thighs and palmed her sex, rubbing her erect clitoris through the fabric of her black panties. She writhed against him, wanting him inside her with a desperation that staggered her.

Pulse thudding violently, she watched as he grasped the waistband of her panties and slid them off her legs, dropping them on the floor. Then, holding her gaze, he eased two fingers inside her, groaning with arousal as her feminine walls gripped him.

"You're so wet," he whispered thickly.

A helpless whimper was all Celeste could manage.

He removed his probing fingers and draped her right leg over his shoulder, then lowered his mouth to her drenched sex. She cried out and threw back her head, spasms of pleasure tearing through her pelvis. Her stomach muscles clenched as his tongue flicked over her clitoris and lapped at the swollen folds of her labia.

"*Grant...*" she mewled as her hands tangled in his curly hair, first pulling him closer, then pushing him away.

He raised his heavy-lidded eyes to hers, his lips glistening with her nectar.

"I want you inside me," she said hoarsely. "*Now.*"

She didn't have to ask twice.

He quickly yanked off his sweatshirt, toned muscles flexing, golden skin gleaming.

Celeste trembled with lust as he dug inside his pocket and retrieved a condom, then tugged down his pants and dark briefs. She was riveted by the sight of his thick, engorged penis. He tore the foil packet apart and quickly rolled the condom over his erection, then surged to his feet.

Unable to resist, Celeste curled her fingers around the base of his shaft and stroked him sensually.

Groaning with pleasure, Grant lifted her off the floor. She curved her arms around his neck and wrapped her legs around his waist, shivering as their genitals connected. They stared into each other's eyes as he grabbed her hips and thrust into her, impaling her against the door. She let out a wild cry.

Grant shuddered deeply, gritted his teeth and closed his eyes, looking as if he were trying not to climax too soon. Celeste knew the feeling. He felt so good inside her that she seriously doubted she'd last very long.

Slowly opening his eyes, Grant began pumping into her with long, deep strokes that sent waves of ecstasy crashing through her. She moaned and gripped his shoulders, her nails digging into the whipcord muscles.

His hands slid around her back and moved downward, cupping her butt cheeks in each large palm. She gasped as he drove into her harder and faster, their bodies rocking against the door. The sound of skin slapping on skin filled the room.

With each rhythmic thrust of Grant's hips, Celeste's orgasm built and swelled. She could feel every ridge of his shaft as he pounded into her. The delicious friction intensified her pleasure until her body exploded, clenching around his penis.

"Grant...*Grant!*" she sobbed out, her hips bucking furiously against his.

He shoved into her one last time, then came with a guttural shout. Shaking all over, he dropped his head forward and buried his face in her hair.

They clung together, panting, their chests heaving as they fought to catch their breath.

It was only then that Celeste's gaze landed on a book that had fallen out of her tote bag when she dropped it earlier. It was an autobiography of Marcus Garvey that one of her coworkers had loaned to her for Marcus, who'd been wanting to learn more about his namesake.

Oh, God, Celeste thought as an image of her young son flashed through her mind. That was when she realized the enormity of the treacherous act she'd just committed.

As a hot wave of shame and horror swept through her, she squirmed frantically against Grant. "Let me go."

He raised his head, his green eyes probing hers. "Celeste—"

"Let me go," she said in a sharper tone.

He hesitated, then reluctantly withdrew from her body. She quickly unwrapped her legs from his waist as he set her down and stepped back.

He tried again, "Celeste—"

"Please don't say anything," she begged, bending down to retrieve her discarded clothes. "Anything you say will only make it worse."

Grant frowned. "Don't do this, sweetheart. Please don't."

She hurriedly tugged on her panties and jeans, then refastened her bra and shrugged into the ruined blouse. She assiduously avoided looking at Grant's naked body, afraid she'd be tempted to stay if she did.

"I don't regret what we just did," he said quietly, "and neither should you."

"Are you serious? I'm a married woman who just had sex with—" She broke off as a hysterical sob caught in her throat. Clapping a hand to her mouth, she stumbled over to her fallen tote bag and stuffed Marcus's book back inside, then stood and raced to the door.

"You're forgetting your shoes," Grant called after her.

Swearing under her breath, she turned and rushed back over to him, snatching her clogs out of his hand. Catching a glimpse of his semi-erect penis, she blushed furiously, then spun away and ran from the office like Cinderella fleeing the ball at the stroke of midnight.

But Celeste was no storybook heroine, and after what she'd just done, she didn't deserve a fairytale ending.

Chapter 8

The tension was thick around the dinner table that night.

Michael and Marcus were uncharacteristically withdrawn, pushing their food around their plates disinterestedly. Celeste alternated between picking at her own meal and stealing worried glances at them, visibly unnerved by their brooding silence.

Seated at the head of the table, Sterling quietly observed his family, not unlike the way he'd watch a suspect from the other side of a one-way mirror before he entered the interrogation room. Halfway through dinner that evening, he'd realized two things. The first was that Michael and Marcus were still upset about the argument they'd overheard between their parents two nights ago. The second—and perhaps more troubling realization—was that Celeste was nervous about something. *Very* nervous.

Sterling didn't want to speculate why.

"Just three more days until school starts," Celeste announced, her voice breaking an uncomfortable stretch of silence. She smiled cheerfully at Michael and Marcus. "Aren't you two excited about going back to school and seeing all your friends again?"

"Sure," Michael mumbled around a mouthful of meat loaf.

Marcus didn't even bother to respond.

Sterling shot him a stern glance. "Son, your mother asked you a question."

Marcus stared down at his plate, raking his fork through the buttery mashed potatoes that had turned into a lumpy puddle. "Yes," he answered, barely audible.

"Yes what?" Sterling prompted.

"Yes, I'm looking forward to school."

"That's good." Celeste smiled approvingly. "I'm expecting another year of straight As from you *and* your brother."

This was where Michael ordinarily pled his case, citing the challenges of being a student athlete and claiming that his classes were getting harder, so he shouldn't be penalized if he didn't make the honor roll every quarter.

But this time, Michael said nothing.

Celeste's smile faltered. She briefly met Sterling's gaze, then glanced away and reached for her glass of sweet tea. "Marcus, have you started reading the book I gave you this morning?"

"Not yet."

"Maybe you could take a break from playing your Atari and read one or two chapters this evening," she suggested. "With school starting in a few days, you need to get back in the habit of reading every night anyway."

"Yes, ma'am," he parroted.

Another heavy silence descended over the table.

Sterling watched as Celeste nudged her food around her plate before forking up a bite of meat loaf. She chewed slowly, delicately, her eyes roaming around the small dining room as if she were seeing details for the first time. The peeling wallpaper, the faded drapes, the rusted chandelier that hung from the ceiling—all contrasted with the beautiful mahogany curio cabinet they'd received as a wedding gift from Mama Wolf.

When Celeste's roving gaze came to rest on Sterling's face, he had the uncanny feeling that she'd been buying herself time. As if she had to work up the nerve to look at him.

"You've been rather quiet since you got home," she observed. "Is everything okay at work?"

Sterling gave her a wry look. "I'm a homicide detective. Nothing's *ever* okay."

"Right." She smiled weakly. "Of course."

"But I know what you meant." He took a sip of his drink, watching her over the rim of his glass. "I guess I'm just a little tired. I didn't sleep well last night."

"I'm sorry," she murmured. "I tried not to wake you up when I came home."

"You didn't. I was already awake." At her surprised look, he explained, "I couldn't get into a good sleep for some reason."

"Oh." She held his gaze for a long moment, then looked down at her plate and carefully resumed eating.

Michael and Marcus exchanged glances across the table, then turned to their father.

"Can I be excused?" both asked at the same time.

Sterling frowned, glancing at their plates. "You haven't finished your dinner, Marcus."

"I know," he mumbled.

"You didn't like the meat loaf?" Celeste asked anxiously. "Was it too dry?"

"No, Ma. It was good. I'm just not very hungry." He glanced at Sterling. "So can we be excused?"

Sterling nodded.

The boys shoved their chairs back from the table and stood.

"Oh, wait," Celeste blurted suddenly.

When everyone looked at her, she plastered on a bright smile that had an edge of desperation to it. "I have some great news to share," she announced.

An expectant silence greeted her.

"I got a bonus at work." She paused. "Two thousand dollars."

Michael and Marcus's eyes bulged incredulously. "*Two thousand dollars?*"

Celeste beamed. "That's right. I found out this afternoon when I went to pick up my paycheck. Isn't it wonderful?"

"Heck, yeah," Marcus enthused.

Michael grinned. "Congratulations, Ma."

Stunned, Sterling could only stare at Celeste.

She continued, "So you know what this means, right? You boys are getting new back to school clothes and shoes—"

They cheered.

"—and something else you're really going to enjoy." Celeste paused for dramatic effect, smiling mysteriously. "Can you guess what it is?"

Michael and Marcus quickly shook their heads.

"Here's a hint," Celeste drawled, making an exaggerated show of studying her manicured fingernails. "What are you boys always rushing home to watch after church every Sunday?"

They stared at each other. "Football," they chorused.

"Exactly." She grinned at them. "That's why I bought you tickets to an Atlanta Falcons game in October."

Whooping with excitement, the boys high-fived each other across the table, then rushed over to their mother and hugged her, one on each side.

"Thanks, Ma," they told her. "You're the best!"

Celeste clung to them, her eyes closing in an expression of poignant gratitude. As if she were savoring something she'd nearly lost.

Watching her, Sterling felt his chest tighten with some unnamed emotion.

As Michael and Marcus pulled away, Celeste grasped their hands in hers, looking at each of them in turn. "I love you boys so much. No matter how tall or strong you become, or how deep your voices get, you will *always* be my babies. Do you hear me?"

They nodded. "Yes, ma'am."

"Good." She smiled, glancing at Sterling. "I bought four tickets to the game. I figured you and the fellas could take Quentin."

"You don't wanna go, Ma?" Michael asked.

"Heavens, no," she said with a mock shudder. "You know I don't like football. Quentin's mama and I will treat ourselves to a massage or something."

Michael grinned. "Sounds good. I'm gonna run down the street to tell Q."

"I'll go with you," Marcus said.

The two brothers raced out of the kitchen. Moments later the front door opened and slammed shut behind them.

Alone, Sterling and Celeste stared at each other across the dining table.

He was the first to speak. "A bonus, huh?"

Her chin lifted a notch. "That's right."

"Just out of the clear blue?"

Celeste shrugged. "The hospital's been receiving more financial contributions from donors. I guess they finally decided to share the wealth with their employees. Anyway," she added almost defensively, "does it matter *why* they gave us bonuses? Our family needs the money, so I, for one, am not going to look a gift horse in the mouth."

"Neither am I." Sterling smiled at her. "So now that I've gotten over my shock, allow me to congratulate you. You work damn hard at that hospital, babe, so you deserve every red cent of that bonus, and then some."

"Thank you, Sterl," Celeste murmured. "I appreciate that."

"And I appreciate you," he said sincerely. "You've made our sons the happiest boys in the world tonight. They've always wanted to attend a Falcons game, and now you've made it possible. So thank you."

Her expression grew tender. "You don't have to thank me. I'd do anything for our children."

"I know. You're a good mother, sweetheart. Michael and Marcus love you, and so do I."

She gazed at him, her eyes shimmering with moisture. "I love you too, baby. I'm sorry for the hurtful things I said the other day. I was speaking out of frustration—"

"We both were," Sterling gently interrupted. "In hindsight, I wish I'd handled the whole situation differently. I should have told you up front that we didn't have enough money to cover the application fee. I apologize for keeping you in the dark like that."

"You have nothing to apologize for," Celeste said vehemently. "*I'm* the one who should apologize for putting that kind of pressure on you."

"It's all right." He hesitated. "I've been thinking about what you said, about finding the right time for you to go back to school. Maybe we can start planning for the spring semester—"

Celeste's eyes brightened with hope. "You really mean that?"

He nodded. "I'm not saying it's going to be easy, but as my grandmother always says, 'Where there's a will, the Lord will make a way.' So whenever you're ready, we can set aside some time and start exploring our options. How does that sound?"

"It sounds wonderful," she whispered. "Thank you."

"You don't have to thank me," Sterling said quietly, echoing her own words. "I'd do anything for you, sweetheart."

She shook her head, tears shining in her eyes. "I don't deserve you. You're too good—"

She broke off as he suddenly pushed back his chair and stood. She stared up at him as he rounded the table to reach her side. When he held out his hand to her, she placed her palm in his. He pulled her gently to her feet, then lifted her into his arms.

As he started from the kitchen, Celeste murmured half protestingly, "We didn't clear the dishes from the table."

"Let the boys take care of them when they get back." Sterling winked at her. "*We've* got more important business to tend to."

***

"You've been avoiding me."

Celeste glanced up from the course catalog she'd been perusing to watch as Grant walked into the nurses' lounge dressed in a white shirt, gray tie, and black slacks. Her pulse quickened at the sight of him. She hadn't seen him since the morning they'd made love in his office four days ago.

And he was right. She *had* been avoiding him. She couldn't face him after what they'd done. She could barely look at herself in the mirror every day.

Her mouth went dry as she watched him pull out a chair at the table, turn it around and smoothly straddle it. When he smiled at her, her treacherous heart skipped several beats.

"You've been avoiding me," he repeated softly.

"No, I haven't," she lied. "It's the first week of school, so I switched shifts with another nurse so that I could be home in the afternoons when Marcus gets back."

Grant's eyes glinted. "Fair enough. How have you been?"

"Fine." Another lie. "And you?"

"Lousy. I can't stop thinking about you."

Her belly quivered. Blushing deeply, she shot a furtive glance toward the doorway. "We shouldn't be talking like this. Someone could walk in at any moment."

"I know. Which is why I came to ask you to meet me for coffee when your shift's over."

She was already shaking her head. "I can't. I need to be there when Marcus gets home."

"Doesn't he have a key to let himself in?"

"Yes, but that's not the point."

Grant leaned across the table, pinning her with his intense emerald gaze. "Ten minutes, Celeste. All I'm asking for is ten minutes of your time so we can talk in private."

She bit her lip, wavering. "I really shouldn't."

"Please," he coaxed gently.

She swallowed hard, looking toward the doorway again. She could hear the phone ringing at the nurses' station down the hallway, could hear the slap of crepe-soled shoes against linoleum as her colleagues went from room to room checking on patients and dispensing medications.

She glanced down at her watch. Twelve more minutes until her break was over.

She lifted her head, forcing herself to meet Grant's imploring gaze. "I really can't. I'm sorry."

A look of disappointment swept over his face. Slowly he leaned back, staring down at his hands clasped over the back of the chair. Her mind conjured an image of his hand gripping a scalpel as he carved a perfect incision into a patient's skull. A moment later she remembered that very same hand snaking between her thighs as he slid his fingers inside her.

It was enough to bring a hot, wanton flush to her body.

"You're still having second thoughts about what happened between us," Grant said quietly, searching her face.

"Of course," she whispered. "It was a mistake."

"Was it?" he challenged. "Or is that what you've been telling yourself because you're too afraid to admit how much you actually enjoyed being with me?"

Heat flooded her face. Without answering him, she closed the course catalog she'd been studying and shoved it inside her tote bag with trembling hands.

"I'll take that as a yes," Grant murmured tauntingly.

Her temper flared. "What do you want from me?" she hissed at him. "I'm married with children. I have *everything* to lose. What about you?"

He gazed deeply at her. "I've already lost the only thing that matters, Celeste."

"What?"

"My heart."

She let out a soft gasp, staring at him.

"I love you," he said in an achingly husky voice. "I want to be with you more than anything in the world."

Oh, God. She closed her eyes, fighting back tears of anguish mingled with undeniable joy. How many times had she fantasized about hearing such a passionate declaration from him? How many times had she secretly yearned to run away with him? To start a new life with him, free of guilt or shame?

"I know how difficult this has been for you," Grant continued, low and urgent. "I know you have a family to consider, and you have to weigh the consequences of any decision you make. But—" He broke off abruptly as another nurse entered the lounge, cheerfully humming Blondie's hit song, "Call Me."

Seeing Celeste and Grant at the table, she grinned playfully. "Hey, you two. That looks like a mighty serious convo you're having over there."

Thinking fast, Celeste reached inside the tote bag on her lap, pulled out a notepad, and blurted, "Dr. Rutherford was about to go over his preference cards with me. I'll be assisting him with a craniotomy later this week."

"So you were talking about work?" The tall, blue-eyed brunette wrinkled her nose in disappointment. "Too bad. I was hoping you were swapping juicy gossip about some brewing scandal or another. Guess I've been watching too much *General Hospital*."

Celeste and Grant shared a tense chuckle.

"Anyway, don't mind me," Theresa said lightly, opening the microwave door. "I'm just gonna make some popcorn, then I'll be out of your way."

For the next four minutes, Celeste pretended to take copious notes as Grant dictated to her what he wanted in his operating room for the fabricated surgery. Out of the corner of her eye, she could see Theresa stealing curious glances at them. It was all Celeste could do not to jump up from the table and flee the room. Becoming fodder for gossip and speculation was the absolute *last* thing she needed. If any of her colleagues found out that she was having an affair with Grant, she'd not only lose her good reputation. She could also lose her job.

After an agonizing eternity, the microwave oven dinged. Theresa carefully removed the bag of popcorn and opened it, releasing a cloud of fragrant, buttery steam.

She turned, shaking the bag at Celeste and Grant. "Want some?"

"No, thanks," they politely declined.

"Suit yourself." Flashing a grin at them, she popped a fluffy kernel into her mouth and left the lounge.

After a lengthy silence, Celeste exhaled a deep, shaky breath and set down the pen she'd been gripping tight enough to sever the circulation to her fingers. "I can't do this," she whispered faintly. "I'm not cut out for lying and sneaking around. That's not who I am."

"I know," Grant murmured, keeping his voice low just in case Theresa was loitering near the doorway. "And I don't want to turn you into that person, believe me. But sooner or later you're gonna have to make a decision about us."

Celeste swallowed with difficulty. "I know. I just—"

She was interrupted by the sound of his pager beeping. As he grimaced and reached for the device, she couldn't help reflecting on the irony of her loving two men whose professions frequently pulled them away from her at a moment's notice. One of them saved lives. The other sought justice for those whose lives had been taken.

Returning the pager to the waistband of his pants, Grant said apologetically, "I have to go scrub in for surgery." His lips curved wryly. "Turns out I really *am* performing a craniotomy today."

Celeste smiled at the reference to the fib she'd told Theresa. "Good luck," she said as she and Grant rose from the table together. "Not that you really need it."

"That's not true. I could always use good luck." He smiled at her. "I'm leaving for Minnesota tomorrow."

"Oh?" Her tone was deliberately casual. "Business or pleasure?"

"Business. The head of neurosurgery at the Mayo Clinic has been courting me for months, inviting me to come for a visit to tour the facilities." He shrugged one shoulder. "I've got a few days off, so I finally decided to take him up on his offer."

Celeste went still, staring at him. "You're not considering accepting a position there, are you?" she asked, her heart plummeting at the thought of him leaving Atlanta. Leaving her.

"I guess it depends," he said slowly.

"On what?"

He held her gaze. "On whether I have a compelling enough reason to stay here."

She swallowed tightly, receiving the message loud and clear.

He touched her cheek, a gossamer caress that sent shivers up and down her spine. "I'll see you when I return in a few days," he murmured.

Celeste nodded wordlessly.

As she stared after his retreating back, she wondered how she'd be able to let him walk out of her life, when she could scarcely bear to watch him leave a room.

Chapter 9

One week later, Celeste was awakened from a deep slumber by the sound of the doorbell.

She groaned, opening a bleary eye to glare at the alarm clock on her nightstand. It was 12:34 p.m. She'd worked a double shift the day before to cover for a sick colleague, so she'd been trying to catch up on her sleep ever since she got home that morning.

When the doorbell rang again, she seriously considered ignoring it. It could be one of those annoying door-to-door salesmen, or a Jehovah's Witness. But then she remembered that Mama Wolf often liked to send them surprise gifts through the mail. If that was the postman at the front door, and he left the package on the porch, there was no guarantee that it would still be there when Celeste woke up in a few hours.

With another deep groan, she dragged herself out of bed, threw on her pink satin robe, and trudged downstairs to answer the door. But when she squinted through the peephole, it wasn't the mailman, or a salesman, or a religious zealot seeking converts.

It was the last person on earth she'd expected to see on her doorstep.

It was Grant.

A shocked jolt went through her, zapping all traces of fatigue from her body. She hastily combed her fingers through her disheveled hair and blew into her cupped palms, checking her breath. Wrinkling her nose in distaste, she raced upstairs to the bathroom and rinsed out her mouth with a capful of Listerine. Satisfied that her appearance—and oral hygiene—passed muster, she dashed back downstairs and quickly opened the front door to stare incredulously at Grant.

"What the hell are you doing here?" she demanded.

He smiled slowly, peering down at her over the rim of his dark sunglasses. "Hello to you, too."

Poking her head out the door, Celeste swept a quick glance up and down the street. "Where's your car?"

"I parked a few houses away and walked."

"Thank God." She grabbed his arm and yanked him inside the house, then slammed the door.

Grant tucked his hands into his jeans pockets, looking sheepish. "I know I should have called first—"

"No," Celeste interrupted, "you shouldn't have come here at all. Do you have *any* idea what could happen if one of my neighbors saw you walking up to my house in broad daylight? *Do you?*"

He grimaced at her shrill tone. "I'm sorry for taking such a huge risk, but I had to see you."

She heaved an exasperated breath. "What could be so urgent that it couldn't wait another—"

"I'm leaving Atlanta, Celeste."

The air whooshed out of her lungs as if he'd punched her in the stomach. Stunned, she gaped at him. "W-what did you just say?"

There was an excited gleam in his eyes. "I've accepted a position in the Mayo Clinic's neurosurgery department. They're doing some groundbreaking things over there, and I want to be part of it."

"I see." Celeste scraped a trembling hand through her hair. "Well...I guess congratulations are in order."

Grant's expression softened. He took a step toward her. "Celeste—"

"Would you like some coffee? I'm going to make some coffee." Abruptly she spun on her heel and marched toward the kitchen, her bare feet slapping sharply against the hardwood floor.

"I want you to go with me," Grant called after her.

She nearly doubled over. Somehow she managed to stay upright and reach the kitchen, where she quickly busied herself with brewing a pot of coffee she didn't even want.

She didn't know why she was so shocked by Grant's announcement. He'd already warned her that he was considering this move. But she hadn't expected him to make such a momentous, life-changing decision so soon. She thought she'd have more time.

She *needed* more time.

Grant followed her into the kitchen. "Did you hear what I said, Celeste? I want you to go to Minnesota with me."

"I heard you." She kept her back to him. "You're asking me to leave my husband."

There was a long silence. "Yes."

She closed her eyes, tightly gripping the coffee canister. "I'm not ready."

"I think you are," Grant countered softly. "Your reaction to my news tells me you're more ready than you even realize."

Celeste swallowed hard, saying nothing.

He came up behind her, sliding his arms around her waist and pulling her back against him. She shivered as his warm lips nuzzled the side of her throat, sending currents of sensation charging through her body.

"Come with me," he whispered urgently against her ear. "You've told me how you always intended to leave Atlanta after graduating from college. You've been feeling trapped here, but it doesn't have to stay that way. Come to Minnesota with me. We can start over fresh, just you and me. I'll buy you any house you want, and we'll travel around the world together, see all the beautiful places you've always dreamed of visiting."

Celeste whimpered, stunned by how desperately she wanted the things he spoke of. An escape from the drudgery her life had become, a new beginning. All she had to do was say yes, and she could have everything she'd ever desired.

Sensing her weakening resolve, Grant slowly turned her around, keeping her in the circle of his arms. Her breath caught in her throat as she stared into his glittering green eyes, filled with promise and unmistakable love.

She didn't resist as he lifted her onto the counter and stepped between her legs. At the feel of his thick erection pressed against her belly, a slow, sensual heat spread through her veins, pouring into her groin.

Sinking his hands into her hair, Grant lowered his mouth to hers. Her eyes fluttered shut as he parted her lips and slid his tongue between them, stroking and retreating in a wickedly carnal dance. Her pulse thundered as she deepened the kiss, erotically gliding her tongue against his.

Suddenly she couldn't remember why this was so wrong, having her lover there, in the home she shared with her husband and her children. All that mattered was that she loved Grant, and she needed him more than anything she'd needed in a very long time.

Her head fell back as he kissed the column of her throat, then slipped his hand between the folds of her robe and cupped her breast through her satin nightgown. She shivered, electric fire sweeping over her skin. He stroked her erect nipple, and when touching her wasn't enough, he lowered his head to suck the beaded flesh into his mouth.

A broken moan erupted from her throat. She arched against him, craving more of the pleasure he offered.

She was so far gone that she didn't hear the front door open, didn't hear the approaching footsteps until it was too late.

"What the—"

Her eyes flew open to find Marcus standing in the kitchen doorway, taking in the intimate scene with a look that Celeste knew she would never forget for as long as she lived.

By the time she and Grant sprang guiltily apart, Marcus's shocked horror had morphed into a savage rage that launched him forward like a missile fired from a cannon. Snarling furiously, he took a hard swing at Grant that caught him squarely in the chest, knocking him backward.

"Marcus, no!" Celeste screamed, hopping down from the counter and landing awkwardly on her ankle.

"You son of a bitch!" Marcus shouted viciously at Grant as Celeste hobbled forward and tackled him around the waist. "Who the hell do you think you are?"

Grant held up a restraining hand. "Now just hold on there—"

Marcus lunged forward. "Don't tell me—"

"Baby, please!" Celeste cried, wrestling her enraged son to the floor and clamping her legs around his, as if she were restraining a violent patient at the hospital.

She glanced up quickly at Grant. "Please go. I'll take care of this."

He hesitated, looking concerned. "Let me help—"

"*JUST GO!*" she screamed at him.

He took one last glance at Marcus struggling in her arms, frowned deeply, then turned and strode out of the kitchen.

Marcus yelled after him, "You ever come back here and I'll kill you!"

"Stop this!" Celeste pleaded desperately. "You don't understand, baby. Just listen to me. *Please*."

Tears sprang to Marcus's eyes, and he let out a choked little sob that broke Celeste's heart. And then suddenly, like a powerful storm wreaking a path of destruction before subsiding, he went limp in her arms.

And that was the moment Celeste realized that he would never be the same again. Her baby boy had lost his innocence.

And she was to blame.

"Darling, please," she sobbed brokenly, rocking him back and forth in her arms. "Please try to understand. I didn't remember that you had an early dismissal today. I *never* would have let you see me with Grant that way if I'd remembered!"

Marcus sniffled, then untangled himself from her and climbed slowly to his feet. She eyed him warily, as if he were a wild animal whose next move she was trying to anticipate.

He wouldn't even look at her. "Does Dad know?" he asked in a raw whisper.

Celeste hesitated, tugging her robe protectively around her body. "I was going to tell him, Marcus. I *swear*."

"Why?"

"Because he deserves to know—"

"NO!" he roared so loudly that she jumped. "I meant why'd you do it? *Why, Ma?*"

Bitter, scalding tears streamed from Celeste's eyes, blurring her son's image. "Marcus, there are so many things about your father and me that you don't understand. We've been having problems—"

"So you brought another man in here?"

She shook her head quickly. "Darling, please listen to me. I'm your mother—"

She broke off at the look of scathing contempt that filled his face. He stood over her with his small fists balled at his sides. Half man. Half wounded boy.

Looking her in the eye, he said coldly, "I don't have a mother anymore."

Celeste died a thousand deaths. As an anguished sob welled in her throat, she burst out hysterically, "You don't mean that! Please, baby—"

She tried to launch herself at his legs, but he pivoted sharply on his heel and stomped out of the kitchen. As she scrambled to her feet, her ankle screamed in protest. Ignoring the sharp pain, she stumbled after Marcus. But by the time she reached the living room, he'd already stormed out the front door, slamming it so hard that the family portraits on the wall rattled and crashed to the floor.

Sidestepping broken shards of glass, Celeste hurried to the door, flung it open, and limped onto the porch.

"*Marcus!*" she called after him as he stalked furiously down the street. "Baby, please come back!"

She watched as he stopped at the home of the Nigerian woman who used to babysit him and Michael. After several moments the front door opened, and Marcus disappeared inside.

Wrapping her arms around her heaving midsection, Celeste turned and hobbled back into her house. She'd barely crossed the threshold before shame overtook her, sending her to the floor in a crumpled heap of sorrow and regret.

Sterling had just strode through the door of his office that afternoon when his phone rang. Reaching his desk, he snatched up the receiver and grunted, "Detective Wolf."

There was a pregnant pause. "Sterling, this is Mrs. Akonye."

"Oh, hey, Mrs. Akonye," Sterling said warmly as he dropped into his chair. "How're you doing?"

"I'm doing fine, my dear. I hate to bother you at work, but I wanted you to know that Marcus is here."

Sterling smiled. "Uh-oh. Did that boy forget his key again?"

"Well—"

"Celeste is probably sleeping. She worked a double shift yesterday. Just tell Marcus to knock harder so she'll hear him."

"He didn't forget his key," Mrs. Akonye said in a carefully measured tone. "He went home first, and then he came here."

A dagger of alarm shot through Sterling. "Why? Is everything okay?"

"I'm afraid not. He's very upset, Sterling. He won't say what happened, but he doesn't want to go back home."

Sterling frowned. "Put him on the phone, please."

"Just a minute. He's in the bathroom."

While he waited for Marcus, Sterling eyed his desk, which was cluttered with files and crime scene photographs and lab reports that needed his immediate attention.

As soon as his son came on the line, nothing else mattered.

"What's wrong, Little Man?" Sterling asked with concern. "Where's your mother? Why aren't you at home?"

On the other end of the phone, Marcus drew a deep, shuddering breath and croaked out, "Can you come get me, Dad? Please?"

Sterling was already on his feet, grabbing his jacket off the back of his chair and charging from the office. "Sit tight, son. I'll be right there."

He knew, with a grim sense of fatalism, that the end he'd been bracing for had finally arrived.

Chapter 10

"I'm so sorry."

Celeste looked like hell. Her face was ashen, her eyes were puffy and bloodshot from crying, and her hair was a tangled mess. In all the years Sterling had known her, he'd never seen her looking so thoroughly wrecked. If the circumstances had been different—if she hadn't just ripped their family apart—he would have felt sorry for her.

But of all the emotions raging through him tonight, compassion wasn't one of them.

Leaning against the dresser with his arms folded across his chest, he regarded his wife as coldly as if he were looking at a complete stranger.

She sat propped against the headboard with her bandaged foot elevated on a pillow to alleviate the swelling in her ankle, which she'd apparently sprained when she hopped down from the kitchen counter too fast.

Dear God, Sterling thought, his gut tightening with fury at a mental image of Celeste and another man locked in a passionate embrace, so caught up in each other that they hadn't even heard Marcus enter the house.

Celeste continued remorsefully, "I know there's absolutely nothing I can say or do to erase the pain I've caused you and our children—"

"Did you fuck him in our bed?" Sterling demanded bluntly.

She shot him a stricken look. "No! Of course not!"

"So you drew the line somewhere." His lips twisted mockingly. "How decent of you."

She flinched, her face reddening with humiliation. Dropping her gaze to her lap, she murmured, "I know I deserved that."

"Damn right you did."

She swallowed visibly. "You may not believe this, and I know it doesn't make any difference, but I only slept with Grant once."

Sterling's eyes narrowed. "Where?"

She hesitated, biting her lip. "At the hospital."

Sterling stared at her, struck by a horrible realization. "It happened a couple weeks ago, didn't it? The night you were on call, when you came back wearing a different shirt. Yeah, I noticed," he added caustically when her eyes widened with surprise. "I know you've always kept a change of clothes at work for legitimate reasons, and that morning wasn't the first time you've come home dressed differently. But it stuck out to me this time, and now I understand why you were nervous as hell over dinner that night."

Tears swam into Celeste's eyes. "I'm so sorry, baby," she said earnestly. "I never meant to hurt you or the boys. You *have* to believe me."

"I do," Sterling said, surprising both of them. "As shocked and angry as I am right now, I don't believe you intentionally set out to hurt anyone. But you did, Cel, and that's something we're all gonna have to live with for a very long time."

She leaned back against the headboard and closed her eyes as tears rolled down her cheeks and dripped onto her robe. "Do you think Marcus will ever forgive me?" she whispered piteously.

Sterling was silent, thinking of the sullen boy he'd encountered that afternoon when he arrived at Mrs. Akonye's house. Since Marcus had refused to return home as long as Celeste was there, Sterling had taken him to Burger King, where he'd coaxed the whole harrowing story out of him. What devastated Sterling the most—even more than Celeste's betrayal—was the thought of the irreparable damage she'd caused to their son's psyche. No child should ever have to endure what Marcus had suffered that afternoon.

"Do you?" Celeste prompted, breaking into Sterling's painful reverie.

He met her anxious gaze. "Do I think Marcus will ever forgive you?"

She nodded.

"I guess only time will tell."

She looked crestfallen. It wasn't the answer she'd wanted, but it was the only one he could give her.

A heavy silence lapsed between them.

"Thank you," Celeste whispered humbly.

Sterling frowned at her. "For what?"

"For not flying into a blind rage when you found out what happened. For not screaming at the top of your lungs and hurling vicious insults at me, the way I rightly deserve. For not pulling out your service revolver and blowing me to kingdom come."

Sterling smiled grimly. "Don't think I wasn't tempted."

They shared a low, tense chuckle that seemed utterly incongruous under the circumstances.

After another moment Sterling glanced at his watch, then pushed out a weary breath. "I'd better head back to the station. Got a lot of work to catch up on."

Celeste nodded. "You'll check on the boys before you leave?"

"Yeah." Michael and Marcus were spending the next couple of nights at Quentin's house, a decision they'd made on the way back from the community center where Michael had intramural basketball practice three days a week.

"He wouldn't even acknowledge me when he came home to pack his clothes," Celeste said mournfully.

"What the hell do you expect?" Sterling growled. "He's just as hurt and angry as Marcus is. If you're looking for any sympathy from me, you'd better look elsewhere."

She flinched at the harsh rebuke.

Impatiently straightening from the dresser, Sterling stalked to the door.

"Sterling?"

He stopped and looked over his shoulder at her, his jaw clenched.

"You may not want to hear this right now, but I love you," Celeste said softly. "You're a wonderful husband and father, and the most honorable man I've ever had the privilege of knowing."

Sterling's chest tightened painfully. Steeling his emotions against her heartfelt words, he asked in a low voice, "Do you love him?"

An expression of guilt crossed her face. "Please don't make me answer that."

Sterling stared into her eyes, thinking of the sixteen years they'd spent together, the triumphs and struggles they'd shared, the hopes and dreams they'd never realized.

"I hope you do love him," he said quietly. "Otherwise, you've just ruined a lot of lives for nothing."

And with that, he turned and walked out on her.

****

Two days later, on a deceptively bright and sunny Saturday morning, Celeste moved out of the house.

She hadn't told Sterling where she planned to stay, and he hadn't asked. When he ran a secret background check on Grant Rutherford, he wasn't surprised to learn that the doctor drove a Porsche and owned a penthouse in Buckhead.

Celeste had apparently struck gold.

On the morning of her departure, Marcus sat on the porch steps watching as Sterling and Michael loaded her belongings into the Volvo. The boy could have stayed inside the house, but instead he'd chosen the role of spectator, as if he wanted to make sure that his mother really left. His expression betrayed none of the anger and sorrow he must be feeling.

If anything, he looked eerily calm.

When they'd finished loading up the car, Celeste hugged Michael hard, clinging to him until his arms reluctantly lifted to return the embrace.

When they at last drew apart, Michael's nostrils were flaring as he fought back tears.

"I love you, sweetheart," Celeste whispered to him. "Take care of your father and brother."

Michael nodded shortly.

After kissing Sterling's cheek, Celeste turned to face her youngest child. Her eyes glistened wetly. "Will you at least kiss me goodbye?"

Marcus said nothing, staring at her with that impenetrable expression.

Celeste looked beseechingly at Sterling, silently asking him to intervene.

He just shook his head at her.

Choking back a sob, she hurried around to the driver's side of the car and climbed behind the wheel.

Marcus sat watching until the Volvo disappeared down the street. Then, just as calmly as he'd ventured outside to watch his mother's departure, he stood and went back into the house.

Sterling and Michael looked at each other.

"He's going to be okay," Sterling assured his son, because he had to. "We all are."

Michael swallowed tightly, his Adam's apple bobbing in his throat. He was almost the same age Sterling had been when his parents passed away. And just as he and his brother had survived that unspeakable tragedy, he knew his sons would survive this ordeal.

Stan's words suddenly drifted through his mind, a cruel irony in the face of what had just happened.

Nothing's ever gonna break up the Wolf Pack.

Remembering his own response at the time, Sterling now repeated the words to Michael. Quietly at first, then again, with more conviction. "Long live the Wolf Pack."

Michael frowned, eyeing him skeptically. "You really think everything's gonna be okay, Dad?"

"Not right away," Sterling admitted. "Probably not for a long while. But eventually, yeah."

Michael mulled this over for a minute, his brows furrowed, a muscle working in his jaw as he stared off down the street.

Finally he nodded, as if he'd reached some sort of understanding with himself.

"Long live the Wolf Pack," he echoed softly.

"Hear, hear." Swallowing a hard knot of emotion, Sterling looked around the block of row houses. For the first time, he noticed several people gathered on porch steps, watching their unfolding family drama with unabashed curiosity.

A grim smile curved Sterling's mouth. "Guess we'd better head inside now. We've given the neighbors enough of a show for one day."

"Yeah," Michael agreed, glancing around. "Guess so."

With their arms draped around each other's shoulders, father and son turned and walked back toward the house, knowing that their lives would never be the same again.

*****